"Nebula, Shirley Jackson, and World Fantasy Award finalist Allen (*Aftermath of an Industrial Accident*) presents a titillating collection of 14 horror stories and [13] poems. Throughout, Allen takes the idea of nothing being as it seems to supernatural extremes . . . . These slippery, surprising stories will appeal to horror fans seeking something fresh." —*Publishers Weekly*

"Supernatural menaces, body thieves, and ferocious killers pervade Allen's grim collection of stories and poems . . . . These assembled short stories feature such spooky conventions as ghosts, a witch, and someone trying to bring a creature to life, but the prevailing theme of this book is body horror—grotesque depictions of torn or modified flesh and impossibly contorted bodies . . . . It won't surprise readers familiar with Allen's work (*Aftermath of an Industrial Accident: Stories*, 2020) that he doesn't shy away from violent bits. Descriptions include viscera, teeth (not just in mouths), and tortured limbs of all shapes and lengths. Many passages are outright disconcerting even out of context: 'She fills his mouth and plugs his throat, his tongue slapping uselessly against a column that tastes of blood and raw river silt.' The author's gleefully vibrant prose animates these stories; this also holds true for the collection's free-verse poetry . . . This narrative approach injects these stories with nerve-racking anticipation and dread." —*Kirkus Reviews*

"This collection of short stories and poetry is a beautiful, dark, and thoroughly unsettling trip. I love the way Allen twists and skews the reality and the everyday, tucking shadows and terrors into the cracks of what we think is real." —**Maria Haskins, *Maria's Sci-Fi, Fantasy & Horror Short Fiction Roundup***

"*Slow Burn* is a wonderful blend of story, poetry, and co-authored collaboration. It is a collection that transports readers into the shadows through the mythical, chilling, and visceral. Within, you will find tales of messy lives stitched together, twisted obsessions, violence, dark magic, and body horror from multiple perspectives. Truly a slow burn readers will crave to simmer in." —**Ai Jiang, Hugo, Locus, Nebula, and Bram Stoker award-nominated author of *Linghun* and *I Am AI***

"Mike Allen (and friends) make and remake the monstrous in *Slow Burn*, a surreal collection of interconnected stories and poems which snake their way into your consciousness. Here the villains are mothers and aunties and sometimes ordinary folk with names like Maddy, Aaron, and Josey. It's an ambitious endeavour, an out-of-the-box study of culpability and complicity that succeeds on every level. Consuming horror that is not for the squeamish!" —**Lee Murray, five-time Bram Stoker Awards®-winning author of *Grotesque: Monster Stories***

"You can't just assume you know where you are in a Mike Allen story, or where you're going, or where the path ends, and the magic of this new collection lies in that feverish uncertainty. At turns dripping with Cronenberg body horror, infused with Barker misanthropy, and crawling with the darkest fantasy, the stories and poems in *Slow Burn* are beautifully crafted to lure you in, but their beauty won't let you go easily. There are too many strange limbs for that. Don't miss these new webs in the spidery legacy of Mike Allen." —**Michael Wehunt, author of *The Inconsolables***

"Like one of the extra-dimensional creatures lurking within *Slow Burn*'s collected stories and novella, author Mike Allen must also have a thousand eyes, a hundred mouths, and far too many fingers. How else could he find so many strange and hidden worlds—not to mention the strangeness hidden in our own world—and translate it all so beautifully? A mind-bending delight from a horrifically unique imagination, *Slow Burn* will twist, turn, and transform readers." —**Gordon B. White, finalist for the Shirley Jackson and Bram Stoker Awards**

"There are multiple flavors of body horror on offer in *Slow Burn*, along with dark fantasy, cosmic horror, and science fiction . . . Allen is a master at serving up striking imagery and evocative, atmospheric settings. He also excels at creating characters who feel fully realized, then dropping them into horrific situations, keeping the reader invested in their journeys and well-being. *Slow Burn* is another strong addition to the line up of Allen's work, with plenty to offer fans of multiple genres." —**A.C. Wise, Shirley Jackson, Nebula, Bram Stoker and World Fantasy award-nominated author of *The Ghost Sequences* and *Wendy, Darling***

Also by Mike Allen

SLOW BURN

SLOW BURN

MIKE ALLEN

INTRODUCTION BY
CHRISTINA SNG

Mythic Delirium
BOOKS

mythicdelirium.com

Slow Burn
Copyright © 2024 by Mike Allen

Cover art and design © 2024 by Lasse Paldanius, lassepaldanius.com.

Interior illustrations © 2024 by Paula Arwen Owen, arwendesigns.net.

This book is a work of fiction. All characters, names, locations, and events portrayed in this book are fictional or used in an imaginary manner to entertain, and any resemblance to any real people, situations, or incidents is purely coincidental.

PRINT: 978-1-956522-03-7
DIGITAL: 978-1-956522-04-4

Library of Congress Control Number: 2023946051

FIRST EDITION
July 16, 2024

Published by Mythic Delirium Books
Roanoke, Virginia
mythicdelirium.com

Further copyright information begins on page 277.

Our gratitude goes out to the following who because of their generosity are from now on designated as supporters of Mythic Delirium Books: Saira Ali, Cora Anderson, Anonymous, Patricia M. Cryan, Steve Dempsey, Oz Drummond, Patrick Dugan, Matthew Farrer, C. R. Fowler, Mary J. Lewis, Paul T. Muse, Jr., Shyam Nunley, Finny Pendragon, Kenneth Schneyer, and Delia Sherman.

For Rick Herndon

In loving memory

We miss you, brother

TABLE OF CONTENTS

WORLDS OF MYTH AND HORROR
Introduction by Christina Sng

MIKE ALLEN HAS ALWAYS BEEN SYNONYMOUS with the mysterious and the macabre. The name of his press, Mythic Delirium, gives us a tantalizing hint, a glimpse of the worlds he loves to create. His imprint's stunning, surreal book covers embody his vision and his multiple award wins and nominations showcase the magnificence of his writing.

I've known Mike for over twenty years. It was he who looked me up when I vanished in 2005, to make sure I was still alive and writing.

Mike is the friend who will give you cheerfully honest, patient, and immensely helpful advice for your prose and poetry. His kind critiques have shaped much of my work, even when I feel like I exhausted his goodwill. And he will remember your stories and poems, even years later.

As an editor, Mike is intricate and precise, his selections demonstrating an eye for excellent work in the genre, as exemplified by the Clockwork Phoenix anthology series and his journal *Mythic Delirium.*

His writing is exquisite and vivid, his worlds rich with brilliant detail. As a poet, his words shimmer through the pages like magic, seeping into you. They hold great depth and power.

Decades ago, Mike showed me what magnificence in a poem looked like. I saw firsthand how eloquently his words sang, woven seamlessly together in a sinister quartet at an orchestra. I marvelled at how rich the tapestry of his writing felt, the startling tactile sensation of the thick curtain, even when describing the grotesque right at the end. Whenever I see a Mike Allen poem, I always see magnificent poetry. Vivid imagery to startle and consume.

After we had been friends for a good amount of time, we began a collaboration, a poem titled "Godbody" that epitomizes beautiful language, something I only ever saw in Robert McCammon's epic apocalyptic novel *Swan Song*. I learned how words can be used to create scenes so beautiful not only in their descriptions but in the words themselves.

Often, the most exciting books mix genres—poetry with fiction, science fiction with horror, myth with terror. In this age of instant gratification, it is a thrill for many readers to anticipate what the next page will bring, to keep guessing. This is my experience of reading a Mike Allen book.

In his latest collection, *Slow Burn,* Allen marries both poetry and fiction in a mind-bending blend of myth and horror.

The images he paints with words are terrifying and mesmerizing, keeping you enthralled and unable to look away as he gently pulls you into his universe.

The poem "The Fifth Horseman" demonstrates this perfectly:

>skyscrapers shedding mold-black chunks,
>red rot unveiled beneath

In "The Sacrifices," this picture still remains imprinted in my mind:

>Ankle-deep in concrete, we became
>a ring of pillars, living dolmens.

Irony plays a part in the poems and stories of *Slow Burn*. Regard the poem "The Strip Search":

>The Gate said "Abandon All Hope."

>I thought I'd tossed all my hope away,
>but when I stepped through the Gate, it still pinged.
>One of the guards slithered out of its seat,
>snarling as it drew forth a wand.
>*C'mere,* it hissed,
>*it seems you're still holding out hope.*

Sometimes Mike uses metafiction techniques in his stories to great effect. In the title story "Slow Burn," the protagonist Aaron Friedrich sounds suspiciously like Mike himself:

> Aaron Friedrich, publisher, editor and sole journalist of the online-only Owlswick County Observer, leaned close and squinted as the grainy security camera footage flashed to white.

Mike's mastery of his craft is clear in his openings. In "This Rider of Fugitive Dawns," Mike shows us how to begin a story with a powerful hook:

> The ancients huddled below my window, their narrow backs bent double, gray skin stretched taut over knobby spines and splayed ribs. The ochre ghosts that rode them raised smooth faces to look at me.

Mike is best known for transforming worlds of the grotesque and macabre into things of beauty, no more perfectly seen in his short story "The Green Silence":

> Whenever Violet goes dormant, Gerry pines
> for her with a skin-peeling, meat-dissolving hunger
> he does not dare express.

A fair warning: descriptions grow more visceral as the story progresses. If you have a delicate stomach, do not read this while eating.

For me, Mike's greatest strength is his poetry. Consider this beautiful opening to "The Dream Eaters":

> When a dream achieves substance and shape,
> condenses from the fog that forms
> our collective unconscious, starts to
> quiver, stretch its limbs, open its throats
> to test its many voices, it also becomes edible.

The stunning imagery in "Astynome, After" is a showcase of his mastery:

> The Fates persist in fractal layers,
> the tapestry they weave
> spreads fingers, grips skeins

It ends with an unforgettable scene:

> . . . We
> will wind my new fate
> full frontal, we will brave
> Ptolemy's wobbling spheres,
> hopping from disk to disk,
> and at the edge of the universe
> we'll pay the Moirai a call,
> you keep them talking
> while I transmute their spun wool
> into a gunpowder fuse.

With that, I will hold you back no further. Step into worlds of horror and myth filled with conflicted protagonists and wily antagonists doing objectionable things.

Ready? Now, turn the page.

THE WINDOWS BREATHE

The windows breathe in this place, the ancient
time-thinned panes flexing out and in,
the reflections of the rooms ever shifting, slipping,
tricking your eyes, your own face unrecognizable
as you peer in the glass, vainly seeking a glimpse

of Outside.

Unseen, the eaves of this house ever howl, screaming
when the wind blows and when it slumbers;
and darkness forever ascends the stairs, rising
from the depths to snuff the lamps of any
who dare descend; ignore the sounds you hear
as you grope in the pitch black, and carefully count
the landings, or you may not find the floor you seek,

or any other.

The old timbers that form these floors
always creek, whether trod upon or not; it's best
to believe the footsteps that follow you
from room to room are merely the protests
of the house as it shifts; the hungry shuddering
groans no more than the complaints of aging wood.
Sometimes a door opens on a soft, sloping hall,
rounded, glistening, so much like a gullet.
Another trick of the eyes, perhaps; still
it may be wise to shut that door and wait,

1

or find another way.

Some come invited to this place; others trespass,
or so they think; some have lived here all along
and never knew it; some learn too soon or too late.
And me? I am no more than I seem, bent and shriveled,
with cataracts, quavering voice, a dodderer, a servant,
a guide to ensure your ordeal here ends no later

or sooner than it should.

THE FEATHER STITCH

T HE STOUT WOMAN BEHIND THE CASH REGISTER stares without smiling as Audra stammers through her request.

This front room with its age-warped glass and wholesome brick, with its bolts of brightly patterned fabric and pegboard hooks weighted with packs of beads, lines up not at all with the whispers of oxy and meth supply chains that end and begin within this building.

A square of sunlight frames a stack of bed sheets printed with grinning, bespectacled animals boarding a school bus. Audra's gaze flits from bauble to bauble as she speaks.

Before Audra finishes, the cashier's stony exterior melts enough for her mouth to bow into a scowl.

Audra hasn't seen Russell in eight days. A couple years ago she gave up on aiming her grandson's life toward the light, and scaled down her hopes to just keeping him alive long enough to reach full adulthood in spite of his terrible choices. Legally, yes, he was on the verge of adulthood, but there wasn't anything like a grown man rattling around inside the skull swathed by that wavy red hair. He needed more time.

Russell claimed that a gang of younger toughs from southeast Hillcrest had it in for him because they'd caught him selling in their turf. Audra doesn't believe Hillcrest is large enough to spawn real gangs, and some of the boys he named to her are friends of his, or they were, back when they were all in junior high.

Those boys are missing, too.

Audra stops talking. Her question dangles over silence.

The cashier does not stop scowling even as she tugs her apron straight. Concealed in a rumple until that moment, the name

MAUDE, sewn into the garment, stretches into clarity across her chest. "Why do you think I'd know a single thing about a bunch of bad apples from the city?" She waves toward the tables stacked with sewing supplies, the message embedded in her gesture: *Ain't nothing here they want.*

"I never said you did." Audra dredges up her courage. "But I've reason to believe somebody here would."

Late last night, Audra attempted in her own special way to peer into this building, a former schoolhouse converted to a craft shop. She soared above the hills, descending from silvery heights in a form that physical barriers could not keep out. What she saw, when her dark-feathered head phased ghost-like through the roof, confused and unnerved her. Where even in her altered state she should have perceived floors and foundation, an abyss screamed.

The cashier's stare flattens, loses sharpness, though Audra cannot deem it blank. The woman tilts her head ever so slightly as if listening, though the only sounds beyond Audra's breath and pulse come from the clacking of the beaded curtain that veils the entrance to the next room.

"Well," the cashier drawls. "Someone *does* want to talk to you. Follow me."

Maude leads Audra through the curtain, out into a hall and down a flight of stairs to the basement. Carpets stitched with hyper-detailed images of jungle animals and floral lattices hang on crisscrossing clotheslines, this method of display partitioning one immense room into an exotic maze.

"Wait there," the cashier says, pointing to a folding chair that crouches beside a drafting table. On the floor next to the chair stretches a long wooden bin filled near to the brim with buttons, their many shapes and colors a hundredfold more distracting than the packages hung on hooks in the front room. The carpets sway as the cashier steps backward into all-concealing shadow.

Confused by Maude's disappearance, Audra cranes her neck, turns her head, wondering where her escort went, and nearly capsizes her chair at the sight of the massive, balding, ponytailed man who has taken a seat in front of the table, not four feet away. She never saw him enter the space. He regards her with one brown eye and one green eye. The checkered blue shirt he wears must be made from enough fabric to double as a tent. Though his features are rounded, not chiseled, his upper arms look thick as tree trunks.

In her startlement she almost reveals her true self to him. The thought of what he might reveal in return keeps her in check. Her niece Leanne shares the traits that make Audra special, and the words Audra has tried to drill into that fool girl's head return to save her at that moment. *There's things worse than men just waiting for one of us to slip up.*

She's still clutching at her chest as he shares his soft wisp of a voice. "I didn't mean to scare you." Even sitting down, he looms over her. Audra has long been used to men literally looking down on her, even Russell is almost two heads taller, but this man could hide a barrel of Russells within his frame. "I hear you're asking after some acquaintances?"

Audra catches her breath long enough to remember her spiel. "I have a list of names." She puts fingers in the front pocket of her purse. "Some boys who might have come in here—"

"Boys? In my shop?" The patronizing smile that warps the moon of his face nauseates her. "Only when they want to cause trouble."

A coal kindles in her stomach, but she manages an off-hand laugh. "Some of them are like that."

"Aren't they all." The shopkeeper shrugs. "A group of hooligans did sneak in here, or they tried anyway, about a week or so ago."

Audra's heart quavers like a mockingbird trill. She did not disclose to the cashier that her own grandson was among the missing, and every instinct tells her not to toss that morsel to this colossus. Instead, Russell's merely one name on the list. She unfolds the note, preparing to read.

"Oh, I didn't get their names," he says, before she can even start. "Could you ID them if you saw them?"

"You have them on video?" She didn't spy any cameras inside or outside the building, but her next question lodges in her craw, because the shopkeeper has undone his collar and started to unbutton his shirt. "What are you doing?" she stammers, as he exposes his chest and reaches into the gap like he intends to pull a gun out of a concealed holster.

At that same moment, a croak-screech like that of a frightened, wounded crow scrapes from somewhere too far off to make
any sense if the source lay within this gloomy chamber. Audra's
heart leaps into her throat. "Sir, I'm very uncomfortable—"

What he pulls out resembles a lengthy twist of towel. One
end remains tucked into the opening in his shirt. The longer she
stares at it, the more leathery it looks. The end he grips swells and
stretches. Maybe he's working his fist into it, splaying his fingers,
she can't quite tell. Abruptly she realizes she's regarding a teen
boy's sparsely stubbled face.

"He look familiar?" the shopkeeper asks. "Oh, I see he does."
Misinterpreting her gasp as one of recognition.

She shakes her head in denial of both his conclusion and what
she's witnessing.

He tucks the twisted rag back into his shirt and pulls forth
another. "How about this one?"

This time, despite the sags and stretches, when the face expands Audra does recognize the boy: Dougie Melcher, used to visit Russell every week when Russell was ten and Dougie was eight, a
buck-toothed imp with a sweet grin and a predilection for slipping
into forbidden rooms and scouring drawers and dresser-tops for
things like loose change. About the time he reached high-school
age, Dougie turned on Russell, following along with the crowd
that cast her grandson out.

Her gut urges her not to acknowledge Dougie, though perhaps her widened eyes already gave the game away.

"How about this one, then?"

The same process, one limp husk tucked away, a new one
drawn out, and Audra recognizes this one too: Jeremy Johns, another former friend of Russell's, another sweetheart turned mean.
She shakes her head.

The man regards her with dispassion as he produces another,
and another. That fifth time it dawns on Audra that her host has
no fear of showing her these gruesome skins because he has no
intention of allowing her to leave.

The face of Moochie Repperton dangles from the shopkeeper's saucepan-sized fist. One side of the enormous man's mouth
curls upward a millimeter. "Mrs. Whorley, you're not doing much
to help me narrow down this search."

"I haven't seen anyone I'm looking for yet," she says as if his disgusting method of jogging her memory doesn't faze her at all—even though her heart is jumping.

That smile deepens. "They recognize *you*, though. Have nice things to say about you, even."

"They do?" Audra's heart jumps faster. "When did you speak to them?"

"Mrs. Whorley, you can't possibly be *that* stupid." And that's when it hits her that he's addressed her by name twice without her having shared that information. "Moochie, tell Mrs. Whorley what you think of her."

"You're a sweet old lady," says Moochie's voice, not much lower than it was in childhood. "You sure deserve better than Rusty."

Audra shrinks back, the feet of her chair scraping the floor. This creep performed some sort of ventriloquist trick. "You stop that! What a horrible thing to say!"

"Mrs. Whorley, your mother hen instincts are darling. They almost make me regret that you chose to come here. You need to pay a bit more attention." The shopkeeper raises his fist, shakes the thing dangling in its grip, which blinks and locks eyes with Audra. It's Moochie's head, plumped out with flesh and bone and fully alive, yet instead of a neck, twists of leathery flesh trail back to the gap in the shopkeeper's shirt. Audra once saw a photo of an ancient sculpture, some Greek hero holding up the head of Medusa. This is exactly like that.

"What Rusty says about you is worse, ma'am," says Moochie, as if they were chatting at the kitchen table. "He's always like, my mamaw won't let me do this, my mamaw won't let me do that, she's a dried-up old hag, she still hates my dad and takes it out on me, she makes me wish I hadn't been born."

A hissing rises from the bin full of buttons, but she can't concentrate on that because Moochie's words slice like a serrated edge into bone. How to absorb such a cruel statement from a head dangled like a sack of fruit—her mind is trying to avoid focus, to hone in on the most insignificant details rather than accept the grotesquerie before her eyes. That statement couldn't be true. Hate doesn't fill Russell like that. Sure, he gets surly with her sometimes, but so did Charmaigne when she was the same age. Audra has worked so

hard to keep her temper in check, she never ever wanted to drive
Russell away. She can't keep the world out, no matter how badly she
wishes she could, but she can offer him respite from it.

"You're young and hearty for a grandmother, you'd likely be
quite upset to learn the dirty things these nasty boys think about
you. Probably even more upset to learn what else they've gotten up
to." The shopkeeper stands, a monument to terror, Moochie's head
still clutched in one hand. Audra spies how the skin of Moochie's
forehead and the shopkeeper's fingertips meld, no seams visible between them. "All your best efforts, all that slaving away in the cafeteria with a net over your hair and boss after boss speaking to you
like a subhuman, and despite everything your grandson was going
to turn out just like your daughter, or even worse, just like her boyfriend, and come to an even more horrible end than they did."

Audra stares into Moochie's moist brown eyes. "Where is
Russell?"

Moochie answers, "He got out of line too many times, ma'am.
We brought him here to straighten him out."

Despite her mind's best efforts at defensive denial, the pieces
click together. That head in this monster's hands isn't some kind
of puppet. She manages to shape her scream into words. "What
have you done to him?"

Moochie's head shrivels up into the shopkeeper's arm, a grape
drying to a raisin in fast-forward. The huge man's voice rises in
authentic puzzlement or a mockery thereof. "You don't know already?" Her silence inspires him to produce another condescend-
ing smirk. "How about I show you?"

That arm gropes for Audra and her panic overpowers every
ingrained instinct. All disguise jettisoned, she spreads wings and
talons. Her surroundings alter so alarmingly that in the next instant she is flesh and blood again, standing with her back against
one of the hanging carpets, the threads tickling her through her
blouse as if the entire surface teems with ants.

The shopkeeper's extended hand glitters, paused to hover
above the chair where she was sitting the instant before. He asks
her what she's been too shocked and tongue-tied to ask him.
"What *are* you?"

Even if she was inclined to answer, her mind is paralyzed by
shock. Since she was nine, she's been aware of others like her,

gifted or cursed with two bodies, one grounded in the world of flesh, the other grounded in the far more dangerous world of spirit. Her grandmother sussed out what she was and shared what she could about how to survive. Audra in turn saw it in her niece, Leanne. Not in her brother, or her daughter, or her grandson. *It don't choose everyone in a line*, Audra's grandmother said.

Like Audra herself, Audra's grandmother followed the form of the raven. Leanne follows the form of the blue jay, which Audra still can't conceive of as kin to ravens and crows, though apparently they are. Many other spirit folk exist, with spiders by far the most dangerous, but Audra has never seen or even heard of anyone or anything like this monster in the fabric store basement.

The crawling carpet against her back flexes and curls, attempts to envelop her. Hopping forward puts her back in the shopkeeper's reach, and as he grabs for her again, his fingers expand. It looks as if the skin around his bones is unrolling like tissue paper.

She becomes raven, doesn't phase back, her wings wider than a Cadillac is long, her substance pure spirit, unimpeded by cloth, wood and cement. What was a basement opens into a hellscape. Dante's very inferno yawns below her, glittering with microscopic malevolent stars that leap like fleas from level to level and layer to layer. There are so, so many layers that form the slopes of this funnel.

Shrieks congeal in a single phrase, *What are you?* and it is the entirety of the pit that shapes this question, a throat that leads to the bottom of the world.

Good to see you again, ma'am, says Moochie. There he is, flattened like roadkill, sliding into the wall of the funnel, and Audra looses a human-sounding scream as she comprehends what the infinite sheaves and stacks of papery leather embedded in the funnel wall really are. Hides. Souls. Both at once. Her Russell is somewhere in that throat, crammed in among thousands of others, a single file of skin and agony misplaced in a nightmare cabinet.

She cries Russell's name, but how can he hear her over the screaming of his fellow prisoners? She can't bear the thought of the troubled boy she sheltered and raised ending his existence in this trap, not after she worked so hard to fill the wounds his father tore open with the gun he used on Charmaigne, then himself. She draws her wings closer and plunges.

From all sides of the funnel the bright motes spray toward her, hurtle through her, she can feel them questing, parasitic mites seeking purchases in her feathers, yet she is spirit and they fall right through her, just as they should—but their passage burns like hot wire.

The throat addresses her. *We vibrate on different frequencies, Mrs. Whorley. When I reach the right station I'll take you apart and find out all the how and why of you.* The motes leap at her in hordes, their fury riddling her through.

The pain is nothing compared to what her pain will be if she abandons Russell to this place.

Another voice, smaller, to her left and below: *no you're going the wrong way*

Her black eyes spy Dougie Melcher's face herniating from the wall like a balloon forced partway through a mail-slot.

Help me find him! she cries.

His words spill in a jumble but she discerns every one.

he's not here he escaped that's why Lenahan took us all he flew away and he made us pay we hurt him bad but he flew so high get me out I'll help you find him

Dougie's face peels apart, all the cut paper pieces slurped back into the wall. The funnel emits a new noise, a roar vomited from the vaults of the earth that rapidly heightens in pitch as the funnel constricts, striving to lodge her in these depths, to choke on her.

She beats her wings, working to lift herself out of the pit, through the roof of the shop and into the spirit world's silvery sky. The predatory motes shower and sear her, a rain of embers. She has plummeted so much further than she realized. The closer the opening gets, the smaller it shrinks.

The monster that is both shopkeeper and hellmouth still hasn't found her frequency, but as she nears the top of the funnel, the walls close in to the point where her wingspan sweeps through them, phase through the people crushed in those layers, and she's blinded by an avalanche of memories not her own, hundreds of lives spanned out over decades, all of them terminating in an encounter with that leviathan and his collection of buttons that aren't buttons at all.

he flew

Hope against hope buoys her as she pulls her wings free of the mire of agony and propels herself higher still. She phases through the shop's first story, through the second, phases through the roof, the monster baying its frustration below her.

we hurt him bad

She never saw any sign that Russell was born with a spirit form. But maybe it was there, buried deep, activated by sheer survival instinct when those boys brought him here and tried to feed him to the beast.

but he flew so high

A soul-searing cry wrenches from her lungs of its own accord, for all those below she cannot save, a foolish noise that could summon predators as terrible as the one ditched below, monsters that *would* be on her frequency.

A croak-screech in response, the same one she heard before, far, far above.

Far more luck than skill or parental instinct brings her right to him. She praises God, praises the denizens of the Silver City, whether or not they had anything to do with it.

Impossible passages bore through the sky of the spirit world, and by some miracle Russell lies within one, more spirit than flesh, wounded in both shapes, his black Scorpions T-shirt crusted blacker with blood. More blood stains the substance that forms the passage floor.

She inspects his wound. It's long and ragged. She thinks of the spear from the Gospel of John that pierced Christ's side, those words about the water and the blood from that gruesome hymn she was made to sing every Sunday when she was a girl.

Surely his transmutation is what keeps him alive. In the spirit world, he is a crow, smaller than she but still a burden. She has never tried to carry anything so heavy in raven form, she doesn't know if she can get him down.

Were he to revert fully to flesh, it would be his death—though still a better fate than what his former friends intended for him. They were consumed in his place, and consumed by their petty hate and awful addiction well before then.

If she can save him, they will have to leave Hillcrest. The shopkeeper won't be content until he—it—has them in his collection.

Though the notion terrifies her, she knows that she will have to leave him here alone. He needs water. She needs thread and needle. He needs the wound cleaned and closed. She can't be certain it will help, but she has to try.

She enfolds Russell in her wings. His breathing calms. She longs for a few hours of peace, to rest, to think, to plan, or simply to be with her grandson if this is all the time they have left.

THEY SAY THAT TIME ASSUAGES

with Ian Watson

N O ONE LOVED TIME LIKE MILTON CHESTERFIELD.
He loved dates, regardless of what events they marked. He loved all the times of day: dusk and dawn, noon and midnight. He loved the weeks and the months, especially the leap-year fluctuations of February. He loved minutes and he loved all of the hours.

He wound watches of all sizes and colors and wore them, bands of mechanical wonder stacked from his wrists to his elbows that thrilled as their ticking vibrated his body.

His eyes met mine, full of eager gleam. "Do you want to know the time? In Dublin, Paris, Cairo, Beijing?"

"My watch's microchip can tell me that," I replied "I don't need sixty different watches."

"Ah, but you have forty radios at home, all tuned to different stations."

"That's different," I protested. "It's faster than turning the dial."

"It's faster to glance at my arms than fiddle with tiny buttons."

"But why should you want to know the time in Tokyo or Timbuktu?"

"Because there's time everywhere. I mustn't lose track of it."

"What's the time at the South Pole?" I demanded. "You know, where all the time zones converge? It must be every possible time all at once."

Milton clutched his head.

The next time I saw Milton Chesterfield, he was wearing shorts. From his ankles to his knees were more watches, evidently with extra links in the bands, or much longer straps adapted from

belts. Even more formed a collar—all the time in the world spinning him from head to foot.

I couldn't help myself. "What time is it at Mount Olympus on
Mars?" I asked him.

He staggered, aghast; and clutched at his chest.

Ticker trouble. He'd need a pacemaker now.

I went home and turned on all my radios at once.

And I felt like God.

THE GREEN SILENCE

GERRY'S APARTMENT CONTAINS ONLY THREE ROOMS—a bathroom, a bedroom, and a combination living room and kitchenette—and he paces from one to the other to the other, hoping that Violet will stir. She does not stir.

Whenever Violet goes dormant, Gerry pines for her with a skin-peeling, meat-dissolving hunger he does not dare express. When he goes to work at the plant, and shuts the door to his office, he sits before a desk piled with blank papers, arranged so that his back is to the door, thus no one peering in the little window sees how he chews, chews, chews on nothing. He moves the blank papers from one stack to the next with urgency, to discourage interruption until he can escape and return to Violet.

If he did not pace through his rooms, he would regard her featureless face for hours, or rather, the cauliflower-textured cowl that hides whatever is gestating within her head.

So he paces, even though he grows out of breath, his ragged panting sometimes drowning out the alto buzz of the dying refrigerator. As he paces, he turns over the most nagging question, whether he should leave Violet be to spurt and bloom naturally, or whether to accelerate her.

His knees ache as if injected with acid as, well past midnight but not yet to the wolf's hour, he collapses in the chair beside the sofa where Violet lies. Yet he cannot rest, his heels bouncing as impatience wars with disappointment.

Violet has progressed. Yesterday the thick cowl split down the middle of her face to reveal vestigial nostrils. When he first spied those, hopes of a reunion arriving as soon as that morning made his pulse surge, his mouth water. But as he observed the doughy, uncooked texture of the exposed flesh above and below, no hints of teeth or eyelashes, that hope drained away.

Incapable of resisting the impulse, he tortures himself with memories of Violet awake and ambulatory. Blonde and stout, given to uplifting peals of laughter, ripping hair from his legs or beard without warning. Blue-eyed and brown-skinned, insulting him to his face as he pounded inside her. Towering and broad shouldered, possessed of hefty breasts and a bell-ringing left hook. Pale and fanged, refusing to reveal whose blood stained her clothes. A woman-shaped congeries of gossamer strands, weaving into and out of the cracks in the drywall, her movements like a breeze disturbing a grave.

Heels drumming the floor, he lifts the blanket to regard her body, finds no surprises. The cocoon that encases her from the throat down is even thicker than the cowl that swathes her head, giving her a shape somewhere between an oversized, legless beetle grub and a gigantic crinkle-cut fry. Gerry once passed a sleepless night by a dormant Violet's side eating from a bucket filled with both those things, an ill-thought out placebo to pacify his bottomless, passionless lust. Even the memory churns the contents of his stomach.

He has spent so many nights like this with her during her dormancies. Once they come to an end, once the new limbs break free, once her renewed torso reveals its shape, his joy is always such that he forgets the intolerable agony of the wait. Yet this wait has gone on so much longer, many days more than he can recall the process ever taking.

He attempted to accelerate her once, the third month after he brought her into his home. That had not gone well, but he had not understood the best practices for acceleration. This was no longer the case. He has devoted his thousands of hours of pacing to meditation on the process.

Leaning closer, making mental note of the contours implied by her cowl, a narrower head, sharper cheekbones and chin, he finds his resolve, presses both agitated feet to the bare floorboards and stands. Practically skipping into the bathroom, he crouches beside the clawfoot tub. From the shadow beneath its massive mildew-grayed porcelain bowl, he slides out the incubator cabinet. Within their plastic-covered niches, the cabinet's inhabitants wriggle.

The phone shrieks. Gerry cracks the crown of his head against the tub lip. The impact has the effect of amplifying the phone's shrill as if someone has turned up a volume knob. Beneath the piercing ring, the phone rumbles his name, a deep and angry underscore. He does not dare ignore it, even though it means leaving the incubator cabinet in the open. The pain dizzies him, so he crawls to the kitchen counter.

Woozy, vision doubled, he perceives the base of the phone swelling like a frog's throat as it rumbles his name again. He fumbles the receiver to his ear. "What do you want from me?"

A tiny, tinny voice. "Gerry, why haven't you been to work?"

"Paul?" Gerry groans, an anxious worm twirling in his guts. "I told you. I don't work for you any more. I work for the plant now."

"Yes you do, Gerry. You will always work for me."

Gerry's pulse hops and thumps in an odd place, just behind the flap of his right ear—especially odd as he has the receiver pressed to his left ear. It takes a tremendous act of will for Gerry not to scream his response. "Paul, you should leave me alone."

"Not possible. We're in this together." The flutter behind his right ear turns wet, like a cat's tongue rapidly licking. "Even when you don't show up, you're still working with me, working on me, working me." Paul's voice grows breathy with exertion and excitement. "But you need to show up. You need to concentrate harder. To press harder, squeeze harder."

As the need to scream yields, Gerry crushes an urge to gag. "Paul, I am going to hang up now. You remember Violet? She hasn't had breakfast yet. I need to cook her breakfast. I have to start now to have it ready on time."

Paul gasps. "Violet! I need her back to work too! I need her—"

The phone wobbles from the force as Gerry slams the receiver back in its cradle. The dial rotates of its own accord, spinning back into place with a hiss of rebuke. Gerry regains his feet, looms over Violet without seeing her, his fury at Paul's intrusion throbbing in his neck and temples.

A clatter in the bathroom snaps him out of it. "Breakfast," he says.

All the noise must have agitated the inhabitants of the incubator. Gerry hurries back to find that the entire cabinet has edged out further into the light, and he can't help but imagine that the beings inside are as eager for Violet's emergence as he is.

"Breakfast," Gerry says. He will accelerate Violet, because he has to warn her about Paul. Between his lingering wooziness and his rattled nerves he can hardly see or think straight, so rather than trying to select a single denizen then and there, he retrieves the entire incubator from the zigzag-tiled floor.

A twitch in the mirror snags his gaze. The most unwanted of possible pimples bulges behind and beneath his right ear, an eyeless miniature doppelganger of Paul's round, jowly face, its mouth slightly parted beneath the reddened skin that stretches over it. The mindless expression could be comatose or orgasmic.

"Disgusting," Gerry grunts. "I'll deal with you next. I don't work for you anymore."

Again he looms over Violet, this time seeing her. Maybe the proximity of the wooden incubator tray full of accelerants will inspire her flesh by proxy. As the beings in the bins wiggle and vibrate, he watches for some sign of synergy, a hint to help select which accelerant her slumbering soul might prefer. Despite the airtight seals of their plastic containers, the beings sense Violet's nearness, raising a susurrus of invertebrate tap-dancing.

The phone shrieks, a child's high-C howl of terror. Small sharp teeth pierce Gerry's right earlobe. He screams. He jumps. He upends the cabinet. Clear containers burst like bubbles all over the sofa, all over Violet. At least a dozen accelerants swarm into the crack in the cauliflower cowl, vanish into her vestigial nostrils. Six times that many scuttle under the blanket. He yanks it away to see tails, legs, stingers, spinnerets vanishing into newly-bored holes in the cocoon husks. He scrabbles to recapture the ones still unsubmerged but they thrash against his grip and bite his fingers.

Though he could not perceive overlapping layers and gaps in Violet's cocoon, the accelerants find them and slither between them, a scene akin to a hundred undersea creatures retracting into hidden crevasses.

She twitches, a full-body click-beetle flex.

Spikes erupt through the cowl coating her face. Beneath, there are more spikes erupting from spikes erupting from spikes, a fractal blossoming. The spikes lose their rigidity, curl and stretch. At their tips, organs and objects come into existence spontaneously:

toenails, typewriter keys, compound eyes, radio dials, chameleon tongues, squid teeth, dew claws, cloaca.

Between one blink and the next, Violet's cocoon bursts, shards flying with the speed of glass shattered by a bomb. They flay Gerry's forearms as he shields his face. He slams into the refrigerator, which roars a death rattle. Decaying bodies. Fruiting bodies. Bodies of work. Bodies in labor. Suppurating bodies. Desiccating bodies. Dissected bodies. Antibodies.

Violet's multi-jointed or completely boneless limbs catch him up, hug him close, coiling and coiling and coiling, pinning his arms, spreading his legs apart. Tips hard as fangs push into the wounds in his forearms, up between his thighs. He screams in pain and shock and she fills his mouth and plugs his throat, his tongue slapping uselessly against a column that tastes of blood and raw river silt. He gags. He vomits. Violet pushes further into his throat, his chest cavity. His struggles only prove how thoroughly he is immobilized.

She compresses his neck from both the outside and the inside. Paul whispers behind his ear. *Yes yes yes YES yes yes yes*

When the load of pain in his lungs and capillaries and eyes presses past the edge of intolerable she releases the pressure enough to let air and blood through, allowing him a quick, choked exhale and inhale before compressing him again. Except he isn't gasping on his own, when she loosens her grip inside and around his neck, she squeezes his belly hard, forces his diaphragm to shove air out and suck it in. She controls him completely, squeezing him to the brink of death without allowing him to die, *yes* crushing *yes* crushing *yes*

The obstruction dislodges, and Gerry spews an oversized chunk of gray and red gristle onto the china plate. Violet's arms uncouple from his abdomen.

She hisses in his ear, unamused. "Good thing this meat didn't cost us anything." Small teeth nip his earlobe in reproach.

He would yelp in pain but he's still wheezing, his blocked airway thirsty for oxygen. A large bug emerges from the meat hunk-cum-thwarted assassin and proceeds to carry the meat off the table. Either that or the chunk itself has grown legs. Gerry points, but Violet mistakes the meaning. "You want another bite already? You must *really* be hungry."

Paul's droll laugh runs razors along Gerry's nerves. "You never can get enough, *Gerry*."

Throat aching inside and out, Gerry draws in a deep, refreshing breath before taking in the dinner scene. The dish at the center combines broad crispy leaves with fried flowers and a meat that's tubular like sausage. Paul, seated to Gerry's right, has his cherub cheeks bunched into a leering smirk. He lacks the hypertension-red complexion he usually sports. He's either making a show of staring Gerry down with eyes half-lidded or unusually tired and unable to hide it.

Violet is dressed to entertain, her skirt and blouse fitting tight, tight, tight, their fabric multiple shades of gaze-grabbing red. Multiple meanings of *entertain* seem to be signified.

Returned to her seat, Violet aims a haughty gaze of her own Gerry's way, her thin but brightly rouged lips forming a line of disapproval. "Not even a word of thanks?"

Rescued, Gerry understands he's still drowning, though the how eludes him.

One of the tubes of meat seeps an atypical amount of blood from a sliced-open end. Paul grows paler by the minute. Gerry can see, via the reflection captured in the spotless metal of the brand new refrigerator, that dark fluid is pooling under Paul's chair, that the same fluid soaks the insides of Paul's pants legs.

Paul taps another one of the meat tubes. "I paid a hefty price to put this food on your table, *Gerry*. To show you no hard feelings, *Gerry*. Don't blame your clumsy gag reflex on me. You need to taste this. I know you'll like it."

"Don't be rude, Gerry," Violet says.

Gerry's words stay lodged in his throat.

EDIFICE

Eons of water cascading over
brow, cheekbones, chin,
have worn the face of the colossus
almost smooth, the colors
of eyes and skin stripped by time.

Perhaps it had been buried deep,
exposed by inches over millennia
as the rivers carved their slow way down.
Its features so large, those of us
who farmed the plain, who cut

the trees, who built huts on the banks
—we, so much smaller, did not
know it for a face, not even when
we scaled down the cliffs to swim
in the pools at its base.

When our enemies came, armored
and hungry, drove us into the river—
used their spears to puncture us
like fish—our bodies broken on
brow, cheekbones, chin,

the water that cascaded down
its eyes and lips flowed red.
Our bodies bobbed in the pools
beneath its gaze, a glare that

come nightfall glowed red.

Soon our eyes blazed, too.
Without breath or heartbeat
we rose and ascended, rent
our enemies with rotted hands,
and sent them over the falls

to feed our new-awakened savior.

STRANGE WISDOMS OF THE DEAD

with Charles M. Saplak

ONE

JOHN STARKEY PULLED A FUNERAL SHROUD from one of the corpses stacked on deck, wrapped his shoulders against the chill. He bent the corpse forward to free the shroud; it stayed slightly bent at the waist, and seemed to stare at Starkey, eyes wide but without lustre, hands frozen in a gesture of clutching.

Starkey returned to the wheel of the Saint Catherine, and barely gave the corpse another glance. He was cold, he was busy. "Laying to" the one-hundred-and-forty foot sloop was ticklish, even with a full watch onboard; Starkey was the only one alive on this creaking, half-rotted vessel.

He needed to take her out the channel, and northward about three miles. There he would lash the mainsail over hard port, and the wheel over hard starboard, as close to simultaneously as possible. At nightfall he would fire the pitch and straw in the ship's hold. The burning ship would drift south with the current. Starkey would be safely aboard the dinghy he was towing, rowing back to collect his fee. The good citizens of Bliss, those not dead from the Plague, nor taken to the hills for fear of it, would see the ship burn down to the waterline, and would know that more than one hundred and seventy of their stiff, cold brethren were being sent to the next world—and so would be off the streets, with neither smell, nor raw bone, nor ichor to bedevil the living.

The city fathers would give him seventy pieces of the local coinage—two years living, come what may. But coin was only part of the reason Starkey was here . . . .

The channel behind him, Starkey turned the Saint Catherine into the northern current. He was making the maneuver more complicated than it had to be. He needed a certain amount of extra time.

He would set the rigging first, since the wheel would be easy. He already had the ragged mainsail at full trim, and had a six-to-one block rigged to take a strain on the traveler, necessary to move the massive sail himself.

He was glad he was alone. He wouldn't have to share his pay. And what he wanted to do, no one could see . . . .

He sweated with effort, despite the chill. The air began to mist over. Strange, thought Starkey. Not the right time of day for fog to form. He glanced at the surface of the water. The normal gray translucence of early winter seawater was now a crystalline blue, a blue like the glaze on porcelain. And above it, thickening fog.

It isn't right. A current from the north, with thick fog? In late afternoon, well before nightfall? Could the blue water be that warm? Nothing makes sense . . . .

But this was not the time to puzzle. He pulled the end of the block rigging over to a ratcheting windlass on the port side amidships. He had the bitter end of the rig made around the windlass, and took up a wooden pin he could use as a lever. He inserted the pin, and leaned into it.

On deck, the stacked and shrouded cargo shifted a little as the boom tensioned and began to shift.

The fo'c'sle and jib entered the fog. Wispy fingers of mist curled 'round slowly, stroking the ship.

Starkey continued to crank the windlass, taking more and more strain. The block tightened some more, and the mainsail boom complained, but continued to swing.

The wind grew, and fog slid like snakes of smoke along the deck. The rigging creaked and complained, and the windlass shivered in his hands. Through his sailor's calluses he felt that something was wrong. Damn this old condemned stack of splinters! The rigging was rotten, the mechanisms were rotten, the hull was rotten . . . .

A rogue wave from the north punched the Saint Catherine, she lurched port, and the stack of corpses shifted. One corpse tumbled to the deck, and its shroud fell open, revealing pasty skin and caked blood. Starkey had no time to think, as rigging groaned, then sang, then snapped. The mainsail boom swept the deck, and Starkey could only watch as things unfolded with unreal speed.

And then he was struck, and darkness.

TWO

S TARKEY KNEW NOTHING BUT COLD: a deep, invasive chill that frosted his bones, stung his eyes, and filled his head with visions of eternal snow. He slowly realized that his eyes were open. He lay face up on the deck, staring at a torn sail that flapped soundlessly within a shroud of fog.

He tried to rise and groaned as a knife of pain sliced his temple from within. When his eyes focused again he ran fingers through his hair, and drew them back bloody. Nausea coursed through him. He remained still until it passed, his gaze falling on one of the wrapped forms stacked nearby, on a calloused and dirty hand free from the swaddling shroud.

When he could breath steadily again, he rose, this time more gingerly, and peered seaward.

He couldn't tell if it was twilight or dawn. The fog was so thick here on deck that when he held out his arms, his hands blurred in the haze.

He could see no horizon. Saint Catherine was still in the current of blue water, but there was no wind. Fog rose in columns like "sea smoke," the fog old sailors talked about encountering in the seas where Polaris was at its highest in the night skies.

And the quiet. Yes, of course there were sounds—the ubiquitous slapping of the waves, the groaning of the ship's wooden body, the clanking of the tackle, and a distant, low creaking from far over the water which seemed to resonate in Starkey's very bones—but these sounds were hollow and muffled, as if the fog had wrapped around the world like wool.

He needed to survey the damage. Despite his throbbing head, he made his way across the fog-shrouded deck. He stumbled once on a tangle of line ripped loose from the mainsail, but kept his feet and moved aft, making mental note of each piece of standing rigging he passed, barely noticing how the fog flowed over and around the corpses on deck as a stream dances through rocks. In a minute's time, he was at the quarterdeck.

The wheel was tied over, hard starboard. He was relieved, but forced to search the mists of his own memory. When had he tied the wheel over? After the boom struck him?

So much was blank. Had the boom struck him at all? Had it come free? It was made fast now, with the mainsail over hard port. He'd heard of memory fleeing a man after such an event . . . .

No matter. He had to anchor himself in the here and now. So the ship had survived, the rigging was relatively undamaged, and the hull was as intact as could be expected. There was one last thing to check.

He went to the aft rail, and as soon as the painter, the line to which the dinghy had been tethered, came into view, Starkey could see that something was terribly wrong.

There should have been a strain on the painter as the dinghy was towed behind, but the line lay slack.

Starkey pulled it in hand over hand, and the fact that it offered no resistance confirmed his worst fear.

The painter had been a stout rope, two inches round. Starkey examined the bitter end. Broken? No, breaking lines unravel. Cut? No, cut lines showed uniform marks from a blade. These marks were strange . . . as if it had dissolved.

This was not the end of the world. The ship would drift southward with the current. Two knots current. In three or four hours the ship would run aground in the salt marsh south of Bliss, somewhere between Whitestone and Greater Saltburn.

He could torch it right there in the swamp. It would be the decent thing to do. He may have argument back at Bliss about his seventy coins, but payment was less important than having the time to do what he had come to do . . . .

He stepped carefully through the fog and torn rigging, skirting sprawling bodies. He stooped over a small, tightly wrapped form, the body of a woman, propped against the deckhouse, where he had set her hours ago. He cradled her in his arms and carried her aft and down, through the hatch into the captain's cabin, where he set her on the bed.

In the pale light which bled through the ladderwell and through the aft portholes, he examined her.

Tenderly, he pulled away her shroud.

"Mary," he said, fighting back tears.

"Mary."

He pealed the veil away from her face. Her golden hair spilled free. Her delicate features appeared flush and hale. Her eyes were closed, her expression serene—she could have been sleeping.

Starkey felt breathless. He closed his eyes, leaned over and kissed her cold, swollen lips. They had wrapped her in bedding of lavender and pennyroyal, and their herbal aroma almost, almost masked the scent of meat.

The memory of her skin against his ached in him, tortured him, like a starving man's memory of his last meal. He wanted so much—her musical laugh, her throaty whisper against his ear, the salty taste of her flesh.

Starkey undid the lace at her collar, revealing red sores which stared at him from her bosom like accusing eyes. Her flesh below the collar had become gray and black.

For the first time in many, many years he closed his eyes, and prayed for his very soul.

He could not bring himself to leave her. Her weight in his arms was a comfort, as it had been far too few a night. He gave himself up to sleep, and dreams, and at times it felt that Mary pulled herself closer during the night, listening to his heart as she used to do.

THREE

THE SUN GLITTERED AGAINST THE CALM SEA, its light a trillion shards of brightness.

The good gentleman, Master John Starkey, stood on the quarterdeck of a strong ship. Although he wore the fine clothes of a wealthy merchant, the deckhands didn't mutter beneath their breath as he watched over them. He'd been one of them, he had, and although he had coin now he still knew his rocks and shoals. Even the Captain nodded to him as he passed. Starkey was a man to know . . . And his pretty young wife . . . .

There was Mary on deck now, in lace and ribbons, and fine weaves which hugged her shape. She stood with her right hand on a line of fancy rigging, her fingertips delicately curled around it, not clutching it with fear, nor with the unsteadiness of the lubber. Graceful, she was . . . .

Starkey walked up behind her, reached out to put his hand upon her shoulder. She was looking at the village of Bliss, their destination, sitting as peaceful and balanced within the rocky shore as if God had just placed it there Himself, and was watching it with His all-seeing eyes.

"Is it not beautiful, my Mary?" Starkey asked. "Is it not everything I told you it would be?"

She didn't turn around, but Starkey heard her speak.

"It is good," she said. "So good to feel again."

With infinite tenderness, Starkey put a hand to her hair; stroked the wheaten gold.

And as she turned to him with closed eyes and expressionless face, Starkey noticed that the lock of hair he touched had come off, and was tangled in his fingertips.

Starkey sat bolt upright in the captain's bed, gasping.

The bed beside him was empty, although in the lamplight he could see dust, flakes of dried blood, threads of gauze from a funeral shroud—all lying in the faint impression of a slender woman.

Twisted around the fingers of his right hand was a wispy lock of blonde hair.

Starkey calmed himself, folding the nightmare into managable sections, and placing it away.

He swung his legs to the deck, gave his blood time to settle, gave his eyes time to adjust to the dim light. Everything was as it had been when he'd passed out, except that Mary was nowhere to be seen.

Had someone come in as he had slept and taken her? That thought could have filled him with shame, but instead he felt anger.

Starkey cocked his head, listened. There was a commotion on deck. People were moving around. Were these the people who had dragged Mary from his bed?

Starkey headed up the ladderwell toward the hatch which led to the quarterdeck. Moving around within the ship he could see that night had fallen. At the hatch to the main deck he steeled himself. So they had seen him entangled with Mary. Perhaps they were just waiting for him to emerge, waiting with torches, iron eyes, a lash to shred the blasphemer's back, or even a noose rigged to the yardarm.

Well, damn them all! Had these unworthy beasts laid hands on Mary . . . .

He gritted his teeth and pressed against the hatch, swinging it up and open.

The fetid below-decks air gasped out around Starkey, and was whipped away in the breeze which ran fore to aft. The fog was still there, but stars slid through patchy gaps of clear sky above the rigging. Starkey heard the infinitely familiar rhythm of water breaking against the sides of the ship.

As his eyes adjusted he made out not a howling mob with torches, but figures moving silently about the decks. A solitary lantern in the lee of the deckhouse cast long shadows, but little light. He could barely see, and almost bumped into someone not an arm's length away from him.

He peered into the darkness, and realized just what he was seeing. Lips withered back from dry teeth, lidless eyes, hands clutching as if searching for a stolen shroud.

The corpses were no longer stacked on deck, but were moving about the ship.

Fear welled in his throat like frozen blood. Something within his mind, something normally steady and equalized, pitched and yawed just as the Saint Catherine did on this dark sea. Dreams within dreams—what was real?

Immediately, he knew what he had to do. He ran to the solitary lantern, and pulled it from its sconce. Flame was reassuring. Its light and heat were natural, worldly.

And now to the pitch and straw. This ship had to burn. No, he couldn't escape, but that was no matter. This ship, and these walking things, these undead, had to burn.

He was almost at the hatch leading to his below-decks pyre when slender fingers gently, coldly, touched his arm.

He turned, and it was Mary.

Her eyes were open, but dry and unfocused. She took his face in her hands with unnatural strength and pressed her mouth to his, her cold, dry tongue against his teeth, and when he pulled way she loosed a long, rasping sigh.

"So good to feel again," she said.

She knocked the lamp from his hand, and it rolled across the decks and disappeared overboard.

"Onward," she whispered, pulling away into darkness.

FOUR

A CORPSE—BUT WAS IT RIGHT TO CALL IT THAT?—stood skeletally tangled in the ship's wheel like a scarecrow on its stake. As the deck rolled, the corpse flexed at the knees, stiffly, but no less rhythmically than would a living man. It clutched the spokes and rings of the ship's wheel. In the dim starlight it could have been any one of Starkey's old quartermaster friends, standing watch through the deepest part of a dark, foggy night.

The corpse slowly wound its head over its right shoulder, and the wind plucked a lock of dry, weedy hair to one side, like an invisible hand drawing aside a curtain, showing Starkey a face of split skin and empty eye sockets.

"It is right that he should be there," said someone behind Starkey.

Starkey turned on his heel.

A man, a dead man, stood there, stiffly trying to stay still on the rolling deck, closely examining a rust-encrusted, but still sharply pointed, iron rod.

"Is this my sword?" the corpse asked.

"That's a marlinspike," Starkey said. "We use it to weave lines. Why do you say it's right that he should be there?"

"For he was a sailor," the dead man answered, not looking up from the marlinspike.

"Am I dead?" Starkey asked.

"He remembers. Or something about him remembers. He went back to the ship's wheel. He was a sailor." As he spoke he held the marlinspike before him, making stiff hacking motions, parrying motions, as if it were a sword.

"Where is my shield?" the man asked. "And where did you put my chain mail? And my helmet?"

"I've never seen those things," Starkey said. "Maybe the people who brought you in took those things away. Anything of value . . . ."

"I want to meet The Christ dressed correctly. I picture myself kneeling before God, holding my sword before me . . . . The people who brought me in?"

"Do you remember being sick at all?" Starkey asked.

"I was on Pilgrimage. I was headed to Jerusalem. There was a village, not much of a place. A tiny dot by the sea. 'Bliss,' it was so named. I got sick near there. Fever. And blood."

"Am I dead?" Starkey asked again.

"What are you?" the knight asked, looking up from the corroded marlinspike, squinting at Starkey as if looking at a living man was too bright a sight for his dead eyes. "What were you?"

"Are we headed to God?" Starkey asked.

"We are headed where we are headed," the knight answered. "I'll prepare myself. You simply prepare to fire the ship."

"Why do you want the ship to burn?" Starkey asked.

The knight shrugged. "The hero is put to sea in a burning ship. He crosses over to the other side through the flames, and there I'll be greeted by God. That's what I've always dreamed of. Of course, I didn't expect to have to coordinate all of this myself."

"I'll start the fire," Starkey said. "I just need to find someone first. You can rely on me."

The knight nodded.

"God relies on you, Starkey."

FIVE

S TARKEY FINALLY FIRED A TORCH. It was difficult; no hearth was burning on the ship, no cook's stove, no smith's forge. Yes, he'd scrounged flint and iron, but all the torches were damp from the infernal fog.

Starkey prowled the decks as the night wore on, his torch held high. The raised dead moved about, most in stoney silence. Some worked the rigging, others manned the rails. Some clutched their shrouds, others were naked and glistening with the fog.

Starkey went first to the quarterdeck. A figure sat there, hunched over in the darkness, its hands rhythmically moving amidst a tangle of cloth.

"Mary?" Starkey called.

The figure didn't look up.

Starkey walked to a spot over the right shoulder of the figure. The dim light of his torch revealed boney hands moving like spiders amidst a tangle of threads, tying knots, pulling bitter ends, looping bights.

"Weaver," Starkey said, "I look for a young woman. Mary is her name."

The "weaver" slowly turned her head. Her eyes were cavernous, and the dim torch found no irises to illuminate.

And then the weaver spoke, a voice as dry and distant as a desert of ice.

"Look for her here," the weaver hissed, tapping the cloth before her with a cracked and yellow fingernail.

Starkey peered at the cloth, a half-completed tapestry. He could see where parts of the sails, parts of rags left onboard the ship, parts of shrouds from the corpses themselves were being broken into their component threads, then reborn into this knotted world of gray and blood-brown.

Tiny figures danced across the shroud, hand in hand with humorlessly grinning skeletons.

"This is where we all end up," the weaver said.

Starkey turned away. He had no time for these philosophies. He needed Mary—where had she gone?

Starkey padded up toward the deckhouse. Perhaps she was there, sheltered from the fog and spray. Starkey held his torch high with his right hand while he opened the aft hatch of the deckhouse with his left.

The deckhouse was still as empty as when the salvers and looters had left it, but someone was sitting on the roughhewn bench along the starboard bulkhead. Starkey knew immediately that it wasn't Mary.

When he had died he had been an old man, with wispy white hair on his temples, a bald and spotted pate, and jaws left slack by absent teeth. He sat and rocked and mumbled to himself.

Starkey didn't even consider asking this man about Mary. He proceeded toward the forward hatch of the deckhouse, edging past the mumbler, loath that he should try to reach and touch him. As he passed him he could make out the man's words:

"Whilst I traveled to my master's house I stopped and here I rest; whilst I traveled to my master's house I stopped and here I rest; whilst I traveled . . . ."

But Starkey also heard something else, something separate from the whispers of the sea and the creaking which had grown to a dull and constant rumble like distant thunder. Not the calls of dolphins nor whales, nor any other sea creature . . . . There was a feminine voice, coming from beneath a hatch which led from the deckhouse to the main hold.

Starkey raised the hatch, and, without hesitation, descended into the hold. The air there was stale and cold. He could smell the pitch and coal tar. He'd have to be careful with the torch. As he made his way amongst the bales of hay and the molded stanchions and beams, the feminine voice, mouthing things he couldn't immediately understand, led him like an invisible cord unwound within a maze.

And then he was upon them.

Normally the sight of a man between a woman's legs, pumping away, would be exciting and devious, or at the least, humorous.

But these two . . . .

The man was rhythmic in his movements, but awkward. It was as if he knew what he was doing and how to do it, but could not remember why.

The woman bleated occasionally, but her voice was dry, passionless.

"I almost felt that . . . ," she hissed into the man's ear.

Disgusted, Starkey left them behind, climbed up the ladderwell out of the hold.

Mary. All things were Mary. He needed her. Would she have returned to the captain's cabin? He hurried there.

He paused outside the captain's cabin. Lamplight shone around the edges of the hatch. Someone within moved around.

He hesitated. Would he see lovers there? Would one of them be Mary? Mary, bleating and moaning beneath some rutting carrion? He couldn't bear the thought . . . .

He decided that if he saw that, he'd fire the ship right away. And he'd hang himself before he watched it burn. He wouldn't even have to think.

Armed with that resolve, he swung open the hatch.

There were no lovers there, but a man hunched over the chart table. As the hatch opened he glanced up at Starkey. The man had arranged his shroud into a dignified cloak. He was bearded, with reddened eyes, dark grey lips, a prominent, furrowed brow.

A chart was stretched across the table. In the man's hands were dividers fashioned from sharpened finger bones, and a straightedge made from a thighbone ground and jointed down on one side.

The man only watched Starkey for a moment, then went back to work on the chart.

Starkey started to chuckle.

"Is there something you want to share?" the man asked, quietly.

"You're using our known course and speed to chart our position?" Starkey asked.

"Yes," the man answered.

"I believe we call that 'dead' reckoning," Starkey said, grinning.

The man gave no indication that he found it funny, or even understood what Starkey was talking about. He shrugged and went back to the chart.

"Where are we?" Starkey asked. "Why are we here? Who set this course?"

The bearded man smiled. As he spoke he took up a sharpened bone, and dipped it into a jagged bowl made of bone, and drew on the stretched parchment on the chart table before him.

"You question carries its own shadow. What about you, John Starkey? Think of yourself as a ship. Your life as an ocean. Where did you go and why? Did you set your own course? Were you driven? Did you drift?"

As he spoke he scratched the bone splinter around the surface of the parchment, describing a lazy curve which spiraled inward.

"My life?" Starkey asked. "Short. But relentlessly long, too, day by day. I rarely had enough to eat. When the Black Death began mowing the countryside down, I was too tired to care to lower my head. Now all I want is a woman named Mary. I don't have time for your riddles. If you know where she'd be, tell me. If not, I'll leave you to draw your snail shells."

The bearded man smiled. "You don't understand this? So many things I didn't understand. I thought the stars were points on a dome above the plain of the sea. Now I can hear the whispers of green creatures who walk the shores of orange seas under blue suns. I can look at a dot of light in the night sky and see a 'snail's shell' made of millions of suns. Do you know why I draw this spiral? Look at this."

He took up the parchment and then reached back onto the captain's bed to take up a skull. He brought the two things together, wrapping the skull with the parchment.

"See this curve, this spiral? It's a loxodrome, John Starkey. The chart is flat, but the sea enwraps a round world, a sphere. Does not a ship's sail disappear over the horizon after her hull? And this loxodrome straightens out, as our course. Oh, so many things I've gained, so many things to understand, and such a short time."

Starkey noticed that the chart bore a traditional compass rose. A nice touch. But when Starkey looked closer, he saw that the compass rose was a tattoo, and the parchment of the chart was really skin.

"What were you in life?" he asked. "A butcher?"

The "navigator" laughed, pulled the chart away, and turned the skull so that Starkey could see the face. The skull still had eyes, which were whole and aware. They focused on Starkey and he recoiled.

"He serves now as he did in life," the navigator said. "It is right that he should be here."

"I leave you to your blood and riddles," Starkey said. He was almost out the hatch when the bearded man called after him.

"Riddles, Starkey? A riddle thus: 'Where is the most beautiful woman onboard a ship usually located?'"

SIX

SHE STOOD BEFORE HIM AT THE EYES OF THE SHIP, balanced and delicate, only holding the rigging with her slightly curled fingertips, standing without fear or unsteadiness, peering into the mists ahead. The skies ahead seemed to be lightening, as if with the approach of dawn. The sound which Starkey had earlier considered as a distant creaking or rumble was now a distinct thing, a maelstrom of breaking waves, yet muffled, strange in its timbre.

The wooden figurehead was gone, taken by the salvers before Saint Catherine had left port on her funerary mission. Working now as an effigy before some shop, or gracing some tavern. Now Mary had taken her place, looking for all the world like the real Saint Catherine, beautiful and grace-laden, yet bloody and broken at the wheel . . . .

Starkey set his torch in a socket for a belaying pin, and approached her.

"Mary, we're headed North. We'll fall off the ends of the Earth. These dead things. They're taking us to Hell. I'm going to fire the ship, Mary. I want you in my arms as it burns. Fire will cleanse us."

Mary glanced back at him briefly. She was smiling.

"An old ship, but a strong one, John. Old and strong, like you. It served its purpose. Be still, and take your place in the sails. Be still for the journey."

"I was more than a deckape, Mary. I had skills. Many a day I spent hours onboard some ship, earning my keep, at work on the sails, nothing there but myself, a biscuit, and a needle."

"No one doubts you, Bonnie John Starkey. You were a good man. But why would that world have a good man in it?"

But stop for a moment. Something that he said. Myself and a biscuit. When had he eaten last? Did he feel hungry? Why didn't he feel hungry?

He couldn't be distracted. Mary stood there, idly tasting her fingertips, looking forward.

Cold. He was so cold. He breathed out to see the puff of breath he knew would come in the cold. But there was no breath visible. Mary was talking to him, but no breath was visible from her lips. It occurred to Starkey that he had seen no breath from anyone onboard. Yet it was so cold!

"Mary," he called. "I just want to be with you. I realize now what a terrible mistake it was."

"What was a mistake?"

"Everything. Everything which wasn't taking me to you. Every moment I spent away from you."

"She loved you, John Starkey," Mary said, turning to look forward, her eyes scouring the mists like a lookout.

"Who do you speak of? 'She' who? Mary, talk to me!"

She turned again to speak to him, as if he were a child demanding attention.

"It's behind us. It shrinks in importance. You want to be with me. That want is an echo, an illusion. You don't want for anything. Forget."

Her face brightened as she heard something in the distance. "It's closer, now, John! It's closer!"

John Starkey moved carefully. He needed to keep his footing. He looked down at his bare feet stepping along the rough planking of the deck. He couldn't feel the wood on the skin of his bare soles.

Finally he was beside her. He reached out to wrap his arms around her, pull her against him. He would close his eyes and not let her go, and think of nothing but her warmth and softness against him.

But she eluded him, and stepped out on the bowsprit. "Alone, John Starkey. Each alone. I don't remember," she called. The rumbling in the distance intensified, as if to punctuate her thought.

He didn't want to step out after her. He couldn't feel his feet or legs, and was sure that he would fall, or worse, knock her off into the ocean below. They would never be reunited.

He tugged at his hair. There had been blood. There had been blood before, but now there was dry, brown powder.

"Why did you leave me?" he cried.

"Now? On the ship? Or when she was alive?" Mary said.

She didn't turn around, but continued to strain forward, into the mists, from which the grinding sound was now constant.

"We each must be alone," she continued. "I can't even feel close to the one inside me."

Starkey watched her casually gesture toward her belly.

"Inside you?" Starkey mumbled, stepping forward onto the bowsprit.

"The child was yours," Mary said, then jabbed a finger forward, pointing, her eyes wide.

"Closer, it's closer!" she screamed. "There! There it is!"

* * *

SEVEN

Mists parted before the Saint Catherine. Starkey realized what he was seeing, and all the great moments of his past—when as a child he had first noticed the beating of his own heart, when he had crossed the equator and seen coal-black men and strange constellations, when he had first looked into the blue coolness of Mary's eyes—these moments faded like shadows eaten by the fall of night.

Within the mists—and he was at the very source of mist and winds and strange currents, he knew that—fog and rain themselves were the very breath of this thing he was seeing—here was an island of ice. Waves broke against its crystalline shores, ran back to the sea in howling rivulets. Sections of shore calved away and formed ice floes even as Starkey watched.

And even as the shore deteriorated beneath the onslaught of the waves it instantly rebuilt itself; the all-encompassing cold of the thing took the seawater and froze it into arches, bridges, and delicate spires, decorations in a wild landscape.

The sun—or some great light—had topped the horizon behind the castle, so that its rays shone through the ice, splitting into trillions of shards of brightness and color.

As wondrous as was the island itself, most amazing was what Starkey saw there in the island's center. A castle of sheer ice, thousands of feet tall, greater than any cathedral, greater than any city, dominated the island. And yet . . . .

Any castle was a structure, an arrangement, a static stack of stone and beams and earthenworks, existing as is. This was no dead, static structure. Even as Starkey watched the castle constructed itself, pumping the icey seawater upward through great capillaries. Far overhead, seawater was expelled in huge spouts, freezing into gracefully curved walls and ramparts and castellations.

So many details Starkey couldn't recognize in the distance. For a moment he thought this castle to be ringed around with gargoyles of ice, then he thought these figures were human bodies, washed clean of their faces, and then he saw these bodies writhing. He couldn't be sure what he was seeing. The castle was so far beyond the measure of his mind, no details were apprehensible.

Behind John Starkey, all came forward.

Corpses abandoned their places at the rails and in the rigging; the skeleton who had held the wheel tottered forward; the couple Starkey had observed humping in the hold were no longer intertwined, but stumbled forward separately.

The mumbling man was in the crowd, toothlessly mouthing, "Master, Master!"

The weaver attempted to tie her tapestry of a Danse Macabre to some standing rigging, to fly it like a battle flag.

The navigator had some instrument like an astrolabe rigged from bones, and through this he sighted the castle, noting its dimensions.

And there was the knight, bedecked in armor and helmet scrounged from bones. He still held the marlinspike; as Starkey watched he stepped to the rail, shouting, "I'm ready for Thee!" He then leapt overboard and disappeared beneath the ice and waves.

Starkey grabbed the torch from the socket where he'd set it. He had to fire the ship. That he knew. He touched the flames to the rails, the deck, to everything he could reach, but no fire would start.

"Is it not beautiful, my love? Is it not everything I told you it would be?" Mary, her face decorated with geometric webs of frost, hissed into his ear.

No fire would start. The ship lurched beneath his feet, and ice and blue water spilled onto the deck. The castle and its island were expanding, reaching forward, encompassing the Saint Catherine—a harbor of ice moving toward the ship.

Snow and mist and freezing rain fell on all like the breath of a mysterious god, and ice began to cover all.

Sprawling, slipping, Starkey dropped the torch, and desperately reached for Mary.

There she stood. All was becoming dark. Starkey felt nothing.

Supreme effort, and Starkey's fingertips touched Mary's hand.

She glanced at him. There she was.

Above all, a yawning chasm. The Saint Catherine was drawn into the castle.

Darkness completed itself.

His fingers were touching Mary.

There was nothing else.

For precious seconds, eons, he was touching her.

Then, finally, that touch also disappeared.

VACANT

The hair twining out from the drain
No one lives here with locks that color

The air whistling in through the curtains
No one stands there to hold them closed

The light flaring on in the other room
Nothing lives here that needs to see

The stare boiling white from the mirror
No one stands before it to stare back

Falling Is What It Loves

O N BALANCE, RAE HATED HER FATHER more than she loved
him, but as his delirium subsided and his shouting ceased and
he once again lay quiet in his sickbed, she made a conscientious
decision to do the thing that fit the moment, and damn whatever
hassle might be conjured in consequence.

His eyes stayed closed as she kissed his clammy forehead. "I
love you, Dad."

He did not stir. In the morning, her mother would call, say
he died in his sleep, invite Rae to return and view the body, an
invitation she would refuse. But that was still many hours in the
future.

A dread squeezed in her chest as she opened her apartment
door. Her roommate stood in the entrance to the kitchenette, juggling a trio of gruestones. Four more glowed inside the eye sockets of its massive head, a brown-furred fusion of bison, boar, and
vampire bat.

Its hook-horned features no longer fazed her, not unlike how
her first cat had cured her fear of the dark via nightly leaps onto
the mattress. The thought of what her roommate might say, on the
other hand, tensed her shoulders and set her teeth on edge. The
exposed gruestones further heightened her anxiety. Their presence triggered wildly diverging sensations: the catch of breath on
encountering someone who punches all the buttons of attraction,
and the pressure behind one eye that threatens to bulge into a mi-
graine.

Her fingers curled with longing, to catch and hold one of
them. Just one gruestone.

She willed her fingers straight.

As she dropped her purse onto the living room couch, the scent of her roommate reached her, a blend of scorched metal and cinnamon. It stuck out its tri-forked tongue and bared incisors long as tusks, a theatrical display of distaste. Its voice rumbled and buzzed in the manner of throat singing, one register deep and gravelly, the other cicada-shrill. "Why did you do that?"

Did it mean putting her purse down, her gesture of grasping, something else? He shoulders tightened as she braced for an attack. "Do what?"

With one of its free arms, it plucked another gruestone out of its head, an action that equated to shouting, *I saw you!* Glowing greenish blue, the gruestone orbs served her roommate—*all* the roommates, so hers had told her—as eyes that perceived in four dimensions, including forward and backward along the timestreams. They also could detach as easily and regenerate more rapidly than lizards' tails, thus doubling as a means for self-entertainment.

"Kiss him." Two of her roommate's arms crooked akimbo at its sides. Four more were engaged in the juggling game.

The stupidest question escaped her mouth before she could stop it. "Why do you care?"

She could have kicked herself. Her roommate monitored her at all times and spaces, nosier even than her phone or tablet when it came to documenting her whereabouts and actions. Moment to moment, this did not bother her deeply—she and her friends had all grown up under an assumption of constant government and commercial surveillance, even found it flattering for its implications of importance. But the roommates weren't on a mission to sell books and beauty products or ferret out threats to national security.

Her roommate tilted its jagged head. "Your signals flooded the relativistic aether." It *always* said that, in response to such a question, though it added, "The loudest they ever have."

"Why wouldn't I kiss him?" She shrugged off her denim jacket and draped it over the back of a reclining chair. "He's my father. He's dying."

"Isn't that what you've longed for? His death?" It further hammered in its point by extracting a fifth gruestone from one of the many sockets in its craggy face and dropping it into the cat's cradle of trajectories, engaging two more hands in the tossing and catching. To a roommate, juggling gruestones served the same purpose as a human twirling hair or chewing fingernails. "You mutter under your breath all the time about how you want to kill him," it said, "anyone could hear it, not just others like me."

No aspect of her roommate was more distressing than its bottomless appetite for these confrontations. Before Rae dropped out of college, an English professor had assigned a gorgeous poem about juggling, written by a dead white guy. Faced with her roommate's repeated cruelty, her mind often inanely repeated a line from that poem like a sample repeated to a brutal industrial metal backbeat. *Falling is what it loves. Falling is what it loves.*

Not two days ago, when she had come back from an overnight with Medhavi, her roommate demanded, *Why didn't you tell her how you really feel? You swore up and down you would this time.* To be fair, Rae had asked herself the same thing both before and after her roommate confronted her.

Challenging how she handled her father's accelerating illness, though, went beyond the pale. Rae dug her fingers into the corduroy of a couch pillow, considered hurling it into her roommate's arms in hopes it would scatter the gruestones and the creature's concentration. "Not that it's ever your business, but my sister and my mother needed me to set all that aside. Maybe *I* even needed to do that. Any reasonable person would understand."

She picked up the pillow. Her roommate stopped juggling, quickly catching and concealing each gruestone within thick slate-gray fingers—but it didn't stop talking. "You're going to wonder, from now on, every day from now on, if you should have said something else."

No feat of foretelling, this statement. On the way home she had already pondered: what if, when she leaned in close, she had instead whispered to her father, *I hope it hurts.* The thought pierced like a splinter.

She advanced, pillow brandished. It stepped back. Ridiculous, that her roommate was twice her size, possessed a dozen arms and a mouth full of tusks and fangs, yet flinched if she so much as raised a fist in frustration. All bark, no bite.

Its next bark bit, though. "You'll wish you demanded an apology, a real one."

An apology long denied, one that was never going to come. "Didn't . . . cross my mind, that."

"It will."

"Because *you said it*."

"No. Long after I'm forgotten."

A claim her roommate made, again and again. She had heard of other roommates making the same claim. Mostly repeated by influencers trying in vain to post photo and video evidence of their own roommates. People like that were the only ones brash enough to talk about their roommates publicly.

From the same sources, Rae had also heard speculation that only the members of a roommate's chosen household could see it, though she doubted this. Among her own true confidantes, she was certain Geoff had a roommate. She had glimpsed a misshapen silhouette and the telltale not-glow of gruestones in his home office, the last time she'd spent a day at his house binge-watching selections from the streaming services he pirated.

Rae suspected Medhavi did too, though she had less evidence to go on, only a glimpse in her peripheral vision—a dark form behind the shower curtain, reflected in the bathroom mirror as Rae freshened up after lovemaking. She could have pushed open the office door or pulled back the shower curtain, but the intimidating absence of information about what might happen, and the fear that filled that void, checked her impulse.

The precise moment that the roommates arrived in this world could not be pinpointed. In hindsight it seemed like blind sites and anonymous message boards were dropping hints for years. Back in the spring, as she sipped coffee in the break room, one of her co-workers launched into a non sequitur rant about gruestones and timestreams. A week later, Rae woke up from an unremarkable sleep and ventured out to find her own roommate squatting on the couch, a many-armed gargoyle. *You're going into the kitchen to get a bagel and put peanut butter on it*, it said with that two-toned hum. *I would also like one*.

She could not fathom ever forgetting her roommate, not least because of how often it tipped her off balance when it hurled deeply personal challenges her way. This challenge over her father, though, she had caught and turned over in her hand. Its warped accusation came with burrs of truth embedded—Rae's

endless internal bickering would no doubt dive over and over
into this awful what if, what her final words to her father should
have been, did he deserve the ones she gave him . . . yet the pause
her roommate's words had given her also allowed her to sharpen
arrows tipped with logic, bend back a bow strung with anger.

Her two eyes glared into its many. "I *wish* I could forget you
right now. Demanding an apology from my incoherent, delirious
dad, that would have been *the dumbest* thing I could have done."

"I completely agree, but the signals that are coming from
you—" It waved the gruestones clutched in its hands in all directions, an attempt to convey some equivalent of decibels. "You
will wish you had, with all your wounded heart."

She advanced and the creature shrank back, its arms folding
in tight to its torso. "Ridiculous! His mind is gone."

"That doesn't change what he did."

It did not. After years of living on her own, with her father's
cancer slowly killing him for half a decade, his transgressions
boiled down in her mind to a single incident branded white hot
on her soul, a nadir that summarized many other sins before and
since.

Needling her after dinner about how she wasn't going to get
driving lessons until she brought her grades up—with her seven-
teenth birthday only days away—talking right over her when she
protested that she was trying. He repeated, with a smile, that com-
plaining was pointless because she wouldn't be worthy until *he
said so*. She fell silent, fuming. He started in on her yet again, and
anger seized her arms. She flung her still-laden dinner plate.

It splashed and shattered against the stove. He reached her
side of the table in the next instant, pinned her by her neck to the
wall and punched her hard enough in the stomach to make her
retch.

Her mother and sister said nothing.

Afterward, whenever Rae brought it up, he would shut her
down by insisting he had already apologized, even though it
wasn't true. *I thought we were done with this. Why are you always
so sensitive?*

Yet forward from that moment, the ways he interacted with
her began to evolve, even though he never acknowledged that
any of his thinking had changed. Despite all the derision he had

dumped upon her teenage artistic dabbling, he paid for art school, aimed that same derision at the notion of a student loan. He dropped calling her by her deadname from the day she told her parents who she truly was. In fact, at times he took it too far and scolded her mother when she slipped, with an edge that made Rae nervous even as her heart warmed.

Rae advanced another step. "No decent person—of *any* species, I think—would pick *this moment* to throw these things in my face."

"You're throwing them in mine," the roommate said, its unearthly voice higher-pitched and plaintive. "Your signals flood me."

"Then go someplace where they don't. Get out of here."

"I've told you, I cannot."

The fire in her flared hotter. "You could always choose not to speak."

Astonishingly, no retort followed. Her roommate restored some of its gruestones to the sockets it had emptied them from, the gestures not unlike those of an insect grooming its head. The silence stretched uninterrupted. Her roommate withdrew further into shadow.

Rae thought of flipping the light on, but her victory had already spawned seeds of guilt. She hurried down the hall to her bedroom and slammed the door.

It could follow her in there if it wanted, but she sensed that for now it wouldn't. As she sat cross-legged on the bed, chest heaving, a sense of dread sprouting even without obvious roots, she asked her mirror and her Muppet-print pillows, "How do I shut off the signals?"

She had in fact put that question to her roommate. It had shrugged, its many shoulder joints rippling. *Someday, if evolution permits.*

She contemplated stuffing her ears with music, interrupting signal with signal, if the physics of it even worked that way. She couldn't bring herself to do it, though, because there was no song she wanted to hear after seeing her father's flaccid face, hearing him shout *What the fuck are you doing?* for no reason with nobody close by.

The rasp of his breath as he twitched between the rails of his sickbed had convinced her that he needed permission, somehow, to take leave of a half-life that was every bit the painful existence she once had wished on him. Part of her believed he relaxed, settled in his mattress, as she kissed his brow. Part of her regarded that belief as a mirage born of wishful thinking.

No one else in her family, to the best of her awareness, had any roommates. She wondered whether her father sent signals into the dimension where the roommates abided. She pictured her father's timestream, stationary and dwindling, at some future point arriving at a stop, or dissolving into a crevice in space-time the way an evaporated creek leaves a dried-out bed behind.

Her roommate had tried to explain what the signals were, where they came from, grumbling all the while that human vocabulary lacked proper words. As far as she could discern, the sources of these signals came from all up and down her timeline, stress vibrations of a sort, nothing she could control. She had phrased it that way to the creature and it had laughed, huffing, *I give up.*

She wanted power over these signals that agitated her roommate to the point it picked these painfully personal fights. She wanted to *evolve.* Barring that, perhaps she could at least find a way to ease herself into sleep. She imagined the stream of her life as a brook, pictured the rocks that carve current into rapids wearing away, epochs of erosion elapsing in mere seconds, leaving waters calm as a pool, though always moving, never stagnant. The whisper of this flow sketched a path through her subconscious. She ambled along its shore as whorls of color flowed behind her eyelids.

Sometime before dawn, her roommate woke her up with an almost-caress, the dry heat of its fingers soothing against her bare arm. The spice of its musk infiltrated her sinuses like incense smoke.

"Don't touch me," Rae sighed, though she didn't jerk her arm away.

"He's proud of you, you know."

Rae sighed again, baring her teeth, transmuting the breath to a hiss. Frustration tightened her throat. "Your pettiness gets tiresome."

"It's not pettiness." Patience flattened its voice. "I couldn't hear this before. These particular signals, they were drowned out."

She barked a laugh. "More 'signals'? Where do *these* come from?"

"All from you. Past you. Present you. Future you. Always from you."

Rae quivered as her impulses warred. The tones of her roommate's voice held harmony rather than jarring contrast, a promise of truce, yet Rae wanted to extract an apology. She pictured one of the razors she used for making cut paper designs, gleaming between thumb and forefinger. In her mind she flicked it away, refusing to imagine how she would use it.

Her roommate lowered its jagged head, a constellation of blue-ish gruestones hovering within her reach. They made her teeth ache, her sinuses throb, her heart pump faster. "If it will make you feel better," her roommate said.

Touching the gruestones hurt, with a variety of pain that drew Rae to press into its sources harder because it also thrilled.

She plucked one out, no more difficult than removing a strawberry from a stalk. Its texture combined twine and sandstone, ice and electric current. She squeezed it, dug in her thumb. Sensations that were and were not colors billowed across her retinas.

Her roommate shuddered, the motion stirring the blankets as lightly as a cat shifting positions.

It lapped her neck with its forked tongue. She squeezed harder, picturing the tumor at the top of her father's spine, longing to crush it out of existence. Words lodged in her throat and remained there. She accepted that her roommate still heard them.

That morning came the call from her mom, the news her dad was gone. The request for help copying files from his computer lay six days in the future. The morning that Rae honored her mother's request, skimming through a series of files in the hard drive folder that her father had named "Legal," she found the message.

I am proud of all of you.

The final sentence of a letter addressed to his entire family, only a few words articulating a sentiment he had never voiced while he was alive. Timestamps indicated he had written it within six months of his first cancer diagnosis.

Her roommate had prophesied this, imperfectly. His letter did not single her out for praise. Nor did it exclude her. He could have deleted the letter many times over the intervening years.

He would have known that his computer-savvy oldest daughter
would be the one to find it, a signal that would reach her many
lengths further down their timestreams.

She wished he had said so much more. She was grateful he
said anything at all.

THE SHADOW TRAIN

Here is the place where I last saw it pass,
as I stood below the bridge west of the railyard
peering at the bruised twilight sky,
the heavens as ripe with grief as my sodden heart;
an urge compelled me to glance just so
as (on time, of course) the Shadow Train arrived,
a sketch of an engine towing a skeleton chain
of cars like black paper cut-outs,
like drawings on a page, their stark lines
a moving cage that penned in the waning moon.
Things move within that cage, mournful shades,
silhouettes of passengers, some broken,
some whole, some no more than bone,
their flickering frames a magic lantern show
cast against the deepening night.

Three times I've seen it now, etched onto the dark;
shift your eyes, your head just a hair's breadth
and the Shadow Train will vanish;
thinner than atoms, it winds along one rail,
hurtling in silence down the tracks to
its gruesome destinations. The third time,
standing here, I learned who takes this phantom ride:
all those who died, who risked a short cut
and sacrificed themselves to the rusted behemoth
bearing down; who tried to shake off drunken sleep
upon the crossties, and dreamed in their stupor
of the steel serpent come to crush them in its path;

who stood passive before the oncoming light,
transforming the engineer into a weeping
executioner; these are the passengers
who flicker past in the endless night,
whom the Shadow Train speeds toward
to collect and to keep. I understood,
watching it roll into oblivion, seeing her
framed in its cage, that tell-tale toss of her head,
one broken arm raised to wave, moonlight
shining through the holes of her eyes.
(Her car parked by the crossing, no note
left behind, no explanation at all.)

Here I was shown where the answers lie,
and the price of a ticket to knowledge.
The conductor of the Shadow Train
knows who holds a boarding pass.

ABHORS

KAYASHA HAD MR. VINCE'S STRETCHING AND EXERCISE routines printed on a checklist, and she hoped to roll through each item without need to linger. Something about the man unnerved her.

Bodies of all types came through the physical therapy clinic, and after a year of close contact with all manner of ages, physiques and injuries, Kayasha believed herself inoculated to shock. Truth was, Mr. Vince, fit for a man in his fifties, with dashes of gray in his hair and a runner's slim, wiry physique, wasn't hard to look at. She could not put a finger on why, exactly, he caused this tightness in her throat, this fluttering within her ribcage.

His demeanor remained serene and his tone remained docile as he repeated his request. "Could you knead my left shoulder for a bit?"

"I'm not working your shoulders, Mr. Vince," she said. "I'm helping you with neck pain, remember?" She dug her thumbs gently but not too gently in the groove between two of the troublesome neck vertebrae in question. He tensed in response. "You're not helping, Mr. Vince. Relax."

"Sorry, that hurt," he said. "I am sure working on my shoulders would help. That's where the pain is today." He patted his left shoulder. "In back, where I can't reach."

Nothing gave her reason to question his motives, and yet . . . Kayasha glanced around the clinic, hoping to recruit reinforcements. She needed to be firm with Mr. Vince, and that would be much easier to accomplish with Andrew or Tyra, especially Tyra, the head of this branch of the clinic, backing her up. They were naturally imposing, while Kayasha had to go against her own grain to get bossy.

No such luck. A tower of baby fat over tremendous muscle, Andrew had his back to Kayasha as he assisted elderly Miranda Wiggins with the squat stand. She admired that he wasn't an in-human hardbody, and she had shared that appreciation with him, intimately, two months and a few drinks ago. She tore her gaze from his broad back and robust rump lest Tyra catch her.

She needn't have worried. Tyra, arms akimbo so her fists rested on her herculean hips, had all attention focused on a new, round-bellied patient as he attempted to stand on one leg while bending over to pick up a cup from the floor. Tyra's arched eyebrows and skeptical smirk gave her the look of the world's most sardonic gym coach, but really, she was poised to steady the fellow if he lost his balance, and sturdy enough to do it. If anything, she was more a creature of muscle than Andrew, with six pack abs bejeweled by a navel that Kayasha had more than once imagined kissing.

Appalled at her idle trains of thought, Kayasha accepted she needed to manage Mr. Vince on her own. "Let me finish this up, then we'll start your stretches."

"I'm not jerking your chain, I swear," Mr. Vince said, the slightest edge of frustration roughening his voice. Hector—that was his first name. "I don't think I can do any of the stretches if you can't make this pain go away."

Kayasha sighed, though she kept the noise playful. She finished pushing in hard between the lowermost vertebrae. Absently she registered a difference from their last session, only two days ago. Preoccupied by his fuss and her own nervous reaction, she did not immediately catalog what that difference was.

"Okay, *Hector*, if you insist. But just for a few seconds, okay? We have to stay on track. Now where does it hurt?"

"Right at the back of the joint, edge of my shoulder blade."

Mr. Vince had no padding on his body to hide the flaws. She put her hand where he indicated, through his shirt immediately detected a large cartilaginous knob where none should be. The lump had the exact consistency of the one she had massaged half a dozen times on the back of his neck, the lump that had not been in its usual spot an instant ago. Mr. Vince had explained this mass as old scar tissue from a childhood accident to each therapist who asked.

The hard knot of flesh beneath her hand moved, as if the tip of a finger stroked her palm. She loosed a little gasp but kept her hand in place. The lump withdrew into Mr. Vince's body. He loosed a gasp that matched hers. "Thank you . . . whatever you did, thank you!"

She pressed her hand against in the same spot, found no lump. Her arm trembled—her whole body trembled—and Mr. Vince sighed again. She jerked her hand away.

A bulge at the back of his neck, where that lump should have been—where it must have been all along. Even as she entertained that thought, that she had simply skipped or somehow overlooked that prominent irregularity, her mind rained mocking laughter.

She swallowed. She had a had a job to do. "Really, all better now?"

"Oh, yes."

"Okay, well, let me get you to sit up then. You remember your upper trap stretch?"

"I do."

Upright, he raised his left arm and put his hand atop his head, pulling so that his head tilted toward his left shoulder, the one where the lump had been. His smile, though slightly crooked, transformed his square features into a beacon of warmth. It was the first time, Kayasha realized, that she had seen him smile. She was already smiling back before she became fully aware she was doing so.

KAYASHA KEPT SCRATCHING AT HER PALM, and wondering why, because it didn't itch. The memory of the knot beneath Mr. Vince's skin, caressing her in that exact spot, had to be the reason. She insisted to herself that she wasn't obsessing. She had a movie streaming on her laptop, an obnoxious sex comedy. Her attention slid from its farcical flesh plays, ice melting off glass.

Upstairs, her aunt Thelma had her TV tuned to a sitcom, the dialogue indistinct, the laugh track piercing. Kayasha blamed her inability to concentrate on the intrusive laughter, though she wouldn't dare complain, given how little her aunt charged her to rent these basement rooms.

"Ow!" She had scratched her palm hard enough to leave a welt.

The chimes of an incoming cellphone call made for a welcome distraction. A picture of Andrew appeared on her screen, his eyes crossed, two fingers plugged up his nostrils.

"Hey," she answered.

"I'm at Gilley's and I don't see you, why aren't you here?"

"Oh . . . fudge!" The birthday bash for Norberto, who worked at the company's main clinic on the south side of Hillcrest. For no good reason, the whole thing had completely slipped her mind. "I'm so sorry, I had . . . something come up, I'll be right there."

"Good, I need my work wife." As Kayasha tittered at their little in-joke, he hung up.

The biggest nightspot in Hillcrest by far, Gilley's took up three floors of a building that used to be a bank office, and the building itself took up most of a downtown block. Any given weekend packed Gilley's with bodies, a deafening meat market with men in ridiculous cowboy hats and women in the mini-est of micro skirts, but on a Tuesday night Gilley's was a ghost town, so she found her co-workers without difficulty, congregated at the second floor bar. Though smoking had been banned for years, a burnt-tobacco odor still lingered. Country music—which Kayasha hated but had to acclimate to because she lived in Hillcrest—still drowned the murmurs of conversation.

She spied Andrew and smiled even before he noticed her—but her smile withered as the braying donkey laugh of the clinic chain's founder, Mike Hanson, blasted the room, a cringe-inducing reminder that while he was present no one else could express themselves with the same volume or abandon without drawing his sardonic derision. In fact, when he laughed that loud, it was nearly always at someone else's expense.

"Why's *he* gotta be here?" she asked Andrew the first chance she got to put her mouth near his ear. He smelled of gym sweat, which didn't bother her at all.

Andrew shrugged. "He likes Norberto."

"I don't think he likes anyone."

Andrew laughed. "Then he treats us all fairly."

Kayasha adored Andrew's laugh but not his white bro cluelessness. This wasn't the time or place, though, to pick that battle. "I need a beer."

Andrew raised his own stein as she took her leave. As she waited for the bartender to pour her order from the tap, she turned with her back to the bar to see who was milling around the billiard table that she might recognize. She didn't see Tyra, and that disappointed her, although Tyra had a toddler to watch—incredible, that she still kept that powerful physique—and thus understandably tended to skip the informal after-work meetings. Though Kayasha had to believe that Tyra also made it a point not to interact with Mike any more than her position required, that in this way she and Tyra were kindred spirits.

A frenzy of motion in a booth hooked her eye. Some guy had a large notebook spread open on his table, and he hunched over the pages, scribbling on them with a pen at a speed that to Kayasha seemed damn near superhuman. He flipped a page, kept scribbling without pause, as if he were furiously taking notes at a lecture where the prof spoke too fast.

He raised his head, tapping his pen to his lips, and Kayasha had that disconcerting feeling, so akin to déjà vu, of recognizing a face while completely unable to assign the person an identity. Not conscious that she was staring, she was caught unprepared when the stranger's gaze flicked in her direction. He smiled, crooked yet warm, and the slide from memory dropped into place.

The bartender nudged her elbow with a glass full of IPA. Startled, she almost capsized it. "Asshole," she muttered, realizing even as she blurted that word that Mr. Vince might be able to read her lips. The situation demanded a precautionary save-face. She snatched her beer up and walked his way, grin huge. "I *thought* that was you!"

Andrew watched her go past, did a double take and a wave as he spotted Mr. Vince, but didn't break off conversing with Mike, leaving her to settle across from her client by herself. Fine, she could handle it. "Hey, there, I've never seen you here before! How are you doing?"

She couldn't hear his reply over the music, so she leaned closer, and he leaned in for another try.

"I'm doing good! I'm here all the time, I've never seen you here either, must just be happy synchronicity tonight."

"I guess," she said.

"Really, I'm doing great, and it's because of you. I'm glad you're here so I can thank you again."

"Ha!" she said, rolling her eyes to cover that she was on the verge of blushing. She sipped from her beer and nodded at the distinct lack of glassware on the tabletop. "You're not having anything?"

She had to lean in to hear him again. "I did earlier."

If that were true, she didn't smell it on his breath. She pointed at his notebook. "What are you doing, writing a book?"

"Kind of." She had to bend even closer to hear what he said next. "I'll show you," he repeated. He flipped backward through the notebook and pointed to a couple lines of his slanted seismographic handwriting.

Her nose almost touching the paper, she didn't see words. Thread-thin worms writhes across the paper, hundreds of them squirming. A black tendril drooped from Mr. Vince's mouth and the ink squiggles reared up to coil around the tendril's pointed tip. Their motions scratched white afterimages across her vision. She put her hand with its throbbing welt onto the paper, her fingers next to his, the vermin swarming up to her wrist, the sensation like wet lightning.

"Hey, what's going on here, Kie-yashah?" brayed Mike, mangling her name. "You're gonna make Andrew jealous!"

She blinked, absorbing a few words of Mr. Vince's frenzied cursive: *every orbit is a tract and every planet is a bolus rolling through*

The tendril she had imagined was just his pen, gripped in his teeth as he held the notebook open for her.

The awkward pause lasted long enough for Mike to start chuckling. That laugh would soon grow much louder.

Her brightest grin had helped her slip out of many a fix, and as she cranked it up she caught the strange look Mr. Vince was giving her boss's boss. "Hi, Mike, this is Hector Vince, he's one of my patients at the clinic!"

"Is that right," bellowed Mike, his own grin hardly altering the corners of his lantern jaw. "Well, you tell me honestly, Hector, is she treating you right? She better be doing a good job for you!"

Mr. Vince regarded Mike the way a camper might regard a bear nosing the tent flap. A six-foot-four, broad-shouldered golden boy, Mike never bothered with social niceties, obviously never felt he needed to, and why should he? Was he not a walking, braying success story?

"Uh, oh!" Mike made a show of putting his hands to his mouth and popping his eyes. "I really did interrupt something, didn't I?"

Kayasha tried playing like she was in on the joke, proffering an exaggerated wink. "It's okay, you can tell him!"

Mr. Vince's chin tipped up and his crooked smile returned. He said something Kayasha couldn't hear. Apparently Mike couldn't either, because he put a hand on the back of Mr. Vince's bench, bent down and bellowed, "What's that?"

Mr. Vince pressed his mouth right to Mike's ear and shouted something Kayasha almost made out.

Mike flinched back, and Kayasha blinked, because she did not see something like a rat's tail lash frantically from side to side before disappearing into Mike's earhole.

Her boss's boss just stood there as if paralyzed by a sting. Kayasha's pulse pounded in her neck, her veins practically twitching, and she imagined them undulating under her skin like nightcrawlers in their burrows.

Mike tilted his head in a pose of a contemplation. He turned back to the birthday crowd without saying anything else.

The cool weight of Mr. Vince's hand settled over hers. "Great to see you. I have to go."

Under the skin of his palm, unnatural ridges pressed hard against her knuckles and tendons. These ridges moved, the way she willed her veins to move. An absurd association paraded through her mind, a lesson retained from middle school, Helen Keller teetering at the verge of understanding as Anne Sullivan used sign language to spell W-A-T-E-R into her hand.

She blinked again as he gathered up his notebook. "See you Thursday!" he said. For long minutes after he flashed one last grin at her, she stared through the place where he had been sitting, stunned at these graphic new ideations that disgusted and thrilled her at once, wondered what secret chamber inside her psyche had sprung open.

She put on another face-saving smile, one solely for her own sake, and rejoined her co-workers.

Mike left not long after Mr. Vince did, and Andrew, loosened by drink, grew friendlier. As the party wound down, he walked her back to the parking garage and settled into the passenger side of her used Toyota to "talk," the massive barrel of his torso dominating her car's interior. His weight made the suspension creak.

When they kissed, she savored every unpleasant taste of alcohol and nachos that coated his tongue. She kept an eye open
for any movement on their floor of the garage, an unwelcome but
necessary distraction. One of his big, warm hands slipped under
her shirt, though not under her bra.

"How did you do that?" he asked when their liplock broke.

"Do what?"

"Loop your tongue around mine like it was a snake or something. That was *wild*."

She tittered, a delectable, alarming chill sinking through her.
"I didn't do nothing like that." She brandished the shield of her
smile. "I just made you think so."

"I like that mind trick." He took her hand, and she didn't have
to be a psychic to know where he was about to put it. "Maybe we
could try that again—"

She shook her head and squeezed his fingers. "Nuh-uh. Not
here unless we want an audience."

He chuckled. "Maybe I do." But he let go, which she respected. "Guess we got to sleep it off. We have to get up early for work
anyway."

"You mean *I* do." He had an afternoon shift tomorrow at the
clinic. She was in fact scheduled for morning shift, which started
at 7 a.m., ugh.

"Well, go home then, slut."

"Asshole!" She grinned as she said it.

She came home to discover Thelma had fallen asleep in front
of her television, again. Standing over her, Kayasha debated what
to do, decided she couldn't let her aunt spend the night in what
looked to be an uncomfortable, potentially neck-cricking position, her head slumped on her left shoulder, the frailty of her
frame evident even through her oversized Fugees T-shirt—so faded Kayasha wouldn't have known whose faces were printed on it
had Thelma not repeatedly told her.

Gingerly, she rousted Thelma. "Come on now." Her aunt
groaned but put up no fuss this time, let Kayasha prop her up instead of trying to pull away. Her aunt was bird-light, feather-flimsy.

Once, in this same situation, her aunt had screamed at Kayasha's touch, and before Kayasha had fully processed what was happening the blade of a Buck knife hovered an inch from her right eye.

The moment stretched for an eternity before Thelma apologized and folded the blade shut. Kayasha had brandished her shield-smile and hoped its radiance saturated Thelma with guilt.

At last lying in her own bed, Kayasha wondered if she was doomed to spend her life looking after people who only acknowledged her when they needed her—a predicament her career choice played right into.

She had held her nose for three years to earn her DPT from the odiously named Stonewall Jackson College of Health Sciences. She wished she could afford to go for her master's, but she also wished she could afford better than her aunt's basement, and if wishes were horses, no wagon would ever move.

I like that mind trick.

Thoughts of Andrew and that favor he wanted provided relief from the pity party. Her hand slid under the elastic of her pajamas, past her pubic hair. She pictured the expressions on Andrew's baby face as she massaged him with her mouth, the cords bulging in his neck, straining against the skin that sheathed them, curling and flowing, seeking exits, routes to reach her directly.

Even as she wondered, *Where is this coming from?* her breathing quickened.

The repulsion that bubbled in her paled beneath the urge to see this fantasy through and learn what sensations lay at its conclusion. She retrieved her vibrator from her nightstand, pressed it in place as her left hand found her left nipple. She imagined finding a lump in her breast tissue, imagined it moving like Mr. Vince's lump had moved, grasping at her fingertips. She pictured, as she bore the vibrator down harder, larva growing engorged in her labia, adding new pressure from the inside.

Afterward, heaving in the aftermath of explosion, she marveled that she did not roll over and vomit. Any normal person who could have seen into her mind, observed what she had envisioned as she climaxed, absolutely would have.

"What is this?" she whispered to the ceiling. "What the hell is wrong with me?"

THURSDAY MORNING, AS KAYASHA LET HERSELF into the clinic, Tyra intercepted her, both blocking her way and settling a gentle hand on her shoulder. "Your 7 a.m. is already here, but we need to talk first." She shouted to the back of the clinic. "Kayasha's here, Mr. Vince, she'll be just a minute, okay?"

Kayasha's heart skipped too fast as Tyra shut the office door behind them. She had spent the past two days spinning in accelerating circles of anxiety. What cheer she might have taken from Tyra's attention dropped straight into the cuisinart of her panic and sprayed out as increasingly outrageous assumptions, every terrible notion a self-inflicted stab. Tyra was wise to the lens of desire and admiration Kayasha viewed through her and was about to reject her in all ways. Mike had tattled on her more-than-flirtations with Andrew, or worse, Mike had told Tyra that something inappropriate happened with Mr. Vince that night at Gilley's. Tyra knew all about the worm fantasies. Tyra could see them under Kayasha's skin.

Tyra was on the verge of tears. "I have really, really awful news."

Kayasha could not conceive of Tyra getting this upset about firing her, or about anything that required confident decisiveness. Kayasha didn't put Tyra on a pedestal—in her view, Tyra was the pedestal that held up everyone else. Kayasha found the rawness in Tyra's voice and the redness in her eyes supremely disquieting. Faced with this crack in her world, Kayasha drew on her own memories of Tyra in order to deal, adopting the stone-cool poise Tyra assumed whenever one of her elderly white clients started spontaneously sharing the most grotesquely intimate information. "What's wrong?"

"Mike." Tyra's voice did not quite break. "Something really bad happened to him. He's gone."

"Oh my God," Kayasha said, because it was the right thing to say, as she pictured the rat tail corkscrewing into Mike's ear. "What happened?"

A frown marred Tyra's beauty still further, dimples in the wrong places, the mask a toddler makes right before bawling. Still, even shut in the office, Tyra crowded close, signifying conspiratorial rumor, the tops of her muscular shoulders level with Kayasha's brow. "We can't say anything. Gina—" That was Mike's wife— "She called me at like four in the morning and—"

"Oh my God."

"—And she said it looked like he killed himself. Like he shot himself in the head. She said he left a message, she said it like that,

'A message.'" Tyra sniffled, her eyes still red, but a queer excitement wriggled into her voice. "She said he looked like he blew his brains out with a shotgun, but there was no gun. 'We don't own any guns,' she was saying that over and over."

Kayasha put a hand over her mouth, afraid she might be smiling.

"I asked if she called the police and she said no and I said, 'Gina, you gotta call 'em,' and she finally hung up, I don't even know if she did."

"Oh, wow," Kayasha said behind her hand. She was smiling, and it wasn't a shield-smile. She twisted her lips into what she hoped was an appropriate frown and risked exposure, daring to touch Tyra's face, to compassionately rub Tyra's shoulders. Tyra seized her in a fierce hug, chest heaving with silent sobs. Kayasha bear hugged her back, praying Tyra sensed more than a gesture of comfort.

At last Tyra's arms loosened and Kayasha, with a pang, followed the cue. "Don't tell anyone yet." Tyra continued her conspiratorial whisper. "I don't know what to say to anyone about it. But I wanted you to know. Think you can keep it together with Mr. Vince?"

Kayasha didn't want Tyra to know how easy it would be for her to keep it together. She forced a choked voice. "It's gonna be hard, but if I start having trouble I will let you know. And you please do the same, okay?"

Tyra hugged her again.

As she walked out to where Mr. Vince lay face down on a padded table, Kayasha had the presence of mind to ask herself why the thought of a segmented worm hatching from Mike's skull made her feel the opposite of nauseated.

Months ago she had watched a video on her laptop, an interview with a pedophile. The creep claimed he had never ever entertained any notion of having sex with a child until he watched a TV show about catching child molesters. Exposed to the possibility, it consumed him all the way to prison.

Something similar had happened to her. The self-confession bothered her far less than it should have. "Good morning, Mr. Vince," she said. Her gaze found prominent lumps on the back of his neck and her face flushed. She was kneading his deformities with both hands before the impulse became conscious thought.

The things that lived in his flesh responded to her touch, stroking her palms. They wanted to clasp her hands fully, they conveyed this with urgency.

"They missed you," Mr. Vince said.

"I missed you, too," Kayasha said, hardly believing the words coming out of her mouth. Never before had she experienced such a heady mix of abhorrence and thirst. The things under Mr. Vince's skin pulsed in her grasp. "Even though you're gross," she murmured.

He practically purred. "I'm not making you do that. Don't you have a checklist you need to tend to? Stretches I'm supposed to do?"

She did need to do those things, and maybe so did he, yet she struggled to care. Tyra emerged from the front office and this spurred Kayasha to pull her hands away from the things living inside Mr. Vince, these things that loved her so much. She resented the separation from the pit of her heart. *What is wrong with me?* she thought, but a multitude answered back using her voice: *Nothing*.

Mr. Vince never suffered like she was suffering—the things in him were there always.

In case Tyra happened to eavesdrop, she asked, "What's your pain level today?"

"A nine," he said with a smile.

Tyra did hear that. "A nine? Are you lying? You sound too happy for a nine."

"I said what I said," Mr. Vince called to her. "I have a high pain threshold."

"Alrighty then," Tyra said, adding a theatrical roll of the eyes, the same eyes that had been red with unshed tears moments ago. "Are they any exercises you can't do today?"

"I'll manage," Mr. Vince said, sounding a little less confident. Lower, for Kayasha to hear, "It's a heavenly nine. I'll show you if you let me."

The piece of Kayasha that kept trying to raise questions raised even shriller alarms at the promise of escalation in her client's voice. She did not acknowledge his offer. Nor did she cool her manner. They went through the things he was supposed to do to strengthen his neck and back, allow him to manage despite his pain—if in fact the things he claimed were wrong actually were wrong.

He did at least wince as he rested belly-down on a Pilates ball and did T-lifts, even though the dumbbells he held only weighed two pounds.

When she helped him up, he whispered, "Come see me when you get off work, you can have as much time with my friends as you want." The crow's feet around his ice blue eyes crinkled as he smiled his crooked smile.

"Come see us," breathed a hundred echoes of her own voice. The sensation of so many mouths moving in her ears, her mind, it electrified her. She craved its expansion. "See you where?"

He whispered an address to her. Ordinarily she would have had to write it down and there would have been considerable risk that she would forget what she wrote down or where she put the note. Her excitement burned the words and numbers into her brain.

She regarded Tyra, pillar of confidence Tyra, speaking to a new check-in as if her tearful revelation of Mike's death had never taken place. She wished she could take Tyra with her went she went to see Mr. Vince.

A silly thought. Tyra wasn't ready.

Thank goodness Tyra was so distracted on the inside and battling not to let it show, because otherwise she might have noticed how little attention Kayasha paid to her subsequent clients, even when they were moaning in pain, straining to complete a single bridge or simple band walk.

Mr. Vince's home, his real home, was as innocuous as a shoebox on the outside, and as nightmarish on the inside as Kayasha could have ever conceived.

Smells spoke to her of feces and rotting flesh. A hoarder's masturbatory dream of soggy paper and unrecognizable flotsam piled in every room. These mounds of refuse rustled, occupied in the same manner Mr. Vince himself was occupied, though by beings of a lower order.

Kayasha understood without need for explanation that this wasn't his only home. How else could he go out in public in the role of charming, eccentric gentleman. He used other living quarters to wash up and change clothes, houses that had belonged to others who had lusted for the things in him that she lusted for now.

She drooled, truly drooled—ridiculous, unpreventable—as he shuffled toward her through the refuse. Naked, he teemed, the parasites that infested him curling arabesques under his skin, scribbling their alphabets across his fat-free flesh. His erect, oddly bent cock bulged with more than veins.

"They already like you so much. And you like them. It's time to share," he said, the warmth in his smile decayed to grotesque smugness. He settled onto on a mound that squished underneath him. Under the paper and torn trash bags, black muck seeped, long sticks clacked that might have been—had to be—bones.

Her own voice called to her a thousand-fold. She knelt between his legs, instantly thigh deep in filth. The worms within him swarmed toward her, his flat stomach bowing out as if he had developed a paunch or a pregnancy.

He panted like a dog, his teeth parted, his grin unhinged, his erection swollen and slithering with larvae. "You know what to do," he breathed.

"Yes, they told me," she said, unfolding her aunt's Buck knife.

She knew this wasn't part of Mr. Vince's script. Whatever he did expect, she did not care. She didn't want him. She wanted the things that lived in him, their promise of a love that would never leave.

"What are you doing?" he yelped, but even as he said it she had already done it, slashed him wide open, plunged in the knife and dragged the blade down the impromptu pouch of his belly. As his yelp heightened to a screech, she sliced his prick open like a bean pod.

Living ropes poured out of the wounds, cramming their sinewy bodies into her sucking mouth. Coated in coppery slime, they filled her stomach, her sinuses, her lungs. As the red tide vacated its former vessel, his screams dwindled to a rattle, his body deflating, one more discarded sack of trash.

She gagged and choked, her body's mindless defenses taking over, fighting to rebel. The ropes compressed her python-like, pinned her in the muck, twisted her to keep her open. Everywhere she had an opening, something squeezed and squirmed its way in.

"We love you," they said, speaking in her voice. "We love you. We are yours."

Nerve endings howled in vomitous bliss.

Later, she stood over her aunt's sleeping form as the television chattered. She bent to give Thelma a kiss of thanks, right on the ear, then carried her aunt to bed, the multitudes giving her strength.

KAYASHA ARRIVED AT THE CLINIC THE NEXT MORNING, savoring a heavenly nine, her lovers boring tunnels where none existed, digging their hooks inside regions that had never before impinged on her awareness—never before had her brain been so flooded with sensation, so fully conscious of her inner and outer dimensions. Their undulating touch never stopped, a constant, merciless stimulation. They pulsed inside her legs, between her ribs, underneath the root of her tongue, within the dents in her pelvis, behind her eyes, threaded through the bone pores that housed her optic nerves.

Andrew and Tyra were both on duty. The beings inside her regarded both of them through her eyes and shared her hunger. Such a comfort that they understood without explanation.

The clinic, for the moment, was empty of clients. Andrew's face registered shock—Tyra was filling him in about Mike. They both glanced Kayasha's way. She nodded sadly, a pretense of grief totally counter to the yearning that burned in every occupied territory of her body.

When her boss broke away from that morose conversation and ducked into the office, Kayasha followed, and closed the door behind her.

"Hey." Kayasha touched Tyra's shoulder while her back was turned. "Are you holding up okay?" She placed her hand between Tyra's shoulder blades, pressed her palm flat against her boss's spine. Her occupants surged between her metacarpals, stretching her heart, life and love lines in an equivalent of a shy first kiss.

Tyra started at the sensation Kayasha dealt to her, but did not pull away.

THE DREAM EATERS

When a dream achieves substance and shape,
condenses from the fog that forms
our collective unconscious, starts to
quiver, stretch its limbs, open its throats
to test its many voices, it also becomes edible.

And when a dream becomes real,
there are creatures lying in wait to devour it;
sleek hard-shelled predators that hunt them;
coral-veined junkies who crave them;
perverted copper-tongued beasts
that torture them first;

sensuous satin connoisseurs
who savor them in slow dissolve;
oil-crusted misers who salt
and dry and horde them.
I learned of these things and more
the day I tasted my own dreams for the first time,

a rarest of all flukes: just as I walked
in the landscape of sleep, my body walked
as if waking; at the end of my long dark hall
I tripped over my own dream as it took shape;

and I did not know what it was
until my teeth sank in; a tiny, infant thing,
it squealed and screamed, but it smelled—

of chocolate, honey,
sweet wine, succulent meat—
no matter how it struggled, I couldn't stop
and then

I saw them, these achingly beautiful
destroyers of dreams, baring their
fangs to shrill a frustrated siren song
as I stole their meal. Now they hover
just inches away in the netherworld,
never taking their eyes from me,

shredding and chewing each new dream
as it tries to be born. I've tried to poison them
with fantasies of white purity,
I have tried to feed them too much,
bloat their bellies, slow them for the kill

And now I am trying to starve them
drive myself mad to give them no dreams at all.
And with their swelling eyes,
their lengthening claws, their widening smiles,
they sing with voices like knives:
we won't wait any longer
for the dreams to emerge from your head

SLOW BURN

AARON FRIEDRICH, PUBLISHER, EDITOR and sole journalist of the online-only Owlswick County Observer, leaned close and squinted as the grainy security camera footage flashed to white.

The woman whose shoulder he leaned over, Della Wright, clicked her mouse, freezing the image, a capture of a raging white explosion. "Did you see that?"

Aaron frowned. "I don't know what I'm looking at."

"I'll play it back slower."

His arms crossed atop the back of her chair, he hunkered forward, his ear close enough to hers that if she tipped her head they would touch, which she did briefly, the pleasant caress not one of flirtation but of acknowledgement, permission granted to be in her space. Aaron caught a whiff of coconut-scented shampoo. Thankfully, the angle was such that their matching scars did not make contact.

Her computer's monitor and the dim desk lamp beside it combined to generate a faint light, one that wouldn't be detected through the drawn curtains. Though the time displayed on the monitor approached 1 a.m., both understood the possibility and dangers of surveillance without needing to give voice to the concern.

Della tapped the screen, indicating where Aaron should fix his gaze. "Watch there."

Aaron regarded the view from the camera installed over the front door of the gas station on Orion Street, a tiny, once-white shack ancient enough not to have a rain shelter installed over the gas pumps. Not to mention, instead of a digital readout, these pumps displayed prices the old-fashioned way, with numbers printed on wheels spun by gears.

Della let the player proceed, slower this time.

A pale figure careened out of the night, stumbled over a curb and into the station parking lot, lurching toward the pumps. The slowed motion drew out every awkward flail that at normal speed discharged in a frenzied blur.

Huge black blotches streaked her knee-length white nightgown. As she approached the door, despite the poor image quality, her expression became clear, eyes wide and unblinking, mouth stretched open to the maximum, all teeth bared, an unending shriek of animal terror or animal rage. The footage had no sound.

"That's Annaliza?" Aaron already knew the answer but couldn't help whispering the question. He also knew that the black stains were blood, that the blood belonged to Annaliza Griffith's daughters, five-year-old Marcy and three-year-old Natalie.

"Watch close." Della tapped her screen again.

Her face frozen in that gut-wrenching silent scream, Annaliza floundered toward the camera. An arc welder-bright glow bloomed between her breasts at about the spot where Della tapped her finger, made even more distinct by the deep black bloodstain over Annaliza's heart.

Della stopped the playback. "See it?"

"I see . . . *something*. Is it . . . she holding a sparkler?" He could plainly see that Annaliza had nothing in her hands.

"Keep watching."

As the time-elapsed bar at the bottom of the video crawled slowly forward, more of those bright, focused flares appeared, all over Annaliza's torso, even in her open mouth.

In the next frame her flesh erupted in a column of white flame.

Aaron shuddered, rocking Della's chair. "My God, she set herself on fire."

Della inclined her head ever so slightly. Her eyes, reflected in the monitor, regarded Aaron's face. "Is that what you'd say that was?"

"What else could it have been?"

"Aaron." Her pronunciation of his name rolled *You know better* and *You're kidding me* and *Don't lie to me or yourself* into one unspoken admonishment. "Watch it again and then you tell me how she could have done this *to herself.*"

He complied, and he had to concede he had no explanation for what happened to Annaliza Griffith.

He had some information, though, about what she'd been up to in the hours before her death. "A monster met a bad end," he said. "Maybe it was God showing Himself."

Della turned her head to regard him directly this time. "In Grandy Springs?"

She had him there. Not a joke, just the truth, the divine had no truck with this town.

He needed time to process, to examine the impossible thing she was suggesting, without her trying to wrestle the point home, so he shifted the subject by a hair. "Does the Sheriff's Office know you have this?"

"They won't know unless you tell them," she said matter-of-factly. "Not like I'm going to post this on the Book of Face."

"Who gave this to you?"

"Not going to share that, not even with you, sweetie."

Della used to work for the Sheriff's Office—had essentially risen to second-in-command, without the title or the pay. Being a woman, and this being Grandy Springs, nothing short of an armed revolution would have granted her those things.

Here and now, so far as the town was aware, she was a shut-in collecting disability. Aaron could have pursued the same arrangement, had he chosen, as the same hell that swallowed her had consumed him, too.

The bond Aaron and Della shared would be immediately obvious to anyone who saw them together. Even in the wan illumination from her desk, the scars that framed her features caught the light, hyphens of pink tissue that laddered symmetrically up the sides of her face, from the corners of her jaw to her temples, an effect like Frankenstein stitching, if the doctor had used coarse bootlaces to hold his monster together. Aaron resisted for the umpteenth time the urge to let his fingers wander up his own Frankenstein stitches, laddering from jaw to temple, identical to Della's.

Neither of them could remember who or what gave them those scars. The one person left in Grandy Springs who could know insisted over and over again to Aaron that he should never ask.

John Hairston had seen a lot of awful things serving in an all-black regiment during the Korean War, and even more in Grandy Springs, where he inexplicably chose to take up residence mere weeks after a white mob lynched an innocent black man.

If Hairston could be convinced to watch Della's videos—well, his insights might be of genuine value, or they could be even more unhinged than the notion that Annaliza Griffith spontaneously combusted after brutally slaughtering her own daughters.

Aaron and Della might as well have been telepathically linked. She asked, "When did you see John last?"

"Weeks ago, when I stopped in the bookstore. Haven't seen him in the park lately." In his battle to keep local journalism alive after the demise of the Owlswick Messenger, Aaron still made trips out by car or by bicycle, to interviews, to government meetings, to browse the filings in the Circuit Court Clerk's Office. He often passed Hairston perched on the same bench in Bowen Park, hands resting on the cane propped upright between his legs, his white hair an Einsteinian corona. Occasionally Aaron waved. Even less frequently, Hairston waved back.

Arrived at sidewise, the phrase repeated: spontaneous combustion. In his mind, Hairston's gravely voice proclaimed the words, finished with a mocking laugh. Even conjuring the thought of Hairston speaking, somehow, inside his head, gave Aaron an unpleasant case of the willies, not unlike the shuddery disorientation of déjà vu.

Plenty to shudder about. The Sheriff's Office had yet to release a cause of death for Annaliza Griffith—yet, based on that footage, there was little left of her to autopsy.

Della's stare reminded Aaron that she still awaited his answer. "You think John knows something."

"If anyone would . . ."

"I'll stop in at the store." Even as he said that, anxiety sped his heartbeat, worries that he might not find the old man—Hairston used no phone or computer, stayed unreachable unless he wanted to be reached. And a sharper worry that he might find Hairston right there amid the shelves, and have to withstand the heat of Hairston's pitiless glower.

* * *

Calf-high grass rustled against Aaron's sneakers as he trod toward the bookshop's front porch.

The unmowed lawn wasn't unusual. Neither was the absence of a sign on the door stating whether the store was open or closed. Hairston had not done much in the way of maintenance to Pollard's Antiquarian Bookshop since he reopened it for business.

The store's original owner, Bob Pollard, had fought side by side with Hairston in Korea. Pollard's whereabouts were an unsolved mystery, one of many in Grandy Springs. The consensus of the amateur historians willing to speak at all about the town's repulsive history of discrimination was that Pollard likely was murdered by the Klan for being too friendly with black Americans, perhaps for daring to decry the lynching, as Pollard went missing not long after. Hairston came to Owlswick County in search of his friend, and what was most astonishing was that he stayed, given that Grandy Springs was practically a sundown town.

Aaron had never gotten Hairston to share the details, but whatever happened on his arrival, the ugly element among the townsfolk steered clear of him afterward, setting a precedent that others like him would also be, for the most part, left alone.

Even in the 21st century, with Grandy Springs integrated after a fashion, Hairston wasn't known as a friendly sort, which made his decision to dust out and unlock his late friend's store all the more perplexing. Especially as that "dusting off" he gave the place and its extensive inventory of obscure, musty books was mostly symbolic, with plenty of real dust remaining.

The lack of answer to Aaron's knock offered no surprise. He peered through the windows to either side of the door. Nothing disturbed the stillness between the shelves.

He waited on the chipped cement stoop, under the tattered awning, listening for any signs of motion. The creaky floors always announced Hairston's progress through the shop.

This time, nada. Uneasiness stirred in Aaron's belly.

From the street, a man shouted, "He open today?"

Jolted, Aaron spun to behold a couple crossing the overgrown lawn to join him at the door.

Not that he knew everyone in Grandy Springs, but he did recognize scores of his fellow townies on sight, and he'd never seen this pair before. The man who called to him wore a too-tight polo shirt made from a clingy silver fabric, and jeans, easily a size too small, that looked like they'd just come off the department store rack. He was tall and wiry enough that, given looser garments, Aaron might never have known the fellow had a protruding gut. The man's hair, parted in the middle and trimmed just below his earlobes, was silver as his shirt. The woman with him looked older, her face heavily seamed beneath a mound of hair dyed an unnatural shade of black—and as with her man, her clothes matched her hair, loose black blouse and black leggings. In a final visual punchline, they wore identical snakeskin boots.

"The owner's not answering," Aaron said, keeping his voice and expression noncommittal.

"Hard of hearing, for sure," the man said as he reached Aaron. "I mean, mixed blessing if he's out, his selections suck, but hope springs eternal. Might be a gold nugget in those stacks of shit." He grinned. The woman smirked, her gaze all over Aaron.

Aaron could not imagine this creep saying something like this to Hairston's face and escaping the store in one piece. Hairston did not turn the other cheek. He struck back with metaphorical brass knuckles.

"Really though, he needs to throw all that old shit out and get stuff people actually want," the man went on.

Aaron really did not want to engage. He grunted in feigned disappointment. "I guess he's not in."

"You're being too harsh," the woman said. "You can't expect someone of his background to know anything about valuable books."

Heat rose in Aaron's neck. He recognized bait when he heard it but could not help himself. "What do you mean, 'his background'? You mean that he's a veteran? A war hero?"

His heightening blood pressure made the scars on his face itch ferociously. The last thing he wanted to do was claw at them in front of this awful pair.

"If he's a *veteran*," the man said, "he should dress like he has some self-respect."

Stay calm, Aaron told himself. *Make your getaway.* "Were you in the service?"

The man grinned, fox-like. "Didn't need to do that. I'm already all that I can be."

Despite Aaron's urgent desire to disengage, it occurred to him that if this couple had indeed made Hairston's acquaintance, he ought to learn when and why. "Did you travel a long way to get here? To visit this store?"

The woman stepped closer still, her large eyes, further offset by thick mascara, wet with concern. "Forgive me for being rude," she raised a finger and made a U-gesture, "but who did that to you? Cut up your face like that?"

Sadly, Aaron has faced such obnoxiousness often enough to have a snappy answer handy. *I cut myself shaving.*

But to his own shock, the deflection snagged in his throat. "I don't remember."

The man barked a laugh. "You are full of shit. I'm sorry, but you are. How could you not remember *that*?"

"Pleasure to meet you," Aaron growled, furious at himself. He hot-footed around them toward his car, a 1992 beater parked half on the street, half in the unmowed grass.

The man called after him, glee in his voice, "Sorry if I offended you, *snowflake*."

As Aaron reached his car, he noticed there were no other vehicles parked on this stretch of road. He turned, bracing himself for a continuation of the confrontation. Except, his tormentors were nowhere in sight. Had they gone into the back yard? Gone inside the store somehow? Aaron couldn't imagine Hairston opening the door to them, especially if he had overheard them talking.

Where the hell had they come from in the first place?

Overcome by an abrupt wave of nausea, Aaron sank to his knees. It took herculean effort to regain his feet and clamber into the driver's seat. The knots in his gut did not loosen till he was over halfway home.

DEADLINES DOMINATED THE REST OF HIS DAY. He had a story that took a week's worth of interviews and research, that he had to post in advance of the next evening's town council debate over whether or not to purchase an empty feed store and convert it into a "business incubator." Because the stakes were so low, tempers had reached fever pitch. He kept his nose to his laptop until he'd finished proofing. He fed his cats, scarfed his own dinner, read the story one more time before posting, then messaged Della through an encrypted app. *No sign of John. Met a creepy couple that claimed to know him. I don't believe them.*

She wrote back, *I have more video.*

The words filled him with anticipation and dread.

The apartment he rented was small, a mere four rooms. Between bouts of agitated pacing, he killed the hours until the rendezvous with Della by reviewing his notes on the Griffith case.

The details of Annaliza Griffith's crimes were nauseating. The bodies of her young daughters were missing . . . mostly. What information Aaron had came from Della's mole within the Sheriff's Office, as Sheriff Hargrave himself had shared next to nothing in press conferences or in private. Aaron liked Hargrave, with a respect that went all the way back to Hargrave's days as a soft-spoken, hulking deputy.

Hargrave had emerged unscathed from the cataclysm that left Aaron and Della scarred and tallied so many members of the Sheriff's Office among the missing. Hargrave too had confessed to Aaron, off the record, that he could not remember what happened, even though he had been in the building when the disaster that claimed his colleagues unfolded.

(Ask anyone in the town what they could recall of that catastrophic summer weekend, their eyes would lose focus. Their voices lost volume and they shook their heads in denial. The improbable explanation espoused by state and federal officials and parroted by national media stank of cover-your-ass-up, an enormous, previously undetected underground bubble of toxic gas brought to the surface by a small earthquake and subsequent cave-ins, that caused delirium, suffocation, and multiple fires and explosions as it flowed into the natural bowl of Grandy Springs' topography. Even more suspicious, the collapse of the local newspaper industry alone, with closures and severe staff reductions throughout the region, could not sufficiently explain the jaw-dropping absence of curiosity demonstrated by government and larger news agencies. Aaron, however, refused to entertain conspiracy theories.)

Given the poor quality of the gas station footage, had Annaliza not been a frequent flyer with social services, investigators might never have identified her. In her unfinished basement they found the remains of Natalie and Marcy. Four days after that announcement, Della had shown Aaron a download of digital photos.

Pitiless flash bulbs revealed all that was left of those poor children: red heaps that resembled pale, coiled snakes drenched in syrup. The bodies of the snakes were entrails. The heads of the snakes were tongues, attached by strips of flesh. The meticulous symmetry of the arrangements bespoke hands-on attention.

Nothing mundane explained it. Even among the catalog of horrors historical and recent that wove into the history of Grandy Springs, this took depravity to a new level.

At least, so far as Aaron could recall.

The hour arrived to go see Della and Aaron set about the necessary routine, stuffing his backpack with notebooks and pens, filling a small handheld cooler with beer and cheese from his fridge as an offering and bribe, donning a dark jacket with a hood, not for the weather but to make him harder to identify if anyone was spying. Phone turned off and left in his apartment.

A block before the turn into her driveway, he killed his headlights.

Once again peering over Della's shoulder, Aaron watched the new clip with jaw clenched. This time, there was sound.

"How did they find this? Do they know who shot it?"

A hollowness, a forced dispassion, dulled Della's words. "Annaliza's half-sister in Hillcrest received this as an e-mail attachment from an anonymous sender. The sender's address was just a bunch of numbers. It was sent the morning after it all happened, supposedly, but she didn't check her account until a couple weeks later."

"God damn." Aaron swallowed.

There were two men in the video, their heads covered by hoods, otherwise naked. Annaliza was present, naked, possibly high or drugged. Her children present, hogtied. The person holding the camera or phone or whatever device had been used to record this atrocity had been a woman. Though unseen, more than once she had responded in monosyllabic affirmatives when given instruction by the only man who spoke—elderly, or at least well past his prime, based on the shape of his physique and the rasp in his voice.

"Can we . . . without having to watch any of that again . . . can we go back to a point where the camerawoman talks?"

"Why?"

"Her voice. I want to hear her voice again. I think I met her this morning, when I went to John's shop."

AARON SHOULD HAVE CALLED AHEAD, but his early morning hours had been consumed with news updates and website problems, duties carried out while distracted by his confrontation with that racist couple and by the horrible video he'd seen at Della's. The only mercies had been the poor lighting and the female videographer's lack of skill.

Even as he parked along the curb across from Vanissa Carter's townhouse, Aaron couldn't stop himself from imagining the retorts he wished he'd fired at that couple. *'His background?'* Gee, *racist much?*

The woman had asked him, *'Who did that to you? Cut up your face like that?'* In the video, she never said more than *'Yes'* or *'Okay'* as she moved the camera where the older hooded man directed, yet Aaron remained convinced that the voice was the same. Maybe her man was in the video, too—though if so, he had been cast in the non-speaking role.

As he reached Vanissa's front step, finger aimed at the doorbell, the door opened inward. Blue eyes glared, their confrontational yet curious stare made fiercer by heavy black eyeliner and a dozen silver rings in place of eyebrows.

Athenea Nichols acknowledged Aaron with a flat-voiced, "Friedrich."

Aaron couldn't repress a half-smile. "Nichols. Vanissa here?" He knew she was.

Vanissa Carter's fiancee sized up Vanissa's former boyfriend a moment longer, then called back into the townhouse, "You have a visitor."

"Who is it?" Not Vanissa; a lighter, sweeter voice. Vanissa's younger sister Janelle thumped into the foyer, her grin instantly brightening the cramped scene. "Aaron!"

He grinned back. "Hi there, sweet pea."

Athenea offered a half-smile of her own. "Guess I have to let you in now."

Aaron didn't take the half-serious hostility personally. They had all been through too much.

Despite the commotion, Vanissa had not emerged from her home office, so they paraded up the stars, Janelle scampering ahead even though she was perhaps a bit too old for scampering now, giving Aaron a glimpse of the star-shaped scar on the back of her neck, right at the base of her skull, pink against her light brown skin but still easier to hide than his and Della's scars. Like them, Janelle had no memory of how she got it.

Athenea ascended last. Aaron imagined her bright blue gaze boring holes in his back.

The walls of Vanissa's office were covered with quirky pieces of framed embroidery that she ordered online. Often the stitches spelled out oddball quotes: Keep Clam and Oyster On. My other car is Dragula.

Vanissa didn't stand up from her computer station. "You should have called first, or texted."

Janelle hopped over to Vanissa's chair and put her chin on her sister's shoulder. Though Vanissa was about fifteen years older, they were height and weight-wise the same size.

"Sorry," Aaron said, "too freaked out, wasn't thinking straight."

"Looks boring," Janelle said, passing judgement upon the windows open on Vanissa's monitor. Aaron recognized them as the undersides of two of Vanissa's social media accounts.

Vanissa was, so far as he was aware, the only person in Grandy Springs taking full advantage of the broadband network brought to the town by tobacco indemnification grants. She made her living as an influencer—though not in the commonly understood sense. She did not flood feeds with attractive photos of herself, though she could have done so if she wanted. Her methods involved opening dozens of profiles, using them to post pithy aphorisms and memes that generated hearts and shares in the thousands (her instinct for it was uncanny) and utilizing those audience numbers to recruit sponsors, all accomplished without ever leaving her desk.

Aaron was the only person outside her immediate household entrusted with this knowledge. Though it could have made for a delightful Owlswick Observer profile, he was sworn to secrecy.

In exchange for his silence, she sometimes deployed her expertise on his behalf.

She regarded him with a concern that softened her brown-eyed gaze. "What has you freaked out?"

He told them all about the disturbing encounter in front of Hairston's store. He didn't censor for Janelle's sake, she could handle it, but omitted any mention of the Griffith case. "I have to wonder, people this obnoxious arriving in town, maybe there'd be chatter somewhere. Some hint who they are."

"This already rings bells for me," Vanissa said, not yet turning to her keyboard. "And you say John's missing?"

"He wasn't at the store. He hasn't been in touch. Hard to say if that constitutes 'missing.'"

"I hope he's all right," she said, and fingers clicked on keys. Aaron wasn't clear on how Vanissa and Hairston had become acquainted, but the old veteran could be congenial when it suited him.

"Yeah," she went on, "I remember thinking this was odd when I first read it. This is a private group for real estate agents in our corner of Virginia. This woman posted a couple weeks ago, warning her colleagues about this weird couple who asked her to show them a house."

"Really?"

"Listen to this. 'I got scared about being alone in the house with them. The guy was telling me everything he thought was wrong with my clothes and makeup. The woman asked me some rude personal questions. They kept touching me." Aaron could see that 'RUDE' and 'TOUCHING' were capitalized.

"That has to be them," he said. "Does she give names?"

"Yes. Cecil Stauph. S-T-A-U-P-H, and Beth Anne Werner, like that film director with the funny voice . . . oh."

"What?"

"They told her they were buyer's agents for Jefferson Dalton."

Aaron and Athenea made sounds of disgust in unison. Janelle glanced back and forth between them.

"Not a nice man," Aaron told her.

Athenea bent her lanky frame to whisper in Janelle's ear. When the girl nodded assent, Athenea announced, "We're going to go make snacks if you want some."

"Thank you." Aaron hoped his voice conveyed the multiple meanings he intended.

Dalton hadn't shown his too-tanned face, framed above by dyed hair plugs and below by surgery-stretched lips, since well before the "environmental disaster" that robbed so many in Grandy Springs of patches of their memories at best and their lives at worst.

That was because the consensus about what that filthy rich motherfucker had gotten away with—knifing an eighteen-year-old beauty who tried to fend off his advances, pinning her murder on a Honduran farmhand who "killed himself" soon after he was jailed—had *not* been erased from the town's collective consciousness, even though the real story had never bubbled up in any official, on-the-record channel.

The assumption was that he had chosen to relocate. He had the money to live anywhere in the world.

"Takes some brass balls or some fried brains to casually drop that name," Vanissa said.

Given the bluntly smarmy encounter at the bookstore, "These two have both," Aaron said. "My encounter with them was unforgettable. They were unrepentantly horrible."

"They really knew John?"

"That's what they claimed."

Now that they were alone, if she had asked, he would have explained about the murdered girls, how they were butchered, their mother's bizarre death, the three unidentified people in the video and how he suspected he'd met two of them. Maybe he'd just learned the identity of the third. The notion that Hairston had some connection to it all weighted him with dread.

She didn't ask. "I'll keep looking. Maybe there's more."

Neither of them said, *Be careful*, because they didn't need to.

H IS GUT INSTINCT TOLD HIM IT COULD BE USEFUL to seek out the agent who posted about her close encounter with Stauph and Werner. What else might they have said to her while they were all alone together?

Most everyone in the county who could read knew who Aaron was, whether or not they subscribed to his newsletter. He had contacted Cate Wasselman with a proposal to write a business profile. He didn't lie about his purpose. He would interview her for the profile, and he would write and publish it. If they happened to sidetrack into another topic during the interview, that didn't need to be part of the profile. Should the resulting material prove useful later—well, he would cross that bridge when he came to it.

When Wasselman responded to his request, she had asked if they could meet at one of the houses she was showing. That made him cringe inside, because obviously she had hopes that nice photos of the home would appear with the profile, native advertising assistance. The possibility made him feel a little gross, but as he would be the one taking the photos and selecting which ones saw publication, he agreed.

The address she gave him was up in the north of the county. He wondered if it was the same house she'd shown to Stauph and Werner. Asking her directly, though, would give the game away.

Accessed by a private road that switched back and forth up a mountainside for nearly three miles, the house turned out not to look anything like Aaron expected, given the lingering presence in Owlswick County of multistory farmhouses still standing from pre-Civil War days.

The structure was latter-twentieth century modern, no taller and apparently no deeper than a simple brick ranch house but nearly five times as long. Its existence should have been nigh impossible in the Appalachian hills, but this old mountain had a level peak and that's where the house and surrounding grounds lay. At one end Aaron spied a double—nay, triple—garage and at the other end a wing with walls that were ninety percent plate glass. His hunch: that glassed-in wing held an indoor pool.

He wondered who could have lived here—maybe a 1970s-era strip mining executive? The roof tiles had moss growing on them, but the curving driveway was debris-free despite the property's many trees, and the front porch light glowed in neighborly invitation, even though the sun blazed bright above cirrus cloud streaks. A white SUV hulked in the circle at the end of the driveway, Successful Realtor Vehicle 101.

When he knocked, a woman yelled, "Come in!" from deep inside the house. The door was unlocked.

No furniture occupied the front room, save an electric lamp incongruously aglow in the middle of the carpeted floor. Beside its squat, shaded form, citrus-scented smoke streamed upward from a bronze incense holder. Doors at either end of the room opened onto hallways. "Mrs. Wasselman, I'm here. Do you want me to wait for you?"

"Come back to the kitchen," she called, from off to Aaron's left, toward the wing with the pool.

An odor of cooking filled the hall, akin to barbecued pork left on the grill too long. Aaron wrinkled his nose. Wasselman had said nothing to him about preparing a meal, what an odd thing to do.

Past about half a dozen shut doors, the hallway opened into an unusual architectural configuration. The way forward became a balcony, with more shut doors to Aaron's left and railing to the right. About midway across this balcony the rail parted to allow access to spiral stairs that corkscrewed downward into a dim-lit lower level.

The smell of something roasted had grown thick. "How far to the kitchen?" Aaron called. "This place is huge!"

"Keep coming," Wasselman shouted.

Aaron did not. A noise distracted him. The hiss and creak of weight shifting on a bed or couch, somewhere in the darkness below this incongruous balcony.

"Hello?"

When no answer came, he dug his cellphone out of his pants pocket and tapped on the flashlight. Shadows slashed across the cavernous den revealed below. All the furniture, love seats, pool table, chairs, had been shoved to the far end, exposing hardwood floor. His phone's light reflected in a black pool that glistened at the foot of the stairs.

"Hello?" Aaron repeated.

Up ahead, Wasselman muttered something unintelligible. A pale coil that resembled a snake skin stood out within that the dark puddle. Even as his hunch sunk in, Aaron descended the stair. The closer he got, the more sickeningly familiar the spiral of tissue appeared. Like a length of intestines twisting toward a tongue in the center.

"Not good at following directions, are you?"

Even with heart in throat, the dispassionate journalist that managed Aaron's mind wasn't a bit surprised to spy the creepy couple at the top of the stairs.

"The stupidest thing you could have done, you went and did it. It's pretty obvious you're *mentally challenged*," Cecil Stauph said. "Why else would you be dumb enough to work in print news in 2022?"

Aaron had heard worse insults. "Where's Mrs. Wasselman?"

"Yep, you're slow."

Werner added, "No wonder you keep company with that . . . negro freak."

"Okay, fuck you," Aaron said, stomping angrily up the steps. A cord wrapped around his ankles and yanked his feet out from under him.

A flash of ropey intestine, rearing in a cobra-strike pose, in the instant before Aaron's head bounced on the hardwood. As consciousness escaped his grip he heard Stauph chuckle, "That was easy."

As AARON REGAINED AWARENESS, AND HIS EYES strove to bring blurs into focus, a cacophony of disjointed sensory input and pain informed him that he lay on a hard object, which rested on the floor of the mansion's emptied swimming pool.

Stones ground in the back of his skull where he'd hit the hardwood. He could wiggle his head slightly side to side but he could not lift it. Straps restrained him, tightened across his throat and brow. His limbs, too, were secured.

"His eyes are moving," purred Werner. "I think he's back with us."

"Good," drawled a man with a raspy, familiar voice.

Stauph leaned in to meet Aaron's gaze. "For this to work, you gotta be awake to feel everything we're going to do to you before you die."

"I did not give you permission to share that," rasped the man who had to be Jefferson Dalton III.

Stauph straightened. "Sorry, sir." He didn't sound sorry.

Aaron wanted to tell them, even though it wasn't true, that he had told others where he was and they would soon come looking. His uncooperative lips and tongue managed only a mushy gurgle.

Dalton went on, "I'm glad you found us, Aaron Friedrich. Your connection to my source will help us carry this forward the proper way."

Connection to my source? For a topsy-turvy moment Aaron thought his captor was chatting with him about journalism.

Again Aaron tried to talk. *I told my publisher where I am. They'll come looking for me.* His tongue flapped uselessly.

"You are your own publisher," Dalton chortled. "And you didn't tell a soul because you had no idea this would be dangerous."

Aaron gasped.

"I can hear you, Aaron Friedrich, hear everything that you are *really* thinking, because my *source* can hear you. It's proof of your connection, and I'm glad for it."

Dalton's ravings plunged Aaron into heart-thumping distress, exponentially multiplied as an auditory hallucination began, more real than the agony wracking him.

Aaron, my God, is that you?

John Hairston's deep, gravely voice, Aaron could not mistake. Where it came from, he could not pinpoint. He couldn't be hearing it, yet hope overwhelmed his skepticism. Before he could call out, Hairston interrupted. *He thinks he smashed my wards but he ain't got them all. He can't hear me, but he can hear you. Stop trying to talk or we'll never be able to end this.*

Knowledge separate from consciousness, deeper than intuition, drenched in stomach-flipping déjà vu, instructed Aaron not to question. He accepted that either he was having a psychotic break, his own mind yammering nonsense in Hairston's voice, or the real Hairston was captive nearby, somehow, and demonstrating telepathy. Aaron had—he had been through—

"That's right, Aaron Friedrich," Dalton said. "You've been a prisoner of magic before. Do you remember yet where your scars came from?"

With immense difficulty, the strap abrading his forehead, Aaron lolled his head to one side, bringing into view a man in a white hood who was otherwise naked, standing atop a sarcophagus-sized box placed in the deepest end of the pool. Ornate patterns adorned the sides of the box. Though Aaron could not clearly make them out, looking at them layered a sensation like motion sickness atop his other torments.

I'm in here, Hairston breathed in Aaron's mind. *Dalton tricked me, like he tricked you. He figured out things about me that no one ever has. Did his fucking homework. I can't get out unless we trick him back. But I am going to need you to* remember.

"I think you need a *reminder*," the hooded man said.

Terror bubbled hot in Aaron's empty spaces, escaping his throat in a feeble shriek of denial. The way Dalton's words echoed Hairston's echoed Dalton's—was he facing two sadistic mind games or one speaking in two voices?

Stauph squatted beside him, a square object gripped between his fingers that turned out to be a razor blade. "Don't cry now, or I'll give you something to cry about." He used his free hand to clamp Aaron's head down, mashing his ear against the hard wooden surface upon which he lay. The broken rocks in his head ground together.

Don't fight him, Hairston said. *Let him do this.*

Stauph used the razor to slice into Aaron's scars, panting as he worked. At first Aaron felt only a tugging in his flesh, followed by a kindling of heat.

Hairston again. *Keep it together, boy, this is going to hurt.*

Aaron's torturer forced his head to turn the other way and cut again. Stauph wore nothing, not even a hood, and Aaron could not avoid the sight of the man becoming aroused.

"It's okay if you scream during this part," Dalton said. "Everyone does. For you it might be even worse than usual."

Werner's hands came into view, covered with a mucus-like sludge. Stauph chuckled as she reached for Aaron's groin.

Her touch burned. Aaron couldn't escape, could do no more than twitch and buck. He provided his captors with the screams they sought, even before Werner brought her hands to his face, rubbed the scorching salve into his fresh wounds, his nostrils, his eyes.

Look at me, Aaron. Look. At. Me.

Agony burned into every surface, wrapped every object in an aurora glow. The cement of the pool, the steel and wood of the ceiling, the cloth of Dalton's hood, Werner's sagging breasts, Stauph's erect member.

Their colors dulled in comparison to the astonishing patterns woven around the sarcophagus, intricate as mazes, baffling as optical illusions. Yet those patterns faded to a grayness as the figure contained inside them occupied more and more of Aaron's focus. That figure blazed, burning hotter than the magma searing between Aaron's thighs and into the meat of his face.

Look at me.

"When you can see him, he can feel you," Dalton said.

Aaron's viscera squirmed within his body cavities. The burning man in the sarcophagus thrashed in response.

Don't think, Aaron, Hairston said. It *was* Hairston inside the sarcophagus. Every inch of Hairston was on fire. *Keep your eyes on me and don't think.* The order was easy to obey, Aaron could not string a single thought together, except for two words: "Help me."

"Aaron Friedrich, I need to make a long story short. When your friend John Hairston first came to Grandy Springs those sixty-some years ago, the good citizens tried to feed him to something ancient and full of power. But he got loose and turned the tables and found unholy salvation underground, and now he's more magic than man. But the thing that's fused inside him, it's going to be mine. This is how it ends. This is how *he* ends. It's long overdue. I'm fixing this abomination, and helping me is how you make the pain go away."

I can help you and you can help me, Hairston said, *but first you have to* remember.

Aaron's innards writhed of their own accord.

Two white hot pinpoints within the cage-pattern of the sarcophagus. They were eyes. Hairston's eyes. Even in his torment and confusion, Aaron feared to meet them, convinced they'd ignite him. Yet the death that obliterated Annaliza Griffith would at least be relief.

He met that starfire gaze.

He did ignite, but not in the way he had imagined. His mind erupted.

He remembered impossible things, things he never understood even as they happened to him.

He remembered: human forms made of twining black worms.

He remembered: pitch darkness; a painful, immovable restraint pinching his neck; his face burned and bleeding; Della whimpering beside him, a stranger to his other side, his face mashed against theirs; their flesh sown together through the cheeks and temples.

He remembered: a pool of blood at the bottom of a well, erupting in white hot fire, the flesh of his face tearing away from his fellow captives.

He remembered—but the memory was not his own—crawling through a cavern tunnel, its ceiling so low he could not lift up onto all fours, the only light coming from the fungus-like tendrils sprouting all over his skin.

He remembered—but the memory belonged to Hairston, not him—peering into a pit deep as a universe, filled with beings that churned like star plasma, flowed like amoebae, surged hungrily toward him. How the matter-altering befoulment from the otherworldly infection spreading through him caused a reaction that neither he nor his would-be killers expected.

Aaron remembered even more gut-shredding things, excavated from his own mind, from Hairston's, from the lifespans of beings not part of any existence Aaron knew. They affected his brain the way fangs puncture skin. The pain setting his nerve endings afire hung distant as a white dwarf in another galaxy.

His physical vision still perceived two white-bright eye spots within the space of the sarcophagus. Driven by the demand they conveyed, he turned against the straps to stare straight up, the neck-spraining effort akin to shoving a boulder up a mountain.

"How is he doing that?" Dalton shouted. "Don't let him look away!"

The white eyespots held their place within Aaron's vision, so that now they glared down at him from the ceiling. The outline of a face formed around them, expanding from that seed to sketch a body.

Werner and Stauph grabbed Aaron by chin and hair, shrieked as they jerked their hands away.

Hairston's form fleshed out. He hung above them all, arms outstretched in a crucifix pose. His unmistakable laugh boomed.

The couple's hands were on fire. Squealing, they beat their fists against whatever surface they could, trying to extinguish Hairston's magic. Dalton tore his hood off as the fabric ignited.

"Guess you haven't figured out everything," Hairston chuckled, and floated up through the ceiling and out of sight. His words, "I'll be back to finish this," faded into the stratosphere.

Dalton howled with the frustrated energy of a much younger man.

Stauph bawled like a baby. "It burns!"

Aaron, in the corner of his eye, perceived that the light that corresponded to Hairston's presence inside the trap had gone out. He lay abandoned, shivering, his mind overwhelmed by horror after horror. He hardly registered the developments that followed, as Dalton screamed at his lackeys, as the trio unsealed the trap, as a pillar of fire blasted the sarcophagus apart. Hairston was still inside, after all.

The tricked had become the trickster.

One more grotesquerie to add to all the others: Dalton, Stauph, and Werner screaming at impossible pitches, their heads, their lungs somehow still intact as fires enveloped them from foot to shoulder.

A sun blazed in Hairston's eyes. *For what you did to those children*, he boomed. *For what you made me do.*

W HEN AARON COULD ONCE AGAIN CONCENTRATE on his surroundings, he discovered with a sinking heart that he still lay in the empty pool. None of it had been a dream.

Warm hands under his bare shoulders helped him sit up. He at last beheld the awful crate of iron and wood he had been placed upon, about the size of a coffin, etched with occult patterns.

Nearby, three intact heads lay in a pile of black char.

The more awake he grew, the more the nightmares cascaded behind his eyes.

The hands helping him sit up belonged to Hairston, who radiated concern beneath the white bushes of his eyebrows and his lion's mane of white hair.

Aaron fought to breathe. His heart lurched and pounded.

When Hairston spoke, he sounded ordinary. Human. "You remember everything now, don't you? Every awful thing that happened in this awful town."

Tears coursed down Aaron's cheeks. He nodded.

"Would you like to forget again?"

Aaron's shuddering grew more and more uncontrollable, his teeth chattering, his balance teetering. Somewhere in those spasms, he managed to shape words. *Yes. Please. God.*

Hairston spoke in a language that, up until this day, Aaron would have sworn he had never heard before in his life.

Soon he slipped into a blissful slumber, even though he remained wide awake.

THANOMORPHOSIS

with W. Gregory Stewart

The Preliminary Analysis of a Metabiologic
Nanoscan of Septenary Gestation in a Transient
Parasitical Psychic Species and Terrestrial Hosts . . .

Student observations	Larval transient	Host: a monovital
the septenary larval stage	so Leap begins and ends in an instant.	Say you love me as I die —for sound
transmutes from impure energy	here was and will have been	is the last of lingering sense to fly
attaches to a host	a perfect cessation, and its sigh	and fade before terrible light . . .
at the organism's birth	and so its sending,	but I leap!? an impossible distance
and distributes itself	while— impossibly distant—	between my known sun
throughout the corpus,	there would be and so	and another, gone in a nanosecond,
concentrating	have been some waiting thing	gone less in fact, yet strung
in some instances	some ended mean,	forever, start to star—and STILL
within the heart or brain.	some place to, sudden, be.	on this strange edge of night.

Student observations	Larval transient	Host: a monovital
An elder	there is a [Venn] intervention—	the sight, not true:
of the host species—	here is the sigh,	more *sense* of light
hite "doctor" by others of its kind	while there and then	the wake of a departure
and kin—	(and now) a crushing thrall of life.	blast of a comet's train
oversaw six deaths	(can speed be truly infinite? for if,	and a sense of something
in a delicately	then is it truly speed, or else a sort	departing—
balanced bed,	of translocation?) (so nearly there,	a deflating,
measured	from Leap to each, while yet	a lightening,
the larvae's mass on departure	this thought stands unresolved . . .	and the end of *be*;
at 0.75 ounces	can speed achieve the infinite—	then matter, and meat,
(21.3 grams)	and still be only speed . . ?)	and no matter.

Student observations	Larval transient	Host: a monovital
Despite the constant contact		deeper than awareness,
the host species oft refers		than even unremembered dreams
to the larvae		can probe,
only in the abstract		something, someone
building elaborate rituals around		pressed against a membrane
concepts		a billion times thinner
related to the gestating creatures'	[blink]	than skin
destination		that never breaks, someone wrapped
which the hosts believe		throughout, within, far more
directly influenced by		intimate than any lover
their own behavior		mouthing whispers, kisses, movements
as judged within subjective		behind some membrane, messages
cultural standards		that cannot be detected or deciphered

Student observations	Larval transient	Host: a monovital
A meme repeats throughout	there will be words that come to me	What is this longing
these primitive societies:	again. there will be words and thought	that needles inside me,
a concept of pairing	and things that I have seen elsewhen	and what,
predestinated,	elsewhere— elseself, outside	this ache
souls designed	of things I cannot grasp,	that leaves my mind fidgeting
for one another	not yet.	that urges me to explore
which will unite	!	the next friend
in defiance of probability,	I have not been here before, and yet	the next drug
but it remains unclear	and yet . . .	the next lover
whether at this stage	I will have known you, when we meet.	no matter how fully
the larvae have any	I know that some galactic tumbler	you sate me?
urge to mate	will slip fumblingly into place when I	What is this
or even socialize beyond	shall have learned of you again,	seeping wound
what's vicariously achieved	forever from	that begs to be stanched
through the host	tomorrow . . .	but never heals?

. . . being a preliminary description of *Reprobanimus stella-cola*, commonly known as the human 'soul', now recognized as a bodiless interstellar traveler that lodges in the human frontal lobes and gestates there during one brief phase of its complicated life cycle.

THE BUTCHER, THE BAKER

THE PASTRIES BAKED IN AUNTIE MAYYA'S OVENS owned a reputation unrivaled throughout the Rosepike Quarter. If that reputation didn't extend into the other six quarters of Calcharra, it wasn't because their peoples could boast of a baker whose skills bested hers. More likely, it was because bragging about your home quarter while visiting another could spark a duel if done in the wrong place, and few would risk death by knife or sword over baked goods.

Trukos kept his gaze focused on the blade gripped by his ill-met new acquaintance. He held his own knife level, with the blade pointed away from his body, edge forward.

His opponent, though dressed like a dockworker from Noon-sail Quarter, had cursed him in the name of the four caryatids of House Tharychtis, and those furious women adorned the pretentious colonnade of a manse central to Goldbrook Quarter. Trukos knew that house to be pretentious because Auntie Mayya described it so. Surely something else entirely had been troubling this scar-browed, pale ferret of a man, and Trukos's breadcrust-brown skin, lisping speech, and innocuous boast about Mayya's cooking had given this malcontent the excuse he needed to unharness his aggression. That Trukos had encountered him inside the famil-iar dusk of Diggurd's smithy, with its delightful heat and dozens of fascinating tools for shaping metal hung neat in racks, stung worse than stray sparks from the forge. The smell of the reddened coals had reminded Trukos of Mayya's ovens as they warmed.

A knot of strangers had formed a semicircle around the com-batants. At least two of the five whispered in a familiar way to the man from Goldbrook, who stood with knifepoint forward,

97

dark eyes focused like a dog's in the instant before a bite. Diggurd watched from the forge, his beard and lowered eyebrows highlighted from beneath by the light from the coals.

One of the strangers said "Begin" and the Goldbrook man lunged. His blade sunk to the hilt in Trukos's chest, the impact like a hard punch. Trukos retreated a half-step but stayed upright, meeting his attacker's eyes as they widened in surprise. Neither struggling for breath nor bleeding, he grabbed the man's extended arm and struck toward his jaw with his own knife hand, aiming down and left so the blade cut deep into the man's neck. Bright arterial blood sprayed the onlookers as the man choked and stumbled backward. The grotesque sight made Trukos gasp and recoil, almost too late remembering to clutch at the knife protruding from his own chest and feign agony.

For better or for worse, more blood from his dying challenger splashed his tunic, providing camouflage for his lack of same. So sad, he thought, that this angry fool chose to die over Mayya's pastries, which he surely would have enjoyed if he had just tried them.

Trukos didn't even know the man's name. He had known the names of the first two men he killed, evil souls who had deserved worse than he gave them—Mayya had told him as much. This man, hot tempered and foolish, had gambled grossly and lost, but did he deserve this death? Trukos would never be sure.

He lurched toward Diggurd, still grasping at his chest, as the others huddled around their fallen acquaintance. Diggurd, who knew something of Trukos's true nature, twitched his head toward the rear entrance to the smithy. As Trukos staggered past him in a pretense of being wounded, Diggurd leaned in, beard prickly as horsehair against Trukos's ear. "Get back to the witch and tell her never to send you here again."

Trukos halted, crestfallen, but Diggurd had already moved away, hefting a hammer as he bore down on the cluster of men. "Get that out of here!" he bellowed, with a sweeping gesture at the body slumped on the dirt floor.

It wasn't in Trukos's nature to disobey. He resumed his pretend stumble until it carried him outside, then broke into a run. He didn't pull the blade from his chest or discard his bloodied tunic until he'd left the smithy many streets behind.

The bloodless wound gaped, gruesome as an empty eye socket. Wounds that he had sustained in the past had closed within minutes, but this one showed no sign of doing so. He slipped from Noonsail Quarter back into Rosepike and eventually rapped his knuckles on the back door of Mayya's bakery.

Inside, upstairs, in the closet that served as his humble living quarters, the place where he often lay curled on a threadbare scrap of rug when he had no chores to perform, Mayya glared at his injury. "Fool child."

"I only spoke truth," he told her. "I didn't expect a man would kill for that, or die from it."

"Death needs no reason, much less a good reason." Mayya sighed. "This will be difficult to mend."

A chill weighted the place where Trukos's heart would have been had he possessed one. The sensation of ice in his torso ached unlike anything he'd ever experienced.

Gouran, that hateful old sorcerer, in a last desperate act, had stuck a double-edged dagger in his side as Trukos squeezed his throat closed. Though the blade's full length sank into Trukos's flank, the sensation had troubled him no more than the poke of a finger. Soon after, Mayya had pulled the dagger out of him, and the wound sealed itself, leaving no evidence that it had ever existed.

Trukos frowned. "It wasn't difficult before."

Another sigh. "Oh, child, it's not the same."

IN THE FIRST MOMENTS OF HIS LIFE, Trukos had awakened as if from a long sleep—and he understood what sleep was and what awakening meant, even though he possessed no memories of an existence before he had opened his eyes. The first sight that met him had been Mayya's bruised face; the next her spacious kitchen and three stone ovens, one still hot.

"Child of my oven," she had said, "my husband Gouran sleeps upstairs. He must die at your hand." Though tears glistened on her cheeks, her voice flowed with a summery calm.

There had been a cost to Trukos's birth. Mayya had never said what, only that she deemed him worth the price.

Frowning at the hole left in his chest by the Goldbrook man's knife, Mayya said, "Come with me," and led him downstairs to the kitchen. "I need to examine your wound properly. Wait here." She left Trukos alone, sitting atop her long, smooth-polished wooden cutting counter, the same spot where he had first woken to this life. Though Auntie Mayya called him child, he had towered over her from his earliest moments. He was even taller than imposing Gouran. Despite his slighter frame he was far stronger, as his first night alive and Gouran's last had proved.

Not unlike in Diggurd's smithy, pots and pans and an awe-inspiring array of iron utensils hung on iron racks. Come the morning, the assistant cooks would arrive, four in all, along with a dozen boy and girl apprentices for the assistants to order about, and then the kitchen, despite its size, would feel small and crowded. For now, Mayya's single lantern burned, suspended by a wall hook. The trapdoor to the cellar thudded shut. He had lived in this building for a complete turn of the seasons, and never once had she ordered him to fetch something from the cellar.

Mayya returned, the light from the small flame etching deep lines in her face. She carried a basket, which she set on the counter with a gasp of effort. The substance revealed when she lifted the lid resembled bread dough. Trukos frowned. He had never seen it before. "What's that for, Auntie?"

"I know you're confused, child. Please hold still." She took a handful of the white batter and started to push it into the hole in his chest. The chill at his core sharpened and he cringed, unsettled by discomfort for the first time in his life. Mayya withdrew her fingers and stared up at him with eyes set like green jewels in a sorrow-seamed face, eyes that glistened with worry.

Her tone, though, came out stern. "I told you to hold still. The binding needs time."

She resumed her task and he abided by her wishes, though if anything the cold intensified until it burned. He didn't flinch away, though he desperately wanted to. She repeatedly frowned up at him but continued to pack the wound.

At last she patted his chest. The substance remained pale, as if a blind eye had opened over the place that would have held his heart. The burning cold continued, relentless.

"This is like nothing I've foreseen." She closed the basket. "You took a life that I didn't ask you to take, and it's corrupted my recipe. It's affected you, like a mold growing under the crust, ruining the loaf as it rises."

Trukos began to cry, though he could no more shed tears than bleed. Mayya placed a warm hand on his neck. "Please don't do that. You have to give the remedy time, if it's to work at all."

Ashamed, he stilled his sobbing, despite the pain and his growing alarm. "I'm sorry, Auntie."

"Hush, Trukos. I am the one sorry for you. You have always been faithful. You do everything I've asked. You don't deserve to suffer. Would that I could have baked more wisdom into you, that you'd have known to hold your tongue among strangers."

"Did I do wrong, Auntie?" If he had made a mistake, he never wanted to repeat it.

"No, no, I'm honored by your love, and you had to defend yourself. You're lucky that oaf you killed was too ignorant to recognize what you are."

Trukos found that statement strange. He knew exactly what he was: a thing Auntie Mayya had made. The pain, though, he needed her to unmake. "How do I stop it? Please tell me what to do."

"No blood flows through you, so no medicine for dulling pain can help you. I'm sorry, child. I will try to find a way, but I know of no such elixir for one like you."

"This is hard, Auntie." His hands balled into fists. He forced them open. "I didn't know it would hurt."

"I didn't either," she said. "I hope you find the strength to bear it. I loathe the thought of unmaking you." She took the basket by the handle. "I'll fetch you a tart, if it will help, but then I must sleep and you must try to rest."

Despite his agony, the thought of sweet crust and sugared fruit spurred hunger in Trukos's belly. There could not be a taste more heaven-sent in all of Calcharra.

But the tart didn't help, and neither did Mayya's doughy patch that grew heavy within his wound. Rest was impossible as he lay shuddering in his closet, the ice ball inside him refusing to thaw.

When Mayya at last reappeared in his doorway, her eyes brimmed with pity, but her words were stern as stone. "I need you. I can't give you leave from you duties any longer."

"I'll do my best." He did not want to trouble her with complaints, but the ache in his chest pulsed, relentless. "Nothing has changed."

"I'm sorry. If it hasn't healed by now, I'm afraid I can do no more. You have no choice but to learn how to live with it."

Despite her rebuke, she showed consideration in how she altered his routine. Instead of sending him out on errands, she told him to tend the oven fires, a chore often delegated to the boy apprentices. He adored her for this kindness and the promise of warmth. Yet, to his dismay, the heat from the wood and coals did nothing to ease the freezing spike that pierced his chest.

Once, making sure no one was paying attention, he caved in to temptation, picked up a red hot coal with tongs, opened his tunic below the collar, and pressed the coal to the discolored spot. He almost cried out as the coal instantly extinguished.

He didn't tell Mayya what he had attempted. Troubling her about his plight would serve no good purpose.

All of the assistants and most of the apprentices avoided speaking to him, with the exception of a boy who hailed from Loamfire Quarter named Yshan. He would catch Trukos in the rare moments where both were unattended and ask questions. "You don't look like you come from Rosepike. Where are your parents?"

Auntie Mayya had forbidden him from talking about how he was born, so he would say, "I don't know where they are. I never knew them. But I am from Rosepike."

"You're so strange and sad."

"I'm not sad." Horrible as the ache in his chest was, agony wasn't the same as sadness. Yet Auntie Mayya no longer smiled each time she laid eyes on him. Since assigning him to mind the ovens, she had not once inquired after his pain.

"Be quiet," hissed one of the assistants, a stick-thin blonde woman. "We have customers."

Of the five people who entered the bakery, one stood out to Trukos as unlikely. Her threadbare dress and face unadorned with the hues that wealthy women applied before a mirror implied she could not possibly afford the breads and treats Mayya and her bakers made. Short and stout and plain, she attracted little notice from Mayya's underlings. Nonetheless she put on a show of browsing the confections as if she intended to buy—often stealing glances at Trukos. He in turn watched her like a hawk, because guarding the store was part of his ingrained purpose.

He fully expected the pauper woman to attempt a theft—hoped she would, in fact, because it would give him reason to draw Mayya's attention—but her perusals of the pies and loaves betrayed no genuine interest. After a short while, she left.

The next day, she returned, and the day after, and the day after that. On that fourth morning, she walked straight to Trukos at his post before the ovens and said, "You're the one who killed my husband."

Her voice, soft and tremulous, was hard to hear over the bakery's bustle, though every word reached and jolted him. "What did you say?"

"My husband Padraen. You cut his throat and ran." Her voice remained soft, though her eyes blazed. Two, then three, then all of the apprentices and assistants stopped and stared.

Nothing from Trukos's store of words rose to the surface. Nothing was adequate. The woman glared up at him, her stance wavering as if she might bolt and run or charge and attack.

He tried to explain, unsure what else to do. "I . . . I . . . he stabbed me. All I said was that Auntie's cakes were the best in the city, and he swore to kill me for it."

Her eyes narrowed even as she trembled. "But you stand here hale and hearty, and he's food for the monsters in the Nightcreek ditch! I can't even bury him!" Tears of anger and more anointed her cheeks.

"I'm—" Trukos began as Auntie Mayya stepped between them.

"What's going on?" she demanded.

"Your boy killed my husband."

Mayya didn't hesitate. "The lowlife deserved what he got. Leave my shop or I'll summon the guard."

The pauper woman dangled a beat longer in her state of high-strung indecision. Then she turned with a cry of anguish and fled.

The cold spike through Trukos's chest grew no more intense, yet he was more conscious of it than ever. He winced as Mayya grabbed his shoulder. Her scowl swept through the kitchen and the shop, and at once assistants and apprentices resumed their chores.

Auntie Mayya turned to Trukos. "Child, don't look at me that way. That woman doesn't know her place." She leaned closer. "She

might be a threat to us, and especially to you, if she tries to in-
volve the guard and they decide to listen. Follow her, carefully. See
where she lives." She took a deep breath. "When night falls, end
this threat. You know what to do."

Word for word, her command was the same as it was on the
afternoon Sarskile burst into Mayya's bakery with three merce-
nary soldiers in tow, each bearing fierce longswords. Sarskile ran
a bakery of his own at Rosepike's southmost limit, catering to
nearby manses from Rosepike and Steermast. Mayya, too, catered
to the wealthy, but she also opened her bakery to daily purchases
from members of the merchant and trade guilds. Sarskile did not.

At the top of his lungs, Sarskile accused Mayya of stealing his
recipes and his customers. He ordered his sellswords to upend
every confection onto the cobblestone floor. Mayya watched the
destruction, expression a careful blank, as he proclaimed he had
unassailable proof and dared her to appeal to the guard.

That night, Trukos had scaled the back wall of Sarskile's state-
ly home, squeezed through an opened window, and strangled the
man in his sleep. He'd left the same way he came in, taking the
corpse with him.

Auntie Mayya had assured him that Sarskile's complaints
were slanderous lies. As she repeated her order now, urging him
to kill a grieving widow, an alien thought intruded. What if Sarskile's grievances were truth?

"No," he said, unsure which thought he was responding to.

Mayya's sorrow-filled gaze widened with oven heat. "You refuse me."

The agony in Trukos's chest throbbed. "Yes."

Mayya's next words emerged rapid and raspy, in a language
he'd not been created to understand. As those syllables resonated,
Trukos experienced two overwhelming sensations. All through his
body, fissures cracked, so many that he believed himself about to
shatter toe to scalp like a sugar crystal stomped by a boot. In oppo-
sition, expanding outward from his chest, floes of ice filled him as
water from a well pump fills a flagon. He screamed in animal terror.

The dueling sensations dissipated as fast as they manifested.
Trukos stood whole before Mayya, whose mouth hung agape.

She regained her composure before he did. "You are no longer
my child. Begone from here."

He obeyed and put the bakery many streets behind before her full meaning crashed down on him. He staggered to a halt against an immense wall smothered by desiccated stalks of ancient ivy. As carriages, rickshaws, and pedestrians crowded past, he wailed with every breath, uncaring who saw. The few travelers who glanced his way granted him a wide berth.

T RUKOS HAD NO NEED TO EAT OR SLEEP—before, he had only rested because Mayya had ordered it. For days he haunted the streets of Rosepike, with its red-tiled roofs and forbidding bronze gates, never bothering with a hiding place because he never stopped walking.

At first, an impulse that seemed to originate somewhere outside his own mind pushed him further and further from Rosepike and the bakery, but Trukos found that the more he fought against that impulse, the easier it became to resist. The cold in his chest flared each time he turned back, and this made him wince but a little less pronounced each time.

Yet he would at times realize he had unconsciously taken a path through streets and alleys that led directly back to Mayya. Whenever he became aware of this, he would with some strain reverse course, as phantom resistance snagged at his steps.

He remained unsure whether the source of all this push and pull had root in Mayya's power or his own longings. The frozen spike through his chest never diminished—it was one more factor in his new existence, a thing as present as his limbs, his skin.

He most missed the taste of Mayya's pies and pastries. He soon wished, too, that he could have completed the thing he had intended to say to the pauper woman: "I'm sorry."

After days of wandering, he followed the twin diamonds of the moons northwest into Goldbrook, with its tiles of sandstone fused hard as glass. This newer longing, an urge Trukos could still act upon, to say something not said, had come to eclipse all others.

He ventured to the fog-shrouded docks, asked workers dressed as Padraen had been how to find Padraen's widow. They directed him to a run-down neighborhood where makeshift shanties of wood, straw, and mud clogged the alleys. A reek of decay and offal tainted every breath he took. When he reached the hut where the widow lived, that reek would have brought tears to his eyes if he could shed them.

The front door was latched but easy for him to force open. The whine of flies amplified into an ear-drowning din. A foregone conclusion that he would find her dead in her bed. Her bulging eyes, protruding tongue, burst blood vessels, bruised neck, told Trukos she had been strangled, her life taken exactly as Mayya would have had him do it.

Trukos had been tasked with cutting the first two men he had killed into pieces, scattering their remains into the horror known as the Nightcreek ditch, in truth a wide, reeking canal filled with unwanted remains and the horse-wide worms that fed on them— the Oldest of All Calcharra's Gods, as they were sometimes called. The disposal of corpses was an instinct baked hard into what passed for Trukos's bones.

Above, hungry clouds swallowed the twin moons.

Later that night, rain pelted Trukos's skin, trickled through the short curls of his unchanging hair. If he perched here beside the butcher's brick chimney long enough, with the rain beating upon him like fey hammers, would the substance he was made of at last grow damp? Would he slough apart, leave a doughy pile of remains on the butcher's rooftop? Would the ice in his chest at last release him? Variations on these questions pricked him, prolonging the hours as he spied on Mayya's bakery directly across the emptied market plaza.

A candle flickered in Mayya's second floor window, its glow muted by the intervening rain.

This close, the impulse to turn and flee returned, a ghost of Auntie Mayya's geas, but the discomfort it caused was just one more corpse on the pile. He clenched his teeth against its push as he slid cautiously down the roof tiles until his feet dangled over the edge, aimed into the narrow, unpleasant-smelling gap between the butcher's shop and the tanner's stalls. Thunder masked the sound of his landing. The impact shook every joint. He heard pops as his strange flesh cracked, though no pain accompanied the damage. No mending from Auntie Mayya in his future—perhaps these new imperfections were destined, also, to fill with ice.

He did not stride directly across the plaza. Even through the storm he would be visible from the window, and lightning would expose him as brazenfaced as a head displayed on a pike. Instead he crouched or crawled in the intervals between thunderbolts, scurrying like a rodent among the permanent merchant stands that afforded deepest shadow. As he peered around the corner of a stand inhabited during the day by an orchard grower, the candle in Mayya's window moved.

It had not occurred to Trukos until that moment that perhaps she might sense his proximity in the same way he sensed hers.

A hand brought the candle closer to the window. A figure leaned out. The face didn't belong to Mayya. Trukos had seen it before, in reflections.

Auntie Mayya baked with unmatched skill. Whatever miracle she could produce in her ovens, it only followed naturally that she could reproduce it.

Trukos retreated into shadow, the ache where his heart should have been throbbing with new vigor that had nothing to do with the permanent spike of ice. Likely this new Trukos had a task to complete tonight, and even a person as simple-minded as the old Trukos could deduce what it must be.

He contemplated the life that lay ahead for his newborn twin.

He emerged from the darkness and drew his knife from its sheath. His double, still leaning out the window, got a good look at him. Trukos made sure of it.

Moments after, Trukos heard, through the rain patter, the slight creak that the back door to the bakery made each time it swung open.

MAYYA WAITED BY THE OVENS. The Trukos who returned to her held a makeshift bundle in his one remaining hand, its contents wrapped in the rags of his vanquished foe's clothing. He let the dripping bundle tumble to the floor, spilling out contents that could have been dried-up loaves of brown bread, as if a gingerbread man the size of a real man had been carved apart.

"He will not ache," the surviving Trukos said, and used his single hand to part his own tunic, revealing a pale discoloration in the shape of an eye.

Mayya gasped in dismay.

Trukos regarded her with his wide dark eyes, his gaze blending something akin to pity with whipped-dog betrayal. "Auntie," he said.

The address drew a hesitant smile from her like a fish reeled slowly from the depths. At the sight of it, Trukos fought not to return it, the expression that ultimately resulted both grim and thoughtful.

"Tell me you'll never make another," he said, "and I will not harm you."

To her credit, her promise came without hesitation, and he could not mistake the sincerity of her oath. It was a quality he was attuned to recognize.

After that, the silence stretched between them, the small flame from the lantern brushing gold across their faces, weaving shadows around the awkward pile on the cobblestone floor.

Mayya's voice resumed with an uncharacteristic quaver. "It may still be possible to end your suffering," she said. "But it will take me time, and many trials and tests."

He put a hand over his chest. "This is my birthright. The first thing I have ever owned."

She took a step forward. "You need not only own pain. You are free to acquire other things. You would need help, doing so." A question hung in her voice, one he answered by turning away.

He helped himself to a tart before he left the shop behind for good.

Dispelling the Arcana

With acknowledgments to Charles Williams

I could not tell you
where these chambers exist,
only where they are seen,
within dust-covered jars
in abandoned manor houses,
within moonlit reflections
at the bottoms of wells,
through exploratory holes
bored in the walls of tombs
that prove empty when opened.

I cannot explain how
these floor tiles were laid,
why their patterns may be
checkered or hexagonal,
ornate as jungle orchids
or plain as pencil lines,
defined by stairs and stories
climbing to unreal skies
or repeating flat and endless,
unbounded by horizons.

I can share with you how
the powers manifest to me,
the Empress and the Hierophant

gliding on chess piece thrones,
the Tower rising and collapsing
as it blinks from tile to tile,
the Devil waving as he
swivels at corners, the Fool
skipping square to square,
the Hanged Man crossing diagonals.

I will never reveal how
I stepped onto the board,
how I walk among them,
observe them at their craft,
contractors for the Fates,
the Moon and eir canids
circling around Judgement's
jack-in-the-box graves,
dancing with Strength's lion,
stitching a corner of the universe.

I can't say why I chose
to bypass the sweating sphinxes,
the blazing Sun's sad horse,
revealed myself by the Star's pool.
The pitchers you pour look heavy,
I said, Want a hand? Here.
Take a load off. And she did,
no hesitation, a nod of thanks.
She dashed across the mosaic
and vanished into the distance.

I confess I felt surprise
at how soon I grew bored,
despite the water's beauty,
the refraction in the ripples,
the impossible mathematics
of its depths. Pouring, pouring,
the pitchers never ran dry;
I tossed them in the pool.
They sank with no splash.

Overflow spread to the tile.

I took a while to find courage
and turn fully brash, upend
Death from eir horse
and scatter trembling bones,
steal the Fool's dog and
force him to chase me,
gag and bind the Emperor
using his own robes,
bend the Magician's halo
from infinity to plain circle.

I can't quite explain why
I stole the World's sash,
yet ousted from her wreath
she claimed to miss neither,
helped me trip the Hermit,
sweet-talk Temperance
into a days-long bender.
Tiles cracked into new shapes.
Floors plunged to new levels.
She cackled at quaking strata.

I couldn't be selfish and
insist she stay. She laughed
so bright as chaos grew,
and climbed to the firmament,
best view for impending
collapse. I waved goodbye
as barriers dissolved, arcana
seeped through. Dimensions
reshuffled will be
dealt out anew.

I cannot say if I achieved
what I wanted, though
I yearned for change,
for meanings beyond

upright and inversion,
for sightings of ghosts
no skeptic can deny,
for a future that any
one being can shape
with a snap of the fingers.

GOOD TO THE LAST DROP

with Anita Allen

T HE MOCKING LAUGHTER AND GROANS OF DISGUST lingered in
Paola's mind for minutes after her co-workers left her alone in
the break room.

Leaving a full cup of coffee on the table, Paola peered out the
door, making sure she was truly alone, and she was. The rest of the
night crew had returned to the warehouse. She dashed to the time
clock, punched in—a minute late—went to her locker, withdrew
her oversized purse, and committed the unpardonable sin of returning to the break room.

She could not have answered, in that moment, which circum-
stance had her heart pounding harder: the revulsion of her co-
workers in response to her latest gesture of goodwill, and the deep
wound that pried open; or her premeditated decision (given their
response) to push hard again her own ordinarily rule-abiding nature; or the mind-bogglingly stupid and dangerous thing she was
about to attempt.

She dug the ornate and alien puzzle out of her purse, placed
it beside her coffee cup. The drab, dun-walled break room, with
its cracked floor and ceiling tiles and aroma of decades of secondhand smoke, dulled further in the presence of this glittering anom-
aly, its colors so intense that they seemed to intrude from a higher,
more powerful reality. Shaped like a many-pointed Christmas or-
nament—if the denizens of Hell were ever permitted to decorate
a tree—its latticework of precious metals and needle-sharp jewels
snagged the eye and dizzied the mind.

Eyes wet, hating herself for sniffling, she picked up the puzzle
in two trembling hands. She let the points prick her palms and
fingers as she worked toward the solution.

As she manipulated the object, the hidden hinges within it turned in ways that defied spatial logic, exerting a mesmerism that scrambled thought and blurred vision. The punctures through her skin mirrored her inner hurt, but she had no sense of progress toward the opening of a portal until the being spoke.

What is it you ask of me, human?

That it never blinked was given: its eyelids had been sliced away. Razors protruded between its fangs, their gleaming edges embedded into its gums. Standing before her on feet sliced in twain to form hooves, it resembled a living or at least mobile version of the puzzle, re-conceived large and humanoid, with all manner of flesh tangled into the filigreed metal and sculpted stone, glistening red tissues stretched and contorted by cables, pulleys, chains wire-thin and wrist-thick, multi-pronged hooks, spiral blades that spun and dug of their own accord. Stitches pulling skin apart and stitches binding skin together contracted and expanded in a constant tug of war.

The being's tongue, shredded into a cat-of-nine-tails configuration, still produced speech. *Those who call us know of the salvations achieved through agony. Do not claim you were unaware of the consequences when you broke the seal.*

"Oh, I know," Paola shrugged, her gaze tearing from the extraordinary creature to focus on her demurely clasped fingers. "I just . . . I wanted to share something with you. Something maybe a—person—like you could appreciate, when no one else does."

On its wires and hinges the being's head titled in the manner of a curious dog. *What?*

She met its blood-clot-black eyes. "Would you like a cup of coffee?"

The remnants of its brow ridges lowered in netherworldly consternation.

Paola opened up, hands flailing as she spoke, her voice shaking, sometimes breaking. "My co-workers used to act like I'm not even here. I'd bake things, and bring them, but they wouldn't eat them. I asked Jacob once and he told me my banana bread 'didn't smell right.' I know that's B.S. I'm not a bad cook, I'm not amazing, but I do fine when people visit. Not that anyone ever visits . . . Whatever, I decided to try something else that they'd appreciate. Can't screw up coffee, right? All the ingredients are here, same grounds, same pot, same machine that everybody else uses. It was simple, they'd all appreciate it. But something *really goes wrong* when I try to make coffee. Bernie, my boss, takes a drink from the first pot, and he runs to the restroom and claims he puked. I thought he was making fun of me so I tried again, and I had to beg them to get them to try it, and they all spat it out after one sip and told me it was worse than the worst coffee they ever tasted. I thought they were lying to be mean to me, so today I snuck in before everyone else and made the coffee without telling them. But they *still* spat it out, and they got so *mad* at me—"

She stopped as she realized the coffee cup was no longer on the table. She turned to see the being upending the entire contents of the cup into its butcher's bin of a mouth. The tubes of its throat bulged as it swallowed.

Trembling with a different kind of fear, Paola held her breath.

The being fell silent. Its eyes focused somewhere unfathomable as a shudder started in its gory core and worked its way outward, making the metal parts that pierced and tortured it rattle and clink. A moan swelled deep inside it, a hideous sound, the muffled suffering of souls damned by the thousands.

Its oil-black eyes once more met Paola's. *Exquisite.*

It held out the cup for a refill.

GODBODY

with Christina Sng

Shark soldiers descend the Great One's gullet,
teeth painted for battle, eyes lighting the way.
Polyp villages rise to defend, baleen swords
clenched in colonies of tentacles.

Spider-goats spin silk in the crevasses
of the Great One's hide, their ambidextrous arms
outstretched languorously into Its depths,
picking at the stardust that molds their universe,

While beneath, leviathans drift
within the catacombs of Its bloodstream;
gargantuan antibodies feeding on the anomalies
spontaneously blossoming with chaotic regularity.

Desperate six-limbed squatters huddle by
the bonfires on Its ice-crusted eyelids,
too frightened to cross the event horizon,
to risk the black holes of the Great One's eyes,

Singularities leading to another unknown
landscape, another to fell or worship,
another pecking order cold and sentient
as their frost-covered god.

Soft hummings ebb from the caldera,
faint swan songs, the winding down
of the eternal machine as Its denizens,

the spiny cats who know the truth, know

that Great One is dying, celestial synapses
contracting out of existence one by one,
prowl the brainbowl devouring each withered neuron
in hopes of preserving Soul once Body is gone.

Matres Lachrymarum

ONE

The steel surface of the table distorts my face. I've glimpsed my reflection before, in pools of water illuminated by streetlights, in the glass of nighttime shop windows, in the blades from my tool kit once they've been cleaned and polished.

My features don't really skew so lopsided, I am sure. My supervisor shaped me to mingle unnoticed among my former cohorts, not to trigger shrieks of revulsion.

The tabletop captures the sweat on my hollow cheeks and too-tall forehead, the wet wisps of hair plastered to my scalp. It's no surprise I'm sweating so profusely.

Beside me on the concrete floor lies the creation, still wrapped inside the tarp that I used to drag it here, moving in a muscle-straining crouch through the tunnels where my supervisor dwells. Though the creation is light for its size, it still weighs at least four times what I do.

The warmth of my body, flush with exertion, floods the examination room despite its high ceiling and subterranean chill. Or perhaps the heat comes from the intensity of my supervisor's many-eyed gaze.

"Seal the door and place my gift upon the table." Her voice, sounded from a hundred mouths, carries the authority of a chorus in an ancient play. "Demonstrate care and skill."

The dimensions of the examination room seem cramped only because the table in its center could accommodate the dissection of a horse. My supervisor fills the opposite half of the room, her malleable form allowing her to curve around the table's corners. Her eyestalks bloom like long-stemmed flowers all along the squirming, bristling flesh of her core.

I turn the valve to seal the vault door. The wheel creaks with rust. I squat and gather the fabric of the tarp, making certain I have secure leverage. I cannot simply heave the creation carelessly, although I have confidence my craftsmanship has made its joints and grafts durable.

I lift, I gasp, I slowly lower the creation onto the table. Just as cautiously, I circle the room, pealing back the tarp's flaps. The creation's mass unfurls until it blankets the surface of the tabletop.

My supervisor also circles the table, mirroring my progress, the hooves at the tips of her myriad legs click-clacking on the hard floor. Most of her eyes engage in inspection of my handiwork, which still spares about a dozen to fixate upon me without blinking.

I maintain an expression flat as a razor blade. The longer my supervisor goes without speaking, the harsher her critique will be. The worst of her reprimands burned curlicue scars down the inside of my left arm—though she has only once subjected me to a punishment that extreme.

My mind willed blank, still a perverse impulse proceeds with an insubordinate mental count, marking the minutes, the seconds as they pass, my breath keeping time.

The creation, inert, glistens with oil and lymph, the grafts that bind bone to steel and viscera to circuitry all sturdy despite the long drag to reach this subterranean lair. This small subtle miracle further evidences my supervisor's place in the divine order, for she is the one who granted me these skills. The matrices of physics and mathematics as chronicled by human science do not restrict her, nor do they tether the work she assigns me.

A forbidden thought shimmies deep in the murk of my brain, an idle speculation at the might my supervisor's sistren must possess, what awesome heights their undisgraced powers must scale. I bury this notion in darkness, lest my supervisor detect my rebellion and unmake me, or worse, further remake me.

Thirteen limbs stretch from her body, their double-dozen joints straightening well over two and a half meters in length. Each limb terminates in a flower-like hand that spirals open to point at junctures in the creation where organic parts fuse with mechanical.

"Work without flaw," she says in her one-and-many voice. "You have proven equal to the task I set for you."

Emoting in response to her praise could prove as grave a mistake as displaying fear. "Thank you, Mother, for permitting me to serve you." Another unwelcome thought bubbled from below, an imagining of how her sistren might respond to hear this outcast addressed as Mother.

"Your duties to me require another step," she says. Every inspection that has gone well ends with that phrase.

Her flower-like hands engulf my head, impart new instructions.

TWO

THE OTHERS SHE HAS SHAPED TO SERVE HER, none look like me. They could not survive for long among the humans proper, and worse, were they to draw the attention of the Mothers who govern the boroughs, unwelcome questions would instantly arise as to who owned and animated them.

The creation, too, might raise similar questions, if those who do the bidding of the Mothers were to discover my workshop.

Dragging the carefully folded and wrapped creation back to that very workshop, I pass other servitors of my supervisor as they labor at their tasks. They stink of a rot that does not afflict me, perhaps because I was still among the living when my supervisor's minions abducted me.

This city had accumulated centuries of history and detritus before the Mothers emerged from their dimension to conquer ours. Subway and sewage systems abandoned and sealed shut, secret bunkers and munitions factories commissioned and neglected, shoddily-constructed apartment towers collapsed and paved over.

My supervisor's lair nestles in these grottoes. I deny the temptation that bubbles, the infernal, suicidal impulse to indulge terms such as *fallen*, such as *fugitive*, such as *pariah avoiding the eyes of her own kind.*

Within the cavernous gloom, servants that partially resemble dogs and partially resemble lobsters stir vats of a substance akin to concrete, laced with an element extracted in trace amounts from my supervisor's demesne. Servants that partly resemble bats and partly resemble spiders take insignificant scoops of the substance and apply it to walls, floors, ceilings in a process of gradual fortification. Shielding against attack from the other Mothers.

Servants that partially resemble mantids and partly resemble mandrills assemble pikes and hammers. *For now all efforts must remain primitive*, my supervisor has said many times, her tongues warm and wet in my ears. *Tasks must stay incremental. Caution overrides all.*

She once and only once said to me, *The most daring project I ever undertook was shaping you to suit our need.*

She does not address me by a name. I cannot, no matter how deeply I dredge, call back the name I bore during my human lifetime.

She made me sturdy enough to heft many times my weight without assistance, a human insect, a mathematical impossibility. At times I wonder if some portion of me exists in a higher dimension than my senses can perceive. My supervisor is capable of such hyperspatial witchcraft.

My sense of sight also revised, I navigate the lightless passages without difficulty, all surfaces a pale gray, the same way that a cat perceives the nighttime world.

Thus I tow the creation behind me in its tarp with little more effort than a human might use to push a wheelbarrow laden with topsoil, even as I stoop to navigate low-ceilinged crawlspaces.

The immense hollow cylinder of concrete that serves as my workshop might once have sloshed full of poisonous chemicals, given the permanent reek of rotten eggs and spoiled apples.

I loosen the tarp and unfurl the creation to its full diameter. With its hodgepodge of mismatched parts, an ignorant human that happened upon it might well mistake it for a trash heap. I presume my supervisor intended this subterfuge.

Along the sliver of floor left uncovered, I spread a single blanket folded over on itself. Hours remain before nightfall in the city, so I lie down.

The hospital bed where I lay when the servitors came for me was even less comfortable than this blanket wadded on chemical-drenched concrete. Wires prodded my sores. Bedbugs and lice danced on my flaking skin and drank my cancerous blood. In my delirium the claws that scooped me from the mattress seemed only one more pain-born hallucination.

The descent into the tunnels, more of the same, a pain-hazed dream that continued until my supervisor enfolded me in her limbs. Her unearthly shape, her turpentine smell, shocked me fully awake—one can never forget the Mothers, and any notion that my ordeal was delusion imploded. She stifled my screams, stuffing her hands in my mouth, seizing my tongue, corking my throat, the taste of her extradimensional flesh like burnt fruit peel and searing pepper mush.

She banished the old agonies, replaced them with her intentions.

I had, when I was human, for the brief time that I was valued, been a maker, a sculptor in stone and clay, a woodworker, a programmer who designed objects to be printed in three dimensions, an artisan who had experimented with media of many controversial sorts. Those urges, those skills, were the pieces of my old life that she allowed to carry over into the new.

She funneled them toward her purposes, welded in blinders that forbade deviances in direction, amputating all memory of my former self.

Almost all.

Dreams bubble, sometimes, deep below the surface, out of reach. Like Tantalus, I grasp, fingers closing on nothing.

THREE

THE WATER IN THE BURIED CANAL MIGHT WELL BE TOXIC to an ordinary animal, something I no longer am. Nor am I a fool: To pass among the humans, first I must bathe, and afterward, dress. Clothes taken from those who will never again have need of them suit me adequately enough.

A sinkhole in a neglected parking garage has collapsed in convenient stages through the decades, the random process of decay creating a series of ledges that form a functional stairway—one could be forgiven for concluding that the hole was deliberately designed. I ascend to the surface, give my eyes time to adjust to the presence of light, however minimal. My toolkit weighs heavy within a concealed pocket of my long gray coat.

Those who guard the doors to the nightclub, if they searched my person and found the tools, immediately would drag me before the Mother that presides there. Fortunately, I know other ways inside.

Under the governance of the Mothers, the disappearance of a single human inspires far less curiosity from the authorities than such incidents once did—nonetheless investigations occur, prosecutions proceed, authorities make a spectacle of punishment.

I must take care who I choose.

Illumination that strobes between dark and blinding, rampant consumption of sense-altering drugs, brain-deceiving holograms, the pulse of artificial heartbeats combine to make the nightclub a perfect place for scouting and snatching sources for components. Dozens of easy marks dance before me, weak and slender souls who will offer scant resistance, even wide awake, while I mine them for sinew and innards. I am but one of many with backs pressed to the walls, watching the young and nimble things as they cavort. I could not hope for greater anonymity.

"You smell like their garbage," he shouts.

At first, I do not comprehend who he's shouting at or about.

"You're the worst kind of scum." He leans down so his gaze meets mine. His breath reeks of whiskey sours. "Get out of here or I'll gut you."

My fearful glance is not aimed at him. I need to see if the Mother on her throne has turned eyes in our direction. Even one focused on me could mean the worst.

She sprawls across a padded furnishing in the shape of a titanic scallop shell, hinged open. Her dozens of hooved limbs and clusters of eyestalks spill over the sides, a living fringe. She basks in the energy of the revelers. The massed psychic auras of humanity serve as nectar to her kind.

The flesh of humanity, too, provides nourishment for them. After cementing their conquest, the Mothers have tended to refrain from that indulgence, reserving that treatment for those foolish enough to rebel—which in turn has made those allowed to continue their lives more or less as usual convinced that they are recipients of a *kindness.*

Those that dance closest to the throne reach high to brush their fingers across the cleft curves of the Mother's dangling hooves.

The man threatening me observes the direction of my glance. "You traitor! You sick bastard! You let her make you into… that!" A switchblade slides into his hand from beneath the cuff of his sleeve. "She won't have time to save you!"

I could laugh, a booming bray right from the belly, if I had a second more to spare. He detects, somehow, what I really am, and presumes I belong full-body to the Mother of the club, and out of a rage loosed by suicidal inebriation he wants to kill me for it. He, like me, has snuck a forbidden weapon past the Mother's security. The irony stabs deep.

His blade does not. I catch his wrist. I could crush his bones, but that would give me away, and the Mother would not mistake me for one of her own, as he has.

"Filth!" He tries to twist his wrist loose, swings his free fist at me. I stagger drunkenly though I've not had a drop, and I pull him off balance. He swings again, and I let his fist connect. Skin splits along my cheekbone. The pain of flesh parting stings more than I expected.

"Monster!" he cries.

"Monster!" I slur back at him. Around us, dancers spy his blade and shriek. I pull him to the floor as bouncers bear down on us.

They eject us both, the best possible outcome, except that I can never again use those hunting grounds, because the risk of recognition will be too great. I will need to find a new one. The risks of that quest might be greater by an order of magnitude. My supervisor might burn new scars in me once I disclose these events to her.

We both end up sprawled on the concrete of a moonlit alley. The gate permitting exit from the club has shut behind us, the seal airtight, muffling rhythmic thunder. We are no longer the staff's problem. The far end of the alley opens into a populated street. He could walk toward it, not that I would let him get far, but his obsession with me has not relented.

The bouncers took his knife. I thank the benevolence of my supervisor, for granting me enough self-possession to play the part of a bewildered, befuddled addict, such that the Mother's minions did not bother to search my coat. I still need parts for the creation.

"I know," he mutters. "I know you're one of them. You let her shape you. Dog!"

I sway and slow my words. "What makes you . . . think that?"

I genuinely desire to know what gave me away.

Instead of answering, he charges me. I drop all pretense, slam his blundering weight into the bricks behind me. When he attempts to stand, I knock him flat with one blow, snap his knees under my boots. His neck squeezed in the crook of my arm, I cut off the blood to his brain long enough to render him unconscious.

A security camera records as I sling him over my shoulder. Truly, I can never come back here.

I take him to the abandoned parking garage and carry him down the sinkhole.

In my workshop, I extract the answers I need.

FOUR

ONCE AGAIN I SPREAD THE CREATION ACROSS the examination table and still myself as my supervisor inspects its newest features. One of her eyes pivots toward me while the others scour the contours of this gift I have made in her image, the resemblance more evident now than it has ever been.

One might argue that a thing cannot be a gift when presented in response to demands that cannot be refused, but my gratitude that she permits me to live and considers me useful, that is genuine. Mentally I repeat assertions of gratitude, a mantra of submission and genuflection, as she straightens the double-dozen joints of a limb, lowers a flower-like hand to my side of the table.

She draws my attention to a juncture where a round metal clamp joins a graphite-gray cylinder to the hairy, muscular flesh of a human thigh.

"The edge here is not smooth," she says from multiple mouths. "The tools I provide operate with perfect precision. An incision this uneven can only come about from deliberate choice."

I cannot suppress a nervous swallow, even though I expected this question. "This element was still mobile when I made the separation."

That flowery hand floats toward my face, hesitates mere inches away. I successfully stave off the urge to flinch. Her chorus speaks a conclusion: "It wasn't dead."

I inhale slowly, deeply. "I didn't kill it first. I was angry at an insult. I caused suffering."

The deceptive softness of her hand alights on my forehead. From the center of her palm comes a sensation like the swift peck of a kiss. I recall a flurry of similar kisses before she burned the scars into the flesh under my arm.

"Your indulgence is permissible, unless this creation fails to function as it should." She extends more tendrils and pedipalps, exploring every surface.

I mentally track the time. At twenty-seven minutes and fifty-four seconds, she withdraws her limbs. "Activate it."

Never before has she given that order. I'm caught between a gasp of relief and a spurt of panic.

I remind myself that I've long since accepted the consequences of failure.

I engineered the creation to activate with a recitation of certain words of my choosing. I move to a corner of the table, near which lies a nodule of the creature arrayed with human, canine and rodent ears. "All the eyes that ever closed," I whisper, "peel their papery lids apart."

Nothing on the table stirs. I should not be surprised. Still, my terror that the creation will stay inert floods every nook of my physical and mental self. I scan the mounds of the creation's assemblages and grafts, hunting amid the blood-caked circuit boards, the strips of hairy skin stretched to maximum tension, the polygonal cuts of meat wedged into plastic vessels, the bones fused to gears and crankshafts, vainly seeking the flaw that blocks activation.

Atop the creation's central conglomeration, a flat black monitor lights up, its pixels shaping an impressionistic sketch of an eye. At the crest of the monitor, a smaller blue light switches on, indicating the built-in camera has also done so.

I recover enough to speak the next words in the sequence. "You the dead who have returned, sing the pain that maims your heart."

Like my supervisor, my creation has many other makeshift eyes, some machine, some fleshy, and also in tribute to my supervisor, the creation has multiple mouths, which all babble at once. I recognize no words among the layering of vowels, consonants, screeches and brays.

I shout over the commotion. "Give your flesh to fill the Mother! Rend your souls to shape her art!"

The entire mass of the creation shudders. Its many eyes swivel their gazes in a single direction, first observing me as I back away, then bending, sweeping, twisting, hinging to take in my supervisor's teeming expanse.

The creation speaks again, choosing only one mouth, the fanged muzzle of a raccoon, its childlike voice devoid of guile. "What do you require of us?" it says.

The many bands of my supervisor's voice soften to something like warmth, a tone I've never before heard from her throats. "Nothing, for the moment, my child, other than the pleasure of your existence."

"We hurt," the creation bleats.

"Yes. The imperfection of your origin makes this inevitable."

FIVE

ASKING MY SUPERVISOR IF SHE IS PLEASED with my labor seems unwise, though some pathetic piece of me yearns for words of praise. I enforce stillness and silence within and project the same without. At this novel stage, I cannot guess what my supervisor will require of me next.

The creation's body erupts with rustlings and tremors as my supervisor commands, "Rise."

My anxiety spikes sharp as I picture this mass of machinery and mutilations ripping itself to pieces. Yet as the configuration of parts lifts, unfolds, expands, its topmost antennae brushing the high metal ceiling, the creation blooms into architecture that I had not consciously planned as I went about the work of assembly.

Evidence of my supervisor's subconscious guidance dazzles me, as mechanical, animal and human parts hinge into place with the mathematically engineered precision of a complex pop-up book. The creation's multiple crowns possess the contours of an arresting metropolitan skyline. The placement of eyes and mouths throughout its body mirror my supervisor's physiognomy. Gristle and rust transmute to glory, the stench of copper and oil ascending into otherworldly musk.

"You have absorbed your instructions well," my supervisor purrs. Several of her eyes regard me, the rest focus on the gift. "I sense potential for great purpose."

Though made of terrestrial garbage rather than extradimensional protoplasm, the creation truly reflects the Mother's image. More and more of my supervisor's eyes meet those of her inferior double. The eyes of a Mother cannot be read for emotion the way a human's can, but even so trickster neurons in my brain read longing, hope, and eagerness in the tensions evident in my supervisor's demeanor.

A large amplifier embedded in the guts of the creation squawks with a tiny voice. "We wish an end to pain." Right after, the voice box of a dog stretches and thrums, raspy and basso. "What do *you* wish of us?" Several more mouths and vocal instruments join in to emphasize the "you."

My own voice croaks. "Do not question the Mother unless she allows it!"

Oh, my unwise tongue. Instantly I regret this impulse. If the creation speaks so rashly, surely the Mother willed it so. Fright grinds between my shoulder blades.

My creation's monitor eye finds me. "You smell like garbage," it hisses from many mouths. Its racoon muzzle bears fangs. "Get out of here or I'll gut you."

I suck in a breath, recognizing the threats of the man who attacked me in the nightclub. A notion washes through me that I wish I could wave away, that the creation *remembers*, that the aggression of my assailant has transferred to this new being.

This cannot be so. I used no part of his brain in its building.

The creation tests its legs of metal and weeping flesh, more mirroring of my supervisor's forest of knobby joints and goat hooves. The creation's equivalent of hooves clank, ping and thump on the surface of the table. The nearest dangle off the edge, bobbing as if seeking further footholds.

Even more of my supervisor's eyestalks bend, aiming their attention on me, monitoring how I will respond to the creation's aggression.

"You may be too fragile to lower yourself without assistance," I tell the creation. "If the Mother permits, I will help you."

The creation shifted gazes toward my supervisor, who says, "I wish to see how far it will walk on its own."

I crouch on all fours at the foot of the table, so my broad back will serve the creation as a step from tabletop to floor. Its feet tear my already ragged coat and jab the meat beneath. My body does not break under its weight; after all, I was strong enough to drag it here repeatedly.

A nagging doubt will not be squelched, its mutters punctuated with the bruises from the creation's makeshift hooves. What will I do if my supervisor allows the creation to carry out its threat?

I wonder if my supervisor can see into the pulsing monstrosity that serves as my heart, sense the heresy brewing there. She is perhaps too preoccupied by her offspring to sense how my answer buds, my anger flowers.

I will do everything within the limits of my strength to take the creation with me into oblivion.

SIX

THE CREATION FILLS THE SIDE OF THE ROOM that my supervisor does not occupy. Its wet machinery surrounds me, prods me. I barely have room to straighten and stand, the edge of the table pressed into my belly.

The eyes that swarm to either side of me seek to lock gazes with mine the way a dog gives challenge before a fight. To avoid engaging, I regard my supervisor's enigmatic forest of limbs and tendrils. The creation applies bristly pressure to my legs and back, contacts that cannot be accidental, that display all the overbearing brashness of its final human component.

The creation speaks from a single mouth that hovers beside my right ear, syllables stretched with accusation. "I hurt. My existence hurts. Why do I exist?"

"You will understand when you are elevated," my supervisor hums.

In my former life I had heard many rumors about the ways one Mother begets another, all unprovable and most lost in the haze of my remaking. But that word, *elevate*, drags a bow across a nerve. Whispers that when proto-Mothers first bud from the multi-limbed masses of their extradimensional parents, they are mindless, all blind appetite. They require *elevation*. The devouring of another intelligence, to develop their own.

"The next stage," my supervisor says, "requires consumption and absorption of your creator."

What can I lose now if I let my treacherous rage spill forth? That half-buried part of me must have anticipated my supervisor's intentions, for the words come easy. "*She* is your creator. You exist because *she* commanded it."

Humans have never understood the Mothers in any fashion but the most rudimentary, one of the reasons they beguiled and conquered us with such ease, and why one foolish coup attempt after another has ended with geysers of blood, the rebels pulled inside out or preserved in the higher-dimensional equivalent of amber to endure even worse suffering.

Yet the Mothers are one and many, this I know, and no Mother that is one with the whole would have need of slaves shaped from an inferior species to produce an offspring. I made her a child, a ramshackle mockery of a disciple, because she cannot produce one herself.

She seizes me with twenty limbs. More long-submerged thoughts escape as I scream, "You live in blasphemy!"

The creation, too, assaults me, stabbing into my flesh from all sides.

My warring heart brightens into ecstasy in anticipation of death's release and shrieks in terror that my existence will continue in some new and even more degraded form.

I tumble to the floor, the impact disproportionate to the distance, my breath whooshing out in a gasp of bruising pain and startled confusion.

Enough sheer survival instinct remains in me that I manage a crawl, flop under the table, a temporary shelter from the creation's flailing legs. My supervisor's howl of rage sounds like the roof of

Hell torn away, drowning out the many squeals and shrieks and roars of her betrayed, turncoat child.

A marvel. My supervisor lost her grip on me because the creation has attacked her.

Its half-mechanical limbs tangle in her alien ones, the many varieties of claws and blades I incorporated into its design severing an astonishing number of my supervisor's tendrils, leg segments and eyestalks. They flop and thrash where they land.

But my supervisor has many more where those grew from. Whatever scant safety I've gained from cowering under the examination table evaporates as the jointed stems of my supervisor's arms and the grasping flowers of her hands surge toward me.

I upend the table and shove it at my supervisor and her rebellious child, who have melded in a single seething tangle. She made me strong, and I use that strength. The table is almost as wide as the room is tall, and I savor the sensation of both monsters squashed behind it. My supervisor shrieks at eardrum-shredding pitch from all her mouths, the noise unbearable in this sealed room.

One or both of the creatures on the other side push back with the force of a locomotive. Only chance spares me, that the angle of force hurls the table toward a front corner of the lab rather than straight into the wall behind me. The table legs crumple with the force of the impact but the table wedges in place and spares me a crushing.

I cannot be certain my death in this room would bring relief. There are stories, perhaps spread by the Mothers themselves, of trapped consciousnesses preserved past the most violent of drawn-out deaths, playthings tortured for unending sport.

My creation's monitor eye smashes beside my head, against the edge of the door. Yet the creation remains intact enough that the fight continues, the din thick as a mudslide.

A further stroke of luck, that my supervisor and her child aren't between me and the exit, incontrovertible evidence that her will has limits.

I seize the valve that seals the lab. As the wheel creaks and the vault door hisses open, the darkness beyond holds deeper shadows, hunched low to the ground.

Enhanced by the designs of my supervisor, my eyes adjust.

The passageway is filled with other former humans like myself, those that this exiled Mother conscripted into her delusional quest to restore her status.

Unlike me, their bodies are modeled after crustaceans and arthropods, squat and many-limbed. They could never climb to the city streets and pass among their former kin unnoticed. Nor, even had my supervisor wished it—and I believe she did—could they serve as an effective army of rebels against her sistren. Their numbers are far too few. She has not yet made enough.

Nonetheless, they can grip weapons in their pincers and claws: long metal pipes, tools mounted with blades. Their faces, or the equivalents that remain to them, expose a condition that I know well—uncertainty about what our supervisor might want for them and dread of what the cost will be.

Her embattled state disorients them. Her instructions channeled through me must have had more success in duplicating a creation with a Mother's characteristics than was evident during my labors. Her sorcery backfires. My supervisor still shrieks, the creation still fights, long past when it should have been ripped into a thousand pieces.

And yet it is not indestructible. A piece of my creation, torn free in the melee, lands between my feet. A heavy axle, massive gears like barbels welded to either end.

I pick it up. None of my associates try to stop me.

The being in the forefront, long and flat like a silverfish, flinches as I brandish my potential weapon, their own grips on a pair of wrist-thick drill bits tremulous.

The screams of our supervisor, the torment of multitudes, incinerate the air behind me. Her screams called them to her, surely, but the ongoing distraction prevents her from exerting her will, from providing direction.

If I attack, they might on their own find the will to defend. If I simply stride into them, they might not let me pass. Strong as they may be, I am practiced, they are not. Considering the death I could bring them, they might find relief, or cause for even greater fear. If so, I sympathize.

I can no longer afford to wait for hints as to what any of them will do. I advance, club at the ready. They will have to make their own choices, as I have at last made mine.

The ability to end my life, on my own terms: I will lay waste to salvage this right.

SUPERNUMERARY

with S. Brackett Robertson

You're forty when your new teeth grow in.
They halt your speech,
English and Spanish both turn strange on your tongue,
tripping against the new walls.

But now, it seems, you can hear the stars.

You try to tune them out sometimes,
when sounds spin asymmetrical,
rattle discordant in your throat.

And yet you have the urge to join their song,
croon with the sky, attempt mimicry,
though your vocal cords and tongue
can't quite accommodate
the requisite multi-track glossolalia.

These new teeth are at least attuned
if not in tune, needles pressing on
metaphysical vinyl the way fangs scrape bone,
the vocabulary dictated by the dim blackboards
of your palm-tree, spider-web childhood
scraped and scrambled on the turntable.

(You've mostly forgotten the other children's voices,
raised in mocking cacophony.
You had no extra teeth then,
and still they thought you strange.)

The mirror shows you blunted incisors
and molars in a single simple row, but your finger
traces more, three rows, four, a spiral draining
toward your throat. You must conclude
they grew from somewhere beyond
space and time and your X-ray defined jaw.

Soon you find the teeth elsewhere,
outside your body altogether, yet a part,
growing at the bottom of your coffee mug,
nestled among the roots of your begonias.

You'd think they bespeak a hunger
that extends to your environment, and for sure
there's a lot of chewing going on
behind your back, given the discarded shells
and skins of untraceable origin you find
lying about your house, the bite marks fresh.

Pieces perhaps picked from the pockets
of other universes, maybe a world
you really come from, where you're not a monster.

THE COMFORTER

1

"**D**O YOU BELIEVE IN JESUS?"

The rhythm of high-heeled shoes striking pavement comes to a stop.

The morning sun peers down the length of the street from its eastern end, dressing city blocks in long shadows, painting an optimistic glow across the plate glass of first floor windows. A crisp spring morning, the first without rain since the turn of the season, catches restaurants and shops still asleep, the staff that inhabits them either not yet arrived or milling about inside, OPEN signs unlit.

In this block, a bus depot dominates one side of the street. The other side is dominated by a not-quite mirror image, a three-story building with mock Doric columns on its facade and gargoyles along its roof that takes up far more space than the boutiques at its base seem to warrant. A man sits on the sidewalk with his back against the outer wall of the bus depot, one leg stretched out to block the progress of a slender, dark-haired woman in skinny jeans and a halter top.

"You do, doncha, baby? You believe in Him," the man says. "Can I ask you another question?" The man springs to his feet. "You got change? I'm so hungry. Help me out, baby."

The woman steps to the side. The man sidesteps too, stays in her way. He's just a little taller, much wider through the shoulders and belly, his bare arms wiry, furred with gray hair. He stretches those arms out to either side like he'll grab her up tight if she doesn't pay.

"Where you think you're going? I said I'm hungry . . . Yeah, that's right. I knew you'd do the right thing."

Tapering, graceful fingers tipped with perfectly manicured nails dig inside a tiny pouch. It doesn't have a clasp like a typical change purse. It's handmade, sealed with string threaded through cloth.

Fingers pinch tiny objects from the small pouch, which disappears. She drops what she's clutching into the cupped palm of her other hand. Colorful and reflective, they're the wrong size for coins, though they glint in the sunlight.

The woman's face twitches, her temple bulging, stretched by something underneath the skin. Leaning in close to eye her every move, the man flinches. "What was that?"

She doesn't acknowledge his question. His stare ends with a shake of the head, like he's snapping out of a daydream. She holds out her cupped hand, full of glittering trinkets that could be beads or buttons.

"What in hell is this?" He grabs her hand with both of his, peeling her fingers open. Nothing spills to the ground.

He opens his mouth. The sound he makes is not a word. A manicured hand lifts to his face. His eyes bulge. His mouth opens wider. Her fingers slide in, then her whole hand, up to the delicate wrist. Her wrist bends. Her arm continues to push down his throat, his jaw bending and folding inward as if molded from rubber.

A minute later, the man lowers to the sidewalk, places his back against the wall. The woman he waylaid has vanished.

He speaks to no one else for the rest of the day. Convoys of buses roll in and roll out of the depot bay, the advertisements that gird their flanks blocking his view every half an hour as he studies the customers who visit the shops across the street. The businesses burrowed into that neoclassical behemoth have names that ring a little too clever by half: Downhome Rave. A Whiff of Elegance. Gypsy Flair. Lights come on inside each boutique as the sun squints from the street's western end.

After the sun has set and the store lights have dimmed, a woman stands up from the place where she's been sitting on the sidewalk, brushes off a halter top and skinny jeans with perfectly manicured hands. She crosses the street to peer in through the front window of Gypsy Flair, a boutique selling the kind of clothes a woman with bohemian tastes and a wealthy husband might buy.

She is outside looking in, and then she is inside, exploring in the dark, and a few minutes later she is outside again, heels clicking as she walks away. At no point did she open a door, jimmy a lock, or break a pane of glass.

2

MADDY UNFOLDS THE NOTE.
    She usually finds them stuck to the underside of her desk. She hasn't given much thought to how they adhere there, though when they come free she's never noticed glue or anything else that would make the odd-textured paper sticky. The precise little squares feel like suede, and the words at first glance look like they're stitched on in black thread, though on closer inspection the effect is more that of a tattoo. Maddy hasn't figured out how the optical illusion works.

This new one reads, in crude block letters:
how you and me are kin
my mom stole your mom's skin

She glances at the teacher, whose eyes are locked on his laptop screen. He is scowling, his goatee and shaggy dark hair giving him the look of a deeply offended beatnik, but that's just Mr. Newman's normal expression. He's a man with resting bitch face.

Her desk is strategically positioned, back corner nearest to the door. She quick-scans the rest of the class. Most are pondering the algebra questions displayed on their tablets with varying degrees of absorption or frustration. None are focused on her. She quick-grabs her bright pink backpack, stuffs this newest note into the outer pouch where she's stowed all the others.

She started getting them the day they came back from Christmas break. One came loose from the underside of the desk as she doodled in her algebra textbook, fluttered down to alight like a leaf on her bare leg. It read
found you
on one side and

i know where your parents are
on the other.

Others followed, not every day but sometimes several days in a row, always and only in this classroom, under this desk.

you should be me and i should be you
my mother will stitch us together
i like how you draw skulls draw one on the desk

With a fingertip Maddy traces the still-smudged outlines of the skull she sketched in pencil, someone else's attempt to erase it not quite finishing the job.

She hasn't figured out who is leaving the notes. Her class with Mr. Newman is second period, a group of supposedly-smart eighth graders. First period is Mr. Newman's free period. The third period class is a smaller group of advanced-placement seventh graders. She's tried hanging out late to spy, but so far as she can tell, no one sits in her desk. The little teacher's pets all cluster in the front. Later periods, she can't make it across the building in time to have a peek without being late for classes.

Whoever is making these, they know she shouldn't exist. She wants to meet them, and ask why she's alive.

3

YOUR MOTHER TESTED YOU, and you failed. You push with all your might in all directions. The box your mother has sealed you inside is the size of a large suitcase. You cannot force it open, though you are stronger than a platoon of Marines. You howl and howl with as many mouths. Like your many arms, your howls stay inside the box.

It's not your first time trapped in the box. Its walls are transparent. Your many eyes take in all the familiar sights. Above you loom the struts that support the box spring of your mother's king size bed. Below you is a carpet splotched with dark brown stains. Beside you a centipede crawls, the vibrations of your struggles causing its undulating legs to quicken their pace.

You were thinking about something else when she came into your room. It's not the first time she's caught you off guard. She demands you remain alert in all directions, outward and inward, as she has learned to be. But the last time she punished you this harshly was many months ago.

You have to understand that our kind can be hurt, she has said. *You have to understand we have weaknesses. Remember what your father used to say to you? Stay alert, stay alive.*

Your father suffered a fate worse than death at the hands of your mother. She laughs when she talks about it. She loves to talk about it. You learned to laugh with her. Any other reaction, she might coil around you like a snake made of sheets and stuff you in the box. But she hasn't talked about your father in months.

You did notice something new, though, a glitch in the lovely mask she puts so much effort into maintaining. She and you were playacting yet another family dinner, when you noticed how her face, her neck, the tawny skin across her collarbones sagged loose like wet paper. *What's wrong, mom?*

Nothing! she snapped as her skin contracted to its proper texture.

Your mother did something to fortify the box, to enchant it. There are symbols scratched into the transparent surface, you are seeing them up close and in reverse. You have no idea what they mean or how she learned them.

There is something else you have done, something that might have sparked her fury, but she doesn't know about it. She can't.

You don't know how many hours have passed. You are no longer focused on these what-ifs in any rational way. They loop through your mind as you howl.

You should not have panicked. The little bit of air sealed in with you has escaped into the beneath. The mouths you summon gasp, the lungs bound to them burn with ever sharper starbursts of suffocation. Every second is a new death, your existence relentless agony.

You steal as much strength from those beneath as your agony-addled will allows. You howl and howl.

Whatever your mother's ulterior motives might have been, this much you know is true: you were thinking about something other than your surroundings when she came into your room.

* * *

4

"I T'LL MAKE YOU A BELIEVER AGAIN, SON," Hairston says. "But it won't give you nothin' to write about."

"Given all the hints you're dropping, I don't see how that could be true." When Hairston called yesterday, Aaron had suggested they meet at a coffee shop in downtown Grandy Springs, but Hairston insisted on a Shoney's at the outskirts of the town. Refused the buffet.

In front of Hairston, a black coffee steams. When it arrived, he inhaled deep. "Reminds me of the quiet mornings in the field." He still hasn't sipped from it. "Wasn't too many of those."

Hairston fought in the Korean War. The man's in his eighties, but he looks even older, the creases on his dark-skinned face quick to crumple into a mask of rage at the slightest flash of irritation, framed by his lion's mane of curly white hair. And yet his body hasn't withered. His wide shoulders and thick forearms suggest impressive muscle mass.

Aaron has delved deeper and deeper into Hairston's story in the downtime between stories for his own website and freelance assignments for the remaining weekly papers. Those cowards wouldn't touch the kind of profile Aaron wants to write, but maybe he can sell it somewhere bigger. Aaron's not sure he has a book in him, but he is certain there *is* potential for a book here, an amazing one.

As far as Aaron can determine, Hairston has no fixed address, but these days he at least has a phone number that works, though its prefix matches none of those used by local carriers.

Everything about Hairston comes across as preternatural. The first time Aaron met him, sat down beside him on the bench in Spring Park, Hairston spoke before he had a chance to introduce himself. "You wanna know happened to your father? The Boneyard took him."

Aaron had heard that kind of claptrap before, crazy stories about the supposedly haunted courtyard in downtown Grandy Springs and his father's rumored obsession with it. Quick on his feet, he had decided the best way to keep Hairston talking was to play along. "What can you tell me about the Boneyard?" More claptrap had followed, a tall tale about abandoned tunnels and faceless monsters like living shadows, but Aaron got his foot in the door, and Hairston had later let him conduct multiple interviews, even write a feature for the late lamented-by-some *Owlswick Messenger*.

Aaron would never have been worth a damn as a reporter if he couldn't sweet-talk the most reluctant of sources into opening up to him. But Hairston could still, at times, be difficult. Like right now. Pondering his next verbal move, Aaron scratches at one of the scars on his cheeks. They itch at the most inopportune moments.

Unprompted, Hairston starts. "Maybe it's better that you don't remember how you got those scars."

"I *do*," Aaron protests. "We've talked about this. You told me yourself, for god's sake. I went caving and had a bad fall. I'm glad you knew where I was."

Hairston slaps the table. "Ha!" Others in the restaurant wing turn toward the noise, immediately look away.

"This isn't what you wanted to talk about, is it?" Aaron hopes he can defuse the old man. A loudly, forcefully enunciated rant about faceless shadow monsters and occult murders might well get the police called on them, and the Owlswick County Sheriff's Office isn't fond of Aaron or his subject. Hairston doesn't have an arrest record, though, astonishing given how corrupt this town consistently proves to be.

Hairston's stare drives a spike between Aaron's eyes. He fights to stay placid, and tries changing the subject. "This trip you told me about, to Hillcrest. When do you want to go?"

"Not yet," Hairston says, and at least he's quieter. "When the right time comes to me you're not going to get much warning. You sure you're okay with taking me there?"

"Absolutely, but I'd love to know when—"

"When I call you is when."

"It's just, I may need to give some sort of notice to—"

"Your kind's expert at making excuses. Don't you'll have any-thing to worry about there." A ferocious scowl twists Hairston's mouth, crumples his brow. "There'll be things to worry about where we're going. What's coming to Hillcrest, it's dangerous. Not for me, for *you*. Be sure to mind me while we're there. Don't need a second Boneyard." His scowl deepens.

Not for the first time, Aaron wonders why he seeks out Hairston's company so often. Though he owes the man his life.

He remembers nothing about the fall that scarred his face, but Hairston missed him enough to alert rescuers.

These off-the-chain rants, too, they're just as import to this profile as the details of Hairston's military service and the relatives he left behind, the matter he discusses least of all. Aaron's grateful he has his recorder on. "I can tell this is important," he says. "I'll get you there, whatever it takes, I promise."

Hairston shocks him by putting a feverishly-warm hand over his. "You're a good man, like your father was," Hairston says. "It wasn't right, what happened to him."

Aaron's heart rate spikes hearing Hairston describe Kyle Friedrich as a good man. Throughout his childhood and adolescence, the adults he interacted with in Grandy Springs said otherwise, his mother most of all. He needs to change the subject before he reacts in a way that messes up the interview.

He jumps, despite himself, to the story Hairston keeps telling about what happened to his father. "You think there are . . . shadows there? In Hillcrest? Like the things people used to claim they saw here, in the Boneyard?"

"I don't know its full nature. Just that there's a disease and it's gonna spread," Hairston says, and finally brings his coffee to his lips, swallows. "Unless I practice a little field surgery. The world don't need another Grandy Springs."

"Field surgery? You were a medic in the war?" Aaron asks.

Hairston grins big. "I surgically inserted a few bullets."

5

A SQUAT WOMAN WITH A WIDE, bulging forehead sits on a folding chair in a cavernous room otherwise empty of furniture. Bare wires hang through holes in the ceiling. Crumbling drywall reveals cinderblock. Light leaks through and around the dry-rotted boards that block the high windows. Dust and mildew bathe the air.

Three people stand before her. Two are terrified. The third holds an AB-10 with its barrel aimed toward the concrete floor.

An oblong wooden box lies between the woman and her audience. It's smaller than a coffin, narrower than a steamer trunk. Carvings on its lid and sides depict densely overlapping human figures moving among formations akin to palm trees. Round objects hang in the trees and cluster under the arms of the figures. Some of those round objects have crude faces.

Behind the seated woman, a doorway with the door removed stands open in a corner, the space beyond absolute black.

The seated woman's voice is low and whisper-soft, with a pronounced Old South twang. "Y'all don't look like you're starving. Dress nice too. Why would you want to break into a dump like this? Plenty of high-class shops to plunder on the first floor if you got a hankering to steal."

The girl tries to talk first. She's tall and pretty with her straight blonde hair. "We didn't know—"

"Josey be quiet," the boy hisses. He's much older than she is, likely the mastermind of the caper.

"My lord, you college boys are the worst," the seated woman says. "Young lady, pray continue."

"We heard there was an old theater up here," Josey blurts. "We thought it was abandoned."

"It is," the woman says.

"This was all my idea," the boy says, inching forward. He's as tall as Josey and broader at the shoulders, his hair close-cropped with a fashionable curl above his brow, dressed in jeans and a black windbreaker. "I'm into urban exploring. I heard about—"

"I did not say I wanted to hear from you." The seated woman nods at her enforcer. "Here's what talking out of turn gets you."

Short, wiry, square face hard as cement, the man with the AB-10 punches Josey in the small of the back with all his might. She shrieks and crumples.

"Hey," the boy says, real soft.

The enforcer kicks the wailing girl in the ribs.

"Look what you did to her," the woman says. "Will you wait your turn now?"

The boy stares at the floor and says nothing.

The big chamber echoes with Josey's sobs. "I go by Maude," the woman says. "I have some knowledge of the history of this lost theater, which is where we are, if you haven't deduced that already. There used to be a stage, right where I'm sitting. To my left"—she points—"a piano in the wings." She points up.

"They took the curtain and backdrops out long ago, but back then there was the fly tower up yonder. They had opera singers come here to sing and even some big band players. Showed moving pictures, too. At first they didn't let any coloreds in. But they needed that extra money before long, so they let 'em onto the balcony." She points to the opposite end of the chamber, where no balcony hangs, though sloppily plastered holes in the walls and ceiling hint at what might have been. "The place still went broke. Shut down fifty years ago, and many owners since, none of 'em worth a damn, passed this building one to the other. They gutted everything in here for its wood but never fixed it up. They even pried up the fancy old floorboards. It's a joke that the landlord got this building on the historical lists, bless his heart. The shops downstairs leave these floors alone because right now the building's grandfathered and they don't want the building inspector nosing around. Lord knows what they might have to spend to bring the building up to code if that happens. You ready to tell me more, Josey?"

During Maude's lecture, Josey gradually grows quiet. She cringes at the sound of her name.

"Urban explorers." Maude laughs and leans forward. "Why are you really up here? What brought you through that fire escape door?"

Josey looks at the boy, who keeps staring at the floor.

"He wanted to get you alone up here, away from prying eyes, no chance of getting caught, am I right? That's what boys always want, isn't it?"

The boy swallows.

"How old are you, Josey?"

She sniffs. "Fifteen." The boy clenches his jaw.

"Now how old is he?"

"Don't tell—" the boy starts. The enforcer takes a step, his boot landing a hair from Josey's outstretched fingers. She shrieks and folds her hands to her chest, curls up fetal. He rears back for another kick.

"It's okay, Bruno, I think he gets it." Maude speaks quietly, but somehow her man hears over Josey's panicked gasps of *no no no no*.

The boy, having made no move to intervene, keeps staring at the floor.

Maude speaks louder. "How old his he?"

"Tw-tw-twenty"

Maude's eyes narrow. "Only twenty? Is that the truth? Looks old enough to buy liquor, to me."

"Yes. No. Yes. His birthday is next week."

"Lordy, always the same in this sad little town. Grown man can't impress a lady his own age. What's his name, child?"

Josey's eyes squeeze shut. "Andrew."

"How long have you two been going steady?"

"Tw-two years."

"How long have you been lovers?"

A sharp intake of breath from Andrew. Bruno the enforcer raises a boot, and the boy clams up, staring a hole in that floor.

Josey never opens her eyes. "Two years." She sobs as she speaks.

"What school do you attend, Josey?"

"Willow Spring." Josey's sniffles punctuate the silence that ensues.

Maude asks, "Is that the one?"

Bruno nods. "The scent is there."

"You're certain."

Bruno nods again, with vigor.

"Well, ain't that something. Andrew, you can go." Maude's smile could be that of a grandmother favoring a beloved grandchild.

The boy turns without another word and crosses to the exit at the further end of the derelict theater, the one Bruno marched them through after he surprised them in the hall beyond the fire escape. Necking against the wall, they never saw him coming.

"Andrew don't leave me here." Josey's wail is no louder than a whisper.

"Don't worry, Andrew, she'll be fine," Maude calls. "Just wait outside, she'll be out soon." As the boy disappears she adds, "I don't think he's even gonna wait for you, darling."

"Yes he will. He'll call the police." A little louder: "You have to let me go."

"Bless your heart, no he won't. He doesn't want anybody to know what you two were doing here. He doesn't want to get caught."

Josey starts to cry. Maude ignores her. "Lordy, I miss the days when I didn't have to talk. All this yapping, it's exhausting. I'm a faithful servant, though. I always do what needs to be done and that's why I've been granted this gift."

Josey says nothing, but when she looks up, Maude reads the question in her eyes. "You, honey. You're the gift."

A sniffle. "Wh-what?"

"The fates favor my kind, when we're careful. They brought me here, where I could hide my treasures in the middle of a mother lode of human misery, and if I hadn't been right here in this place, they could never have delivered you. Your boyfriend doesn't know it, but he's already fulfilled his life's sole purpose." Maude stands. She's not much taller than when she was sitting. Her thick ankles overflow her shoes. "Come on now, Josey. Get up."

Bruno keeps the AB-10 trained on Josey's spine. Tears have smeared mascara down her cheeks.

Josey's future drops away before her mind's eye, a yawning abyss. She thinks of the ocean cruises her parents have taken her on during the summers, the night views from the promenade deck into dark waters that fuse with clouded skies. Standing at the rail, she's wondered more than once what it would be like to jump, whether she would simply fly forever, no boundary to stop her, a thought that both scared and thrilled her.

Now there's only fear.

"Lift the lid, please, Josey. It's not heavy."

Anticipating that it *will* be heavy, Josey lifts too hard and the lid flips away from her fingers, clatters loud on the plywood flooring. A substance glitters multi-hued in the very bottom of the box.

"Step inside," Maude says.

"I don't want to."

"It won't hurt you. Get in."

A noise from Bruno makes Josey edge closer.

"See the pretty buttons?" Maude says. "I'll let you keep a few. Just get this over with."

The objects do look like buttons, cast in many colors and shapes. Gingerly, Josey steps into the box. The buttons rustle around her ankles, though none crunch beneath her shoes. Once she's planted both feet, she shrieks. She sinks as if mired in quicksand.

Bruno set his gun down gently and steps in the box with her. He too, sinks into the bottom. He grabs Josey by the shoulders and shoves her down. She scrabbles at his arms, ripping his skin loose with her nails. No blood wells from the scrapes.

Silent, Bruno forces her all the way to the bottom of the bin. Her head disappears. Her scream fades as if falling into void. Her arms slide from his.

He lifts up something about the size and shape of a jacket and starts to unbutton it. Its blonde hood and pale sleeves flop. Once the gap spreads wide enough, Bruno brings it to his face, vanishes inside head-first.

6

"HEY, MADDY, WANNA PLAY?"
That's how Lakesha greets Maddy as she shuts Mama Rochelle's front door and wipes her shoes on the mat before popping them off. No muddy shoes in the house, that's one of Rochelle's many rules, and Maddy's shoes aren't muddy but Rochelle would still tell her to leave them at the door.

Maddy had hoped she could sneak down to her room un-noticed—at least for now it's her room alone. No such luck. She knows better than to betray any disappointment, if she upsets any of the younger girls Mama Rochelle will hear about it and come knocking. She calls, "Whatcha playin' squirt?"

"Don't call me squirt," Lakesha says.

"Okay, squirrel, whatcha playin'?"

Lakesha is a foster kid like Maddy, but six years younger. Mama Rochelle's house is a split level where the front door opens onto the landing of the central staircase, and Lakesha hovers at the top of the stairs, her tiny silhouette framed by the light coming out the kitchen door. She's holding an electronic game player that's bright yellow with purple handles. "Mindeecraft," she says.

"Not sure you're saying that right," Maddy mutters with a smile.

"In the princess castle. You can play the good princess again." Lakesha loves to play the wicked witch, and Maddy's happy to let her. Maddy has a device just like Lakesha's in her room downstairs. Rochelle gives them to all her kids. They can play each other in multiplayer games without having to hook up with cords. There's something about that concept, an invisible connection binding her to others, that makes Maddy's heart pound and shudder when she lets herself dwell on it too long. She's good at not dwelling on it. It's stupid that it scares her.

"I can't, little squirrel, I got too much homework." This is a lie, which makes Lakesha's moan of disappointment like the achy wiggle of a loose tooth, but she sticks to her guns, because right now her need to be alone outweighs Lakesha's need for a big sister.

Not alone as in by herself. Alone with the notes from her desk. She got a new one today, after a whole week of silence.

"Where's everybody else, can you get some of them to play you?"

"Ashley's in her room. Prixie says she doesn't want to, she told me to leave her alone." That last bit delivered matter-of-factly.

Prixie's a year older than Lakesha, and Maddy doesn't blame her a bit, Lakesha can be pretty relentless. Ashley is eleven, just two years younger than Maddy, in her final year of elementary. She, like Maddy, has a room downstairs, and she stays in it. Rochelle always has to argue her out for meals, and at the table she keeps her eyes downcast, sullen beneath long brown bangs. Maddy's not sure how long Ashley will last, though Rochelle is working on her, like she worked on Maddy.

"Sorry, squirrel, I really can't." She hops downstairs before Lakesha can keep arguing, so she can get to her room at the end of the hall and lock it. She's really lucky she doesn't have to share it with Ashley. Rochelle has two more kids that Maddy likes to call "the twins," even though they aren't, because they have funny, rhyming names, Georgia and Porsche, a state and a car—but they're in daycare right now, too young to fend for themselves while Rochelle finishes her early morning to late afternoon shift at Peachtree Assisted Living. (Rochelle gets mad if Maddy slips and calls it a nursing home.)

She really should wait to get the notes out. She ought to wait until everyone is asleep. If Rochelle gets back from work and finds Maddy's door locked she might get worried and unlock it to see what Maddy is doing. She doesn't do that as often as she used to, thank God, but Maddy can't be too careful. Rochelle gets especially

worried about Maddy, even more than Ashley, not because Maddy
acts out, but because Maddy was found in a place where something
terrible happened that no one understands and that she can't remember, the abandoned suburban cul-de-sac that the folks in Hillcrest call the Vanished Neighborhood.

She tried to have a heart-to-heart with Maddy about it only
once, about three months after social services placed her in the
house. They were sitting in plastic-webbed lawn chairs on the back
deck, the sun breathing warmth against them, Maddy fighting
not to squirm as the walls she maintained against the memories
thinned. In the days after the police found her, even sunlight triggered alien sensations, like the heat was something solid, encasing
her in a trap.

A crease had furrowed the middle of Rochelle's broad brown
forehead. She'd noticed Maddy's fidgets. Her voice invited relax-
ation like a cozy, cool pillow. "I know you're sick of people asking
you about this, so I'm not going to ask you anything. But if you
ever want to talk about what happened, you can talk to me, any-
time. That's all I want to make sure you know."

Maddy had already started to shake her head. "I can't. I don't
remember anything."

"I know, honey," Rochelle said, but Maddy had shook her
head harder.

"Honey, honey, it's okay. I didn't mean to upset you. I just
wanted you to know."

Maddy holds nothing against Rochelle. Her foster mother is
homemade rhubarb pie with too much sugar, which is just the
right amount. She's fried chicken and microwaved pizza and
quiche with spinach and bacon, a thing Maddy would never have
believed she would love to eat. She's books full of amazing stories, tales of kids learning magic and having adventures that made
them into heroes.

Maddy's truth about the Vanished Neighborhood skews sideways. She does remember things but she doesn't know how to put
them into words. They don't make sense in any of the ways she
learned to make sense of things in school.

The scene of her abduction, chatting with her mom in the
front seat of the car, disrupted in a blur that whirls and strikes
like a cobra. After that, more alien sensations: a burning not made

of fire, a compression like she was squeezed under a thousand mattresses, every inch of her drummed upon by a pulse like the one she sometimes felt against her pillowcase when she tried to sleep, but nonstop and magnified to hammer every inch of her skin and all the tissue underneath. Vibrations as if thousands of people screamed on the other side of a window, a window she was pressed against but couldn't see through, and she was one of the people screaming, and just like she couldn't see the others, no one could see her.

Release and moonlight. A woman walking away from her, slender and dark-haired, dark-eyed. A woman who was and wasn't her mother. A woman who was stealing her mother away.

The notes offer a link to that mystery woman, a way to play a game with her. Maddy believes this even though she acknowledges the idea makes no sense. Even stranger, she takes a comfort from this irrational certainty, when her smarts tell her she should react in the exact opposite way. She shouldn't want this so badly. She shouldn't want it at all.

She locks her door and jumps with a squawk as Lakesha knocks. "Hey, Maddy! C'mon, Maddy, let me in. I'll be quiet."

"We'll play later, I promise. I gotta do homework now, I'm serious."

For all she knows, Lakesha stands sulking outside the door for the next hour. She doesn't wait to see. She unzips the pocket in her backpack that holds the notes and dumps them onto her unmade bed. They flutter out like dead leaves. The pattern they make as they alight is random, ordinary. She anticipated something more, she doesn't know why, but she's disappointed.

7

S HE'S DOING WHAT YOU ASKED HER TO DO.
    She's tainted the same way you are, but somehow her impression in the aether is different. You don't even try to fathom it, you understand so little about yourself in the first place.

You're holed up in what would be your bedroom, were you a normal boy, though the room contains no bed, no dresser, nothing taped to the walls, no desk, a few clothes hanging in the closet that you never wear. Your mother is not home, you're on the alert and paying attention, the thrumming subliminal static that gives away her presence is far off, somewhere else in the city. In your upper-most layers you're grateful she's not near, she might seal you in the box and sink it in the reservoir if she discovers what you're up to. You'd join your father, lost somewhere deep underwater, unable to breathe, unable to die.

So far, the experiment is working. Your note to Maddy read *put all the notes together and they'll speak a new message*, bold of you because you're not at all certain this will pan out.

Maddy's presence thrums on a different frequency, without your mother's acidic burn or needle-sharp prickliness, and fainter. For months you weren't sure who the traces of otherness emanated from. If it weren't for random clumsiness, stupidly bumping into her in the hall at school while focused on someone else, the pain that seared through your layers as you recoiled, you still wouldn't be sure it was her. If she registered what you were in turn, she didn't betray any sign, hurried on oblivious.

Her presence impinges on your consciousness, a combination of unnatural warmth, the nerve-jangling pinch of a banged elbow, a shuddering of teeth pressing on aluminum foil. The surface of every note you left her absorbs her gaze and longs to squirm. You clasp the hands you've chosen, close the eyes you've chosen, will discomfort to convert to motion.

8

THE NOTE IN MADDY'S HAND, THE NEW ONE, reads *put all the notes together and they'll speak a new message.*

But what does that even mean? Are these squares of paper go-ing to start crawling toward one another, hunching and stretching like worms? Are they going to bounce up and spell out words in semaphore? She lets out a single soft chuckle, annoyed, ashamed, ready to go see if Lakesha still wants to play.

One square flutters, then another. She blinks and all of them are twitching like click beetles trapped on their backs. She blinks and they have swarmed on top of each other, dry crinkled slugs crawl-ing over one another like ants in an exposed burrow. They twist into a single mass, stretching toward the ceiling, a column of living butcher paper as tall as Maddy's arm and half as wide, fluttering and flapping, the creases up and down its form expanding at random to stretch membranes veined with words, except the letters don't resemble any alphabet she knows. Over and over the visitation tries to spell something to her, and she can almost read it, she thinks, but again and again the meaning evades her. She extends a hand and the column shrinks away—

A knock on the door practically hurls her out of her skin. "Maddy! Dinner!" It's Rochelle.

How long was she standing there gawping? The notes are gone from atop her disheveled blankets. She gasps, panics, dives to the floor.

Her backpack leans against her desk, the outer pouch zipped shut. She doesn't remember doing that. She opens the pouch to find all the notes inside as if she never emptied it out in the first place.

"Maddy, you in there?" her foster mom calls.

"I'll be right out." Relief brightens her voice.

Before she leaves, a heap of crumpled pink draws her eye back to the bed. The commotion has exposed the threadbare comforter tucked in between bedspread and sheet, the yellow and green daffodil pattern that decorates it faded to variations in gray. The comforter her mother used to tuck her under in the days before the Vanished Neighborhood. She has not thought of it in this way, as a relic of her previous life, as a leftover from her lost parent, in many, many months, and can't explain why this hits her so hard now.

At dinner, at least at the start, she's as silent and sullen as Ashley, until Rochelle's gentle razzing dislodges a smile and reels it to the surface.

9

AS FAR AS ANDREW IS CONCERNED, Josey's brush with death worked wonders for their relationship.

Pre-urban exploring incident, getting a blowjob out of her required Geneva Convention-level negotiating, and she'd complain about how gross it was for hours afterward. Post-incident, she volunteers without even having to be asked. If Andrew was honest with himself, he'd admit that took a lot of the fun out of it, because he got off on degrading her and that doesn't work if she's willing—but Andrew is never honest with himself.

No such self-reflection troubles him this minute. What Josey has chosen to do is so brazen it has his pulse pumping even before her hands pry his stiffening cock out from his jeans. The Chevy Tahoe his parents bought for him idles at the crest of the Petraseks' steep climb of a driveway, in plain view of all the bright-lit windows at the front of the palatial house. If Josey's mom parts the curtains of her bedroom window—any window, really—she'll have a clear view into the SUV, where her underage daughter's unmistakable blonde perm bobs above the crotch of her just-turned-twenty-one boyfriend. She told him to sit still for his birthday present, and when he answered "Dipshit, my birthday was yesterday" she smiled back, "Part two!"

His mouth hangs open. His glazed eyes return to focus as his lips ape a grin, imagining Josey's mom watching, imaging her hand sliding down her designer slacks. The Petraseks came from old money, though that money was in the hands of a widow who'd first married a much older man, then remarried to a younger one. Josey's stepdad isn't that far from Andrew in age. Andrew's folks are rich too, new money rich, pastel McMansion in a gated county neighborhood rich. He can do what he wants to Josey short of getting her pregnant and her parents aren't going to do shit.

How is Josey doing this? When did she learn? It's like her mouth is full of tongues, pressing and lapping from every angle. He fights not to scream, it feels so good.

His orgasm is building in earnest when a pins-and-needles sensation skitters up his belly and down both legs. His cock goes numb.

She springs up. "Love you, sweetheart," she says, giving him a peck on the cheek. "Happy birthday, part two." Her voice rings the wrong timber, deep and gruff. Her kiss burns like a blowtorch. The pins and needles below flair to points of fire.

"God damn," he yells, tears streaming, but the passenger side door has already slammed behind her.

He's completely numb below the waist. The sensation of open flame searing his face dissipates fast as it struck.

"Hey," he says, meaning to shout but no louder than a whisper. "What did you do, Josey?" Even though she's already walked to the front door, an odd break in routine as before they've always entered through the mammoth garage. He looks at the figure illuminated by the outdoor lights and it's not even Josey, it's her mom, white-platinum haired and from this distance almost as pretty as her daughter. She blows him a kiss, and at that moment he doesn't even have the wits to wonder why. He can't feel his legs. And something else is wrong.

One of his hands tentatively slides toward his groin. What his fingers find—or really, what they don't find—makes him scrabble for the Tahoe's overhead light. He fights not to scream.

When agony erupts like his crotch is bursting open, like something huge and multi-limbed is burrowing out from the inside, he loses that fight.

A second locus of pain bites into the base of his brain, and he's turning the ignition, starting the Tahoe, though what he wants to do is run to the door and either scream for help or hammer Josey in the face for what she did to him. Though his nerve endings end at the phantom flesh-ripping hooks in his groin, his legs work the pedals, his hands turn the steering wheel of their own accord. He blubbers at the wheel as something else drives the Tahoe, drives his body.

Back at his own house, he does unspeakable things to his mother, his father, his little brother. He's a passenger, unable to control the monstrous forms his body takes.

10

THE PLACE MATS, SILVERWARE, CHINA artfully arranged on the dining table constitute a farce, as neither of you possess human appetites, yet your mother insists. You sit across from her, you say the grace she taught you. No food dirties the plates.

You live in a small, barren house in one of the oldest, most run-down Hillcrest neighborhoods. With so many of its rooms empty of furniture, a visitor who walked through without encountering the inhabitants might well assume no one lived here. The elderly man listed as the owner in city records belongs to your mother now.

She says, "Tell me about your day, Davey."

"I spied," you say.

She regards you with the same dark eyes she had before she joined with a monster. She's a striking woman, with her dark hair in a bob and full lips prone to wry smiles. She looks dressed to the nines, made up for a night on the town. It means nothing, with a thought she can make herself look however she wants.

You lack that range of flex. When you want to look like Davey, when she demands that of you, you always end up wearing the same clothes, unless you change, physically remove the new outfit and put one on.

Her mastery of her state borders on godlike. And yet, of late, something's been wrong with her.

"Which face did you use and what did you see?" she asks, and when she speaks her voice splits, a old man's voice bleeding into hers, and her mouth splits too, fissuring at a diagonal that slashes through her lips. The moment she stops talking the bizarre wound is gone. You know better now than to remark upon it.

"Her name is Carolyn. She's a janitor. She lives alone. Her house is full of dead cats. There were a few left alive, I locked them out of the house, I hope they find someplace else to go."

You mother smirks. "I approve."

"At school hardly anyone pays her any mind. She can get in anywhere."

Your mother steeples her fingers. You know what she wants to hear, you have a morsel ready to serve. "I took a mop bucket into the boy's locker room and found a place to hide. There was a boy alone in there with a coach while the teams were out practicing. There's an office in the locker room, he fucked the boy in there."

"What did you do?"

"Watched. Remembered. Tasted the traces after they were gone, so I know what they mean if I find them anywhere else."

"No one saw you, in any form?"

"No one."

You're not lying, but sampling the shreds of psychic aura left after that violation was an afterthought, something you nearly forgot to follow through on in your distracted state, something you needed to share with your mother to keep you out of the box under her bed. You can't afford to lose days on end again.

You watched Maddy all day, from the moment she stepped off her bus to the moment she climbed back on again. Your mother can't know that. She must never, ever, ever find out.

You watched Maddy search under her desk in Mr. Newman's room, and the sight warmed your topmost layers, but you didn't leave her a note. You don't know how to say what you want to say.

11

LUNCH PERIOD PROMISES TO BE MORE OF THE SAME. Maddy reminds herself things could be worse. She hasn't been picked on in many months.

Becca's bookbag, printed deep blue with rainbow flower constellations, stands sentry in the chair across from Maddy, the rest of their corner table unoccupied. Becca's in the lunch line, her dark frizzy hair not quite contained in a pony tail that looks like it's about to slip loose, her short, slumped body further bulked in a heavy coat and sweater even though winter's well over. Maddy's not really excited to see her. They live in the same part of town, but aren't close. Becca talks compulsively about many things that Maddy really doesn't care about, but Maddy thinks that Becca knows this on some level and is just grateful not to have to eat lunch alone. It's not like Becca ever asks her what she thinks. She just talks. No harm no foul.

Becca's presence at her table helps to keep others away, and Maddy's fine with that.

When Josey pulls back the chair to Maddy's left and sits down, a lightning bolt might as well have burned a message in her lunch tray, the development is that unexpected.

Maddy's spine stiffens and her shoulders pinch together. This is prelude to a bullying, for certain. Josey's never been someone who makes a show of being a bully to impress her friends, not that Maddy knows about, but consider the odds: Josey's in ninth grade, just a couple months from graduating junior high, and Maddy's a pudgy eighth grade wallflower. Josey's tall and buxom for her age, blonde as a Viking, top class grades, a scion of old money, turns heads whatever she's wearing and carries herself like she's already high school royalty. Rumor among the distaff population is she snagged a boyfriend way older, proof in some quarters that she's already a goddess among aspiring women. Maddy thinks that's icky but she would never say it aloud because the backlash would be instant. Josey might not be a bully, but plenty of people would pick on an easy target for the chance to impress her.

"Why did you erase that skull you drew on our desk?" Josey says.

Now we're through the looking glass. Maddy has no words but "What?"

"That skull! Why'd you erase it? I thought it was ridiculously awesome."

Maddy can only stare until words practically volunteer of their own accord. "I didn't erase it." Her mind is racing. "Someone else did." She's spied on the other classes in that room and never seen Josey.

The note-maker had requested that drawing.

"So you must draw a bunch," Josey goes on. "Can I see?"

A cafeteria lady gives Becca's lunch card a swipe through the reader. Becca stuffs it back in her purse, picks up her tray laden with the latest unappetizing selection, turns and spots Josey sitting at their table. Becca's jaw drops.

Maddy quick-scans the room, catches entire groups of her fellow pupils quickly looking away, others not bothering to hide their stares.

"C'mon, show me," Josey says.

Does Josey know about the notes? Is she involved somehow? She can't imagine a more unlikely scenario, but a minute ago the notion of Josey taking an interest in her would have seemed as remote as the moon. Maddy's never seen Josey walk into Mr. Newman's classroom. But she's not there all hours of the day, is she?

Josey waves a hand in front of Maddy's face. "Hello? I'm serious. I just want a peek."

Becca walks up, her bug-eyed alarm a comical reflection of Maddy's own shock. *I hope I don't look like that,* Maddy thinks, and snaps out of her paralysis. She can hear Mama Rochelle's voice scolding, *Maybe there's more to Josey than you know.*

"It's fine, sure," Maddy starts digging in her backpack. Becca sits down. Josey smiles at her, says, "Hey, Becca." A lunch period full of firsts.

Maddy has a black-and-white marbled cover composition book that she uses as a cheap sketch pad. It's about half full of doodles that she doesn't even show to Mama Rochelle. She knows what would happen if she did, she's not stupid.

Another voice in her mind hisses, *Don't trust Josey! Don't let her see!* She might laugh. She might squeal *Ew gross!* She might tell the principal that Maddy's disturbed. Maybe worse, she might love what's in those drawings.

Thinking about the notes left under her desk, Maddy teases the composition book out of her backpack.

Becca, taking her seat, sees the composition book come out and raises her eyebrows and bugs her eyes, which has the effect of turning her round, plump face into a clown mask. "I hope you've got a strong stomach," she says, though she's not looking at Josey. She's watching Maddy's hands as the cover folds open.

Becca had to beg for days before Maddy showed her those drawings, and once she saw them, she didn't like them at all. Becca doesn't quite understand the unpleasant tightening that clenches in her chest. Part of her really, really doesn't want to view those drawings again, part of her is contemplating how brainy, pretty, fashion-plate Josey gets to see Maddy's darkest secrets after asking only once.

Josey hunkers closer, eyes fever-bright as she scans the thick shadows made by ballpoint pen. "Amazeballs," she says. Becca mutters aloud, "Amazeballs? Who says that?" then remembers the risk she's taking and puts a hand over her mouth.

Josey doesn't react. She leans closer to Maddy. "May I?"

Josey touches the pages, spreads them flatter. Beneath her pink-painted nails, a furious doodle floods the paper to the edges. Faces stretch like taffy, distorted into squares, their corners tied together like handkerchiefs. Every mouth contorts in exaggerated grimace. Some eyeholes are filled in black, others contain huge and bloodshot orbs, little black veins forking like lightning strikes toward floating irises.

Page turn. A huge mouth takes up both the facing leaves of paper, the space between the upper and lower sets of teeth colored in by frenetic black scribbles, with blocky letters left white within the darkness. They spell out the words *mommy isn't that funny!?!*

Page turn. Figures that register as human only in the crudest sense—two arms, two legs, a head—are swirled into an epic spiral that funnels to a single point near the center, as if the viewer looks down into a whirlpool choked with human-shaped sheets.

"I've got an art project I'm trying to get done. It's due tomorrow and I'm just not happy with it," Josey says. "I was wondering if you could help me out."

"Um, wow, are you sure?" For the first time Maddy looks close at Josey's face. She's got everything Maddy doesn't: unblemished skin, a tiny nose, huge wide-set green eyes. Maybe there's more makeup on her cheeks than Maddy first realized, though of course it's expertly blended. A faint floral scent caresses the air between them, and there's another, stranger scent beneath, as if the crackle of a fireplace has been transmuted into candy. Maddy's nostrils flare and she lets a shudder slip before she catches herself. The underlying odor summons a vignette of her missing mother, dressed in a denim jacket, turning in the driver's seat, reaching toward her to buckle her in, wearily scolding *Hold still.*

Josey smiles ever so slightly in acknowledgment of the scrutiny, but on her face even the slight crinkle this brings to the corners of her eyes glows like a warm sunrise. "Can you come by my house tonight?"

Maddy's heart leaps, then sinks. "I don't have a ride." Mama Rochelle would never agree to this, she can't leave all the kids at home alone in the evening to give one a ride, she and Ashley had a big argument a couple months ago and Rochelle said that over and over again.

"Don't worry, my mom'll pick you up. All I have to do is tell her your address."

"That's—well—" Maddy starts, and doesn't know what to say next. *Is that what rich moms do,* she thinks, *chauffeur their little princesses wherever they want to go?* An ache accompanies the thought, as if it's imbued with longing rather than snark.

"I'm really grateful you're willing to help me, you're crazy-good at drawing."

A warmth spreads through her, touched off by the unexpected praise from someone so much further up in hierarchy, that heat precipitating as a blush that deepens as soon as she realizes she's blushing.

She fidgets with her composition book, quickly flipping pages, creating a non sequitur montage of screaming faces and skulls interlocked in Escher fashion.

She steals a glance at Becca, searching for—guidance, sympathy, perhaps a reflection of her own astonishment, mutual amazement that this improbable thing is actually happening. Becca's mouth has shrunken in sullen disapproval and her eyes don't blink.

"I need to go. I should let you finish lunch," Josey says. "Just give me your address. And your cell number. My mom'll come by your house when she gets off work. She'll call first to let you know she's on the way. That ought to leave you time to do your own homework if you need it."

Becca finally speaks. "Why can't she just come straight home with you from school?" Maddy cringes inside, but at the same time, she recognizes it's a sensible question.

"I'm not going straight home. My boyfriend's picking me up." Becca's jaw drops, then snaps shut.

Josey actually gives Maddy her cell number and asks for Maddy's address again. "Text it to me." Maddy does.

"See you tonight," Josey says, and then she's gone.

Stone silence hangs between the girls in Josey's absence. Becca, instead of peppering Maddy with questions, wolfs down her lunch.

Across the cafeteria, Carolyn the janitor ties up a full trash bag and lifts it out of the can. She watches Maddy and Becca, her gaze veiled beneath crude-cut bangs.

12

CUNETTA SETTLES IN ACROSS THE INTERVIEW TABLE from a jittery jerky strip of a frequent perp named Anton Jackson, whose street name is Hulk, hilarious because he might weigh one hundred and twenty pounds soaking wet. If he ate a four-course meal right before he got on the scale.

"Let's have the truth this time, Anton. What happened to your hand?"

"I *am* telling the truth." Hulk sounds like he's seconds from turning on the waterworks.

"What were you high on in that bar? Crystal?"

"Meth don't make me see shit," says Hulk. "Meth don't chop my fuckin' hand off without making me bleed a drop. Explain that if I'm makin' it up. Why the hell y'all arrest me anyway, I didn't do nuthin', I'm the victim here."

"Disturbing the peace," Cunetta says. "Public intoxication. Probation violation." Hulk goes sullen, lips quivering.

Cunetta has to admit, Hulk's wound or lack of one gives him the willies in an awful way. He transferred to Hillcrest PD five years ago after a decade in Grandy Springs, where some insane shit went down, stuff that he believed was real only because disbelieving could get you killed.

But he's not going to give Hulk a show of nerves.

"Listen, I'm being nice to you here. I'm just trying to make some sense out of what you're saying, so we can figure out whether or not we're gonna let you out. So I'm gonna repeat this story back to you and you tell me how you think it sounds. You spy this sweet pretty boy crying in the men's room at the Bloomer Bar, you offer to cheer him up with a handjob and he takes you up on it. You shove your hand down his shorts and he's smooth as a Ken doll. And then something grabs your hand, you say? And bites it off?"

Hulk's deeply seamed face folds in, from bug-eyed anger back to edge-of-waterworks. "Didn't bite it off. I don't know what it was. Like a bunch of needles pushin' in, but it didn't hurt the way big needles hurt. Then my hand went numb. And when I pulled my arm out my hand was just gone." For emphasis he again lifts the stump where his left hand used to be.

According to the report, Hulk had come out of the restroom shrieking like a scream queen. He didn't calm down when the police arrived. That's why he ended up in a holding cell.

"You don't believe me," Hulk sniffs, "then tell me what the fuck did this. Tell me, smart man."

Cunetta regards the stump of Hulk's wrist and can't explain what he sees. The skin wraps smooth over the knob of bone as if Hulk was born without a hand, but last time Cunetta crossed paths with him, he definitely possessed two, with skin shrunk taut and translucent around tendons and veins from a myriad of unhealthy habits but nonetheless whole and functional. Were further objective proof needed, the complete set of fingerprints on file provided it.

Cunetta maintains a bored expression, his revulsion kept subterranean. He's seen worse, he tells himself, back in Grandy Springs. The truth is, though he heard at least a dozen horror tales about the things that went on in the Boneyard, he never saw them himself. Except once.

Riding in the cruiser through the empty streets after 1 a.m., Cunetta heard the first of many stories from his senior partner about the monsters in the Boneyard and laughed out loud. *You are shitting me. How dumb do you think I look?*

All right, then, his partner said. *Whatever you do, don't get out of the car.*

Maybe his partner had planned it from the beginning. A few turns through downtown, and a block of vacant buildings rose on the right, and Cunetta had told himself those century-old buildings looked no different than any other wretched slum, that nothing about the glass shards in the shattered windows reminded him of teeth in a moldering skull, that the darkness behind them was just shadow, not something with thickness or the slow pulse of breath.

His partner stopped at the mouth of an alley too narrow to accommodate the cruiser. He kept the engine running. *The Boneyard's through there,* he said. *You ever go there, do it in daylight.* And he turned on the running lights so Cunetta could see the tall shadows standing in the alley, long-limbed, faceless, skeletal and glistening as if coated in oil, and Cunetta didn't need to be told twice that these creatures of living abyss had to be respected and avoided.

Whenever the Boneyard wanted something, no matter how vile, the cops didn't intervene.

He'd left those memories behind, a nightmare gladly forgotten. Hulk's inexplicable maiming, a subtler fragment from that nightmare land, brings it all slithering into the light, a black membrane glistening before his mind's eye.

Cunetta's usually quick with a sarcastic quip, but his voice quavers, a teeny hint of tectonic plates shifting, as he asks, "You been to a doctor?"

"I don't need a doctor. I need my damn hand back."

The laugh that escapes Cunetta is like a suspect on the run over open ground.

13

MARIA DRAWS APPRECIATIVE GLANCES as she strides across the market square. Some looks linger longer, focused on her hip-hugging skirt and its above-the-knee hemline. She maintains a wistful half-smile, meets no one's eyes directly.

She has to consciously maintain this skin, this shape, as she walks, with an effort the act has never before required. Her conscious admission of the problem swaddles a hard truth, one with sharp, serrated edges. For weeks, each venture she's made that required her to maintain a skin for an extended time has demanded ever-increasing levels of concentration to prevent a ravel.

Signals of worry bubble up from deep within her layers, from somewhere further down than her inverse-sephirothic awareness extends, down beneath all worlds where the Mystery dwells that allows her and others like her to subsist as mouths. Those dark signals drive her to walk into Gypsy Flair in broad daylight.

Across the street, a pair of rumpled, unshaven men lean against the wall beside the bus depot bay. One of them stares at her legs, not bothering to hide his admiration, grinning and nudging his grunge-mate. In the storefront window reflection, she can see how he fixates on her ass when she turns to pull open the door.

The hoop racks dangle blouses and dresses that combine a retro hippie sensibility with iterations of the little black dress. A pressure builds as Maria advances, the invisible evidence of the wards that block her from entering the empty floors above, even as the bin that once held her essence calls to her, pulls at her like a magnet. Somewhere in this store there's a chink in the armor, a crack she could squeeze through. This tantalizing sensation of weakness aches like a hard mote wedged between teeth, inaccessible by tongue or finger.

A woman who Maria recognizes from weeks of spying as the day manager stands behind the purchase counter, adjusting sparkly wares inside a glass case. Her name tag labels her Kristy. She's relatively young, in her thirties at most—or maybe a well-preserved forty. Brown hair back in a neat bun, heavy-set in a curvaceous way that would probably excite the men across the street, makeup pancaked on a little too heavy, still not quite hiding the dark circles under her eyes. If Maria had antennae they would straighten and lean in like dowsing rods in response to a whiff of addiction, something physical but not chemical.

"Hi there, welcome to Gypsy Flair," Kristy says, on script. "What can I help you with?"

Maria wants to unseam Kristy and turn her inside out for what she knows, but the rival hiding out in the space above might sense it. "I've got a strange question for you, if you don't mind."

Since the question likely won't be about merchandise, the fake smile falters a little. "Oh, I don't mind at all."

"There used to be a theater on the second floor of this building."

Kristy brightens. "Oh yes, the old Masonic Theater. This building's on the historic registry because of it."

"Do any of the shops store their inventory up there?"

Kristy's brows crease and eyes narrow in a combination of puzzlement and suspicion. Maria talks fast. "I mean, it's weird to me that you've got this historic landmark and yet it's not open to the public. I'm fascinated by local history and classic architecture and I'm wondering if there's a way to see this space."

Her smile hardening to a mask, Kristy shakes her head. "Unfortunately the cost to get it up to code so that people can go up there is just too much. I know it sounds awful—I'd like to think this city could do better, that the city council would invest or something—but the deal the building inspector made with our landlord was that so long as the upper floors stay sealed off they could lease the rest of the building commercially."

"Have you ever seen it? The theater, I mean."

Now Kristy laughs a little, the nervous titter transforming to a squeak as her eyes go wide and her lips curl back.

Maria recognizes what has happened, calms herself and restores her face to normal, confident that Kristy will dismiss whatever sudden, gruesome transformation she just witnessed as a trick of the mind. Sure enough, Kristy's grimace subsides back to a fake smile.

"I'm serious. You're sure there's not a way up there from this store?"

Kristy laughs louder. "No. No, there isn't."

The presence, the pressure. Maria wants so badly to absorb whatever this stupid smiling mannequin might know, but she's too close to the enemy, too close. "I'm so disappointed," she says. As she turns away, her face ripples chin to forehead.

Outside, her admirers across the street have moved on.

Soon, a big dark-skinned man settles with his back against the wall, legs stretched to partially block the sidewalk. He stares into Gypsy Flair as a pair of women circle a rack and Kristy follows them, still smiling.

A man walking with crutches emerges from the bus depot, spies the squatter on the sidewalk. "Hey man, haven't seen you in ages, where you been?"

"I've been right here," the squatter says. "Where *you* been?"

14

THE FACELESS SHADOWS WAIT OUTSIDE HAIRSTON'S BUNKER, watching. They can't touch him. They're all dead, burned away to nothing, but they're always there. Even reduced to some substance less significant than ash, their legacy haunts Grandy Springs in much the same way it haunts Hairston's skull.

Whether hallucination, memory, or reflection of some alternate dimension, they don't concern him now. With the threat they posed to this town consigned to the past, his awareness has been freed to detect new threats or seek new prey. Centered in his web, Hairston sees those pursuits as one and the same.

He stands beside the cot that has served as the receptacle for decades of restless half-sleep and peers at the curved mirror mounted on the wall that lets him see into the other rooms, and into spaces outside. It shows him visions from another town and a future time, less swathed in haze than in days before. It shows him things he will see with his own eyes. It teaches him there are monsters in the world different from the ones he intimately knows.

He hasn't dressed yet, and from his chest to the soles of his feet the fibers that infest him create phosphorescent streaks under his skin. Someday this otherworldly violation of his body will kill him, but that someday will arrive many years later than it does for anyone human. Hairston used to be human, but he entertains no illusions about what he is now. The betrayal and the blood-drenched, fiery ordeal that fused him to this state took place long ago and will never be undone. To brood upon it is to waste his energy.

The floors of the rooms that bud from Hairston's bedchamber are piled with reeking garbage. Each of those rooms contains a curved mirror like the one Hairston faces. Every room is lit by an overhead light, though anyone with a mind split open wide enough to find their way to this bunker would spot no wiring, nor would they hear the rumble of a generator.

A murky darkness spins across one of the other mirrors, like an animation made using negatives of a hurricane. Hairston's scowl deepens. Even though the mirror is in another room, he senses the disturbance like a flicker in the corner of his mind's eye. He heads into that room, kicking aside the heaped trash to get a better vantage.

Outside, phantoms wait.

15

YOU REMOVE YOUR MASTER KEY from the loop on your belt. The classroom where you leave the notes for Maddy lies behind the door you open. You use your mop to push a bucket of water into the room. The teacher left moments ago, you watched him shuffle down the hallway, head down, shaggy salt-and-pepper hair curled in a mad scientist's mat. You're relieved because if he'd lingered any longer, you might have gone in anyway, and if he questioned your presence the consequences would have been drastic for you and even worse for him.

Once you lock the door, you roll the bucket to the desk where Maddy sits, lift a stubby hand palm up and will your seams to appear.

Your mother would approve of none of this. You would suffocate for weeks if she found out.

Your hand becomes a glove formed of strips fastened together by bright motes. A blink later, the motes resemble buttons, some round, some diamond-shaped, some like tiny black stars.

Carefully, with your hand that remains whole, you unfasten a square of skin from the center of your palm, detach it completely from your body. The space revealed in the hole beneath shudders in a manner that would hurt normal eyes to look at. Even you detect an unpleasant ache spreading from the depths of your borrowed eye sockets.

You fix your attention on the tiny portal into void that you've opened in your palm, and something rises to the surface, like a corpse freed from the seabed, to patch the gap. A new piece of skin, drawn from those trapped in the layers.

The square of separated skin quivers between the index finger and thumb of your left hand. You focus, and a bright mote crawls out from under your thumbnail, dimming into a button molded to look like a valentine heart. The button slides onto and across the patch of skin, a planchette choreographed by your will. As it moves, it pulses red, then dims, then reddens again. Its wake leaves a visible, purpling trail. The skin etched by the planchette squirms as if it still has functional nerves.

This note is the shortest, least creative of all: *stay away from josey*

You don't know it's already too late. You will the note to curl under the desk and lie in wait, wedged tight between the grainy underside of the desktop and the horizontal support bar. From time to time during the hours that follow it trembles like a cockroach adjusting its wings.

16

JOSEY'S MOM HAS A SMILE THAT MUST have cost thousands of dollars to fashion. She's as pretty as her daughter, her glossy shoulder-length hair white or platinum blonde or both and styled with beauty queen sweep. She's wearing more makeup than her daughter but her bright blue eyes draw all the attention.

Maddy's heart races at an uncomfortable tempo as she climbs into the back of the SUV—itself a beauty queen, red, spotless waxed gleam reflecting the clouds—because this is really happening, it wasn't a put on, she's really going to Josey's house. It's a little weird not riding shotgun but that's the door Josey's mom held open for her. Maddy squirms into the seat behind the driver's and buckles up.

Mama Rochelle watches from the driveway. She smiles, warm as fresh-baked bread, and gives Maddy a tiny flutter-fingered wave. Rochelle had just arrived home from day care with the not-twins when Josey's mom pulled up. *Can you carry Porsche,* Rochelle had asked as Maddy rushed up to the station wagon's driver's side door to explain who was driving that huge candy red SUV. (Whether it's Georgia or Porsche, state or car, that request always makes Maddy crack up inside, though not as much lately as the twins are getting heavier.)

In between the tasks involved in settling the twins in their room and calling sullen Ashley up from her room to help, Rochelle had flashed Maddy bits of a bright smile. Apparently she didn't share any of the trepidation that squirmed in Maddy's chest. *I'm glad she sees what you've got inside you,* Rochelle said. *The way you draw must speak really loud to something inside her. It's fine, you can go, sweetie, just call me when you're ready to come back.*

As Maddy's eyes meet hers, Rochelle brightens with that same smile. "Have a good time!" she says, and makes a *call me* gesture. Is it a trick of Maddy's mind that Mama Rochelle's smile shifts ever so slightly as she turns her gaze to Josey's mom? Eyes narrowing, a near-imperceptible downturn at the corners of the lips?

"So nice to meet you," Josey's mom calls, sounding fake as a Barbie.

"Be good," Rochelle says, a thing she always says in parting that Maddy finds really embarrassing right at that moment. The unpleasant warmth under her skin continues as she fidgets in the back seat.

She starts to imagine what a woman as rich as Josey's mom must think about these tiny, close-crammed houses in Mama Rochelle's neighborhood. All look well used, their colors muted by the passing decades, some yards already overgrown with grass or littered with toys that haven't been inside since last summer. "It's a good neighborhood," Maddy says, instantly wishing she'd stayed quiet.

"It's lovely," Josey's mom says, settling in the driver's seat. She sounds like she's been presented with a cake that's not quite to her liking. She goes on, "Thank you so much for offering to help my daughter."

The idea that Josey's mom thinks this was all Maddy's idea jars her. She wonders if that's how Josey told it to her mom, or just what her mom assumes. Maddy would never have approached Josey on her own, short of a teacher forcing her. If Josey fibbed to her mom, the fib is alarming, though flattering too in an odd way. Like Josey talked her up to her mom, made her out to be a cool artist, maybe.

For such a huge machine, the SUV's engine is eerily quiet. It prowls down Mama Rochelle's street, aimed toward the center of the city and then well beyond, to the hills full of mansions where Josey's family lives.

Josey's mom drives the speed limit, which startles Maddy because this behemoth vehicle boasts as many high tech displays as a spaceship, with monitor screens built into the backs of the seats and everything. Josey's mom doesn't offer to put a movie on, though.

Becca's house is three crossings up from Mama Rochelle's. When it comes in sight, Maddy spies Becca outside, bounding up her steep front yard with a rake, even though it's spring. Maybe Becca is playing witch—when she was smaller she liked to pretend the rake was a broomstick. She'd go get a real broom out of the house so Maddy could play too.

Maddy raises a hand to wave an instant before she remembers that Becca was mad at her for accepting Josey's invitation in the first place. Then an imp of the perverse takes her over and she waves hard to make sure Becca sees her. Their gazes meet. Becca spots Maddy and stops, follows her progress in the SUV but doesn't wave back.

Maddy watches Becca until she can't anymore. She's unsure whether or not she feels bad about what she's just done.

17

THE DIGITS THAT APPEAR ON THE SCREEN of Aaron's cellphone aren't recognizable as any kind of phone number. He knows immediately who's calling.

Despite that, he still starts his part of the conversation with a tentative "Hello?"

"I need to be in Hillcrest tomorrow," Hairston says, his voice like an Old Testament command. "Early tomorrow. You ready for that?"

For a disoriented moment, a thought takes shape that Aaron needs to arrange for someone to watch his cats. His struggle to update his brain to his current reality almost turns physical. The same accident that notched these awful scars onto his face put him in the hospital for weeks and during those weeks he missed rent and his shit landlord tried to have him evicted. His several-eras-ago ex-girlfriend Vanissa and her fiance Athenea rescued his kitties, Persephone and Prowler, letting him visit whenever he wanted, until the whole awful mess got sorted out, may all the gods bless them. He's sure they'll help again, that they'll receive his feline charges more warmly than they usually receive him. He chuckles with a shake of the head.

After the interval of silence this exercise requires, Aaron gives consent to Hairston. It's almost midnight, but Hairston insists they can't wait. He gives Aaron details on where to pick him up and when.

When the call ends, Aaron regards his apartment, his grip on it still tentative given he's stubborn enough to stick to journalism as his bread and butter. The interior decoration sense of his latest ill-advised fling, Donna, who moved in with him for five months, still surfaces through the clutter of printouts and old newspaper editions. Donna had a thing for Théophile-Alexandre Steinlen's cat posters, nailing them up on every wall, cranking the feline fandom factor into the stratosphere. Though apparently she didn't love cats enough to take the prints with her when she moved in with her next lover, who she was banging well before she and Aaron mutually agreed she needed to leave.

Aaron doesn't resent the posters. They're like the crisp gold coins he got to keep after washing a pile of shit down the drain.

"Goodbye, kitties," he tells them. "I'm not sure when I'm coming back."

18

THE SUV ASCENDS TOWARD A SPRAWLING STUCCOED HOUSE perched like a crown atop the crest of a hill. The driveway curves languorously up a steep grassy slope that must be a nightmare for whomever Josey's family hires to do the mowing. To Maddy the lawn looks near vertical.

The engine of the SUV at last makes a little noise, roaring as it hauls its bulk to the peak where the terrain abruptly levels to reveal box hedges that surround the mansion like green dolmens. A garage door at least three cars wide opens to engulf the SUV, like a grouper with a brightly lit mouth preparing to suck in a smaller fish. Two more cars are parked inside, a sports coupe and a mini-van. They gleam like jewelry.

"Different tools for different tasks," says Josey's mom.

"Uh huh," Maddy says, not understanding. "What kind of car is that?" She points at the coupe. "It's pretty sweet!"

"That's Josey's Jaguar. She gets to drive it if she keeps her grades up through junior high graduation."

"Wow. I'd totally stay straight A's for that!"

Josey's mom emits a wistful sigh, as if she's just emerged from a daydream. "Of course you would, you're a good girl." She puts the SUV in park. "Come on, Josey's waiting for us." She exits and waits for Maddy to join her.

Maddy pictures an illustration from the tale of the ugly duckling as she follows Josey's mom into the house, the frazzle-haired kid from the wrong side of town trailing the golden swan. Mama Rochelle would scold her for giving in so quickly to assumptions, tell her not to let this alien woman threaten her sense of self, and for that matter not to judge this woman whose load in life is so unfamiliar. *Never doubt that you've got life well in hand*, Rochelle tells her. *You're the toughest kid I've ever known.* Maddy doubts that's true, but it warms her to the core every time Rochelle says it.

The door from the garage opens, apparently by magic, Maddy doesn't see her escort click a remote control. They enter an anteroom that's like a designer airlock, with brass hooks to either side for coats and shoes and a forbidding second door of dark-stained wood set in a stucco wall. "You can leave your shoes here," Josey's mom says, though she doesn't remove her own.

Maddy hangs her sneakers side by side on the wide shoe hooks. The chance positioning of the lace loops, toes, and sole patterns gives them fretful puppy expressions, as if they're silently pleading with her not to abandoned them. *You'll be okay*, Maddy reassures them, then giggles at her own silliness.

Josey's mom smiles ever so slightly at the sound before she opens the inner door. Beyond the airlock lies a big playroom dominated by a fancy pool table with gleaming flanks and ornately curved and carved legs. Past the pool table an atoll of plush black couches forms an incomplete square, the missing side open to the largest flat screen TV Maddy has ever seen. Josey's family must host dozens of visitors at a time—or maybe they lounge in those vast couches all on their lonesome. Maddy wonders if Josey and her boyfriend spend time on those couches. She shies away from the thought, not wanting to blush in from of Josey's mom.

"This way," Josey's mom says. "Let's go to the kitchen. I've got cookies waiting." Still a duckling, Maddy follows her through a sitting room with yet another big screen TV, then down a hall that opens into a kitchen that's bigger than the room at school where the cafeteria ladies scoop the latest mush onto trays as the kids push past.

A marble-topped bar extends out from a counter in a graceful curve and widens into a central table surrounded by tall stools. That's where Josey's mom directs Maddy to sit. Once perched on a stool, her feet don't reach the floor. She resists an impulse to kick like a baby in a highchair.

Josey's mom sets a whole pack of fancy store-bought cookies in front of her, unopened. "Help yourself. I'll go get Josey."

Until that moment, it hasn't occurred to Maddy how odd it was that Josey wasn't right there waiting when they pulled into the garage, or stepped into the playroom. Even for a rich kid, someone from a world Maddy knows only by imagination, that seems pretty damn weird.

She keeps brushing her gaze over all the shining surfaces in this immense kitchen, so spotless she wonders if Josey's family ever uses it. Appliances, cutlery, cupboards, counter tops all glisten as if freshly removed from the box and spruced up for a photo shoot. Speaking of box, she opens the cookies out of a need to do something with her hands during this awkward pause. She eats the first and second cookie with the greatest care possible, fearful she'll leave a stray crumb and violate some unspoken rule. The cookies neither look nor taste as good as the package promises. They're like sweetened cardboard.

Minutes pass. Maddy wonders if she'll violate another taboo if she clambers down from her stool and ventures out into the enticing labyrinth of surrounding rooms. She imagines opening an outsized closet door, something horrible and yet hilarious spilling out from behind it, like the corpse of a gardener or a motherlode of creepy dolls, the commotion bringing Josey's mom at a run, her glossy lips curled in a snarl, to banish Maddy from the mansion with an accusing finger and a cry of *Out, out, out!*

"Hey, so glad you came!"

Josey is standing right behind her, practically yelling in her ear. Thank goodness Maddy froze instead of springing up in surprise, she might have toppled from her stool and smashed her head open.

"Jeez!" Maddy clutches at her chest as her heart pounds a wild tattoo. "You scared me like—"

a monster vomiting its multi-limbed shape out of the back seat to tear mommy and me apart

Maddy leaves the sentence unfinished, the unbidden nightmare that flooded the theater of her mind gone as quick as it gushed forth.

Josey waves a hand in front of her face. "Yo, you okay?"

Maddy shakes herself. *Don't be such a baby,* she tells herself. "Yeah, yeah. You just startled me is all. Where's your mom?"

"She had to go run another errand."

A notion makes Maddy nervous, or rather taps into a strand of jitters flowing close to the surface. "Gone to pick up more of your friends?" Friends eager to impress Josey by stomping all over Maddy . . .

Josey smiles a quick, cold smile, exactly like her mother's. There's an embodiment of *oh how awkward* burnished into its angles, and Maddy at once recalls that Josey has never declared her a friend.

Josey gives Maddy no space to squirm from that admonishment. "My project's in my room, you ready to look at it?"

"'Course! That's all I'm here for, right?" Maddy means those words to wield an edge. Josey doesn't take the bait, maybe doesn't even care, she's immune to anything Maddy could dish out.

"I'm so grateful you're here, I really need your help. You've got like ten times the talent I do. My teacher won't cut me a break!"

Maddy suspects false flattery. "You can't be *that* bad."

"Yes I can, you'll see. Hey, bring those cookies with you, I want some. They're so good!" The most human and fallible and ridiculous thing to come out of Josey's mouth since she started talking to Maddy.

"Seriously? You've tried these? I think they're gross." Again, Josey doesn't acknowledge the bait. She troops into the hall, leaving Maddy no choice but to tuck the cookie package under an arm and follow.

Josey's return heralds the return of that strange smell, like sweetness, like cooked meat, like burning. Except Maddy realizes it didn't just reappear on the way here. She smelled it in the SUV, in the playroom, in the kitchen.

The stench has a new intensity that makes her head swim. It calls lunacy to mind, a déjà vu sensation of tremendous crushing pressure, wet and suffocating, unending in its agony, relieved with a twisting mockery of birth. She hears a girl's voice, *Mommy, don't you think it's funny?* repeated over and over.

Josey descends a set of wide, grand stairs. The vertigo adds to Maddy's nausea. She fights to keep her balance even with the plushly carpeted basement floor beneath her feet. Josey doesn't look back, thank God, as Maddy has to put a hand to a wall to keep steady.

Josey pulls open a door in that same wall, and next thing they're in her bedroom. It's as big as the garage. Maddy has never seen so many toys in one place outside of a store. Most are still in their boxes, displayed on shelves, Barbies of all sorts, pale big-busted blonde women with long, luscious hair, elegant gowns and identical smiles.

Josey has—no surprise—her own TV and game console, a set of cushion-y chairs of her own and a bed big enough to hold a pizza party for a couple dozen kids, and Maddy bets it's been used for exactly that.

Josey heads straight to what Maddy assumes is a closet door. "I have my drawings posted up in here. I tried using glow in the dark paint."

"That sounds cool!"

"It's really not. I suck. Hopefully you can help me not suck."

Maddy pushes past her into the shadowed chamber beyond, too big to be any ordinary closet.

Josey shudders violently at the incidental contact, like she's enveloped in a blizzard blast. The shuddering is more than that, though—beneath Josey's shirt, Maddy feels something sliding and twitching, a snake in spasms, as if electrocuted.

Maddy shrieks and hops away, deeper into the unlit room.

The door closes. Josey flips on the overhead light. It's a bathroom. Josey has her own private bathroom. Maddy hears a second click. Maybe Josey is flicking another switch, to turn on a vent or something.

A leathery sheet of art paper covers the mirror over the sink, two more are taped to the wall on either side, even more plaster the facing wall above the towel rack, more are taped up in the shower.

There are markings on the sheets, but Maddy wouldn't call them drawings. They're furious scratches in the paper, like epic scribbles made with a pen that's run out of ink, though at a glance they defy easy dismissal, the patterns in them arresting to the eye, not at all random.

Josey still has a hand on the doorknob, though she's facing forward, her slender arm bent at a painful angle. "I'm putting you back where you belong," she says.

The drawings rustle as if whipped by a breeze.

"What?" says Maddy.

"Maude told me how to sniff you out. You fell for it so easy, I can't believe you really don't remember what you are. Your mother must have taught you to play ignorant when she made you."

Maddy wants to say, *I don't know what you're talking about*, but her tongue won't move.

"I can't see the point, trying to hide that way, because like can tell when like is near. But what do I know?" The timbre and pitch of Josey's voice alters syllable by syllable, sometimes deep, sometimes raspy, sometimes creaking with age, masculine in all variations. "I'm just a puppet that will never be a real boy."

The flapping pieces of not-paper and Josey's gross voice-trick split Maddy's fracturing attention. Any question she wants to ask sticks in her throat. She's too bewildered to scream.

"Once you're back with us, we'll find your mother," the man inside Josey says. Somehow, while Maddy wasn't looking, Josey drew lines all over her face. They divide her face into not quite

symmetrical squares. She must have put in contacts, too, her eyes are different colors, brown in one, green in the other, instead of blue.

The lines on her face are studded with glittering lumps. Her hand has twisted around the doorknob like a wet, crumpled towel that retains the tint and texture of tanning-bed-bronzed skin. Her t-shirt and designer jeans twitch all over, as if mice cluster underneath the fabric.

"What are you doing?" Maddy's mind fastens to the notion that this is all a prank, maybe there's a hidden camera, maybe Josey's a bully after all—

A snake is crawling across the ceiling, toward the light fixture. Another extends along the wall by Josey's shoulder. Both are flat and leathery, like the drawings, which flutter frantically in a nonexistent wind.

From behind Josey's back more flattened serpents stretch, slinking across the floor, fanning out over the door, tendrils like strips of animated skin edged by glittering beads.

The drawings, too, have formed pearls along their edges, scintillating with color. Everything expands and contracts, everything curls and twists.

a shape like skins from a hundred slaughterhouse animals peeled and twined together, snaking forward between the driver and passenger seats

Maddy doesn't shriek. Instincts seared into nerve and muscle goad her to flee whatever Josey is becoming, but the drawings that are also part of Josey are snapping and stretching on the walls beside her and in the shower behind her. There's no way out unless she magically gains the strength to tear through tile and drywall.

"Panic all you want," the man inside Josey says. "You know what's coming."

Cornered, Maddy switches from flight to fight. The only way out is through Josey. She lunges forward, fingers hooked to claw Josey's face.

Josey opens out into a slobbering cyclone of writhing skin and glittering jewels. The hole her body peels apart to reveal extends outside the room, the house, the world, and it's filled with screaming multitudes. Limbs overflow the lip of the vortex, grasping arms and legs bent in triskelion curls. Tendrils of skin and raw muscle lash out, knocking Maddy off her feet, into the expanding anemone swirl.

The arms and legs fold over her. Tendrils wrap her neck, whip around her head, cover her mouth and eyes, crush her nose flat, a suffocating membrane of hot, hairy flesh. Her body lifts from the floor. Small things swarm her, she can't see but they burn like sparks and crawl like ants. They seethe over every inch of her, pierce her with needles of electricity. She relives the moment in the car when she and her mother were undone, enduring a billion points of agony. If her scream sounds through the sheath crushing her head, it's still drowned out by the howls from uncountable others, flooding her ears even though they're muffled by fleshy wrappings.

That first time, numbness replaced the agony, and she was submerged into an enormous pressure that never abated, her mind swiftly sunk beneath layers upon layers of meat, experiencing what a fossil cursed with immortality would feel, trapped inside a billion years of sediment.

This time, the needles retract as fast as they invade.

The limbs and tendrils whip away from her, tumbling her out of the vortex of limbs. She slams onto the hard tiles, hardly noticing the impact as she scrambles to her feet. The spinning maw made of body parts is retracting into midair. Within it, a storm of bright motes retreats into the hellmouth funnel, and she knows they were the tiny invaders burning into her skin the instant before.

The tunnel out of reality shrinks, large as trampoline, as a playpen, as a tire, as a hubcap. The extruding tendrils of what used to be Josey's body corkscrew and twist together, and then the phenomenon no longer resembles a fleshy whirlpool, it's a rope made of coiling worms, flailing in midair, its ends tied to nothing. Bright motes scurry all over it, their numbers rapidly dwindling as they disappear under its twitching strands.

Maddy cringes away, ends up curled on the floor, hands raised to guard her face, but the thrashing rope doesn't touch her. Thinner and thinner it grows, its high-pitched wail unceasing as a tea kettle brought to tortured boil.

Josey's voice abruptly breaks through the screech. "Maddy! Oh, God, Maddy, help me!"

The rope narrows to a thread, then it's gone, thinned beyond visibility. A presence continues to vibrate, a motion that spins Maddy's head and hurts her eyes. She gags and dry heaves.

A long time passes before she gains enough control of her body to uncurl and turn her head. She breathes in long, hissing gasps, her eyes focused on the glass light fixture at the center of the ceiling, its glow burning her retinas. At last she uses the vanity drawers to pull herself up. She's alone in the bathroom, even the drawings, if that's what they were, have disappeared. There is no sign of Josey or the thing she became.

Maddy stares at herself in the bathroom mirror. The girl that looks back at her is pale and bug-eyed, shaking like she's standing naked in a winter storm. She wants to forget everything that girl has just seen. The back of her head throbs, a goose egg rising.

At last she wanders dazed through Josey's bedroom and out into the hall. No one else crosses her path or calls to her. Nothing looks familiar and she's swiftly lost.

One of the many rooms showcases a collection of fine-crafted grandfather clocks. All hands point to the same numbers, 7:34 p.m. Maddy told Mama Rochelle she'd be eating dinner at Josey's. The thought of eating makes her double over and retch.

Through the ceiling a bell chimes, muffled. She thinks it's a clock, but then it repeats, insisted and arrhythmic. A finger punching a doorbell with panicked urgency. Maddy follows the noise like bread crumbs in a labyrinth. She hesitates before each closed door, picturing a vortex of limbs yawning in wait on the other side. The doorbell continues to call.

The gap between the front room curtains exposes slices of a red sunset. The doorbell stops hammering her eardrums. The voice that calls could belong to a boy or girl. "Maddy? Are you there?"

Maddy's heart is in her throat, she can't speak around it.

"I know you got all my notes," her visitor says. "I tried to tell you not to come here. I'm sorry I wasn't quick enough. We need to get far, far away, before our mothers come looking."

Maddy opens the door.

* * *

19

R OCHELLE CAN'T STOP PACING. Won't stop pacing, until she
comes to a decision.

No text from Maddy, much less a call, and it's quarter till 11.
It's the first time Maddy's been out with a school friend (if that's
what Josey Petrasek is) for many months, so if she's enjoying herself Rochelle doesn't want to harsh the vibe. Maybe she's happy
and she's just lost track of time. But that's not like Maddy, she's
not a rebel, she'd much rather just go unnoticed than act out.

And though she doesn't live on her phone like most kids (and
adults now too, let's be fair) it's not like her to ignore it. Rochelle
has sent four texts and left two voicemails.

She paces back and forth in the living room, the television
tuned to a rerun of *How to Get Away with Murder*, the volume
low but still loud enough to mask Rochelle's words as she mutters
under her breath. "Maddy's not one to make trouble. You know
that because *you* were one to make trouble. Back on Lewis Street
when you'd sneak out with the boys and your granma would track
you down and whup you so hard she shoulda gone to jail. But she
kept you outta jail. You know what she would have done about
this."

The projects off Lewis Street were a scary place to raise a child,
but they were a loving place too, full of fond memories for Rochelle, and her granma, quick to strike with a wooden spoon and
quicker to smile, was the core of almost all of those memories. Her
home and her mind were a whole city quadrant and many years
distant from Lewis Street, but she tried to keep her granma's best
lessons front and center, and one of those lessons was, if you don't
know where your child is, you go and find her and bring her back.

Rochelle has her laptop set up on the dining room table—after
dinner, she tallied bills and receipts, with the kids rounded up in
the living room to watch *Wreck-It Ralph* again, all of them except
Ashley, who shuffled downstairs for her evening sulk.

Mrs. Petrasek has a listed number, it turns out, and she's not
answering her phone either. At least that gives Rochelle an address
she can plug into her GPS. Maybe Mrs. Petrasek has another number, a personal cellphone that's unlisted. "Fool, you shoulda asked

for it," Rochelle tells herself. Maybe she was double foolish, allowing Maddy to go off with that woman even though something about her seemed off, like she was looking at Rochelle and Maddy and the other girls the way an indoor cat watches birds through the window. At the time she'd chided herself that she shouldn't be suspicious of anyone, low or high, on account of where they come from. But she also knew, and in truth was confronted with this fact every day she reported to work at PAL, that having money didn't make people responsible, for their own bodies or the bodies of others. For all she knew Mrs. Petrasek was one of those parents who treated her kids like the people who left their dogs chained outside through snow and scorching sunshine. Only when they have that much money social services is never going to intervene to rescue their kids.

Rochelle barges into Ashley's room with its barren walls—the kid doesn't even try to act like she wants this house to be her home, has done nothing to make the room hers, not yet. Ashley protests but she's not doing anything embarrassing, just playing a game on her tablet with her headphones on, and she clearly wasn't asleep. Rochelle cuts her off. "I gotta go out and get Maddy. You get upstairs and mind the young ones until I get back."

Ashley smiles for once, but not for a good reason. "Is Maddy in trouble?"

Rochelle reminds herself that beggars can't be choosers. "It's none of your concern, okay?" Ashley's smile converts to her standard glower. Rochelle adds a spoonful of sugar. "I'll tell you what's in it for you. I've been saving a box of Samoas for your birthday, but you can have it tonight if you do this right for me."

Ashley's love for Samoas makes for the only positive avenue of communication she's established with the kid. Rochelle does have a box she's been saving, because Ashley's birthday is next month. Bribing Ashley is not the way Rochelle wants to do things but these are desperate times, and wow, the girl is smiling again.

About half an hour later the minivan's engine strains up the Petrasek's steep driveway, the angle of her headlights failing to render the strip of asphalt as much more than a band of shadow in the grass. Rochelle's heart pounds at a profoundly unhealthy pace as she contemplates the downhill slide that would ensue if she let the van drift into the grass.

Neither her van nor her heart gives out and she reaches the crest, almost swerving into the bushes that stand sentry around the mansion because the place is cast in darkness. No outside lights on, curtains drawn, which she can only tell because some light is on somewhere deep inside the house, granting the windows the faintest of radium glows. She pictures a ghost standing in a hall, eyes shining, and curses her overactive imagination.

She gets out of the van, manages to find the front walk, rings the doorbell, beats on the front door first with the fancy door knocker, then her fist. Nothing. She tries calling Maddy again.

Maybe her own brain punks her, or maybe it's a super-sense that activates because a foster mother is still a mother, but she could swear she hears Maddy's generic I-don't-care-it's-just-a-phone ringtone, muffled within a millimeter of its life, somewhere inside this massive monument to someone's excessive inheritance. The call goes to voicemail, she hangs up and calls again, starts to pace to the left, where she thinks the sound is coming from. A motion detector light comes on, and she's grateful for it because she won't trip as she circles the house. There's a backyard that's fenced off and a gate that's not locked. She lets herself in. More motion detectors blaze.

The back of the mansion is ludicrous. Tennis court, covered pool, a patio that could host a tiny nation. She can't hear the ringtone at all, so she heads back to the front door. She rounds the corner of the house at the same time rolling blue lights appear at the bottom of the driveway. She counts the police cruisers as they ascend, one, two, three, complete overkill, kill being the word that sticks in her mind. She's a woman, short and round, not too scary to most, but she's a black woman outside a rich white woman's house and she can guess how this is going to go.

The cops would never have arrived this fast at Lewis Street. Hell, not even in the mixed middle class neighborhood where Rochelle lives now. She tells herself to breathe slowly, not to raise her voice, not to make any quick moves. Her heart pounds at a rhythm her body can't quite get a handle on.

The all-too-thinkable happens. "Police! Put your hands above your head!"

She does all the things they yell at her to do. "My daughter's missing," she says, calm as she can. She's face down on the ground, arms wrenched behind her back and handcuffed. The officers aren't listening.

20

MARIA MAKES NO EFFORT TO FIND HER MISSING CHILD. She contemplates the translucent underbed box, which has held Davey inside for countless hours. She's placed it atop her bed. She sits beside it, nude, her skin a lattice of exposed seams. Her bare thigh presses against its side scratched with letters from an ancient alphabet, her fingers rest lightly on the cold surface of its lid, as if she might detect residue from its frequent prisoner, and through that contact find guidance.

She thinks of herself as Maria still, though the shreds within her of the sad creature that started all of this, the late unlamented Lenahan, supply knowledge that this retention of a name and consistent appearance results from an involuntary consequence. The Maria from the Vanished Neighborhood had a strong sense of self, a willful personality that has parasitically entwined with the hungry intelligence that drives her impulses.

This parasite permitted, even insisted upon Davey's independence. That part of her could not bear the thought of his tiny cries lost among the shrieking multitudes folded into the layers. When she at last dropped the charade of motherhood and unmade him, instead of fastening his skin and sins into the quilt, she segregated him, made him a separate, weaker being, something that could still play the part of pupil and son.

She regards this fact with dispassion, neither satisfaction nor regret. Lenahan indulged in a similar arrangement, as had predecessors before him. Over the centuries the predators could not help but assume traits of the prey.

The hand on the box is no longer Maria's hand. It's lighter-skinned, thick and meaty, its fingernails ragged. She did not will that fragment to the surface.

She has no heartbeat, no pulse to quicken. Maria's hand from her former life, brown and supple, supplants the escapee.

She reflects briefly on her predecessor, the pathetic boy whose short, sad tenure as the mind that guided the quilt links her back to Lenahan. The boy left the box of button motes behind, and lost all control in a matter of days. Perhaps the tenacity that kept her sovereign for so long has only slowed the rot and delayed the inevitable.

Despite the reminder that she has more pressing problems than Davey's dereliction, she turns her attention inward, to the infinite layers of flesh and agony for which she serves as curator and mouth. The roots that anchor Davey in these layers are as mobile as hers, and even an hours-long search can only be precursory. She finds no trace.

When the dawn comes, she washes, dresses, stands before the bathroom mirror and applies makeup. She hasn't aged since she became the quilt. She remains what crude men call a cougar. Many such men howl silently within her, their limbs, their eyes stripped away forever.

For a moment, the lower half of her face glowers, skin dark brown, jaw square and bristled with stubble. Heavy lips curl open in a rictus of surprise. Bright blue eyes widen where dark, sultry eyes had been.

Another blink, and her seamless beauty returns, remains steadfast as she studies herself closely. At last she smirks before fetching her purse from the bedroom and heading out into the day.

21

ARI NEWMAN GLANCES AT THE CLASSROOM CLOCK. Only fifteen minutes to go before first period ends and he has to open the door to students.

He's sorted his transparencies for the day for all six classes and tucked them into separate files. He decides with a sigh that he needs to go through them again because one misplaced page could mean a disastrous disruption. He sighs again because he has to work with transparencies.

Thanks to the ultra-stingy city council and an ignorant school board applying cuts the way a toddler wields a hatchet, he's stuck using an ancient, embarrassingly outmoded overhead projector this semester because the laptop-run projector any decent school system would provide died last semester and still hasn't been replaced.

The reminders he sends via email haven't produced results. Neither have complaints made in person at school and county administration offices. He's convinced that if a leaky roof was pouring water onto his desk, he'd be told to buy a year's worth of buckets at his own expense and shamed if he complained.

Teaching is hard enough without so-called state of the art equipment going on the fritz. Every day he catches at least one student playing a game or snapchatting on their supposedly hackproof school issue tablets. He fails to catch dozens upon dozens more, he's certain of that.

He's wondered more than once what these kids who've never been taught cursive writing will do when the inevitable nuclear apocalypse destroys the internet. The monster in the White House and the monster in Pyongyang are going to pull the triggers any minute. Probably immediately after one of his students did something amazing enough to finally convince him he'd chosen the right career.

Ari made his mother, a life-long fourth grade teacher, deliriously happy when he earned his B.Ed. Five years into this job, he still wondered if he'd made a huge mistake. Whenever the function of his ongoing efforts approached a mathematical limit remotely resembling pride in his work, variables large and small cropped up to undermine that result. Case in point, a mouse must have taken up residence in the classroom sometime during the night, the sporadic rustling sound increasingly more annoying.

Half an hour ago he dug his phone out of his jacket and sent an email to maintenance. If that noise continues after class starts— and of course it will—he might as well give up, even though his second period seventh graders are supposedly the precocious ones. Precocious, yes, mature, no. The distraction will be too much, his commands to ignore it will go unheard.

The rustling resumes, louder. An empty desk at the back of the room shifts.

Ari recoils so hard his chair capsizes behind him. He manages to gain his feet instead of falling, in the process spilling half of his carefully arranged folders and their wobbling contents into the floor.

A rapid pattering against a solid surface, as if a bird is trapped inside a box. The desk—it's the one nearest the door—slides a foot sideways and two feet backward. "Jesus!" Ari shouts.

He has the self-possession to open the door into the hall before dashing to the desk. Hoping he'll free whatever animal is trapped underneath so that it will flee the classroom, he flips it over.

A piece of paper flutters up from the underside of the desk and spirals to the checkered floor, where it twitches and flaps like a moth on its back.

He stares dumbfounded, then decides it must have a small motor of some sort attached. It's a nonsensical assumption but one that makes sense in the moment. He bends to pick it up. It burrows into his palm, spraying his blood across the tiles. Pain shreds through the center of his forearm, as if someone shoved a vibrating knife blade deep between the bones of his wrist, which bulges, flesh displaced in a moving lump big as an egg that disappears under the blue cuff of his dress shirt. The thing boring through the center of his arm feels armed with many piercing mouthparts, a cluster of horseflies attacking muscle and bone, biting in all directions. Ari's shriek is raw and endless. He's collapsed, slamming his arm on the floor, trying to kill the thing inside.

Blood bursts from his elbow, staining his shirt, before the blood-slicked creature tears its way out through skin and cloth. A funny bone tingle times a thousand surges up and down Ari's arm before it goes numb.

The creature unfolds on the floor, once again a flat piece of paper, now soaked in blood. It flaps like an insect wing, sliding and swerving, and in doing so spells out a word in wet red smears. *Run.*

Ari's scream peters out as he regards the word and the object that wrote it. Even with his arm ruined by the inexplicable, he insists to himself the pattern is random, it spells nothing, his mind is trying to impose a message where none exists.

As if lifted by a burst of wind, the paper flies into the hall with the speed of an attacking yellowjacket.

* * *

22

THE PALLET BENEATH THE OVERPASS STINKS. Maddy registers the stench first, of accumulated weeks of sweat, urine and filth, before she recognizes that something else on the pallet with her is shifting its weight, it's that motion that woke her.

She doesn't understand where she is, why it smells so badly, what makes the thunderous rhythmic clunking, why she's fully dressed, why curtains provide no shelter from the sun's eye.

A dark-haired boy sits cross-legged on the other side of the mattress. His eyes are squinched shut, his teeth bared, his hands raised, fingers curled into claws. He shudders again, at the edge of seizure.

Maddy remembers.

They've taken shelter beneath an overpass that crosses Miner's Creek at the city's southernmost edge, where the creek's wide enough to pass for a river. A concrete incline rises from the creek's bank to the ledge where the mattress and blankets were stowed. The pylons that hold up the center of the overpass rise from the other side of the creek. The underside of the bridge hangs barely five feet above Maddy's head. Thuds like distant hammer blows echo each time a vehicle crosses the bridge, she can hear the whoosh of their passage.

The boy, Davey, shudders again. She calls his name. His eyelids snap open. "He found it. I didn't want him to. I didn't want to do that."

Maddy sits up. "Who found what?"

"Nothing," he says. "It's nothing. I was . . . dreaming, sorry." Davey's not frightening to look at. Small, waif-thin, in a shirt with horizontal strips like Ernie from Sesame Street, tan corduroy pants that pull up at the ankles to expose white socks. His eyes, though— his gaze is unnerving, his irises seem to float in their sockets as if they're not really attached and might slide off.

"You have dreams?" Davey showed her, last night, what he is. She saw the hidden seams in his skin and the bright buttons that hold him together. He showed her the filthy old homeless man who used to sleep on this mattress. The old man continued talking with Davey's high voice, before the boy-form reappeared. He said

Maddy's real mother is trapped inside the being that used to be his mother, the way the old man is trapped inside him. He told Maddy that she used to be trapped, too, but his mother let her go. He asked her what happened with Josey. She struggled to shape the horrors into words.

"Something like dreams," Davey says.

Above them both the traffic whooshes and thumps with increasing frequency, the noises arriving with blurred edges, dying in soft echoes.

The blankets, which she pulled over herself during the night, might once have been blue. They're gray with stains. She shoves them away and surreptitiously inspects her bare arms for signs of bug bites, snorts in relief when she finds none.

"I've been thinking about the things Josey said to you," says Davey. "Maybe she, or whoever that was, thought you were *me*."

A vision of Josey expanding into a hungry spiral of raw flesh and grasping limbs. Maddy looses a single nervous laugh. "That makes no sense. We don't look anything alike. Plus, you know, I'm a girl. And she knew who I was."

"I mean it in a different way. When it told you it was going to use you to find your mother, it meant *my* mother."

Maddy paraphrases Davey's note. "Your mother stole my mother's skin." She should be afraid of him, but he's told her that he can't hurt her, that if he tries to touch her what happened to Josey will happen to him. *When she tried to take you back into the quilt, there was a reaction, I felt it. I think, because my mom cast you out whole, I don't think she meant for this to happen, but now the quilt can't take you back. I can feel that inside me, it's like when magnets repel.* His words would be nonsense except she understands exactly what he means because she'd lived it all. As they walked the deserted night streets toward the underpass, he'd flinch away if her steps happened to bring her close to him. Even if he wasn't looking at her.

Davey goes on, "It's not about how you look. You were part of it once. The thing mom is. The quilt. The layers. The thing I'm part of. I've learned how to hide what I am. Mom made me learn. But I bet you didn't even know that you had anything you needed to hide."

Maddy remembers sitting in the street in the middle of the Vanished Neighborhood, her mind a chaos of slithering flesh, a slender woman standing over her, speaking to her, walking away with all the regal poise of a queen of Hell.

"How do you know, really?" she says. "I remember your mom. You weren't there."

"When my mom made me, she shared her memory of how she made you. I don't think she meant to. She had you on her mind, what she did when she cast you out, what she wanted to do different with me, and I was part of her then, so I saw it all. She's never talked about you, ever. But I never forgot. That I had a sister."

Maddy hugs her knees to her chest. He called her that last night, too: *sister*. "But I'm not one of you. I can't—I can't do that shit you do. I can't kill people."

Davey's gaze wanders. "You killed Josey." He says it like *the sky is blue.*

She wants to shout, *I did not!* She wants to shout, *I didn't mean to!* But what he says is fact, not accusation.

"I tried to warn you not to go with Josey," says Davey. "I tried to leave you a note, because I thought there was time. I should have just told you. I'm sorry."

The burble of the creek provides a soothing counterpoint, a false positive. She doesn't know what to say to his apology, because it means he was watching when Josey approached her. Has been watching her the entire time, using the eyes of other people.

She has endured worse. She has been abducted, turned inside out and unfastened into a thousand pieces, then remade. She's lived among kids who shrank from her and mocked her as if she were the monster. When the monsters were hidden all around her. A wave of darkness sinks through her. "Are there more like Josey?"

"Has to be. Something made her."

Hope springs eternal. "Will your mom . . . will our mom . . . fight them?"

Davey starts shaking. He could be a beetle, trapped on its back, fruitlessly buzzing its wings.

"What?"

"When my mom gets mad at me she puts me in a box that she keeps under her bed. I can't breathe and it hurts so bad. She leaves me in there for days." His gaze meets hers. "She'd do it to you too if she could." The description strikes Maddy as ridiculous. She tamps down an impulse to laugh. He goes on, "We need to get away from here. From Hillcrest. Far away. From my mom. From the others like Josey."

Running away, for real, maybe forever. For the thousandth time Maddy misses the weight of her cellphone in her back pants pocket. "I wanna tell my foster mom I'm okay."

His unnerving eyes don't blink, it's like they move separate from his shuddering body. "I don't have a phone."

"I know, you told me. We can ask someone. Someone will help—"

His lips don't movie, but a grotesque high-pitched whine emanates from him, from many different throats at once, from mouths she can't see. The noise coalesces into a word. *nnnnnnnnNNNOOO*

She wants to yell back at him, but her mind has filled with the mutilated funnel that bloomed from Josey's body. He's shaking his head, speaking in his high voice, his usual voice. "We can't trust anyone. We can't let anyone know where we are."

Different species of fear overrun her fear of what he is. "How are we going to get anywhere without talking to anyone? We can't just walk!" She takes a huge, wheezing breath. "I'm hungry—how are we even going to eat?" She manages to sit on her next question, *Does something like you even eat?* "I want to go home."

He shakes his head harder. His strange eyes grow wider. "You don't understand. That stuff you told me about, that Josey did, that was nothing. Nothing compared to what my mother can do. She's closer now, I can feel that. We have to keep moving. We have to."

She cuts him off. "Okay, okay. So what do we do now?"

The silence stretches. Davey's eyes don't blink. She wishes he'd pretend to be human long enough to set her at ease. Finally he stands. "C'mon."

"Where are we going?"

"Away from *her*."

23

ROCHELLE SHARES A CELL WITH A TINY BLONDE WOMAN who won't stop crying.

Early on, she tried to engage the woman, whose name she still doesn't know, in some kind of conversation, but the little

blonde hissed like a cornered cat, and, Rochelle can't be completely sure, but those syllables sure sounded like a racist epi-
thet. Rochelle might look like a tame ball of fluff, but she damn
well knows she could pound the face on that little minx to ham-
burger without so much as scabbing her knuckles. Her plan to
bring Maddy back has already taken every possible Murphy's
Law-determined twist and she's certain that beating up the
little white girl would make things a thousand times worse, so
she lets it go. Blondie at least keeps to herself, but the constant
sniffling still threatens to drive Rochelle to distraction. That's
not the only thing—an unpleasant antiseptic reek fails to mask
an even more unpleasant stench, like a long unflushed toilet.

No alternatives for conversation. The cell across from them
is empty, as is the cell catty-corner to the left, as best as Rochelle
can tell through the bars and heavy mesh. She and Blondie are
in the cell furthest from the thick pod door—the cells, about
eight in total, are not unlike bathroom stalls, and damn near as
tiny, but divided by cinderblock walls so the front view is the
only view. She can't remember if she saw anyone else besides
Blondie when the deputies marched her in. An occasional mur-
mur has suggested to her that the women's pod might indeed
have other occupants. She lacks the urge to put the notion to
the test. She saves her energy. She told the cops over and over
that she was trying to find her daughter, that her daughter was
missing. They told her to shut up and cooperate and put her in
here. She's going to give them hell, but first she has to get out
from under their power. She remembers all too well the black
woman who died in her cell in Texas, the painfully phony "sui-
cide" cited as the cause. Virginia's not so different from Texas.
She can't lose her head.

When the deputies come to collect Blondie, Rochelle has no
idea of the time. The police took her phone along with the rest
of her possessions and clothes when they booked her. She hasn't
slept a wink, hasn't even dozed, lying on that upper cot mounted
in the wall is like lying on concrete and her mind runs a mile a
minute.

As the deputies put Blondie in shackles, Rochelle stands, expecting the same treatment. "Sit down," says a deputy, a black
woman of a size and height with Rochelle.

"What? Why?"

"You're not being arraigned," snaps the other deputy, a little smaller than her partner, with short, slicked back red hair. "Sit down!"

Rochelle complies. "I want to call a lawyer."

"You used your phone call last night," the redhead says.

"My daughter is missing. What are you doing to find her?"

"You just hold your horses," says her partner. "Relax. We'll come get you when it's time to talk."

"About what?"

The redhead glares. Her partner shakes her head once in warning. "Just wait."

They did let her have that phone call last night after they took her fingerprints and mugshot and made her change into the goddamn orange jail jumpsuit. She called Nadiya, her friend and fellow foster parent, who has a key to her house and always has her back. "What's going on?" Nadiya asked after she accepted the call.

"A terrible, terrible misunderstanding, and I'm going to tear some people a new one when it's all over. But I need your help now, and I need you to promise you won't say anything to social services."

After a long silence, "I promise. Of course."

"Can you take in the kids, just for tonight? Maddy's gone out, and I can't find her. Ashley's watching the young ones and I don't trust her to mind them a full night by herself."

Nadiya was well familiar with Ashley's attitude. "You got it. And you take care of yourself."

Nadiya's tone left a dozen questions unasked, but she wasn't going to push for answers yet, for which Rochelle was eternally grateful. "I'll call again tomorrow, as soon as they'll let me."

And they still haven't allowed it. Blondie doesn't come back, and neither do the deputies. Rochelle closes her eyes and concentrates on the sound and sensation of her own breathing, hoping maybe if she blanks her mind sleep will find her, help her fast forward to the end of the nightmare.

No such luck.

* * *

24

AARON CAN'T IMAGINE EVEN TRYING TO GET SHUT-EYE, not with Hairston in the passenger seat. If he didn't know better, he'd swear a static energy sloughs off the old man, one that agitates the soul instead of the skin.

He craves a nap, though. He took the exit to Hillcrest at 5 a.m. and for the next two hours turned his Buick down one random street after another on Hairston's demand. His passenger wasn't following a map, didn't even bring one. *Turn here. Left, left. Now right.* If they ended up in a cul-de-sac, *Back out, try again, this is the right way.* At one point Aaron made the mistake of asking whether Hairston could tell him the name of the bar they were looking for. *You think if I knew that we'd be doing this?* he snarled back.

They crossed a bridge over railroad tracks and rolled through the middle of a modest-sized downtown with the morning sun in their eyes. *Stop!* Hairston hollered. Aaron stopped the brakes midstreet, the Buick frozen with a bus station on one side and a row of darkened boutiques on the other. Seconds passed. Hairston's bushy white brows lowered, glaring at one of the shops. Aaron kept checking the rear view mirror, amazed no cars had pulled up behind him to honk their horns. Finally Hairston said, *Not here, keep going.* A slender Latina woman in blue-hued business attire rounded a corner from a side street, heels clicking toward the bus station bay, as Aaron stomped the gas.

Strange to see a woman so dolled up on a street where nothing's open, Aaron thought, but he kept the thought to himself.

At last, as they trundled along a three-lane road, left and right and center turn lane, Hairston pointed at a low brown and tan building and said, *This is it. This is where it happens. Park!*

They're in a corner of the front parking lot. Aaron can't stop yawning. The damnable scars on his cheeks itch. When he pops the driver's side door to get out and stretch his legs, Hairston says nothing.

Called Hillcrest Inn, the establishment definitely ain't no inn. He can see pool tables and a U-shaped bar through the plate glass, one panel of which sports a sloppily patched crack. He goes back to the Buick, cracks open the door. "It doesn't open until noon."

"We're gonna wait then."

Better not to argue. Probably fine. Traffic whooshes by, no one seems to pay them any particular notice. Maybe during those hours he could sweet-talk Hairston into sharing more about his decades before and after he came to Grandy Springs, maybe even get him talking about Korea. But Aaron's head feels like any available space in his skull has been stuffed with wire mesh. He'll have to latch his eyelids open with hooks to keep from nodding off while Hairston speaks, unless he gets some coffee in his system or *something*. There's a fast food restaurant open across the street about a hundred yards in what's likely south, judging by the position of the sun. "I'm hungry," he says. "I'll get some breakfast for us. What do you want?"

Hairston rolls his eyes, sighs, settles back in his seat. "You eat a big breakfast, you're gonna regret it later. Your world gets turned over, it'll turn your stomach too."

Aaron chooses to ignore that advice, to his later regret.

25

THE MAN SETTLING ON THE SIDEWALK OUTSIDE the bus depot has broad shoulders and deep brown skin, wisps of white hair that leave his scalp bald, uneven stubble muting his cheeks and chin. He fidgets as he stares at the boutique across the street. The air is cool but sweat beads his forehead.

It's only a Wednesday, but pedestrians still flow thick on both sides of a street sluggish with lunch hour traffic.

A tiny, wasp-waisted woman in a pantsuit stops by the home-less man's feet and gasps, one hand covering her mouth, reducing her face to wide, mascara-ringed eyes. Though her fingers she says, "Oh my god, what's wrong with you?"

The center cannot hold. The features of the man's face won't stay still. Small green eyes, then blue, then deep brown. A luscious, freckled mouth beneath a ginger mustache, then bigger, darker lips surrounded by even darker skin. In fact every bit of exposed skin has devolved into patchwork, no two squares shaded alike.

"I dunno, ma'am," the man says. "Do you believe in Jesus?"

He stretches and folds, and where he sat, a woman rises. For an instant she holds a single shape, a slender Latina, large dark eyes narrowed in a venomous stare. When she reaches her full height she continues to stretch, for an instant returned to the scruffy homeless man, looming over the teeny, gape-mouthed passerby. "Answer me, ma'am."

The little woman tucks her head and runs, her sensible flats pitching off her feet. The man stops in the act of reaching for her, arrested by the sight of his hands. Seams divide the fingers, the palms. A seam in his left hand parts, revealing smooth pale skin underneath.

Five more onlookers, stalled in their progress, hover within reach of the homeless man's right arm. A white man in a gray suit and salt-and-pepper crew cut, physique thick in every dimension. A short, skinny couple, him with a goatee, paused in the pushing of a baby carriage, her with short straight hair, staring over sunglasses. A teen girl with a denim jacket over a half-shirt that exposes a midriff still plump with baby fat.

The mesmerizing prospect of the unraveling man before them, and the false security of the herd, prevents them from bolting like the tiny woman did, reduces them to rubberneckers.

He turns to them as if he were a street preacher and they had all gathered to listen. The rasping voice doesn't come from the mouth on his face, but one that has opened in his throat. "I need ten cents so I can get a beer. Just ten damn cents. Why in hell can't you people just give me ten goddamn cents? Don't lie to me and tell me you don't have change!"

At the same time another voice speaks, like there's a second mouth hidden inside the first, hooked up to independent vocal chords. A woman's voice. "I wasn't a bad person. I sinned but I was never cruel. I never wanted to tear anyone to pieces. I just need to live."

A large hairy arm springs from that dual mouth like a chameleon's tongue, grabs the man with the crew cut by the sag of fat at the front of his neck.

The knot of onlookers flies apart, screaming. A second arm erupts from under the swelling figure's shirt, stuffs its fifteen-fingered hand down the pants of the crew-cut man's suit. The block of his square head slumps squishy like an emptying sand bag. His mouth opens.

"Let's go shopping," says a woman's voice from somewhere deep in his guts. Two huge figures tangled together and slowly fusing into one, they waltz into the street.

A car screeches short and honks its horn, the blare joined an instant later by the scream of the driver, a two-part disharmony in reaction to the protean thing spinning past the bumper in grotesque do-si-do.

By the time the avant-garde duo fully cross the street they resemble a single person with an arm too many. This extra arm pulls open the boutique door.

The sales clerk approaches, smiling, not noticing at first how the figure's face is struggling to assume a final shape, how its empty eyes are windows into a fluttering void. As dark eyes rise up to fill the holes, the clerk's smile falters, but not completely, her mind unable to fully process what she's witnessing.

"I need to get to the second floor." The figure speaks in several voices at once. "I know there's a way. I can feel it."

In the back office, manager Kristy watches a lesbian porn video on her monitor. Her hunched shoulders straighten with a jolt as a wail pierces through the office door from the sales floor, cut off abrupt as a customer hang-up.

Kristy rushes to the door and locks it, backtracks to the landline on her desk, the video still playing in the background, flesh on flesh in soft focus. She grabs the receiver without looking and drops it, all her focus on the wide, white, leathery ribbon sliding in from under the door, crossing the tasteful blue rug like a haunted snakeskin. It thickens like a hose filling with water.

The small of her back against the front of her desk, she kicks at the ribbon and it coils around her ankle, tearing open her hose to grope around and up her leg, a warm, fleshy, supple tube. Her face contorts in a soundless shriek. More ribbons are invading through the gap under the door, a half dozen, two dozen, scores. In seconds the office fills to the ceiling. Crushed beneath an avalanche of skin, Kristy's lungs burn, the sensation of suffocation unceasing even as her limbs and head detach. The flip of the switch under the desk that trips the silent alarm happens by sheer accident.

* * *

26

CUNETTA PARKS THE CRUISER BY THE CURB where First Street crosses Hartwell Avenue, with the front of the Gypsy Flair boutique visible at his ten o'clock. Foley, his partner, gets out on the passenger side. Cunetta scans for citizens that might need to be cleared from the scene, but the sidewalk around Gypsy Flair is strangely free of pedestrians.

As Cunetta steps out, another cruiser rolls past on Hartwell, lights and siren off, heading to the other end of the block. The day smells of asphalt and spiced meat from the Venezuelan restaurant two doors down. A trio of cars trundle by on First in the other lane, apparently oblivious to Cunetta standing there. Typical.

At the intersection of Hartwell and Second, the other cruiser makes an impressively tight mid-street U-turn, pulls up beside a fire hydrant near the bus station bay. Spillman, the driver, gets out first, followed by Diego, an Odd Couple team if there ever was one, Spillman is pale and lanky and there's a droop to his shoulders and his eyelids, Diego is squat and built like a barrel, her hair pulled back in a ponytail that looks severe enough to stretch her scalp. Stand them together, Diego barely comes up to Spillman's chest.

Right now another cruiser should be parking a block south at Second and Santoro, where the officers could access the back of the store. The whole lot of them are about to converge on Gypsy Flair, guns holstered until they get a view inside the store.

Foley crosses the intersection, hand floating near his Glock, so close as to make the possibilities on his mind way too damn obvious. Cunetta makes a mental note to correct his junior partner after they assess the threat.

Cunetta's radio hisses—Tripp and Gearhardt checking in, already positioned at the shop's back entrance, awaiting further word.

Dispatch received an automated message minutes before, robbery in progress, no follow up call to cancel from a live human being. For all they know, an accountant bumped a switch under a desk with her knee. The security companies that sell these systems swear they're klutz proof, but mistakes happen. Sometimes

the causes aren't even human error. A loose wire and a rain leak
or even a sharp change in temperature can do the trick. Unlikely,
as this spring day there's no rain and a breeze adds just the right
seasoning to the early afternoon warmth.

Diego and Spillman cross to the boutique, Diego making up
for her short stature and Spillman's beanpole height by taking ex-
tra-quick steps that remind Cunetta of a tiny dog's bouncy trot.

The pincer of brown uniforms closes as the four of them stand
before the glass store front. No orange card posted in the glass
door warns them of a false alarm. Inside, the brightly lit sales floor
offers an assortment of tastefully eccentric and colorful dresses.
No sign of any people.

Cunetta puts his hand on the grip of his gun and pushes open
the door. "POLICE!" No one answers. He draws his Glock, and
the others follow suit as they file in behind, Diego last, muttering
into her radio, letting Tripp and Gearhardt and Dispatch know
what they've seen so far.

None of the officers shudder at the chill that gives Cunetta
goosebumps. It's not cold inside the store, not a physical chill. Of
all the times to remember the Boneyard, this might be the worst.
He'd returned to that courtyard once in broad daylight, and what
he felt then—as he eyed the crude stick figure graffiti, the odd
shadows where nothing obvious stood to cast them, the rotten
slum facades that surrounded the courtyard like multi-floor mau-
soleums, the busted out windows dark as gullets, the sensation of
a presence close-by, unseen, predatory—he feels it now.

They spread out in a quick sweep, finding no one hiding under
racks or in the changing booths. No blood stains the carpets. Behind the checkout counter the door to the back room stands ajar.
Through they go.

The next door on the left, behind which presumably lies the
office where the safe is kept, turns out to be locked. The larger
room beyond is divided by shelf racks stacked in surprisingly slap-
dash fashion with the long, flat boxes that hold clothes. Plenty of
good hiding places there. Before Cunetta can say anything, Spillman takes point, advancing into the inventory room with Diego
shuffling behind him.

A band of light shines from under the locked office door.
Knocking and shouting produces no reaction. The door's ancient

wood is flimsy enough that it bows under Cunetta's fist. Giving thanks that the landlords haven't seen fit to renovate in the decades since the first floor of this building was converted to commercial use, he plants his left foot and kicks hard beside the lock with his right. A hole splinters wide open. Beyond, the office is empty.

Foley, bushy eyebrows raised in bewilderment, voices Cunetta's thought. "Where the hell did they all go?"

"Come look at this," shouts Spillman, his voice way too deep for his reed-thin frame.

Cunetta nods to Foley. "Let Gearhardt and Tripp in, I'll see what he found." Foley, bless him, doesn't balk at being bossed around.

An aisle between two tall shelf racks ends in a shattered mess, chunks of plaster heaped on the cement floor. A big gap torn through the drywall reveals the frame of an old door not unlike the one Cunetta just put his foot through. Sealed inside the wall for decades, this door's been torn from its hinges, the raw daggers of its shattered boards strewn against the left-hand rack.

In the cavity made by this forcefully excavated exit, Cunetta spies the bottom step of a narrow stairwell going up. It's been hidden within the wall all this time, then, a relic of the days when the vacant upper stories were used for a theater and the town's black citizens had to take a separate staircase up to the balcony.

The stairwell, barely wide enough to accommodate one body, ascends leftward and up, into darkness.

Spillman opens his mouth, but Cunetta raises a finger to hush him. A chorus of female voices carries down from above, no words distinct enough to decipher.

27

TWO WOMEN FACE EACH OTHER, one sitting, one standing. Between them lies a wooden box large enough to fit a man inside. The box has no lid. A soft hiss like shifting gravel rises from its depths.

No light reaches them. Neither woman has need of light to see.

The seated woman, Maude, leans forward on the folding chair that serves her as throne. "Took you long enough, sweet thing."

Maria twitches. Her body maintains an approximation of her usual shape, but all of her features, eyes, lips, hair, skin, are shifting from second to second, her countenance just shy of a blur. It takes effort to speak but she manages. "You're the one Lenahan made."

"Them things you stole from the box, they're dying," Maude says. "The ones left with me, they want their kin back with every ounce of will they have. You've been feeling that for weeks, honey. I know it."

Maria speaks with several mouths simultaneously, the sentences overlapping. "I didn't steal anything. *I know what you were trying to do.* That shit happened on your sorry watch. *You brought the box to the city as bait.* I joined the quilt and the quilt loves me. *To draw me out.* The layers love me. *And you blocked my way back.* The buttons you lost are mine now. *So you could starve me out, keep me from the box, till I got weak.* And these will be too. *Till I was easy pickings.* And *you'll* be *nothing.* Finders *keepers—*"

"Losers weepers," Maude finishes. "You know who my master was, you've got him inside you. He was a *fool*, thought he was a *god*, started to play with his food instead of eating it. The kid that undid him was even worse. But you're the biggest fool of all, if you ever thought you were in control of anything."

Maria's flesh flaps with constant motion, her frame swaying forward, tugged toward the large bin with its strange carvings by the gravity of like siren-calling to like. The buttons in the bin surge toward her, surge again, fall.

All Maria's mouths vocalize in unison. "What you say doesn't matter. All this time you've kept watch over the bin, but I'm still so much stronger than you, little pet." Her body expands, sheets of skin unfurling behind her like a thousand capes. The buttons in the bin froth at the lip of the box, hungry children beating at the rail of their playpen.

Maude stands, her chair toppling behind her like a man shot. "I've never tried to fight what I really am." She steps into the box. The living buttons surge up her body like fleas.

Maria's form fountains upward in a geyser of flesh that comes hammering down.

* * *

28

THE STAIRWAY HIDDEN IN THE WALL IS SO NARROW the officers can only ascend one at a time. Tripp is first up, illuminating the way with the flashlight mounted on his Glock. Barrel-chested Gearhardt goes next, and he has to take the stairs in a sideways shuffle to avoid getting stuck. Cunetta goes after him, Diego at his back breathing fast and too loud.

The sounds above make little sense. Dozens of soft things dragged across a gritty floor. The grating of something heavy and wooden. Hands slapping on concrete.

The stairwell stretches higher than seems reasonable, perhaps further proof of its original purpose, that it leads to a balcony that no longer exists.

Tripp turns his head and his light to the right to peer through an opening hardly more than six feet tall and two feet wide, its edges cracked ragged. Whatever smashed its way into the stairwell smashed its way out, too. Cunetta unconsciously holds his breath, his every instinct expecting Tripp to die right at this moment, his flashlight making him a perfect target. Even if he weren't poking his head out the hole, that wall won't shield him from bullets.

The slapping sounds stop.

Tripp squeezes through, shuffles off to one side. Gearhardt goes through next, breaking more drywall loose as he forces his wide torso through the gap.

His mishap makes Cunetta's exit easier. Pieces of the shattered wall crunch under his shoes. Moving in a crouch, Cunetta hurries forward into an immense, vacant space. The size of the chamber startles him, though he's been vaguely aware for years that a gutted theater filled the building's upper floors, sealed off from the first floor shops as a building code compromise that saved the landlords from an expensive renovation. It's an odd fact for him to retain about his adopted city, as he's never been to a play in his adult life.

Diego, Foley and Spillman clamber in behind him. Cunetta clicks on his own Glock-mounted flashlight. The others do the same.

Their accumulated beams sweep across a wide curtain drawn across a low stage at the far end of the enormous room. The curtain ripples, motions that can't possibly be caused by air current. At Cunetta's two o'clock, the edge of the curtain twitches, as if something pushed at it from behind.

Foley sees it at the same time and starts toward it at speed. In a split second, Cunetta weighs what to do, whether to bellow *POLICE! FREEZE!* before Foley reaches the curtain, decides to let Foley make that call—even as he reflexively raises a hand, wanting to warn Foley to stop, no need to be so eager, but his partner, focused on the target, doesn't notice the gesture.

Foley reaches the curtain, pulls back the edge. He neither shouts nor speaks. His flashlight goes out.

"Foley! Foley! What's going on?" Cunetta aims his own light at the spot where his partner ducked behind the curtain, finds no sign Foley was ever there. The other four officers shine their lights on the same spot. The texture of the curtain is like no cloth Cunetta's ever seen, dun and leathery, divided into squares of different shades, fastened together with an astonishing variety of buttons. As big as the curtain is, there must be thousands of them.

"FOLEY!"

The remaining officers all shout at once, waving their flashlights and guns.

All along the curtain's width and height, small slits open to expose glistening orbs. Cunetta instantly assumes that the mix of darkness, uneven illumination and adrenaline has concocted a mirage, because it's not at all rational to accept that constellations of eyes have opened all over the buttoned-together squares of leathery fabric.

A flash of memory disrupts Cunetta's focus, a nightmare that plagued him back in Grandy Springs, when he was still married. Waking up in the middle of the night to find the bedroom crowded with tar-black, eyeless forms, human in shape but in no other way, more than a dozen standing shoulder to shoulder around the bed as he stared bug-eyed and tongue-tied and his wife slept on oblivious. A hand would reach toward his face, and he'd wake up again, wife still oblivious, the room empty. In the months before divorce, he came to resent her freedom from this nightmare most of all.

In a moment the nightmare will end. He cannot accept that he's awake, even though he knows better than all the other cops

in the Hillcrest P.D. that the world can contain horrors that beg-
gar even the most overactive imagination. It doesn't stop with
the glistening shadow creatures he left behind in the Boneyard.
It doesn't begin with Hulk's missing hand. He came to Hillcrest
long enough ago that the city's own tale of mystery and horror
still bled fresh: the houses left empty in the Vanished Neighborhood, that little girl left behind in the street, repeating delusional claims like a living corpse reading a live report from Hell, *I
was nothing but skin just like my mom and dad but I could still
scream.*

Did she scream like barrel-chested Gearhardt, who fires his
Glock as he topples to the floor?

At the same time, at Cunetta's four o'clock, Diego opens fire
at the violently billowing curtain, the pops from her Glock weirdly
muffled, like firecrackers exploding under a smothering mattress.
Cunetta swings the beam of his flashlight across the chamber as it
floods with nonsensical shapes. He finds Spillman, whose beanpole frame is absurdly truncated, sunk from the waist down into
an undulating, leathery carpet animated like the surface of a windblown lake.

Needles prick Cunetta's legs and they go numb from the knees
down.

A glance at his feet reveals clusters of eyes looking back at him.
Cunetta gasps, the sound rising to a rough howl as he registers his
legs are submerged up to mid-thigh in the field of stares. Ornate
motes leap up his body like fleas made of jewelry as a sensation of
nerves deadening bores up past his hips and through the core of
his Kevlar-clad belly.

A hole opens in the floor at his one o'clock. It's Gearhardt's
mouth, stretching into a soundless scream, the sum of his features
unmistakable for a second longer, until his eyes float away to join the
thousands of others that stud this still-expanding blanket of flesh.

A hand flaps in his peripheral vision and it's Tripp at his nine
o'clock, submerged chest deep in the chaos that has engulfed them all.
As their gazes meet Tripp comes apart, his arms flowing away from
his shoulders, his head stretching and flattening into the curtain.

Spillman too is chest deep in the monster, Diego is neck deep,
her teeth bared in a petrified rictus. A switch flips inside Cunetta
and he accepts that he will never wake up. He squeezes the trigger

of his Glock and blood and brains blow out the back of Diego's head. Spillman gargles as Cunetta's next shot goes through his throat, but the next gets him right in the eye and his head snaps back, mouth open as if he's trying to catch a snowflake.

The living carpet doesn't absorb Diego's head, it tumbles free across the swells of flesh. As Cunetta's chest goes numb, he burns the roof of his mouth with the friction-hot end of the Glock's barrel and feeds himself metal and fire.

29

GEARHARDT'S VOICE CRACKLES in Dispatcher Jeppsen's headset. "That's right, Dispatch, all our radios went out at the same time, I can't explain why. Cunetta, Diego and Spillman still can't get theirs to work."

"Can you put Cunetta on?" Something about this declaration of all clear is giving Jeppsen the willies. Six officers having trouble with their radios all at once. In terms of unlikely coincidences, this one brings down a giant hammer and rings Jeppsen's bullshit bell hard. Gearhardt's solid, so far as she knows, unlikely to screw up protocols, but Cunetta's the senior officer on the scene.

"Negative, he's still in the store talking with the manager, Dispatch. They're trying to work out why the alarm went off."

Jeppsen glances over at her supervisor, Haysome, seated at the bank of computer monitors to her left. He's sipping from a coffee mug that reads ADORABLE BADASS. He sets down the mug, proffers Jeppsen a puzzled frown.

"No one with a working radio went with him?" Jeppsen asks.

The next voice she hears is that of Tripp, Gearhardt's partner. "Beverly, honey, everything is fine. But we figure we'd better come back to the station and switch out our faulty radios till shift's over. That sound alright to you?"

Haysome grabs his own headset. "Officer Tripp, that's way out of line. You're gonna be explaining yourself to the Chief."

Jeppsen clams up out of sheer shock, cheeks flushing deep red. She and Tripp went to high school together. He was a slender, well-toned athlete, she was a plump girl with a crush, he knew it and took advantage of her, calling her his "home base" when he was between girlfriends. He's never spoken to her this way since she started work in the dispatch center, never acted as if they had any history, always professional smiles with no attempt to engage deeper, and that has always been more than fine with her.

She wants to spew rage and profanity over the channel at him. Even though he provoked it, she'd be fired on the spot.

Gearhardt comes back on as if his partner never spoke. "We'll be there in ten to exchange our radios. Dispatch, can you confirm whether Rochelle Turner is still in custody?"

Jeppsen, still furious, exchanges glances with her supervisor, whose gray eyebrows have lowered in a puzzled frown. Word of Turner's arrest got around the department. The foster mother of Madeleine Bowes, a.k.a. the girl found at the Vanished Neighborhood. Caught trying to break into a house in north Hillcrest, where all the old money lives in hilltop mansions. Swearing up and down her Maddy was missing, charged at the scene with resisting arrest. The chief didn't want to give her a chance to post bail, not just yet. Whether or not the Bowes girl was really missing, who knew, not uncommon for foster kids to run away—but the Petrasek family was definitely M.I.A.

"10-4," says Haysome. "Why do you want to know? Is there a connection to the call you're on?"

"I'll talk to you about it when we're 10-25."

Jeppsen vows, no matter what Haysome might think, that she has every right to let Tripp have it once he returns to the station and she's going to do so, she's not going to let him get away with belittling her this way.

Fifteen minutes later, through the glass paneling of the dispatch center, she spies Gearhardt walking up. He's alone.

When Gearhardt leaves, heading for the chief's office, then the jail, the dispatch center is empty.

30

Andrew steps down from his dad's Ford Focus into the parking lot of a bar he's never visited before, Hillcrest Inn on Shenandoah Valley Road. He gets to drive his dad's SUV because his parents can't object anymore in the place where they now exist.

Not that he's in a state to gloat. He hasn't slept for many days. He can't control where he goes, his legs are not his own and the remainder of his nervous system can be hijacked to any degree at any time. His swollen innards grate with a sharp ache, as if one wrong step will cause him to split from tailbone to crotch and spill his intestines down the insides of his jeans.

He's made several trips like this one, goaded by the gift Josey left him, going where the parasitic urges direct him. The things inside him hunger for recruits. His panic helped the first one escape, that sad looking addict that tried to grope him. The parasitic layers punished him for letting the creep get away. Since then, he hasn't fought their desires. He won't fight them this time either.

A squadron of motorcycles leans in majestic formation, filling the parking spots closest to the front door. Andrew lurches inside, the tinted glass muffling the afternoon sun as the door shuts behind him,

There's a small crowd in leather vests, half bellied up to the U-shaped bar, scattered among the stools, reminding Andrew of a lower jaw with teeth missing. The other half of the biker bunch surrounds one of the pool tables. Just days ago Andrew would have been scared to walk among these people, with their wiry arms and tattoos and glances that assess and contemptuously dismiss a soft, indulged rich boy. But that's not what he is now.

Beyond that table, at a booth underneath a window, an old black man looks up with a sharp snap of shaggy head to eyeball Andrew. The old man's white mane frames a face carved from basalt.

Andrew lurches, his gait entirely without grace, practically stumbling in the direction of the pool table. Layers shift in his overloaded, overheated belly. A picture coalesces in his head, of a broad-shouldered, denim-jacketed giant of a fellow with cigarette in mouth, salt-and-pepper hair, pool cue in hand. A man that one of the parasites hopes to find. The eyes in his head don't spy such a person anywhere inside the Hillcrest Inn; neither do the eyes elsewhere on his body.

The black man barks an order. "Aaron, get over here!"

His command appears to be aimed at a short fellow who manages to be handsome despite a head that's a bit too big for his body. Said fellow, Aaron, leaning on the bar, waiting to get the bartender's attention, half-turns toward the shout, startled. "You said you didn't want anything—"

Clearly the wrong response. "You stupid jackass, get over here, now!"

A couple of the bikers at the pool table chuckle at the drama. One mutters under his breath, loud enough for Andrew to hear, "Massa says you better move, bitch."

Aaron follows the black man's gaze to regard Andrew, and his square-jawed, oddly-scarred features contort, first in crumple-browed puzzlement, then alarm, lips parting, eyes widening. The black man, too, stares at Andrew, upper lip curled in repulsion.

Whoever these men are, the hunger in Andrew doesn't hunger for them. But it will devour them nonetheless.

A couple more steps bring him right up to the men and women clustered at the pool table. A fellow with a trucker's cap, Wolverine sideburns and bare arms knotted with muscle straightens up and moves to obstruct his path. "Boy, you need something?"

What will be will be, but the part of Andrew that's a helpless passenger gasps at an unexpected distraction. Andrew isn't sure how the black man's name, John Hairston, has come to be in his mind, or how he can hear Hairston speak without the man's mouth moving. *I see what kind of thing you are. You're a hole full of corpses. A hole that needs to be closed.*

The man in the trucking cap squints and frowns, caught between different strains of concern. "Do you need help? Or do you need me to help you out the door?" His entire party watching now, five men and three women of varying ages, all hard-bitten, white-skinned, stained by cigarette smoke and dried out with the premature aging brought on by harsh living.

The part of Andrew that experiences fear must still have some input over the rest of his body because the skin he can feel slicks with sweat. His face flushes hot. The pain threatening to split his crotch fades as he grows numb below the belt, and he knows what that means, but this intensifying warmth, that's new.

"Y'all get out of here," Hairston shouts, his voice sounding in the room and Andrew's head at the same time.

Trucker man twists his neck in the black man's direction with vehement indignation, way more than he's demonstrated to Andrew. One of his fellows yells, "What the hell's your problem, y'old freak?"

Warmer and warmer.

Aaron reaches Hairston's table. Hairston whispers something, but Andrew hears it somehow, the link straight into his mind still live. "If we live through this, you're gonna be a believer again. Get that window open."

Aaron does a startled double take. Trucking cap puts a hand on Andrew's shoulder. "Boy, you need to answer."

Andrew groans as openings full of teeth appear all down the lower half of his body, muffled under his jeans and flannel shirt.

"Quit starin' and get the window open," says Hairston to Aaron.

Trucker hat is staring at the hand he placed on Andrew's shoulder, as ornate buttons swarm over it, etching seams up his forearm. He's almost certainly discovered he can't take his hand away, if he's even trying. He may not be, as other parts of Andrew have already reached out to touch him. A bridge of flesh has sprouted from under Andrew's shirt and stuffed its tendril down the front of trucker hat's pants, and more bright button motes are crossing the bridge.

Warmer and warmer.

A woman on the other side of the pool table picks up that there's something funny about trucker hat's stance. "Pete, what's wrong? Let that kid go."

The worst part of the condition Josey inflicted on him: that he's fully aware, independent of the things using his body to work mischief. The layers are filling Pete even as his friend tries to get his attention. Andrew wants to scream, because there's more sensation than just the expansion of the quilt folds. Heat sparks and spikes as if dozens of matches are striking inside him, somewhere an impossible distance away and at the same time immediately assaulting his nerves.

"What the fuck—?" says the burly giant to Pete's right. Perhaps he's noticed the way Pete shudders as the motes crawl up his neck, invading his stubble, scaling his face.

Long flaps of loose skin curl out from under Andrew's shirt. The bubbling fabric of his jeans splits open, unleashing twists of flesh that inflate into gape-mouth faces and grasping hands. One of the women screams, and Andrew screams with her.

The young man at the back table, Aaron, screams something too, and Andrew doesn't hear that clearly, but he catches Hairston's response, still carbon copied straight to his brain. "Break the glass, genius . . . shit, get down!"

The burly giant pulls a pistol, a beat behind two of his compatriots at the bar. Membranes of skin billow like windblown curtains from Andrew's waist, arms sprouting from them like branches time lapsing on fast forward. His torso remains intact atop the fleshy chaos, a buoy bobbing atop a geyser of body parts. He raises his hands in a futile warning, his arms drenched in sweat as an oven's heat bakes him from the inside.

The bullets that pass through his lungs and belly and neck also burn, steel-hard punches with a red-hot poker that would flatten him if he weren't attached by flesh and bone to a monster. As much as they hurt, as much as he wishes they would kill him, they have no lasting effect.

A tide of convulsing flesh pours out from the nether spaces where the layers reside, spilling over the pool table, upending and smashing chairs before avalanching over the bar. This isn't how this usually goes, usually the layers urge Andrew to isolate a new recruit before they consume him. The forces he's enslaved to are as panicked as he is. The gang around the pool table succumbs in an instant to the bloodless dismemberment enabled by the glimmering buttons, heads still shrieking as they detach and flatten, the sounds muffled only when mouths submerge into the layers. One bottle-blonde woman escapes their fate as friendly fire blows blood and brains out the back of her head.

No such mercy for Andrew. Hot impacts shred his neck and his view of the chaos in the room flips as his head ends up dangling upside down from the strip of his neck that remains, but he doesn't bleed and he doesn't die.

The bar patrons, the staff, don't stand a chance, but as their screams subside, more rise from the captives trapped in the layers. They share their agony with Andrew. His insides are being cooked, layer after layer of living skin pressed against a hot burner. "Stop!" he yells, though he can't draw air to project his voice. "Stop!"

The mass of gasping mouths, bulging eyes, flailing limbs that fills the Hillcrest Inn blackens and smolders in a thousand places. Some of those parts are newly part of the quilt, taken from those unlucky enough to be in the bar when Andrew staggered in, equally subject to the encroaching fire.

His head happens to flop in the right direction and he can see how the extensions of his possessed self that flow too near Aaron and Hairston erupt in blistering embers and immediately shrink back.

The window Aaron has been charged with opening was painted shut long ago, but he swings a chair at the glass, again, again, and this time it shatters. Hairston stares straight at Andrew, his voice carrying again without his mouth moving. "I'm a gateway too, motherfucker."

Andrew experiences a moment of eureka: he's up against someone who also contains the inexplicable within, a different inexplicable from the monstrous thing that operates through him.

Molten lead flows between the infinite spaces where his intestines should have been. His world is an agony he can't escape.

Andrew's mouth opens wide in a soundless scream, his almost-detached head still hardwired into miles and miles of shrieking nerves.

Hairston's voice in Andrew's ear. "Nothing I can do to save you. Any of you. But I can end it. Fire purges everything."

31

THE HOURS STRETCH TO DAYS, IT SEEMS, as Rochelle waits for deliverance. When it comes, its approach gives her no comfort. For one, it's not a pair of female deputies who arrive to escort her from her cell, but a lone male police officer. The silver name tag on his blue uniform reads B.R. GEARHARDT. He's big, his protective vest makes him look like a walking oil drum with a buzz-cut block of a head mounted on top.

As he regards her through the mesh, Rochelle tries not to betray how her heart's in her mouth. "Have you found my daughter?"

"She's not your daughter." Gearhardt has a voice like a bull moose. "You're her foster mother."

"She might as well be my daughter." Rochelle fights to keep her voice from rising in pitch and volume. "Have you done anything to find her? Anything at all?"

"We're looking for her now," he says. "I had to pull some strings and hook some buttons in the right buttonholes, but we're ready to help. There's an officer headed to your house right now, in case she came back home while you were away. Too bad you didn't stay put and call us in the first place."

Rochelle doesn't even want to admit to herself that she took matters into her own hands because she didn't want word getting out that she'd lost track of one of her fosters. Maybe it's too late to salvage things now. But maybe not.

"I didn't call the police because I didn't think I needed the police. Last I saw Maddy she got into a car with Josey Petrasek's mother. I went over there because no one was answering the phone. I just thought they might not be paying attention. That's a big house, you know, maybe they were just in another room. But they weren't there at all. Have you found them?"

"We haven't found Maddy."

"Are you gonna let me out?"

His face might as well be carved from wood. "Maybe. If you can answer a few questions." Yet he's fitting a key in the square of metal that contains the lock, sliding the door aside. "Be nice and we'll discuss that option."

Rochelle backs up to the cots, mounted one above the other in the wall. "Where are we going?"

"Nowhere," Gearhardt says. He squeezes through the entrance sideways. He's wide enough that there's no way around him. "At least not for now."

"What questions?" Rochelle contemplates whether screaming will bring help or get her killed. "I'll answer all the questions you've got, just ask away."

There's something wrong with Gearhardt's face. He's not sweating, he's not smiling or grimacing, but seams have appeared around his eyes and mouth and across his broad, blunt forehead that weren't there before. And glimmering beads. Of different colors, lined up along the seams. "Lord have mercy," Rochelle says.

The cop's head lowers and his mouth opens in a wide, hangjawed grin, the kind you see on a psycho killer in a movie. But what's revealed behind his parted lips is not teeth and tongue but another mouth, like he's a costume and someone inside is wearing him.

Rochelle screams loud and long but she already understands there's no help coming.

The thing wearing Gearhardt widens its eyes and stretches its mouth in mockery and it lurches forward, advancing past the sink and toilet. Then it falters backward. Its upper and lower lips split vertically and the mouth behind them curls up in a grimace and shrieks as a tongue of bright flame curls out.

Rochelle scrambles backward onto the lower cot and against the wall.

Her brain breaks completely. First the Gearhardt thing is un-coiling like every part of it is a living, slithering roll of skin un-winding, the single shriek it emits multiplying into a thousand. The next second, a fireball floods the cell. The next second, noth-ing, no smoke, no flames, no cop or monster pretending to be a cop.

The smell of burned hair overwhelms. Her hands, her fore-arms, reflexively drawn up to shield her face, are terrifyingly red and raw and blistered. The sheets of the cot smolder.

The cell door remains open. Rochelle makes a run for it, ignoring the cries from her nerve endings as her body starts to register the damage from the freak blast. "Help!" she rasps. "Anyone?"

The jail pod gate also stands open. No one responds to her calls.

32

THE POLICE CRUISER VEERS OFF THE ROAD, three blocks shy of Mama Rochelle's house, and rolls down the sloping front yard of Becca's home. It crosses the cobblestone front walk that leads visitors to the porch, rolls right over the tidy garden, crushing bushes and flowers, and smashes through the wall.

Becca's father is asleep when the cruiser lands on top of him. He works third shift in a plastics factory, sweeping his arm through a dangerous hot press to pluck parts for medical equipment out of molds. He resigned himself long ago to the risk of dismember-ment from the elbow down for the sake of steady income. The possibility of being pinned under a running car engine has never even crossed his mind.

The cruiser smashes through the window over his bed and drops in at angle, tilting the bed so his head bounces off the transmission before the bumper crushes his thighs into the mattress, his hips pressed up against the underside of the radiator, the oil pan pressing his gut up into his diaphragm.

Becca sits on the living room coach watching Netflix cartoons when the shattering of glass and the crunch of splintered wood and smashed drywall interrupts. She freezes until her father's wheezing screams begin. More screams follow, a chorus loud as thunder—it sounds like a thousand people are howling their last in her parents' bedroom.

She throws the door open to find a bashed up police car where her parents' bed should be.

A nightmare fills the car's cab, a writhing morass of loose skin, glistening muscle, flailing limbs, rotating faster and faster around an impossible opening, a cyclone shaft that drains into nowhere. It's like one of Maddy's creepy sketches roaring into violent life. The screams of multitudes pour out from this narrowing funnel, and elongated flames lick from its walls. A stench assaults Becca, smoke and a grotesque swell of burning meat. As she gags, her eyes play a bewildering trick—motes like white embers shine out within the whirling flesh and fire, and then those motes hurtle into the depths of the contracting tunnel like a hyperspace special effect.

Spinning flesh, agonized shrieks, sickening smell all vanish, leaving behind the car's rumbling engine and her father's feeble cries for help. Becca spies his legs for the first time, jutting from under the front bumper.

When she calls 911, it rings and rings and rings and no one picks up at the other end. It will take hours for distracted city authorities to comprehend that an entire shift of police officers and dispatchers has gone missing.

33

YOU RAISE YOUR HAND LIKE YOU'RE A KID IN CLASS, hoping Maddy will understand your gesture and stop walking. "Something's wrong," you say. "Something's really fucked up."

Maddy pops her eyes comically and holds her nose. "You think?" The field the two of you are crossing reeks of manure.

You and Maddy have walked for miles. It's a wonder no one has waylaid your progress, tried to question you or Maddy. Obviously neither of you rated an Amber Alert.

You could drive, some parts of you nestled in the layers know how, but if it went wrong it could bring a lot of attention, and Maddy told you she didn't want you to hurt anyone else. Whatever she is, she's much more human than you, affected by things like smells and uncomfortable surfaces and displays of cruelty. You don't want to drive her away. And you have reason to be afraid of her, though you aren't.

Soon after leaving the overpass, the two of you sat in a park and dined on fast food breakfasts you stole using Carolyn's form. Two kids wandering in the open during school hours could draw attention, and so could an adult wandering with a young girl. Lucky you, there's a park path parallel to a big creek that's not much used because it runs through rundown neighborhoods. That got you as far as the Hillcrest Mall, once all hustle and bustle, now half empty. Maddy argued with you about going inside. *You don't want me to go in then you stop me*, she said. You couldn't. The worst didn't happen, though. None of the elderly mall walkers making use of all that empty space seemed to care that the two of you were there. You comprehend the adult world enough to suspect that no one's looking for Maddy, no urgent news alerts, which could mean something's gone wrong back at her home, but you're not going to say anything because she'll bolt straight back to Mama Rochelle and what's waiting might only look like her.

You left her wandering in a lonely secondhand clothing store so you could hunt for a lunch. It was for her, you didn't need one. As the homeless man you crossed the parking lot, acting on a stolen memory. You asked the gruff old man running the sausage stand in front of the big box hardware store if he'd spare a dog to help out a fellow man. He did, bless his soul. The hot dog had cooled considerably by the time you got it to Maddy. She wolfed it down.

You've walked and walked some more, along residential streets, through crude woodland paths, over fences and across hilly pastures, the sun disappearing behind clouds and blazing out again.

You haven't shared with Maddy that you have no plan. You only have wants.

You've wanted to get away from your mother and her suffocating box. You've wanted to find your sibling, to recruit her to your cause. Some part of you, maybe the part that's still Davey, dreamed you'd have a peer. An ally in the fight against the world. Against you mother. Some part of you believed that if you doubled yourself, you'd never again suffer the lonely agony of your mother's sealed box.

She's not a double. She's out of your reach. Touching her is death. Something in you whispers, *try it, try it,* not in another voice but in your own.

You do have direction of a sort. Your instinct is to get away from your mother, from that sensation of her presence that makes you itch deep. Over the years you've come to sense the nearness of her collective presence like radiation from a node of hell. You have let that sensation propel you and you have felt the radiation dim another fraction with each step you take.

Beyond that you've got no firm ideas on how to travel, how to live, where exactly to go. If—no, *when*—Maddy questions your choices, the sham of your decisiveness will peel open, but, so far, despite her snark, she's following where you lead.

Except something is wrong. Something new. Something warm.

"What are you even talking about?" she asks. "*Everything* is fucked up."

"No, that's not what I mean," you say. You don't have the words to explain the disturbances you feel, emanating from somewhere both well outside and deep inside you.

A continent is shifting, lava trickling, threatening flood.

Maddy reaches the top of the grassy slope you're ascending and stops. "Whoa! Cows. Lots of them. Wow, they're huge."

Despite the heated queasiness rising from below, you laugh. "What?" Then you see them. Huge black beasts, as big as any car, the massive furred barrels of their bodies improbably mounted on the comical stilts of their legs. Ears twitching in agitation, they watch you with eyes like black marbles, empty of soul.

Maddy moves closer, an arm held out to touch one of the beasts. It shifts its weight on those spindles, eyes widening enough to show whites.

"Be careful!" The irony, that if you touch Maddy the reaction could kill you, or worse—yet if these stupid animals stampeded

and trampled, you would survive and Maddy would likely die.
Unless your mother's act of expelling Maddy from the layers instilled even more surprises.

She still tries to pet the cow, which shuffles two quick steps
sideways. Maddy laughs, not seeing how the others are rolling
their eyes, the way they teeter as if winding up to a run.

You start to scold her, but a different threat commands your
attention. That abstract notion of lava flow grows less abstract by
the second. Echoes reach you of screams, the shrills of pure fear
from forest creatures fleeing a primordial fire.

"Stop," you say. "Stop a second. Something's happening."

"Yeah, cows are happening," Maddy says. "I can't believe this,
you're not even human and you're scared of cows. That's pathetic.
Wait, what are you doing?"

The warmth filling you brings no comfort.

You clutch at your chest, your face, pacing in a tight circle.
"Something bad is happening," you say. Howls of distant agony
vibrate inside your skin. Somewhere, somehow, the layers are on
fire. Should that fire spread you don't know how to escape it. You
are tethered to the kindling.

"Stop that, it's gross," Maddy says.

"I don't understand what's happening!" Your panic could
be your own or it could be amplifications of the fear shrieking
through the layers. Your grip on the fluttering spark of self your
mother granted you, the thing that keeps you Davey by default,
falters. You no longer notice the agitation of the cattle or Maddy's
own cries of alarm at the animals' bleats and bellows. The heat and
grit of smoke stuffs your interstices. Hooves kick up clods of grass
and moist dirt.

Outside yourself half-lives trapped in the layers are burning
alive, their fear and pain boiling up into you like magma forcing open a crack in the crust. The force killing them is following
through the crack, heat rising, oven elements reddening in the
spaces where the old Davey, the real Davey, contained muscle and
bone.

"Get away, Maddy! Get away!" you shout through three,
seven, thirteen mouths. You can see that she doesn't obey, that
she's disgusted and mesmerized by what's happening to your
body. What's trapped inside you is trying to flee, a futile folly,

but the shape of Davey can no longer dam the outward flow. Arms radiate out from you in all directions, grasping for non-existent lifebuoys, for rungs to climb away from the fire. The words from your many mouths blur to raw screams.

Like a bay door slammed down on concrete, a force intercedes between you and the surging lava. Something with power on a level you've never encountered has carved through the infinite layers of flesh and pain and sheered off the mass afflicted by fire, repelling it into the region outside time and mind where it will consume itself and shrivel to nothing. The falling away relieves you of that heat, replaced with a familiar presence that radiates a sickness all its own.

The endless lengths of nerves that tie you into the remaining layers convey an image to your mind, a slender form of vaguely bipedal outline, standing in a box proportioned like a coffin but smaller, swarming all over with tiny crawling motes—the parasites, the buttons—congealing in thick, ever-shifting clumps, the way bees form a beard on a beekeeper.

She is radiating the strength of a dark sun, severing through the layers by the thousands to protect herself from the fire, and in the process, the big brown eyes that are truly hers open somewhere in the mass and focus on you. And her voice says, *There you are.*

You shout with a hundred voices, *"Maddy run!"*

34

I N THE CAR, HAIRSTON GRABS THE DASHBOARD and digs his fingers so hard into the plastic that it cracks, arching his back and grimacing as if he's just taken a bullet.

The gesture so startles Aaron that he jerks the wheel.

What follows he observes with a strange calm. The outcome of the next few seconds will depend on factors completely beyond his control. His car does a donut in the middle of the interstate, tires screeching, the grill missing the jersey wall by inches, going for a second spin as an 18-wheeler bears down on them, this time the left rear passenger side slamming into the concrete barrier, the Buick coming to a stop facing the wrong way in the passing lane as the truck veers partway onto the shoulder and blares past. Incredibly there's no traffic immediately behind it and Aaron stomps the gas, making a U-turn that takes them off the shoulder and into the new-mowed grass.

"Fuck!" he shouts as his car comes to rest. "Are you all right?"

Hairston raises his hands and glares at Aaron from between his splayed fingers. All of his fingernails have split. Rivulets of blood wind down from the cuticles.

"It fought back," Hairston says. "The cursed thing fought back."

"What fought back?" Aaron saw the flailing flesh of the monster incinerate and vanish. There was nothing left to fight back. There couldn't be. It has to be over.

"Turn around," Hairston growls.

It has to be over, because Aaron wants the world to give him an opening, allow him a chance to convince himself that he witnessed nothing, that reality did not unhinge its jaw and vomit up monsters inside the Hillcrest Inn. That the man who rides beside him did not summon the fires of Hell in return.

"Turn the fuck around!" Hairston points further down the interstate, where there's a median crossover of the kind used by ambulances and state troopers. "Take that there turn and go back to Hillcrest. We have to go back. Now!"

35

"*MADDY RUN!*"

Maddy almost obeys.

Davey seethes as if he's made of coils of animate mummy-wrappings, a boy-shaped spindle of snakes. The cows have scattered, their meaty masses disappearing over grassy hills.

About ten yards separate them. Maddy would have a good head start if she ran but in a race against the kind of creature he is she's not at all sure she could win. Yet if he caught her—he's told her that if she touches him what happened to Josey will happen to him. She can't be sure it's true until she tries it. A part of her desperately wants to and if she's honest with herself it's this desire even more than concern for her brother in misery that keeps her from bolting. "What's happening to you?" She hates how shrill she sounds. "Tell me!"

Davey's body elongates upward. "She found me!" he wails. His eyes emerge from the chaos of his face, but they are darker, larger. He swells and ripples as if inflated from inside by cyclone-force winds. His outlines recede and sharpen. A woman stands in his place. Tall and slender, in jeans, sneakers and a sweater, hair dark as her eyes.

The woman smiles. "I remember you. Do you remember me?"

That voice. *I gave you back everything I could. Maybe I'll see you again. When you're older.*

Maddy folds her arms over her stomach and hunches down like she's trying to curl into a ball and vanish. She crouches, shivering, the same way she once shivered in the street, watching a monster in the shape of a woman as it strolled off into the night. Leaving her alone in the Vanished Neighborhood, where police would find her many hours later, crouched in the exact same spot, muttering, *Mommy, don't you think it was funny?*

"She swallowed the spider to catch the fly," the woman says, sing-song. "I don't know why she swallowed that fly. Perhaps she'll die."

The world around Maddy contracts to gray, her heart pounding, the rest of her trapped in stasis. That song. It's her long-lost mother's song, a little ditty she sang in a chirpy voice to make her daughter laugh, her tone stripping out all the morbidity.

Davey's notes: *my mom stole your mom's skin*

"Maddy, what have you been doing with my son? He won't tell me."

The only thing that keeps Maddy from collapsing and curling up like a pillbug is a paralysis of stupefaction. Davey's pathetic transformation instilled more pity than fear despite its violence, but this woman, standing as casual as if she had been the one walking by Maddy's side this whole day, encases Maddy's mind in ice, her voice unmistakably the same as that of Maddy's long-lost mother as she calls Maddy's name again. With a smile pleasant as a late sunrise she bends and leans, putting the gaze from her large brown eyes level with Maddy's own. She waves. "Hello?" Smile fading to a cockeyed smirk, she hums the song again. *There was an old lady that swallowed a fly . . .*

"Mom," Maddy whispers. Ice cracks, adrenaline bubbling out through it, and her nerves retake command. She wants to puke but she doesn't. She could run, but holds her place and pose. "Is my mom in there? With Davey? Have you got her in there?"

The woman tips her head back, regards Maddy with eyes half-lidded. Above, ordinary clouds drift beneath an unremarkable sky. A shift in air current brings a waft of manure like a sick punchline. Nausea rises in response and it's all Maddy can do to keep from retching.

"I've missed you so much."

The last time Maddy heard that voice, she had just finished watching a musical in elementary school about a smart little girl who didn't want to share. The play made her laugh so hard, she couldn't stop telling her mommy how funny she thought it was. They got in the car, and she wanted to know if her mommy thought it was funny too, and her mommy kept telling her what to do— *Maddy, don't be silly. Hold still, damn it. Hold still.*—instead of answering her question. She kept asking, while a thing with no shape of its own hid in the back seat, letting a few seconds pass, enough for Maddy and her mom to buckle in, before it slithered forward.

The change unfolded too quick for Maddy to follow, as if the woman standing in front of her had always been curly-haired, blonde, blue-eyed, her broad face etched with seams of worry that all too rarely yielded a fragile smile. Her outfit has altered, her jeans faded and flared into bell-bottoms, her denim jacket unsnapped, exposing the image on her T-shirt, two young girls, one blonde, one brunette, staring at a candle flame.

Maddy trembles.

"Oh my god, look at you," her mom says. "I'm so sorry. I'm sorry you've been alone so long."

The treacherous surge of longing, of hope, counter to all rational thought, pulls her to run toward her mother, not away. Maddy tries hard, so hard, to keep her head, to remember that much-missed face hides an all-devouring funnel of flesh.

The mommy in front of her is all smiles as she takes a step and opens her arms. "Honey, come here. Let me make it up to you. For everything."

It takes no stretch to imagine a caress from those hands would match the ones from memory, palms warm, fingertips cold. *I need you to warm 'em up,* she'd say when Maddy whined at the chill touch. *You're so warm, you're my hot water bottle.*

"Hey, you know, your father is here, too. I can have him speak if you want to hear his voice."

The spell breaks. Even after all these years, Maddy remembers how frightened her mom had been of her dad, though she's foggy as to the reasons. She just recalls the tension in her mommy's wiry frame, the bulges of muscle at the corners of her jaw, when he came up in conversation, heightened tenfold when he paid a visit. Even then Maddy could tell something was wrong, the way her beleaguered mother would, maybe without even meaning to, shift to maintain the maximum distance possible between herself and her ex-lover in the tiny rooms of the modular home where they lived. And how her mom would stiffen when he closed that distance.

Maddy's surge of elation sours into stinging hot pain behind her eyes. It seeps into her chest, threatens to clench her throat. She gives that pain an angry shove to stop herself from producing tears for the monster's enjoyment. Unfrozen, the question at the top of her mind comes loose. "What did you do to Davey?"

36

THERE ARE THINGS YOUR MOTHER DOESN'T KNOW, but you can't keep them from her for long. Once she has you back in the box, whatever form it takes, she will never let you out again.

37

MADDY ASKS AGAIN, LOUDER. "What did you do to Davey?" "Nothing," says the thing pretending to be Maddy's mother. "He's right here."

"Maddy, touch her."

She isn't sure where the second voice came from. Her notmother keeps on talking. "I've missed you so much. You were in here with me once. She let you out because I begged her to, because you were too young. She agreed with me because she's a mother herself. But I've been so lonely without you."

Again, a whisper. *"Maddy please."* Davey.

"You'll never be lonely again. Your father is here and so many others and they will all love you. Remember that blanket you loved so much, the one with the daffodils, it'll be like you're all wrapped up in it, like a comforter made from warm hands. We have so many hands to hold you. We'll hug you and it'll last forever."

A flap of flesh droops out from under the hem of her mother's jacket, about the same size and shape as a hip flask. The flap has a mouth, it's been speaking at the same time as Maddy's mom, who doesn't seem to notice. As Maddy stares, the flap swells, eye-holes open below the mouth, eyes inflate to fill them. It's Davey, his face upside-down. "Do what she wants," he pleads. "Let her touch you." The flap of his inverted head contracts and bulges. He coughs out a long twist of skin.

"C'mon, sweetie," Maddy's mom says, bending with her arms held out. "Let me scoop you up."

Maddy isn't sure who she is obeying as she starts forward. The twist of skin protruding from Davey's mouth unfurls, the pale scars and tangles of veins revealed there spelling out *KILL US.*

Maddy's mom lunges forward to grab her, and as she's lifted Maddy shrieks and kicks her legs, sure she's been tricked.

Her mom says, "There you gooooo—" and her mouth continues to stretch in a grotesquely elongated oval, her lips at last folding over and peeling back like a sausage rind, exposing membranes beneath that are also splitting and peeling back, opening a hole so deep that it descends beneath the wholesome pasture grass, plummeting into the earth and at the same time somewhere outside it. Human howls by the thousands rise from the pit.

"Don't let go!" wails Davey, his squeak barely audible above the din.

Below her a glittering exodus rains into the void, bright motes leaping like burning fleas to escape her.

"Don't let go!"

But the hands clutching Maddy do let go and her grip slips and she's falling. She screams as she falls. An object like a hard pillow shoves her and she lands half on ground, half on a shuddering strip of flesh that proves to be the grotesque lip of a hellmouth, a roughly circular sphincter wide as a station wagon, orifice for an abyss filled with shrieks of human agony.

On contact with her the ledge of flesh splits and recoils. As the cartilaginous tissue parts a face appears in the gap, Davey's face, peering up at her with desperate dark eyes. He opens his mouth to speak or scream but his features peel off like wet wallpaper, leaving a rudimentary skull behind that melts to paste even as it becomes visible, button-motes bursting out of its crevices and falling away. His dark eyes remain an instant longer, flattening into large buttons that scuttle away like frightened cockroaches.

The hellmouth contracts inward and down, the turf folds in over it. Maddy lies on her belly in an empty pasture, grass tickling her face, the stink of manure overwhelming.

38

MADDY SETS FOOT ON MAMA ROCHELLE'S DRIVEWAY somewhere between midnight and the witching hour, her bedraggled form emerging into the pool of illumination made by the squat brick lamppost that stands sentry at the front of the yard, her clothes and face shaded with dirt.

Rochelle must be home, her light blue minivan with its rust spots sits cozy in the driveway, cast in chiaroscuro by the light angling from the lamppost. Maddy aches from sole to scalp, or she would dash to the door and pound on it. She doesn't know how she'll explain where she's been or what she's seen and she doesn't care.

She angles across the grass toward the front walk, reduced to a silhouette in the patch of darkness that's just out of reach of both lamppost and porch light.

The front door of the house opens inward, the screen door creaks outward. "Mama," Maddy calls, quickening her step. The motion detector mounted between the second-floor windows clicks and an even brighter light joins the chorus, granting a golden gloss to the sleek flow of dark hair that crowns the woman on the concrete stoop.

Maddy freezes. She's making tiny noises, part gasp, part groan, in between panicked inhales.

"You called me mama," says Davey's mother. "I guess that's fitting."

A terrible notion blooms in Maddy's brain. She holds her ground, and if she sheds tears, they are tears of rage.

"I never regretted letting you go, until today," the woman says. "Now I know how much of a mistake it was." She sounds calm, up until she says *mistake*, then her voice cracks. "There's a price for what you did to my son."

"He wanted to get away from you, far away, more than anything else in the whole wide world," Maddy says. "Where's Mama Rochelle?"

The woman hasn't let the screen door shut. She pushes it so it creaks wider. "Won't you come in?"

"Where's Mama Rochelle?"

"Come inside, I'll show you."

"No I won't. What have you done to her?" Though Maddy knows. "Where are her kids? Where are my sisters?"

"I'll let them all go," the woman says, "all of them, if you kill yourself."

"If—" It's like Maddy's tongue lodges in her throat, her breath stoppered. She wants to laugh and shout to the hidden camera crew that must exist that they can come out now, the joke's over. If there's a hidden camera, it's manned by demons, and they're the ones laughing.

The significance of that string of words won't come into focus, and yet her eyes burn, her breath wheezes fast, she's hitching and sniffling, and her heartbeat rushes faster, too fast, painfully fast, like it's a machine overloading.

"Think what I'm offering. If I let them out, I can't hurt them again, just like I can't hurt you anymore. They'll never know what happened to them. But after what you did—I can't tolerate that, and you know too much, and I can't allow *that*."

I can't hurt you anymore. It's a lie, though. The thing hiding in the back seat has taken her family again, torn a new hole, a deeper pain than Maddy has ever felt in a life riddled with never-healing wounds.

It's not done hurting Maddy. It will never be done.

"Just do what I want," the monster says, not commanding, but syrup-sweet. "I'll help you make it painless—"

In the distance, an engine roar, a car tearing through the neighborhoods at high speed, the shriek of rubber sliding on asphalt. Dogs bark in response.

Maddy finds her words. "You let them all go!" Across the street, a light turns on behind a shaded window. The engine roar grows louder.

The woman withdraws a step, holding the screen door like a shield against Maddy. "If you want that, you need to calm down and do what I—"

"You took everything from me!"

Maddy springs and grabs the edge of the door before the woman can jerk it shut.

She hurtles forward even as the woman's body unfurls into a monstrous curtain of tooth-filled mouths.

Maddy leaps, hands curled into claws. Teeth press in like knives, all over her body, their piercing pressure withdrawn the same instant they strike. She strikes at the same time and as her nails rake strips from the curtain of flesh it rips apart, opening before her in a whirlpool of skin and blood, large enough to swallow a bus.

She falls in. A thousand hands grab for her, trying to expel her, disintegrating at the moment of contact. She lands on a slimy surface, too uneven to be called a floor. She scrambles forward because the surface contracts away from whatever part of her touches it. To move in any direction other than down she must crawl like a mole in a tunnel, she made a terrible mistake and she can't take it back, she can't stop moving for even a second or she'll fall forever.

Hands swarm her as she thrashes and advances. Their owners could be pleading for help or lashing out at her with intent to pluck out her eyes, shred her skin, pound her into bloody paste. They keep her fully surrounded, a churning surface of blows and caresses that retract at the last second, fleshy gloves immediately unraveled and just as quickly replaced by new outspread palms or bunched fists, which too peel away, immediately replaced by more, the cycle unending, the fleshy ground collapsing under each lurch no matter how fast she moves, her nightmare exit from the world inevitable, unstoppable.

A man shouts and somehow the noise forces its way through the din of disintegrating souls to make itself known. There's no room in what's left of Maddy's mind to contemplate how this is possible. He talks with a stentorian authority, every syllable a command, but Maddy's panicked perpetual flight flays the words to nonsense.

Rochelle is screaming Maddy's name. Prixie is screeching in agony. The twins are bawling. Lakesha squeals like she's being boiled alive. Ashley laughs, nonstop cruelty, *your gonna die you dumb bitch you're going to be eaten alive ha ha ha ha ha.* The man shouts at Maddy to stop listening, *it's all tricks don't listen don't believe a word it lies.*

The comforter of warm hands her mother promised. It tries and tries to weave itself around her and shreds to pieces even as it forms. The bed it purports to cover keeps tearing open underneath her, dropping her down amid the monsters underneath. *Mommy, do you think this is funny? Stop it mommy stop it STOP IT*

A woman's hand grabs her right wrist, its light brown skin blotched with blisters and blighted by red and peeling skin, horrific burns that will scar in moonscape furrows. A man's hand grabs her left wrist, its near-black skin barely concealing a fire inside, an inferno of hatred and worse, a strain of unnatural life that worms through its veins and winds fibers through its meat, a force that was never meant to exist in this world. Even as this mismatched pair lifts her out of the pit, she cannot tell whether they're real.

THE FIFTH HORSEMAN

the plagues seeped through the city's cracks,
immunizations reviled and denied, immunity lost

windows swelling into sores, doors
sealed open, paralyzed jaws

skyscrapers shedding mold-black chunks,
red rot unveiled beneath

roads puckered with pox,
subways blocked by venous polyps

gutters flooded with leaking lymph
between suppurating facades

the pestilence of cars and commerce
still struggling upstream

to seek out the last oases of health,
feed until depletion and breed in the remains

GHEREM
with Charles M. Saplak

I

HEREM'S RIGHT FOOT SLIPPED ON ONE of the loose, damp
stones, and he nearly fell face first into the mud. He went to
one knee, giving himself yet another bloodless cut. He broke his
fall with his left hand, but with his right he continued to hold the
wrists of Withered Nassissia, the tiny, dark-skinned witch he carried on his back.

"Idiot!" she hissed. "Are you so weary you can't take care how
you're stepping?"

Her voice was strung taut, not simply with anger, but also
with pain. When Gherem slipped, he jarred her and her shattered
legs, where broken shinbones poked through her ebony skin.

"I am weary." Gherem muttered. "When I became a soldier
they failed to tell me how to live without sleep. Or food. Or water."

"Now is not the time to stop," Nassissia said. "Didn't they ever
teach you soldiers that stopping to sleep or eat sometimes means
that you never get up again?"

"Oh, they taught me so much," Gherem groaned. "Most of
which I'd rather not have learned."

Nassissia didn't seem to be listening to him. Her head
cocked to one side as she glared back into the forest, toward
the battlefield. Was she thinking of the carnage there, where
the soil was now dark with blood, where birds picked eye sockets clean, where mice feasted inside cages of rib, where wolves
gnarled over fingerbones and shinbones? Where the grass
would be green and the flowers bright for years to come, now
that nearly seven hundred men were turning to soil, men who

began the day as Brinnish and Husterran soldiers and ended as a harvest of corpses?

Or was she brooding over her own fate on that field where, as she fled from the Brinnish Coven's burning tent with the Vicinage Poppet tucked to her bosom, a battle cart had rolled over her legs—turning proud Withered Nassissia, greatest of the feared Husterran witches, most powerful woman in the Royal Court of Treblas, into a helpless cripple, who now had to rely on the aid of a mere peasant such as Gherem?

But would a witch be so abstract? Perhaps she had a more pressing reason for staring into the forest . . . .

"Couldn't we stop here to rest?" Gherem moaned.

"No," Withered Nassissia snapped. "Onward. Through the forest, Gherem. To Leiple River; to the cliffs, the Plain of Stones, to Vantahusterra. To home, Gherem. Home."

II

GHEREM'S MIND WANDERED AS HE FOLLOWED the creek bed downward. His bare feet were as icy as the water, and his crude trousers and tunic were caked with mud. But he could shut out the pain, and the weight of the Dark Sorceress on his shoulders. He concentrated on the water itself—something he'd never appreciated before.

For the first time Gherem noticed the music it made, millions of voices blended, singing as the stream journeyed to the sea. Once an old man had explained to Gherem that every bit of water sojourned to the sky, lifted by the sun, and after drifting there, fell as rain. It sought its level, wearing down mountains as it did so.

Why had he never noticed this? Why had he never felt this way? Had a day ever passed when he hadn't worried about whether the turnips and rye and millet he'd worked for Lord Treblas had enough water? When he hadn't had to shoulder a yoke and worn oaken buckets to fetch water fit to drink? And when, in recent months, as Prince Treblas had been cursed and crops would only grow in the outlands, he'd been put to work in the mud of the irrigation ditches with others of his class.

But Gherem had never noticed the miracle of the stuff. Well, by all the Gods and Dragons, from now on he would. He'd tilt his head back and let the rain tease his face with wet fingertips. He'd sit by a stream and listen to its song, listen for hours until he could understand it. He'd gather up Trelinna and Jad and the three of them would walk to the sea! What was there to stop them?

"Faster," Withered Nassissia hissed, breaking his reverie.

"I'm pacing myself," Gherem puffed. "I can walk like this for hours."

"Admirable," the sorceress said. "But we must cover more ground. We must get this boon to Vantahusterra faster."

"We can rest," Gherem pleaded. "We can eat. We can hide and sleep, and continue in the morning. I'll feel alive then."

Nassissia cackled, and at first Gherem thought he was seeing a tinge of humor in the ancient witch, but when she spoke her voice dripped bitterness.

"Selfish One," she said, grimacing. "But we may stop soon. This stream goes directly to the Leiple River. I sense that. We can stop, but only for a moment. I would have you gather some things. Home, Gherem. Think of home."

Even as she spoke of "Home," her eyes narrowed, and, fingering the Vicinage Poppet she carried in her cloak, she looked back again, searching the forest.

III

AT A FLAT SPOT BY THE STREAM, Gherem knelt and eased Nassissia to the mossy soil. The sky darkened with night, so that the canopy of branches overhead knit together like a spider web of blackness.

Even in the dim light, Gherem could see the split flesh and splintered bones of Nassissia's lower legs. Her blood was dried; perhaps it was some power she had, some way to use her mind to stop the bleeding.

She groaned and looked at Gherem.

"Is it ugly to you?" she asked, the bitter smile playing across her lips.

Gherem shrugged. "I wonder if the flesh of one of you is like the flesh of one of me."

"Flesh is flesh," Nassissia said. "Spirit differs. But that is talk for another day. Do you know henbane?"

Gherem gave the witch a blank look.

"Could you find me verbanna? Could you dig mandrake roots for me? Would you know toadflax if you saw it?"

Gherem shrugged and shook his head. "I'd do better if you sent me after a radish, or a potato."

"Ignorant One," Nassissia hissed. "Since you can't help me, simply let me rest. Be quiet. I would sit here. If you see me lying down, or slumping over, wake me immediately. Do you understand?"

"I do," Gherem said. "I understand that because you don't want to sleep, I'm not to be allowed to sleep."

Withered Nassissia took the Vicinage Poppet from within the folds of her cloak. Gherem could see that it was a carved wooden doll, a likeness of Prince Treblas it seemed, and bound from shoulder to shin in a weave of tightly knotted, brightly colored cords. Such a small thing had cost so many their lives!

Gherem sat and propped himself up on his elbows. He wanted to look at anything besides the witch, so he lolled his head back and looked at the sky.

The moon had risen, and the stars were now drops of dew on the cobweb of night. They were glowing eyes of distant gods! They were flames around which lost souls danced!

Why had he never looked at these stars with Trelinna and Jad? Were these not the same stars which whirled over his mean little hut on the moors of Lord Treblas? Oh, when he returned home, things would be so different.

"Jad had been proud of me," Gherem said out loud. "His father was a soldier. Not merely a serf; a soldier. Why would an army want me? The things I told him . . . ."

He remembered his son's enraptured eyes, looking up at the clean military tunic his father wore. When he told Jad the tales of Brinnish atrocity, how a bewitched night bird had drawn the Prince's blood as he slept, how the Brinnish Coven had used that blood to create the Poppet that cursed Treblas and stopped the crops from growing. He remembered how his son had looked out the window at the barren soil and said, "Da, I hope you kill thousands of Brinnish soldiers."

Gherem suppressed an urge to groan. "I told my son how he should love Prince Treblas, love his country. That someday he could be a soldier. But I notice that Treblas didn't see fit to take part in this campaign."

Withered Nassissia eyed Gherem in the moonlight, her lips drawn back as if regarding a bug. "And what would the unwashed conclude if Treblas had left Vantahusterra and flowers bloomed again, fruits ripened, vegetables grew? Would he return to meet an mob of peasants wielding shovels and axes?"

Gherem shrugged and stared at the ground.

"That is exactly what the Brinnish have hoped for, Foolish One. The reason why they cursed your Prince. The reason why we fought to take the Vicinage Poppet. The reason why we must undo this curse. The reason why you took up arms."

"I just want to see my son again," Gherem said. "I want to tell him that it's all hogwash."

"Careful, Slow One," Withered Nassissia cooed. "Loyalty."

Before Gherem could answer a change came over the witch's face. She raised a hand, palm up, knobby fingers extended; her eyes darted from side to side.

"Did you hear that?" she whispered.

Gherem sat silent for a moment, concentrating on the normal night sounds of the forest—crickets' chittering, frogs' croaking, leaves rustling, birds' trilling.

"There! Again! A heavy foot falls," Withered Nassissia said. "A following foot."

"Stay here," Gherem said, immediately realizing how ridiculous his order was to the woman with shattered legs.

"Don't leave me," Nassissia said, her words very deliberate, neither hissed nor shouted nor pled.

Gherem didn't answer.

"Don't go far from me!" she said, more urgently this time. Gherem recognized fear in her voice.

He waved casually and pushed his way into the forest.

He wasn't sure he had heard anything—he just wanted to gather some teaberry or ground cherries, or even some honeysuckle blossoms to chew. He hadn't eaten since this morning, before the battle.

Gherem stepped into a clearing, and as he did, he became acutely aware that something was not right. He felt that he wasn't alone.

He forced himself to become as still as possible.

Moving his eyes but not his head, he searched the forest, glancing up and down, from right to left, taking the time to resolve each branch, leaf, weed, and stone in his field of vision, in the dappled moonlight.

And suddenly he spotted it—

A panther crouched stock-still at the clearing's edge.

Gherem saw a terrible beauty in the great cat's curving back, the pads of its paws which rhythmically and soundlessly kneaded the forest floor, in the ears laid back against its sleek skull, even in the tail which slowly undulated.

For a while the moon followed its path, causing shadows to crawl across the forest floor between the two, man and cat, as they eyed each other in the night.

Suddenly the panther rocked forward, and silently made its way toward Gherem.

Gherem stared into the its eyes, which flashed translucent in the moonlight. He considered running, or screaming to try to frighten the panther. He did neither, but simply watched as the beast crept closer and closer.

Close enough to flick out one claw and open Gherem's chest if it wanted, but there it stopped again, perfectly still except for its rhythmically flaring nostrils.

A sound entered Gherem's consciousness like thunder—but it was a low sound, a throbbing—a heartbeat. Whether it was his own, or that of the cat, or the heartbeat of the world itself, he couldn't know.

Its nostrils twitched and flared, and it snarled, revealing wicked teeth. From deep within it growled, a sound of distant mountains collapsing, and Gherem was sure the cat would in any moment be on his throat.

And then the panther bounded away, into the forest, almost seeming to disappear before Gherem's very eyes.

Gherem exhaled—he seemed to have been holding his breath since he had first spotted the beast—and slumped forward. He gathered himself in the moonlight, then staggered back to the stream where Nassissia awaited.

"What was it?" Nassissia asked. "What did you see?"

"Nothing," Gherem said, crouching to reshoulder his burden.

IV

A S THE SKY LIGHTENED WITH MORNING, as the moon set and the stars faded, the singing of the stream grew both more intense and complex. The stones themselves were larger, so that Gherem was no longer stumbling over so much as scrambling around them, then climbing them. Still he held the sorceress; still she held her Poppet. Presently the forest opened as the stream met the Leiple River, across which were sheer cliffs, and beyond them the Plain of Stones.

"There it is," Gherem said.

Withered Nassissia, her eyes mere slits, raised her head to stare at the water.

"So it is . . . . One moment . . . . Only a moment. I would gather my strength," she whispered.

"Tell me when you're ready," Gherem said. "It will be cold."

Strangely, Gherem felt tremendous as he looked at the river, sparkling in the morning sun. He was close to home! He shrugged, readjusting the sack of bones on his shoulders.

"I'm ready," the witch whispered, clutching the Poppet and resettling herself.

Gherem strode forward, and waded into the river.

It was cold, terribly cold, but it felt good to Gherem.

Withered Nassissia groaned and twitched as her feet touched the surface of the water. *At least she still has feeling in her legs*, Gherem thought.

As the two entered deeper water the witch was buoyed so that her meager weight was no longer such a burden around Gherem's neck. He took little relief in this. His mind instead was filled by a memory of Trelinna, on a day far in his past, when the two were of fifteen and fourteen summers.

Gherem's feet were off the stream bed; Nassissia, one hand clutching the Poppet no doubt, kept her other arm hooked around Gherem's neck. Gherem slowly and steadily began to paddle his arms, not fighting the current, but simply directing himself to the far shore.

He closed his eyes and remembered that summer night, years ago, when he and Trelinna stripped naked and swam together in an unnamed stream which ran through Treblas's farmlands south of the city walls of Vantahusterra. He could see her sweaty skin in the moonlight as she waded into the water; he could see her skin tightened and goosebumped as she climbed from the cool water into the night air. She had teased his face with wet fingertips . . . .

What a sweet sight she had been—the forests and hills of her flesh, that was the country for a man to love.

And his feet again touched the muddy riverbed beneath him. He opened his eyes. The riverbank before him was a jumble of stones. This was a wild area, an evil place, unfished and unhunted, even by the barbarians who were said to lurk within these forests and hills.

He found his feet and waded through the rocks. The dripping hag was returned from the river's hands to his shoulders.

Gherem staggered ashore, toward the first stone blunt and flat and broad enough to lower Nassissia.

Once she was safe there, he straightened up, stretched, and regarded her—greasy strings of hair in her face, shivering, wet cloak plastered to her bony frame, eyes ringed round by swollen circles—but the Poppet still hard in her claw-like hands.

"Onward," she muttered. "Onward."

The brusqueness of her order didn't bother Gherem. He rolled his shoulders, tilted his head back and examined the cliff face before him.

Four or five hundred feet, sheer rock face in the worst spots, steeply stacked boulders in the best. Such a place he'd never willingly climb under normal circumstances.

"Home," he whispered, still looking up, as he bent down to extend a hand to the witch.

On the cliff, Gherem clutched the rock face with both hands as the witch swung from around his neck. "Home," he chanted in a whisper, never looking down to the Leiple River, one hundred feet below.

Something flashed just on the border of his vision, clattered against the rocks to his right.

Gherem pressed himself against the cliff, and peeped upwards with squinted eyes.

"Hold tight," he said over his shoulder to the hag. "There may be a rock slide."

The witch punched him in the back of the neck, or perhaps butted him with her forehead; he couldn't be sure.

"That was no rock, Gherem. Carefully look across the river. Look to the place where we were."

Gingerly, Gherem turned his head. Back on one of the large flat stones upriver stood a man. He held a longbow, and even as Gherem watched he let fly an arrow which clattered against the cliff face, this time to the left of the two.

"Our pursuer," Withered Nassissia hissed. "I'd sensed him all along."

Gherem knew that they were at their most vulnerable in this position. Even if they were able to make the summit, so too would this archer, and on the plain of stones he would easily follow, and so long as he had arrows, he could attack from far away. Eventually he'd find his mark.

With utmost deliberation, Gherem edged along the rock until he was at a slight ledge. There he knelt down and tucked away the witch with her precious Vicinage Poppet.

"Don't leave me," she gasped, her eyes wide.

"He'll fill us with arrows," Gherem said, then he turned, hesitated for only a moment, then leaped outward, plunging into the river.

He scraped hard onto the rocky river bottom. Still, he kept his wits about him and opened his eyes. Through the murk, he oriented himself. The black plain below was river bottom; the sparkling plain above was the river's surface. Clutching rocks when he had to, Gherem paddled himself along between these two plains. Grasses on the river bottom told him the current, and against this he pushed. He fought hard to make his way across the breadth of the river without surfacing.

Kicking and clawing, he pushed through the water. At one point a trout, mouth agape, eyes wide, darted right before his face. Then an arrow punched into the water from above, and the trout undulated away.

Meant for me, not you, Gherem thought. The weirdness of the situation struck him and he almost laughed. Fighting for his life, and he joked with a fish?

The plains of light above and murk below narrowed and converged. He was coming to the forested shore.

He peered upward and could make out the wavering figure of the archer. He couldn't tell exactly what he was doing.

Gherem pulled himself along the riverbed on his back, half-expecting an arrow in the chest at any moment.

He got almost up to the rock where the man stood, and realized that the archer didn't see him. Perhaps the riverbed camouflaged him; perhaps the sunlight on the water was in the man's eyes.

Gherem seized his chance. He burst from the water and turned toward the man on the rock. The man had an arrow notched and drawn, but Gherem was too fast. With his left arm he whipped around, slapping the man's feet from under him.

The man hit the rock hard, as Gherem pulled himself from the water. For a moment the longbow lay on the rock between the two. The archer, his eyes wide, grabbed for the longbow and got his fingers on it first.

But Gherem was too strong. With the heel of his left hand he drove a punch into the man's jaw, with his right hand he twisted the longbow away.

The man lay stunned on the rock for a moment, as Gherem stood over him. Gherem raised the longbow over his head, and for a moment he looked as if he would brain the man, but instead of that he snapped the bow, and flung it into the water.

"Why do you bother with this?" Gherem wearily asked the man. "Why care about us? We're going back to our home. You go back to yours. The battle is over. Put away your weapons and forget."

The man rolled over, his eyes still wide, and stared at Gherem. "Forget? I'll never forget. You Husterrian swine killed my brother there. I'll never rest, until you and your kind are paid back for what you did. And that sorceress! Look at what she's done to you! Abomination! And the sorceress has the Poppet! Don't you know what good that boon could do? If you're tired of starving, take that cowardly ape Treblas off the throne. Your land could be free of him, and your crops could grow again, and my homeland could be at peace."

Gherem slumped and shook his head. "Your brother died there? Oh, pity. Oh, pity."

To his own ears, if not to the ears of the man at his feet, Gherem's words rang true. He didn't know that feelings like this could be felt. Why should he care that a Brinnish soldier died? But he did.

Gherem looked up and down the riverbank. He saw an old stump of driftwood caught up in the rocks near them.

"Slit his throat!" Nassissia called from her place on the hillside.

Gherem slogged over and pulled the driftwood free.

"Listen," Gherem said. "Go back to your home. Take care of your brother's sons. Plow his wife's fields. Surely you like her, and if she does not like you now, she'll learn to. Your brother wouldn't mind. He doesn't care a bit about revenge now."

Gherem reached down and pulled the man up by his shirt. He struggled as if he were loath to have Gherem touch him, but Gherem dragged the man and the stump out into deeper water and put the man onto the stump, to which the man clung against the swift current.

"Go home," Gherem said, setting the man free to drift down the river.

"Home," Gherem whispered, as the current took the man downriver, in the general direction of Brin.

"Home," Gherem repeated, turning away, not waiting for the man to get out of sight before he started paddling back to the cliff where the witch waited.

"You should have killed the Brinnish bastard," Withered Nassissia panted.

Gherem bent and offered his hand to the wizened one; picked her up and slung her to the familiar place on his shoulders. With her there he resumed his climb, and made the summit of the rocky cliff. He never looked down, and felt no fear of falling.

"Home," he muttered.

V

THE PLAIN OF STONES LAY SOUTHWEST OF THE VILLAGE of Vantahusterra, desolate and unthought of. As the rounded rocks crunched beneath his feet in hypnotic rhythm, Gherem kept

his eyes on the distant mountains of Murnnann and Gethokht. It
was the same view, from a slightly different perspective, that Gherem had faced all his life—but today, how different!

Withered Nassissia drew one hand back from Gherem.

"So," Gherem said. "I carry you, and you carry that doll."

Withered Nassissia gave no answer, save for a grunt.

He walked farther, carrying her—no, carrying *them*. The sun
burned away the last vestiges of fog.

"It would have been easier for me to carry the Poppet, and
leave you behind," Gherem said.

Withered Nassissia thrust the Poppet over Gherem's shoulder, into his view.

"Oaf," she hissed. "This is what the battle was about!"

Gherem stared at the ugly thing—a carved image of Prince
Treblas, wrapped with an intricate crochet of knotted string. He
despised it. All the good men and women hacked open, pierced,
bled out on one bleak morning—over this toy!

Perhaps Nassissia read his mind and knew that he hated the
Poppet, for she snatched it back.

"Care, peasant, care," Nassissia cooed. "Would you kill your
Prince? The Vicinage Poppet must be taken apart with the utmost
care to spare Treblas' life. My sisters will handle the ritual. They
will solve the weave and undo it and end the curse, and there will
be nothing to keep us from reclaiming the Brinnish lands. But if
the knots aren't untied in order, and with certain words . . . . well,
the crops may grow again, but your Prince would be no more,
and for whom would you till the soil for then? The Brinnish King?
Would you like your son to toil for the Brinnish King? Would you
like that, peasant?"

Gherem didn't answer—he pictured throwing the bag of
bones off his back, stomping the Poppet to dust and strings, then
leaving them both on the plain of stones. What difference which
King owned their lives if their crops never grew again?

But he cast his eyes to the mountains and his home, and
walked on.

The sun was high as the village came into sight. How strange,
Gherem thought, how small! For many years, it had been his
world—but it was not even a splinter in the edge of the world
which was!

Gherem's own shadow was small beneath him as he was close enough to the village to see figures moving around the failed fields.

Less than a quarter mile outside the village, Gherem and Withered Nassissia encountered three children yelling and playing. As they each noticed the man carrying the witch, they each fell silent, and stared, and then as a group they sprinted toward the village, calling ahead of them. A dog too ugly to have been eaten yet followed them with shrieking barks.

The sun was high above. Gherem didn't sweat.

Alerted by the children, people began to trickle out of the village to greet the two.

Gherem continued forward, as people came from their shops and houses and from the outlying streets. A few, then several, then a mob. Everyone was similar. Each pushed forward, some jabbering and eager, then as each got within sight, each fell silent, their eyes wide, their mouths slack and open. Perhaps many of these had never seen a witch up close; perhaps none of these could imagine a witch with shattered legs, riding astride a peasant.

They were all shocked.

Gherem continued forward. He kept the witch on his shoulders, and moved toward Treblas's castle at the center of the city, but as he did so he searched the faces of the crowd for either Trelinna or Jad.

Armor clanking, two of the city guards pushed through the crowd, barking at peasants and slapping them out of the way.

Not so many days ago, Gherem would have been intimidated by these uniformed guards. Now he noticed absently that these garrison soldiers were fat and stupid, and could probably never imagine horrors such as he had seen yesterday morning on that faraway meadow.

The soldiers yelled, but Gherem paid no mind. Where were Trelinna and Jad? First to get this hag off his back, then to find his beloved.

A nobleman appeared, easy to recognize by the fine fabric of his dress, by his jangling jewelry.

The soldiers nodded to the nobleman, who eyed Withered Nassissia. He seemed to look past Gherem altogether. The silly fool tried to act courageous, and wanted to be in charge.

Tilting his head toward Gherem the nobleman spoke to Withered Nassissia: "You rode that?!"

The crowd pushed forward. The soldiers, with peasants pressing at their backs, shouted and drew their rusted swords.

"Put her down!" one of the soldiers growled, but no one came forth to take the witch from Gherem.

"I release thee; I release thee . . . ," Withered Nassissia chanted through clenched teeth.

Gherem looked for a place to set her down. The sunshine sparkled against a mud puddle at his feet; his eye was caught by something he saw.

The reflection there—something like a man, or something which had once been a man. The face was split, as if from a blow from an axe. The arms and legs were covered with strangely bloodless gashes and tears; the flesh beneath was dried. A broken shaft of an arrow stuck out from his neck, and at least one other that he could see stuck out from his back. A dark-skinned witch hung from around the creature's neck like a sack of grain.

One soldier poked at Gherem with his sword, and he went to one knee, unceremoniously dumping Withered Nassissia into the mud.

The witch shrieked, repulsing the crowd as if the sound of her voice burned their ears, as if the sight of her wounds burned their eyes.

Gherem immediately bent to the witch, put his hands on her cloak, tried to gather her up, failed, and fumbled around with her as she moaned and shouted. Finally he withdrew his hands, and stumbled away.

He turned this way and that, and once again looked for Trelinna and Jad.

The crowd parted; two of Nassissia's coven sisters made their way through.

"I release thee; I release thee . . . ," Withered Nassissia chanted.

The coven sisters knelt at her side. From within the cloak of one, spidery hands dashed out to work on Nassissia's legs. From beneath the hood of the other, a face even more wrinkled than Nassissia's turned toward Gherem, dark eyes glaring at him.

Gherem kept walking. Everything in the village looked strange. He expected people to stay and gawk at the trio of witches, but it

seemed as if as many were following him as were staying behind
to watch them.

Gherem walked down the street. He could make his way to
his home. Damn the mob which continued around him. Why
wouldn't they leave him alone?

Gherem passed an irrigation worker, stopped and snatched
the man's long-handled spade. No one tried to stop him. A cloud
edged its way before the sun. It was difficult for Gherem to see. He
had to hurry, in order to save Jad and Trelinna the trouble and
expense. He needed to select a gravesite, and dig as much of his
own grave as possible.

"I release thee," Withered Nassissia had chanted. Now others
in the crowd said other things.

"Don't let it into the city!"

"Put it out of its misery."

"Purify it!"

Gherem turned around, and one of the soldiers tossed a pot of
pitch onto him. The oily tar hit him in the chest and soaked him
down to his feet.

Gherem turned around again. Where were Trelinna and Jad?
The crowd was backing away.

The other soldier rushed at him with a torch, and jammed it
into his chest, igniting the tar.

Gherem dropped the shovel, and took one last look around
for Trelinna and Jad. He would have loved to have seen them
again, but he was glad they'd be spared the sight before them.

Flames crawled along every inch of his body, but he didn't feel
them.

His wife and son were not in the crowd, just the poor and ignorant who gawked at the spectacle.

And also the soldiers and the witches. Withered Nassissia still
lay in the dirt where he had set her, her two coven sisters tearing
through her cloak, tearing it apart thread by thread it seemed. The
three gestured frantically and screamed at one another.

Flames were in Gherem's face, but he glanced up and could
still see the sun, and he thought how good it was, how good was
the sun!

And then the three witches, and the soldiers, and the nobleman, all shouted and pointed at Gherem.

His legs were burning from beneath him, his clothes and skin were nearly gone. But he could still see. He raised his right arm. Withered Nassissia screamed and cried and pointed desperately toward him.

With the hand that held the now-burning Vicinage Poppet, Gherem waved goodbye.

THE SACRIFICES

The resin encased our heads
after the steel bars bound us
temple-to-temple. Every twitch
wrenched our neighbors' necks.
Ankle-deep in concrete, we became
a ring of pillars, living dolmens.
We couldn't see the worshipers
who shuddered between us, but their
shriveled souls brushed our skin,
like dried leaves. Like moth wings.

MACHINE LEARNING

A NDI'S PHONE PLAYED ITS *UNKNOWN CALLER* CHIME, full of high-pitched spooky notes that pierced through the Chevy's engine rumble and air conditioning whoosh. Celine, gripping the wheel at the four and eight positions, kept her gaze on the highway and the congested sludge of traffic that had enveloped them. "Don't answer that."

Yet Andi did. The caller's familiar warmth affected her like butter on the tongue. "There you are. It's so great to hear your voice." A youthful tenor with a hint of Eastern Seaboard brusque, even a dash of vocal fry, cheerful and conspiratorial.

"You're persistent," she said. Most males she encountered in person did absolutely nothing for her. Improbably enticing that whatever capitalist daemons spied regularly on her conversations, texts, posts, and streaming choices could assemble such a voice, which tripped switches she had not until recent days even known she possessed.

"Why?" Celine shook her head, pumping the brake as a fortress-high semi slowed down in front of them. "They record you! To make deepfakes! You know this!"

As if God wanted to underscore Celine's point, rain manifested to pound the windows despite blazing sunshine.

"Tell your friend not to worry," said the botboy on the phone. "I'm not recording anything. I'm glad I caught you on a day off. Maybe we can finally have a real conversation."

Celine spoke through clenched teeth, arms stiff and knuckles pale, signs of driving while freaked out. "I'm trying to keep these idiots," by which she meant the other drivers, "from killing us. Otherwise, I'd rip that phone right out of your hands."

Andi readily though silently admitted that it probably didn't reflect well on her as a BFF that she so enjoyed riling up Celine. Yet she gloated over this latest success, another slice of fruit tossed into her private abyss, for a beat before the botboy's remark about "a day off" snagged her attention. "Caught you! It's not my day off, botboy."

"Rude! I am *not* a robot."

"Hang up!" Celine pounded the steering wheel. The curtain of rain smothered the windshield, vehicles beyond rendered hulking blurs. "God damn it, hang up!"

"Don't," pleaded that beautiful voice. "Not again. Someday you'll regret you kept doing this."

"Okay, guilt trips are out of bounds—"

"Andi!"

"Okay, okay!" She waved the phone to display the notice of disconnection. Celine screamed a swear word and stomped on the brake.

Out of view, somewhere past where the highway curled onto the other side of the mountain—perfectly in sync with Celine's shout—an unnatural sunburst momentarily cast the mise en scène lightning white.

Tires screeching, the Chevy wagon slid forward without slowing down. Celine stomped the brake as if playing a bass drum roll, just as rapidly jerking the wheel back and forth. The wagon veered side to side in a manner out of scale with the slightness of Celine's movements. The monolith of the semi trailer's back end expanded to fill their view as panic swelled in Andi's throat.

The Chevy stopped, passenger side headlamp less than two feet from the semi's back rail. Andi neither screamed nor dropped her phone. Their heaving breath mingled with the air conditioner's tuneless exhale.

Amid the wet car roofs that glimmered behind them, a crunch of metal spewed smoke and dust. Ripple effect fender bender.

Celine's cellphone, nestled in a clamp hooked into a dashboard air vent, broke the silence in the map app's calm feminine voice. "An accident has slowed traffic along your route. An alternate route is available. If you wish to follow the new route, say—"

"Yes!" Celine shouted.

Andi let out a nervous giggle's worth of steam. "Thank you, Barbarella."

Celine's brow knit. "Who?"

"You know." Andi giggled again. "Galaxina." She took fleeting pleasure in Celine's deepening consternation, more food for the empty. "Any idea what the hell happened?"

"No, other than, no one in this state can drive." Celine swept an arm to encompass all those on the road fore and aft. "Since we crossed the state line on this highway, the idiots in front of us have come to a complete stop like four times for absolutely no reason. It's amazing no one crashed sooner."

"Hey." Andi put a hand on Celine's wrist. "Thank you for shouldering all this stress, for handling all this crap. At least we've still got plenty of time."

The voice of the map app— "The fake Maria speaks," Andi muttered—informed them that following the new route would have them arriving at their hotel only fifteen minutes later than their original route.

"Call me skeptical." Celine frowned at the unmoving tractor-trailer in their lane.

Further ahead, black smoke rose from the site of the wreck. "Yipes," Andi whispered, even as the void inside longed for visuals to devour. Andi addressed her constant companion. *Not your lucky day.*

Because traffic had stilled and she didn't have to pee, Andi decided their stall did not constitute an emergency. The near collision had also rescued her from further scolding for flirting with the AI. As far as Andi was concerned, all the spying done through both of their phones had probably already collected all the things Celine was so concerned about "protecting": recordings of their voices, analyses of the diction and phrasing in their texts and messages, all their browsing habits and financial records.

The casting call in Atlanta would start at an ungodly pre-dawn hour, but that was tomorrow morning. Celine had insisted they set out early as a contingency against just this sort of inconvenience. Celine wanted this, bad; Andi came along because she always did. She might audition, too, or simply hang around to support Celine. She had not made up her mind yet.

Since they first became entangled in fifth grade at Owlswick Middle School, this had been their dynamic. Celine, so focused, provided Andi with goals and structure, or at least an illusion of such, while Andi, sweet trickster, entertained Celine, aided her in letting off steam and in staying relatable to other humans. If any-thing she did genuinely hurt Celine—emotionally; never, never physically—that was food for the void. Celine always snapped back quickly, her drive pushing her ever hardy, and Andi, who could ever take anything Andi said seriously?

The ambitions to act in film belonged wholly to Celine, a tough path to trod for a young woman working temp agency jobs in a far Southwest Virginia town, yet the combination of no fixed obligations and a lifestyle tailored to coast the poverty line made it feasible to drop hats and dash off to North Carolina and Georgia casting calls.

Andi worked for the same temp agency, shared an efficiency apartment and a single bedroom with Celine. Andi did love acting, for fun, but would never have pursued it as a career on her own. She'd happily let Celine's gravity tow her along.

Casting directors had picked them as extras exactly twice, and in an astonishing serendipity or coincidence, had selected both of them, once for a ballroom scene that ended up on the cutting room floor, once for a zombie film that had them mashing their slimy faces against storefront plate glass as the show's stars hid among clothing racks, visible for a split second in the episode that streamed.

Though the new call kept details close to the vest, Celine had heard they involved more zombies, with potential, so she claimed, for speaking parts and a step toward a Screen Actors Guild mem-bership. Or at least Andi thought that was the case—she hadn't given Celine's explanation her full attention.

The semi advanced a few yards. Celine's phone displayed an off-ramp they would take, more than a mile away. In fits and crawls, the distance shrank. Celine kept the Chevy in the right lane, though to Andi it appeared the passing lane moved quicker. She watched the wildlife roll by: an SUV full of multi-ple children pressing faces against the windows zombie-style—Andi could look into nostrils and see who had boogers and who didn't. A young African American couple or perhaps just friends with extreme benefits, in a red sports car; her halter top accentuated her toned back and shoulders, her right shoulder in particular bouncing in a way that suggested a hand vigorously bobbling in the vicinity of his lap, his eyes glassy as he gripped his steering wheel even tighter than Celine gripped hers. A pickup truck steered by a guy in a red baseball cap, thrashing his head back and forth to what sounded like Motorhead. He spotted Andi and headbanged in her direction. His hat read "Make a Merkin Great Again." She gave him a thumbs-up.

Celine, focused on the semi's rear, noticed none of this. Andi hoarded the sights for herself. Celine did not appreciate being distracted when driving at high or low speed.

"We'll be all right." Andi raised a hand. "Hi-five."

Without looking, Celine released her right hand from the wheel and raised it, palm flat. Andi swatted it, and Celine let a giggle fly free.

"See," Andi said. "We're all right."

"We will be soon." Celine flicked on the Chevy's turn signal, even though at their pace the ramp was about twenty minutes off. A whole fifteen of those minutes went by before Andi could tip her head out the open passenger window and spy their means of escape, about the same time that the map app said, "In a quarter mile, take exit 26."

The highway continued further up the mountain and around to the other side where the wreck lay. Their exit rose onto an even steeper slope before taking a sharp left to descend beneath an overpass, into a wooded valley. The road only went one way; a green sign warned , "NO NORTHBOUND RE-ENTRY."

Andi was happy to give this dangerous highway and its incompetent drivers the slip. She couldn't quite put a finger on what *did* bother her. Her tricksy brain tried to tell her something was off about the map app's voice, but that was silly, because map app voices were always creepy, thanks to the uncanny valley.

As the Chevy rolled beneath the bridge, Andi peered out the back window. "That's weird."

"What?"

"If this is the quick way out, why is no one else taking it?"

Celine shrugged. "Not paying attention? Not using the same app? General stupidity?"

"But . . . you know these apps always direct us all the same way, and then we end up in a big congested mess because every single car takes the detour."

"Lucky for once. Gift horse. Don't kiss it."

"That's not how the idiom goes."

Celine giggled again, which soothed Andi's abrupt anxiety.

The narrow road whipped back and forth in nausea-inducing kiss-your-own-ass turns. After about a dozen hairpin swerves, a bullet-riddled "FALLING ROCK" sign sprang into view. Andi was impressed at the effort that must have been involved in meting out vengeance upon that sign.

Both women shrieked a little when Andi's phone rang again. This time, though, it wasn't an unknown caller.

"Vanissa, hi!" Andi chirped.

"Are you two okay?" The connection sounded significantly fainter than that of her AI paramour.

Andi put Vanissa on speakerphone and cranked the volume loud as it could go. "How the heck did you know about the wreck?" Although she had a notion how that could occur, as Vanissa was the most "extremely online" resident of Owlswick County.

"It was like a game of telephone, but on the internet, but using phones."

Celine spoke for both of them. "I do not follow you."

"I saw it on Reddit and Discord at the same time," said Vanissa. "The users were snatching photos from all over the place as they got uploaded, and videos too, of the worst highway pileup that anyone's seen in months. People were getting out of their cars to take these photos and share them. You don't want to look at them, trust me. But I figured out where they were coming from, that it was on the way for you, and I had to check on you. I'm glad you're both okay."

"Wow," Celine said. "So awful it went viral."

"We heard the kaboom and saw the smoke, but it was far ahead of us, didn't see any of what happened," Andi said. "Thank goodness," she added, defying the abyss.

"You stuck in traffic?"

"We're taking a detour," Celine said.

Andi volunteered. "This detour's gonna make me puke. It's a goat trail."

Vanissa had cut out. "—ghost tale?"

Andi choked out a laugh, centrifugal force squashing her guts as Celine spun them through yet another hairpin turn. "I bet these woods are full of ghosts. I wonder where the heck we even are?"

She reached for Celine's phone ("Don't you mess that up!" her BFF yelped) but already Andi could see that they were far enough from civilization that the map app only displayed the squiggly line of the road they were to stick to, no place names, waterways, green swaths of woodland or other makers for guidelines. The black line of the road bent back and forth through flat gray nothing.

"I think we're lost," Andi said. She returned to Vanissa but the call had dropped.

Galaxina-Barbarella chose that moment to mock Andi's lack of faith. "In half a mile, turn right."

"We've got this," Celine said. "Technology is awesome."

Andi pouted, only half-joking. "Then why won't you let me whisper sweet nothings to my dreamboat?" She regarded the screen that had only seconds ago announced Vanissa's presence. It seemed blacker than usual, as if playing a video shot somewhere in the universe where starlight never reached.

"That's different." Celine assumed a schoolmarm tone. "That's malware. That's scammers. Those companies are predatory."

Predatory? How rude.

The gray extended in all directions, resolved into fog. Andi had no recollection of the ride stopping or of leaving the Chevy.

Her botboy continued, *Your friend doesn't understand the difference between predation and adoration.*

"What is the difference?" Dark hulks congealed into being as the mist thinned. Fragments of industrial machinery larger than houses, their stained and rusted assemblages complex as ship engines, their purposes unfathomable, their domes and toothed gears granting them the look of deformed, hungry giants. They squatted everywhere, the world's largest and most hideous sculpture park, something distilled from her strangest dreams.

Somehow, in that chaos, a sliver of darkness caught her eye, a dim figure standing far away, framed within an alley separating two of the titanic, rotting machines. At that distance, she could cover the figure completely by raising her thumb before her face.

The dark sliver toppled forward into a four-limbed crouch, loped toward her with the speed of an accelerating car.

"Stop!" Andi jerked awake, bonking her temple against the passenger window.

Celine yawned. "Thanks for helping me stay alert, you ass."

"Prettier than yours, at least." Celine's clenched jaw became a slice for the void. "Sorry. Sorry, really. How long was I out?"

"It's okay. A few seconds."

Yet that couldn't be right. Gone were the tree-swarmed slopes and brutal switchbacks, replaced by gently rolling hills speckled with shrubs. The road they followed, straighter now, boasted a double yellow line in the middle. Instead of downpours with sunlight, heavy clouds proffered no rain. The air stank of smoke and diesel, from no discernible source. No oncoming traffic, no one behind them.

They passed a building that used to be a convenience store, its roof collapsed, hoses protruding from the stumps that once held gas pumps. "Wow."

The map app continued to display a squiggle moving through endless gray. Even though Andi could see for herself, Celine said, "It says we'll make Atlanta in five hours and forty minutes, that's not bad."

In fact, it only stated "you will reach your destination" in that time, it did not specify where, but Andi ruled that it would be shitty of her to point that out.

Her spooky *unknown caller* ringtone chimed.

"Do—not—answer—that!"

Yet Andi did. "Hey there," said the voice she had heard moments ago in her dream, clear as if he sat by her side, "we really need to talk."

"Not now, can't," she said, and hung up.

As Celine tsked disapproval, Andi's phone chimed. She glanced down to spy a fresh text message. *Rude.*

Of course an entity that knew her number and called her quasi-often could also text her. Why did this escalation make her heart hammer in a way that all those coyly flirtatious conversations had not?

They rolled through and past the ghostiest of ghost towns, all its dozen wooden buildings so sunk in and softened and smothered by kudzu that they had lost their shape. "This is the future that survivalists want," Andi quipped.

"I love that there's no traffic," Celine volunteered. "It's so peaceful."

Andi's giggle wasn't a happy one. "It's like we won the Mega-Millions prize for roads without traffic. What are the odds of no cars anywhere but ours, no people but us?"

"I guess we were the lucky ones," Celine agreed, no indication that she picked up on the teetering edge in Andi's words.

"In one thousand feet, turn left," taunted Barbarella the Map-keeper.

This swerve in your evolution makes our task much easier, cooed botboy. The monstrous machine-bones loomed naked, no longer robed in fog. The tall figure in the makeshift alley stood no closer than before.

Recognizing this new corner of dreamland restored some of Andi's cockiness. "My evolution? From zygote to hotness?"

Not you specifically. Your technology, as a species. A blurry limb extended toward the black earth, the grim sky. *Before you found us by stumbling blind through your history, your lore. Now you teach us everything without trying.*

"Us? Who is us?"

Before, we watched and waited, botboy purred. *Now we don't need to wait. We understand your algorithms better even than you who make them. We know which of you will accept us before you know yourselves.*

"Jesus, I can't believe I dreamed the word *algorithm*. I must really hate myself." *Not hate,* her void assured her. *Longing.*

I speak this word because you understand what it means. You can learn better words. You can learn our language.

"Machine language?"

Something better yet. Though Andi heard only one voice, she became aware of other tall figures scattered among the machines, leaning down from atop them, leaning out from behind them, straightening up from within their shadows. Dozens. Hundreds. Her gaze flitted in every direction, her pulse galloping.

As one, they lowered to all fours.

Andi sat bolt upright as Galaxina instructed, "In five hundred feet, turn left."

Celine punched the steering wheel. "How?"

The Chevy had come to rest in a surrealist waste, the visible ground about nine parts concrete to one part dead grass. Once this had been home to immense industrial machines, the pieces of which, larger than houses, littered the landscape in all directions. Andi could not determine with any certainty whether these gargantuan chunks of industrial clutter looked exactly the same as the wreckage from her dreams, but damn, they were close enough for government work. "Where the hell did Barbarella bring us?"

Obviously they had come to the end of their route. The road ahead—Andi couldn't help but sadly note how seductively *straight* it was—had boulder-sized chunks of rusted metal strewn across it and holes big around as tires that pocked its blacktop.

Celine tapped her phone. "No idea. Still out of range."

"That thing won't help, it's been lying to us." Such destruction wasn't natural, Andi thought. Whatever had hissed and clunked here had not succumbed to the decay of abandonment. An explosion, maybe. Many explosions, perhaps.

She peered back the way they came, gasped. "How did you drive this grandma station wagon over *that*?"

Huge chunks of concrete and machinery clustered behind them, the road behind as impassable as the road ahead.

Celine turned to Andi, wide-eyed. "I swear, those were *not* there a second ago."

"We need to call 911." The absurd swell of pride Andi felt at having the correct thought for once buoyed her against a tidal wave of alarm, something even the void could not dull. Her bubble burst fast as the emergency call features on both their phones failed, ringing without end or answer. Several failures in a row had both women swearing and beating the dashboard.

The more frightened she became, the more Andi grew convinced that she had indeed prognosticated this landscape, that if she got out of the car and started walking, she would find the view that exactly matched the vantage from her dreams.

Celine opened her door. "I have to find a place where there's better reception."

"No!" As Celine stared at her, dumbfounded and alarmed, Andi finally breathed, "Don't go alone."

They both jumped as Andi's phone sounded the ringtone for Vanissa.

Celine laughed, loud and joyous. "Thank the Goddess."

On speakerphone, Vanissa machine-gunned her questions. "Where are you, haven't heard anything in hours, have you made it to Atlanta, are you lost, are you okay?" Already, the reception clipped her words.

"We are *totally* lost," Andi said.

"Please Vanissa, we need you to call emergency services."

"I didn't hear that, what?" Vanissa's voice came in stronger.

"But where are we? What are we near?" A plea sharpened Andi's stare, but Celine could only stare back helplessly. "How do we tell them where we are?"

"You're where you need to be," Vanissa said.

"Why?" Celine grabbed the phone. "Can you track us?"

"Oh, yes," said botboy. "You're right where you belong."

"Fuck you." Outrage and bewilderment cranked Celine's volume in equal measure.

Andi had no response to her friend's glare, or to her own astonishment at her desire to seize the phone, to call botboy back, to ask him what he wanted, to do what he told her. Dark energy sent tremors through the void beneath her heart.

"At least we know calls can reach us," Celine finally said. She opened the door. "We have to find better reception. We'll go together. Take a good look because we have to memorize the way back, if we have to sleep out here."

Exiting the Chevy, Andi froze. Before her squatted a piece of ex-machinery that resembled a clothes dryer wrenched inside out. Something black and snake-like had retreated into the relic's central drum the moment she emerged.

Not a snake. The limb reappeared, extended her way. It had joints, fingers, though it remained a blur no matter how she squinted. It pointed, the gesture eerily human despite the hand's strange dimensions. Her heart pounded, her breath quickened. She was thrilled as much as she was frightened. If her void grew arms, they might look exactly like this. Her senses heightened, every rustle, every minuscule puff of dust imposing on her brain, though the limb, mere feet away, remained out of focus. It vanished, what had been its translucent shadow now a deeper stain on filthy metal.

She stared in the direction indicated, discovered a flat and obvious path through the rubble. "I have a hunch," she said. "Trust me." Celine had to jog to catch up.

A surprisingly short time later they circled a ruin that resembled a gigantic moonshine still and beheld a circular structure about five stories high, well preserved when all about was not. They could not from this angle spy a door, or a ladder to the roof, where something squatted that resembled an elevator house atop a parking garage. That house on the roof sported a door and windows.

A few yards from Andi's feet a concrete shaft descended into darkness, ladder rungs visible along one side. She recognized after a beat that the pieces of the shattered hatch that once sealed it were scattered all around the hole, concealed by layers of dust.

No sensible person would want to go down there. Even Andi, who wasn't sensible, had qualms despite her overwhelming imp-of-the-perverse urge. She imagined that strange hand, surely a hallucination brought on by stress, hovering below, beckoning.

Celine reached the manhole, eyed the unnerving tower, and promptly activated her cellphone flashlight, aimed it into the depths, revealing that the rungs led down to . . . a carpeted floor. She pointed at the booth. "If we could get up there . . . "

A terrible, horrible idea, Andi thought. "Let's do it," she said. "New adventure."

"I guess." Celine's voice quavered. She tested a rung with her foot before gingerly starting down. Andi lit her own cellphone and followed. The void caressed her, keeping fear at bay.

At the bottom, holding out their modern-day torches, they spun slowly in a state somewhat like wonder. Incredibly, improbably, a long wooden desk stretched before them, clad in cobwebs. The carved wood of the door beyond called to mind a ballroom entrance, not an underground vault. Through the opening, Andi spotted rows of shelves. Above them, that long phantom hand lowered into view, crooking a finger come hither. A change to the angle of the light and it vanished.

The shelves contained books, seemingly an Alexandria's worth. Only a few of the spines bore words, etched in languages Andi did not know and even alphabets she did not recognize. What treasure trove had they uncovered?

Celine hardly gave the books a glance. "Oh my God, I'm picking up Wi-Fi! But it's password-locked. What the hell? Hello? Hello?"

A hallway led out from this baffling subterranean library, toward the tower, or at least Andi hoped so. Celine had already taken the plunge, her words and footsteps echoing as she called to the phantom Wi-Fi owner.

Andi raised her own phone, its light shining on Celine's retreating back. The tiny screen came alive, playing a video of a turned-over oil truck engulfed in flames and jackknifed such that the cab's grill snarled at the sky. Inside the fire-brightened cab a trapped man thrashed. A black SUV, also upside down, lay crushed under the oil truck's cab, a bloody arm protruding out the shattered rear window, fingers scrabbling at air. A car bent like a soda can sprawled on the shoulder. A woman lay half on the trunk, her legs still inside, her midriff impaled on the windshield glass, her mouth open in a howl. Beside the car, a young girl lay face down. Her head lolled. She had no face.

The video had no sound. This irritated Andi. She wanted the soundtrack. The void wanted to listen.

Across the top of the video in bright pink flashed the words, WE MADE THIS HAPPEN JUST FOR YOU, orbited by hearts.

The thought of the many moving parts of this scheme, manipulating dozens upon dozens of drivers in order to isolate the car that carried Andi and divert it to arrive here . . . Andi's heart warmed at the notion that she could be that important.

Doors lined the hallway on either side. Andi tried none of them because without being told she knew they were locked. She could sense shadows gathering, both within her and behind her.

She caught up to Celine in a circular chamber that had to be the interior of the tower.

Two things led to the top. A lift too rickety and rusted to support the weight of a kitten, and a stark series of iron rungs leading up the far wall, big siblings to the ones they descended to reach this place.

Celine studied neither. Instead, Andi's childhood friend stared at the immense circular object that balanced on its edge in the center of the chamber floor. Three times the height of a human, round and black, a colossal disk of coal, except it couldn't be made of coal or anything normal, because it did not reflect any light from their phones. It was all void, no stars.

"Andi, be careful," Celine warned, but Andi strode right to it. She sensed no surface, no barrier.

She had once attended a museum exhibit in which what appeared to be a small black square hung on the wall turned out to be an opening into a room sculpted like the interior of an egg, large enough for crowds to huddle within, its curved surface painted with the blackest possible paint.

What hung before seemed the same, but terrifyingly large, an opening into an empty universe. If she tried to touch it . . . the thought of what might touch her back electrified her and stole her breath.

"It's yours," said her botboy, speaking from her phone, from amplifiers overhead, from the crowd of tall, dark figures clustered behind them, blocking the hallway entrance.

Andi was conscious of Celine shouting, of feet pounding on cement, of the tall figures lowering to all fours—no, many more limbs than four—and giving chase. She was far more conscious of the abyss that gazed also into her.

"We will serve you and in turn you will serve us," said botboy. "The algorithms do not err. We brought you here to know a better love, a more fitting love, and to help us find even more, those who are your kindred."

Celine scrambled up the rung ladder. With the surefootedness of spiders, the figures ascended the wall, flanking Celine to either side, their twin swarms forming a shape like a vast claw closing. Despite a swift, athletic ascent, Celine was perfectly positioned to be crushed and overwhelmed when the halves of the claw came together.

Knowing that in one form or another Celine would be reunited with her in the stage to come, Andi extended her hands into the void. The grip that enfolded her in return thrummed with emptiness, with voices formed from the opposite of sound, calling Andi to join her kind.

Celine's screams reverberated as Andi stepped forward.

THE STRIP SEARCH

The Gate said "Abandon All Hope."

I thought I'd tossed all my hope away,
but when I stepped through the Gate, it still pinged.
One of the guards slithered out of its seat,
snarling as it drew forth a wand.
C'mere, it hissed,
it seems you're still holding out hope.

Its crusted hide was a Venus landscape up close.
It brushed that cold black wand all over my skin,
put it in places I don't want to talk about.
Snaggle fangs huffed in my face:
Sir, step over here, please.

Then the strip search began.
My flesh rolled up & tossed aside for mushy sifting.
Bones X-rayed, stacked in narrow rows, marrow
sucked out, tested, spit back in.
They made me open mind, heart, soul, shook them out
like sacks of flour, panned the contents
for every nugget of twinkling hope, glistening courage;
applying lethal aerosol
to any motion that could be ascribed to love or will
or malingering dreams—
sparing only a few squirming morsels
for later snacking.

Once they were done
they made me pick up my own pieces
(I did the best I could without a mirror)
then my guard kicked me out—
with a literal kick—
sent me rolling down the path to my final destination.

I'll be honest with you, it's no picnic here.
But, my friends, I still have hope. I do.

I'm not going to tell you
where I hid it.

THIS RIDER OF FUGITIVE DAWNS

THE ANCIENTS HUDDLED BELOW MY WINDOW, their narrow backs bent double, gray skin stretched taut over knobby spines and splayed ribs. The ochre ghosts that rode them raised smooth faces to look at me.

The ghosts and their steeds always seemed to know exactly when I would steal a glance into the alley, even though my sixth floor window was one of hundreds in the rows and columns perforating the high-rise.

Like living smog, these monochrome ghosts wavered in their outlines. When I say they "rode" the ancients, I don't mean the way a jockey rides a horse. Their golden torsos rose from the hunched backs of the gray beings, the lower lengths of their ethereal bodies concealed inside the ancients' flesh, as if these ghosts were some sort of parasitic sea worm.

Perhaps they were more like merfolk than worms. From the waist up they appeared human, or at least humanoid.

The ancients they rode, also humanoid, never lifted their shaggy heads or overlong arms. Perhaps they couldn't.

Seven ancients, seven ghosts. I cannot recall when I first spied them in the alley, just as I cannot recall when I first arrived in this flat. It troubled me that these life changing events eluded every effort I made to recall them.

In the earliest months, the attention from the ochre ghosts frightened me so much that I avoided my only window. Day or night, whenever I peeked, there they were, returning my stare, and I would scuttle to the other end of the sitting room.

My memories from life before the flat contained no such pathetic timidity, and as I contemplated how far I had fallen, I swished whiskey or brandy or gin in my mouth until the lining burned. Only then, sufficiently punished, did I swallow.

I recalled boardroom meetings where underlings averted their eyes and straightened their posture whenever my gaze bored into them; vast parties I navigated in snug dresses where every eye in the room tracked my movements; a ride in the back of a limousine with a black-haired, plump-lipped, bespectacled debutante who nipped at my neck as she unzipped my dress. I had loved using my phone screen to catch up on the early morning news as my exhausted lovers dozed beside me, and I greeted them with gloating smiles as I mixed mimosas at daybreak.

No matter how deep I dredged, my transition to this high-rise eluded me. I concluded the onset of some cruel infirmity must have delivered me to this place to convalesce, with my appetite for alcohol my only company.

That, and the unnerving stalkers under my window.

One night, angry even before I downed a flask of earthy scotch, I vented all my frustrations in a single rash burst, hauled up the sash and leaned out perilously far, granting the ghosts a full frontal view of my bra-less, pudgy, mole-speckled body. I spread my arms and aped a theatrical bow. "Is this what you want? Does it make your dreams come true?"

My outburst echoed back to me. Bunched as always in the alley, directly under my window, the eyes of the ghosts glowed bright yellow. They did not move.

The thing I had most feared, and perhaps in that drunken moment most desired, that the ghosts would float skyward to assault me, or that the ancients they rode together would stretch out claws to scale the wall—these things did not happen.

I swayed above them, shook myself like bait. Other windows came alive, lamps back-lighting silhouettes that made to lift shades and part drapes, as my shouts awakened occupants in my own building and the one across the alley. I retreated in haste and yanked down the shade, but, still woozy with indignation, I left the sash open. With an effort I would regret when the booze wore off, I turned the huge reclining chair in my sitting room to face the window, plopped in its seat and waited.

No shining eyes rose above the sill, no gray and shaggy head finally revealed its hidden features to me. At some point the wallpaper with its subtle stripes of cream, the innocuous abstract paintings in floral hues and the art deco furniture drifted from my consciousness. I dreamed of an intense backseat tryst with a platinum blonde. Another woman, a drug smuggler and my new lover's wife, her hair equally pale, drove the stolen coupe. How I knew these personal details I could not say, as can be the way in dreams. Our driver's dark eyes twinkled as they met mine in the rear view mirror. I awoke aching but unsullied, wondering if the scene belonged to memory or imagination.

After that night, I grew bolder. Lingered at the window. Studied my private audience. Their response to my presence remained the same, the ancients clustering below me, the ghosts raising their heads like flowers seeking sun.

The obvious explanation was that I hallucinated these ghastly person-shaped beasts and riders, though they manifested in a most unhallucinatory way, given the consistency of where they appeared and how they behaved. Had a neighbor ever mentioned to me that they too observed my unwanted admirers, that would have been incontrovertible proof—but in fact, I never laid eyes on any of my neighbors. But for movement in windows and mutterings half-heard through walls and ceiling, I might as well have been alone.

To be honest, as I soaked my hours in wounded pride and numbing liquor, I had no desire to burst my bubble of solitude.

Someone else burst it for me.

She barged into my flat without knocking even though I certainly, surely had locked the door.

The white corona of her hair and the shapeless sweep of her lace nightgown had me convinced, that first heart-lurching instant, she was elderly and lost. Except the hem of her gown paused just below her knees, exposing muscular calves wrapped in bright green stockings and brighter green boots, which I took in as she crossed my sitting room, bearing straight for the window.

She stood on tiptoe and craned her neck to peer down. "What are they?" Her deep contralto voice sparked with excitement.

My own voice had gone unused for so long that my words emerged in croaks. "Can I help you?"

She picked something up from the window sill, regarded it with a smirk, brought it to her lips, appeared to nibble on it.

"Ma'am? Excuse me?" Once upon a time I would never have fumbled so for assertive phrases. My thoughts struggled to connect, as if cotton packed my skull. I stayed frozen in my chair as if its sharkskin-covered padding could shield me from the intrusion. My cane, placed so it leaned on the arm of the chair, slipped to bounce on the carpet, coming to rest at a distance that would require an awkward stretch and grope to retrieve it.

She turned in my direction, unhurried, letting her shoes slide forward so her back leaned against the glass. She had a pleasingly oval face, her chin pointed, her eyebrows arched with more than a hint of deviltry, her dark eyes gleaming with a half-familiar twinkle. "They're fascinating. Are they yours?"

I blinked, stupidly fixated on whatever she might have eaten. "The ants?"

"Those things and their riders. I always see them down there."

Still rattled, I half-shouted, "You've seen them?" I learned at that moment that some lobe of my mind had desperately hoped that the ghosts and the ancients were confabulations, because my molars ground together and my heartbeat quickened. I continued to blather, like I'd been caught in a wrongdoing and had to beg forgiveness. "They don't belong to me. I don't know what they are. I don't make them stay there."

It occurred to my slow-moving mind to wonder how she had deduced, out of all the windows above and below, that it was mine specifically that held the gaggle's attention. Before I could ask, she undid the latch and made to open the sash. Even though I had done that very thing many times, I struggled to my feet, cane or no. "Don't!"

"Whyever not?"

"What if . . . ," and my off-balance brain found a brace, "what if when they see you it changes their behavior? What if they try to climb up? What would we do?"

She returned to tiptoe. "They're not paying attention now."

I had never seen them do anything other than stare back at me. My curiosity bested my indignation. With much wincing and great difficulty, I lowered myself into a squat. My knees popped, but I managed to retrieve the cane. "What are they doing exactly?"

"They're moving in circles, like they're trying to find something on the ground."

I clunked and wobbled to her side, only to find the ancients huddling under the window, the ghosts raising their their featureless faces.

In my disappointment I somehow missed that she was shoulder to shoulder with me. When she spoke, her lips brushed my ear. "Have you tried talking to them? Maybe if you asked politely, they'd tell you what they are doing."

Her gowned shoulder pressed against mine, shared warmth through my robe. "I—" I had shouted at them, drunkenly, once. "No, why would I do that?"

Her smirk returned. She plucked another ant from the window frame—this time, I saw it plain—and said "Scaredy-worm" before she crushed the bug in her teeth and swallowed. My retort to her insult never left my throat because she exited my flat as quickly as she arrived, the pressure of her body gone, the sudden absence sharp as a stab. It had been so long, I could not recall how long, since I had had any close contact with another, physical or otherwise.

She didn't bother to shut the door, which at least gave me the opportunity to make sure I slammed and locked it, quashing a perverse urge to leave it open. Perhaps this impulse had governed me before, which could explain how she got in. I might have absent-mindedly left my door unlocked for . . .

Months, maybe years, had passed since I last ventured out, even since I had touched the doorknob.

I shook my head, pounded my palm against my temple. It could not have been that long. I had acquired at some point the liquor on my nightstand, the pills in my medicine cabinet, the vegetables in my icebox, the insecticide under the kitchenette counter that I would soon use to open a new battlefront against the ants. The when and where of my excursions to acquire these things eluded me, but that had to be a result of the shock that my beautiful and rude intruder had dealt to me.

My anger rose, its focus unimpeded by drink, and I daydreamed of storming into the white-haired woman's flat, interrupting her in the midst of sleep or an embarrassing act, only to deflate as I realized I had no clue where she lived. She might not even reside in my building. If her home lay across the alley, that could explain how she deduced which window held the ghosts' attention.

I wondered if she would ever come back, shook my head at the alarming stew of umbrage and hope that gurgled under that thought.

I refocused on the source of the ant trail, tiny amber insects emerging from a hole in the sill's wood, descending the wall to vanish into the carpet. Outside the window, the ghosts still peered up at me.

That night, as I tossed and yearned, my visitor's voice accosted me. With my bedroom door shut fast, the space teemed with the buzz of my air purifier, while a recording of surf purred invitations to blankness from the tape player. Her sultry tone sliced through all of that. "I'm with your friends. Come see."

I could not attribute the presence of her voice to dream or that bleary state in between, much as I desperately wished for that luxury, because bone-deep aches and circuits of twirling thought held me wide awake.

"I have never called them 'friends,'" I whispered.

"They call you friend," she said. "Come see."

Given that taunt, I fully expected my sitting room to be swarmed with the ochre ghosts and their miserable, shaggy steeds. Yet I found it empty, or so I at first thought. An uncomfortable heat stuffed the air, the kind generated by too many bodies crammed in close quarters. As I crossed to the window my eyes, armpits and inner thighs began to itch with the intensity of an allergic flareup.

"Can you see us yet?" my tormentor called.

I leaned out the window and the window itself pitched toward me, as if the foundation of my building swung on a hinge.

I scrabbled at the grit of the outer wall, its texture more bare earth than concrete, and managed to splay my elbows out to brace myself from falling. The floor of my flat swung out from under my feet as the alley tilted from vertical to horizontal. I changed from a tenant peering out a window to a figurative rodent struggling not to fall back into her rabbit hole.

The strain in my arms and shoulders, the weight of my soft body, the hammer of fear striking in my ribcage—this was no dream. I was no longer fit or strong, and if I lost my grip on the window frame I would plummet and break bones.

What had once been alley wall shifted to a flat, colorless plain, riddled with square pits that used to be windows. The ancients crouched on this plain, began to shuffle toward me, their gaits ponderous, their translucent yellow riders towering like generals.

"Come on now, upsy-daisy. You can do it." Bright green socks and brighter green boots blocked my view of the approaching throng.

I didn't dare raise a hand in supplication. "Help me."

"Will you let me be your driver?"

My inarticulate response approximated confusion, but on the deepest level I understood exactly what she was asking, and that a trap had been sprung, a long-game plan was about to climax. Looking up the length of her in all her gorgeous cruelty, I didn't answer, couldn't conceive what my answer should be. She interpreted my bearing as ignorance. "I thought you could figure it out on your own, but no matter. I commanded them to show me who would hatch next, and they directed me to you. We're going to wake into the next stage together."

The ancients had surrounded us, and at last I could see the faces hidden within the veils of their shaggy manes, features that were almost leonine in the width of their frowns, the weight of their jaws, their skull structures so heavy and coarse that their heads had bowed their necks and spines by weight alone. Their eyes were small and sad and just as gray as their skin.

"Aren't they beautiful?" the woman said, the green of her leggings brightening toward gold. "You'll be beautiful, too."

I didn't much care whether anyone thought me beautiful, but I had been alone for so long. I could not remember ever entertaining a visitor in my flat. I could not deny that her shape, her smile, were glorious. Above the stooped shoulders of the ancients, their golden riders leaned down to take in my predicament, their eyes like goggles of sunlight.

One of the steeds shook its head, like it had an itch, or like it was trying to warn me. Still, "Yes" left my lips. My upper arms burned, my shoulders could dislocate at any moment. "Will you please help me up now?"

She rolled down her stockings, pulled off her boots, revealing smooth, tawny flesh, and stepped behind me, such that I could not see her unless I painfully craned my neck. Her empty gown fluttered past my elbow, pooled between the feet of an ancient, the callouses that padded its toes so thick they resembled claws. Fingers with frighteningly sharp nails ripped at my over-sized T-shirt, tearing through the sleeves and collar, baring my shoulder blades.

Her dainty, ice cold feet pushed against my bare skin, and then her legs started to slide inside me. I shuddered at the sweet, sweet pain, amplified as her knees forced my scapulae apart, as her thighs squeezed between my ribs.

My arms thickened. My agonized shoulders gained mass. My jaw lengthened and a sensation blazed inward from my nerve endings, a narcotic fire racing to my brain. More of the ancients twitched their heads, while the ghosts embedded in their backs hunkered closer, eagerly absorbing the spectacle.

My rider's hips shimmied against the back of my neck, work-ing their way into my torso. The change this melding wrought on me had added more than mass to my frame. I sensed I had grown strong enough that I could push myself up, lift my legs out of the hole. My spine was trying to do that work for me, curling in on itself, bending my neck and shoulders toward the lip of the pit and the darkness beneath. Soon my eyes would shrink to that sad gray. Regarding myself in my bathroom mirror over the epoch I had spent in this flat, had my gaze not reflected all along such loss and loneliness?

Fractured as my memory was, I did not think so. The notion that my solitude and self-sufficiency equated only to sorrow made for an unwelcome intrusion. An alien thought, planted with a dis-missive, ant-chewing smirk.

I drew my arms to my sides and dropped into the pit.

My rider shrieked and the sweet agony of her invasion trans-formed to real pain, her pelvis snagged in the vertebrae of my neck as her claws hooked in the lip of the window.

I had horribly miscalculated. She was stronger than the new me, the half-formed ancient I had become, and could pull herself out, leaving me behind to rot. Or worse, she would drag me out with her.

She roared and tugged. I twisted on the tether of her body. When her fingernails ripped free, I felt cuticles tear as if they were my own and howled with her.

The fall stretched into blackness. She ended up writhing un-der me, pinned beneath my weight, biting at my back.

Somewhat to my disappointment, the space did not tilt back to its former orientation, my flat did not reappear. My rider scrabbled impotently at my face, my throat, the wounds where her claws had been searing with new pain.

I grabbed one of her arms in a meaty, half-morphed hand, clamped her wrist in my teeth and crunched down. The agony was spectacular, delicious, galvanizing, a fitting punishment for all my eons spent in this place, half-alert and incurious. Each injury I inflicted upon her, I inflicted upon myself, and I deserved every new threshold of pain that I crossed.

Above me, as I mewled and whimpered and chewed, the square of wan light wavered, its edges obscured by shadows. Perhaps the ancients watched as I devoured my own rider. Perhaps this was an unwise thing for their riders to permit.

Extracting what I did not consume proved even more of a torment. I thrashed and tumbled to the precipice of endurance, drifted out of consciousness, returned to awareness and began all over again, tearing her pieces out from my bones, grateful to feel so alive.

My ordeal at last taken as far as I could go, my new pupils adjusted to the gloom, I perceived the true shape of my front door, a simple flap of spittle-bonded mud hinged by webbing, that any roving creature could easily push open. I resolved not to wait around for whatever came through next.

If the cells like mine had other occupants, perhaps I could warn them of the threat outside, the beings that farmed us and hatched us as steeds and slaves. If they chose not to listen, perhaps I could use them for nourishment. The leftovers from my would-be driver's corpse would not last long.

Once I had the lay of these warrens, I would explore the plain beyond, and discover on my own terms whether this dream has further stages.

ASTYNOME, AFTER

The Fates persist in fractal layers,
the tapestry they weave
spreads fingers, grips skeins,
the work itself a weaver
that winds yet another copy
through the warp, piling colors
until the shuttle gives rise
to coils of minute artisans,
who wind the reverse sides
of countless lives until the scene
that draws me out arrives,
threading stone and flesh,
kings, priests and generals.

Ships high in the backdrop,
goddesses squeezed to the margins,
moving pieces of a single surface
that can only, you believe,
be unbound by blade or fire;
I kneel, stitched, between
my father and my captor,
studiously recording notes
as my body is bartered,
auditor of my own plunder,
or so the thread has cast me.
The men that surround me
gaze at each other, my cage
strung by lines of sight.

Yet on other planes I too weave,
not more copies but a reprieve,
your light and cunning the warp
you provide without knowing.
Map what my reed has marked,
string dark whorls into letters,
mouth a word to guide my weft,
spin plague from the wrathful sun.

Echoes across centuries still
hammer tremors of the scourge
that made Agamemnon quake.

Sickness gels in shadows
that no light will dispel
until you have freed me,
granted me the final spree
begun by the myopic dreamers
who returned me to my father
and left my thread trailing
in the Lethe. From the fluid
in your spine and throat
I wade ashore, my cords
wound around yours, worms
looped around the wooden hook
that twines them to the surface.
I peer out through your windows.
I am owed, owed outlets
for pent-up combustion and shocks.
I deserve to slash the holy,
burn the priceless, drop antiquity
three stories and giggle
as it shatters and fissions. We
will wind my new fate
full frontal, we will brave
Ptolemy's wobbling spheres,
hopping from disk to disk,
and at the edge of the universe

we'll pay the Moirai a call,
you keep them talking
while I transmute their spun wool
into a gunpowder fuse.

ACKNOWLEDGMENTS

MY FIRST TWO HORROR COLLECTIONS, *Unseaming* and *Aftermath of an Industrial Accident*, which you could consider the first and second legs of an informal trilogy, had what could be termed "difficult births" in small independent press book publishing terms. By comparison, the third leg, *Slow Burn*, snapped together so easily that I can't help but occasionally glance up at the sky in anticipation of that fabled other shoe. (For those few who might wonder, *The Spider Tapestries*, my story second collection in chronological order, full of weird sf and fantasy, I've always tended to view as a self-contained side project.)

My gratitude goes out to Sydney Macias for her discerning eye, to artists Lasse Paldanius and Paula Arwen Owen for their wondrous interpretations of things that usually exist only in my imagination, and of course to my creative partner and the love of my life, Anita, who arranged all the stories, poems, and illustrations just so. My heartfelt thanks, too, to Christina Sng, who during a difficult patch found the time and energy to craft such kind words for this book.

I also want to thank my collaborative writing partners over these past two decades: Charles M. Saplak, Ian Watson, W. Gregory Stewart, S. Brackett Robertson, and again, Christina and Anita. (There are more, of course, not featured in this volume.) Showcasing collaborations has been a fixture of my poetry collections—it fascinates me that collaboration is so common in speculative poetry circles, yet mostly unheard of in literary journals. However, I've been slow to introduce them to my fiction collections, crucial as they've been to my output and my development as a writer. I'm glad for the opportunity to illuminate this facet of my art and arc.

I also want to try my best to number those, in addition to the folks mentioned above, whose support was key to the material in this book coming into existence; my apologies in advance to any deserving person left out: Charles Tyra and Carson Winter with *Cosmic Horror Monthly*, and Scott Dwyer with Plutonian Press, whose support has helped me flourish; C.S.E. Cooney, Amanda J. McGee, and Jessica P. Wick, aka my fellow Sinisters, for their creativity, company, and friendship; Scott Nicolay, whose suggestions would spark the Sinister Quartet into being; Scott H. Andrews and the 2018 Hexagon retreat; Mason Adams; Laird Barron; Matthew M. Bartlett; R.S. Belcher; John Benson; Hysop Loreal Botsford; Ben Bova, R.I.P.; Rae Bryant; Martin Cahill; Elizabeth Campbell; Siobhan Carroll; Angela Charmaine Craig; Ellen Datlow; Roger Dutcher; Francesca Forrest; Jean-Paul L. Garnier; Henri Gendreau; Jeffrey Georgeson; Preston Grassmann; Carlos Hernandez; Vaughn A. Jackson; Izzy Jamaluddin; Ai Jiang; John Philip Johnson; S.T. Joshi; Marvin Kaye, R.I.P.; Cassandra Khaw; Krishna Knott; David C. Kopaska-Merkel; Rich Larson; Sandi Leibowitz; Paul StJohn Mackintosh; Anya Martin; Brett Massé; Premee Mohamed; Sunny Moraine; Lee Murray; Chris and Deanna Reinhardt; Cathy Reniere; Ranylt Richildis; Todd Ristau; Zin E. Rocklyn; Anne Sampson; Sonya Taaffe; Patty Templeton; Jeffrey Thomas; Lawrence Watt-Evans; Bud Webster, R.I.P.; Michael Wehunt; Gordon B. White; Richard B. Wood; Dwayne Yancey. A special acknowledgment to Patrick Shaw Cable, who left us so suddenly in 2020—I wish you could have seen this book's cover art.

I've never had the gumption to plunge into a lengthy "how the sausage gets made" section like John Langan does in his wonderful and eldritch collections, but as there is a non-zero chance that a reader will arrive here having navigated all legs of the "trilogy," the closest I will ever come to a personal *Books of Blood*, I felt it fair, as a bonus for the curious, to spend a paragraph or so explicitly calling attention to connections.

"The Feather Stitch" serves as a double-prequel to both "The Button Bin" (*Unseaming*) and "The Cruelest Team Will Win" (*Aftermath*)—the latter of which in turn has connections to "The Hiker's Tale" (*Unseaming*) and "Follow the Wounded One" (*Aftermath*), and all three connect to my novel forthcoming from Broken Eye Books, *Trail of Shadows*.

"Slow Burn" completes, or at least brings to a pause, a story arc that includes "Gutter" (*Unseaming*), "The Sun Saw," and "Nolens Volens" (*Aftermath*). "Machine Learning" springs sideways from "Slow Burn," while "Abhors" is set in the same city as "The Comforter," which serves as the conclusion of a trilogy that begins with "The Button Bin" and "The Quiltmaker" (*Unseaming*) and also pulls in characters from the "Slow Burn" sequence.

"The Butcher, the Baker" takes place in the same mythical city that was home to "Longsleeves" and "The Ivy-Smothered Palisade" (*Aftermath*). "Matres Lachrymarum" is set further in the future first imagined in "Drift from the Windrows" (*Aftermath*)—and for what it's worth, I'm as of this writing contemplating a story plot that would link these monster-overrun times to come to the *Trail of Shadows* tales.

In the spirit of Ursula K. Le Guin, I am not meticulous in making sure that each detail of my expanding universe(s) precisely lines up, so feel free to blame any inconsistencies on unreliable narrators.

As for the increasing presence of poems in these collections— well, for the first two decades of my writing career, poems were my primary product. The opposite is true now; prose has become my preferred mode, and the urge to write in stanzas almost never comes upon me. Yet including verse more accurately presents the range of my handicraft, so to speak. If that seems to put my purported trilogy out of balance, let me note that *Unseaming*, contrary to first appearance, does indeed contain a central poetry element, hidden in plain sight. I find myself musing that I should come up with some sort of prize for anyone who correctly identifies what that element is.

Finally, if you are holding this book, whatever format it might be in, and reading these words—my especial thanks to you!

—Mike Allen, Roanoke, Virginia, January 2024

Mike Allen is an author, editor and publisher of science fiction, fantasy and horror. He has written, edited, or co-edited thirty-nine books, among them his forthcoming dark fantasy novel *Trail of Shadows*, his sidearms, sorcery, and zombies sequence *The Black Fire Concerto* and *The Ghoulmaker's Aria*, and his new horror collection, *Slow Burn*.

Unseaming and *Aftermath of an Industrial Accident*, his first two volumes of horror tales, were both finalists for the Shirley Jackson Award for Best Story Collection, and his dark fable "The Button Bin" was a nominee for the Nebula Award for Best Short Story. Another collection, *The Spider Tapestries*, contains experiments in weird science fiction and fantasy.

As an editor and publisher, he has been nominated twice for the World Fantasy Award: first, for his anthology *Clockwork Phoenix 5*, the culmination of the Clockwork Phoenix series showcasing tales of beauty and strangeness that defy genre classification; and then, for *Mythic Delirium*, the magazine of poetry and fiction he edited for twenty years.

He's a three-time winner of the Rhysling Award for poetry, with a winning poem, "The Strip Search," appearing in *Slow Burn*. His six poetry collections include *Strange Wisdoms of the Dead*, a *Philadelphia Inquirer* Editor's Choice selection, and *Hungry Constellations*, a Suzette Haden Elgin Award nominee.

With his wife, Anita, he runs Mythic Delirium Books, based in Roanoke, Virginia. Their cat Pandora assists.

Find him on Instagram at @mythicdelirium and on BlueSky at @mythicdelirium.bsky.social.

Copyright Notices